PENGUIN [illegible]

The Family Farm

Fiona Palmer lives in the tiny rural town of Pingaring in Western Australia, three and a half hours south-east of Perth. She discovered Danielle Steel at the age of eleven, and has now written her own brand of rural romance. She has attended romance writers' groups and received an Australian Society of Authors mentorship for *The Family Farm*. She has extensive farming experience, does the local mail run and was a speedway-racing driver for seven years. She spends her days writing, working as a farmhand, helping out in the community and looking after her two children.

fionapalmer.com

PRAISE FOR FIONA PALMER

'A delightful piece of rural romance.'
BALLARAT COURIER

'A rollicking romance that will have readers cheering on the heroine . . . Evokes the light, people, atmosphere and attitudes of a small country town.'
WEEKLY TIMES

'A moving story that reveals the beauty of the bush and the resilience of rural communities during times of hardship.'
QUEENSLAND COUNTRY LIFE

'A good old-fashioned love story.'
SUNDAY MAIL BRISBANE

'Palmer's characterisation of the town's many colourful identities is delightful and will bring a smile to those who have experienced country life.'
WEST AUSTRALIAN

'A heartwarming romance about finding true love and following your dreams.'
FEMAIL.COM.AU

'Distinctly Australian . . . heartwarming and enjoyable . . . a well-written and engaging read.'
BOOK'D OUT

'A great addition to your shelf if you love strong characters and beautiful Aussie landscapes.'
THE AUSTRALIAN BOOKSHELF

FIONA PALMER

THE Family Farm

PENGUIN BOOKS

PENGUIN BOOKS

UK | USA | Canada | Ireland | Australia
India | New Zealand | South Africa | China

Penguin Books is part of the Penguin Random House group of companies
whose addresses can be found at global.penguinrandomhouse.com.

First published by Penguin Group (Australia), 2009
This edition published by Penguin Random House Australia Pty Ltd, 2016

1 3 5 7 9 10 8 6 4 2

Cover and text design by Cathy Larsen © Penguin Group (Australia)
Cover photography: cover model by Tim de Neefe; farmhouse by Tom Keating/Wildlight;
farm and crops by John White/Wildlight
Typeset in Sabon by Post-Press Group, Brisbane, Queensland
Colour separation by Splitting Image Colour Studio, Clayton, Victoria
Printed and bound in Australia by Griffin Press, an accredited ISO AS/NZS 14001
Environmental Management Systems printer.

National Library of Australia
Cataloguing-in-Publication data:

Palmer, Fiona.
The family farm / Fiona Palmer.
9780143573944 (paperback)
Love stories
Farm life – Fiction
Families – Fiction

A823.4

penguin.com.au

To my husband, Das,
and our children, Mac and Blake

Part One

1

THE old Holden ute squeaked and rattled as it rolled along the gravel road, leaving a billowing dust trail. Isabelle Simpson was glad to see the land around her home district hadn't changed during her absence. The same vast blue sky watched over her, and the unchanged trees were filled with pink and grey galahs and bright-green parrots. Her heart felt free and her skin tingled with eagerness. Not long now. She smiled at the familiar farm signs along the road as if remembering old friends. Izzy was glad that the farmers she'd known her whole life hadn't sold out and moved on. It just wouldn't be home without them.

A high-pitched ringing interrupted her thoughts. Pulling over, Izzy picked up her mobile, saw who was calling and promptly pressed cancel before throwing the phone down. Why couldn't he just leave her alone? Didn't he realise what he'd done?

The phone began vibrating on the seat near her leg. A text message had arrived. Hesitantly, she picked up her mobile.

`We need 2 talk. Can u please call me.`

Like hell, she thought. Izzy had already told him all she was going to say on the matter. Suddenly a sob forced its way out from deep in her throat, catching her by surprise. Her shoulders shook as she clutched the steering wheel. Finally, the bottled-up tears fell in floods. He had ruined everything and she felt so betrayed. Izzy let the tears fall freely, hoping it might help her move on and be done with this whole cock-up.

The familiar road beckoned when she glanced at it through blurry eyes. I'm almost home, she thought. Sniffing loudly, she wiped away the last of her tears and sat up straight. Izzy Simpson was made of tougher stuff than that. Besides, another few minutes and she'd be back home. Back to her parents. Back to the strong memories of her sister, Claire. Back to the close proximity of Will Timmins. Back to another man complicating her life.

Bloody hell. That's all I need, she thought, sighing.

Planting her foot on the accelerator and spraying gravel, Izzy drove her ute back onto the road. She headed through her local town, past the three large grain-storage bins. They were a towering icon of Pingaring and a marker point for Izzy. Her family's farm lay only ten minutes to the east. After days of travelling, it finally felt like she was coming home.

As she peered out of the open window, the breeze flicked her long dark hair about her face, tickling her skin. There was something about returning that made the landscape seem so much more beautiful and bright, highlighting the smell of the warm dusty air, the hint of eucalyptus and the glorious blue of the sky. She knew this route like the back of her hand – the mallee trees and scrub bush that lined the road, and the places where the wildflowers grew in spring.

Taking a deep breath, as if she could suck in all the familiar smells at once, Izzy glanced at her kelpie dog. 'What do you reckon, Tom? Good to be home, isn't it, mate?'

His answer was to stick his head out the open passenger window. Tom's tongue flapped in the wind and his bottom lip blew down, revealing his yellowing teeth.

Both windows were open, and the hot afternoon breeze provided the only relief from the stifling heat. Even though her ute was old, it still ran well. Brown vinyl lined the interior, well worn but clean and tidy, except for the dog hairs that coated the brown seat covers on the passenger side. On the floor below Tom sat his ice-cream container with enough water to wet his chops.

Yes, her old blue Holden was more than just metal and rubber. It was almost like a member of her family. Izzy had bought it when she was fifteen. After four long weeks working on Spud's crutching cradle she had earned enough money to buy it off the local mechanic in town.

Izzy remembered that long month, many years ago. It had been the first time she'd worked off the family farm. Her first day's work was over at a neighbouring property crutching six hundred head of ewes, big fat ones too. It was a stinking hot day full of endless flies and large blowies. Spud, Johnno and Mick were on the crew back then. They crutched the wool off around the tail of the ewes to prevent them from being blown by flies, while she roused and pushed up sheep. She could still remember the clang of the metal flap as the blokes had pulled the ewes from the high race she'd just pushed them up into. The whirr from the hand pieces and the constant bangs, mixed in with Mick and Johnno yelling sick jokes to each other, had caused her ears to ring that day. Then there were the sharp prickles hidden in the wool that had made her already sore and swollen fingers sting as she grabbed the ewes by their thick, greasy coats, struggling to move the more stubborn ones up the race. Not to mention her aching back from bending over all day sorting the crutchings from the shitty dags and half-clean bits of wool.

Izzy had quickly learnt to pack her own toilet paper. It came in handy when you had to squat behind the ute or cradle.

Yes, it had been hard work, but bloody good pay for a fifteen-year-old. Her HQ ute was her reward, and she had spent a special couple of days with her dad cleaning it up. That was before the accident, back in the days when he allowed her to help him around the machinery on the farm. Over the years she'd earned enough money to upgrade her ute if she'd wanted to. But strangely, she felt too attached to ever sell. It held a lot of good memories of times spent with her dad, and of cruising the paddocks with Claire in her newfound freedom.

Slowing down as the familiar turnoff approached, Izzy flicked on the indicator and turned left, stopping just short of a faded sign.

B & J Simpson, Gumlea was etched into a piece of ancient red jarrah, and faded white paint peeled out from the grooves. Gumlea was the name that had been given to the farm long before her grandad had bought it, named, she guessed, after all the salmon gums, which had been planted on the farm many years ago. The sign hung from two small chains off a thicker rusty frame. Her dad would've loved to see the words *and Son* up there. He'd wanted someone to pass his farm on to, and Izzy had wished with all her heart that it would be her. She'd dreamed of running the family farm nearly her whole life. She was twelve when she realised that was what she definitely wanted. Being away at boarding school had been hell and had proved how much the farm meant to her. The only thing standing in her way was good ol' dad. He could be like a mule sometimes, which was the main reason Izzy had been away from the farm she loved for the past few years. He'd have a fit if he knew what kind of work she'd been doing.

Izzy sighed as she moved the stick into gear and headed down the corrugated gravel driveway, intermittently lined with the tall gum trees that she used to climb as a child. Her nerves started to twinge. Crap. What were her folks going to say when they saw her? She knew her mum would be ecstatic – Mum always missed her the most – but Dad was never too keen on surprises.

Tom barked as he spotted the farmhouse, bringing Izzy back from la-la land. Three large paddocks surrounded the farm buildings. Two were in crop, the Halberd variety of wheat making a golden-brown haze, nearly ripe for harvest. The other paddock was bare, and in the far corner sheep huddled in the shade of the nature reserve along the fence line. Large silver farm sheds rose into view like a pop-up book the closer she got. Izzy drove past ancient ploughs left rotting together in clumps – the same ones she and Claire used to play on.

Dad's Toyota Land Cruiser was parked at the house, with the sheep feeder attached behind. He couldn't afford to upgrade his ute like some of the other farmers around, but instead had to wait for a good year or until it died on him. Then they'd need to get a newer one as half the farm work couldn't be done without it. Izzy had spent most of her childhood in that ute. She checked her watch. It must be about smoko time, she thought.

Parking next to the Land Cruiser she noticed the garden was still as amazing as ever. Her mum had planted native shrubs, grevilleas, bottlebrush and other plants that thrived in dry conditions. Water was always a problem, especially at this time of year. But she also had a section of plants that she tended to regularly, from the row of deep red roses to the clumps of irises and daylilies. Then there were the springtime pink and white everlastings and colourful livingston daisies, which incredibly covered the hard ground throughout her garden, putting on a bright display worthy of any garden show. Mum always managed to find enough flowers in her garden to put on the table in Nana's vases.

Looking down at her worn blue jeans and tan singlet, Izzy wondered whether she should have dressed up. She flipped down the sun visor in the car, gawked into the cracked mirror taped on behind it, and applied some lip balm. She would have liked fuller lips and a larger smile, but at least she had straight teeth. Her blue eyes were vibrant against her clear olive complexion. Hastily she retied her hair back into a ponytail. Her hands showed signs of neglect. Deeply tanned, they were callused and dry, but that didn't worry Izzy. To her, each callus was like a gold star, showing how hard she had worked. Poking her tongue out, she pulled a face at her reflection, then flicked the visor back into place.

'C'mon, Tom.' She whistled, then slammed the door behind him as he jumped out. They walked side by side towards the fence and the open wooden slat gate that beckoned you towards the house. Izzy slid her hands into her back pockets to settle her nerves. The soft patter of Tom's paws against the earth led them towards the back of the house. The front door was hardly ever used, only by the odd travelling salesman or Jehovah's Witness. Each step seemed to take forever, but soon she was standing in front of the familiar flywire door. Slipping off her Rossi boots, she placed them neatly beside a rugged pair of her father's. She smiled. Everything on the verandah was how she remembered it. The wooden table that her mum had stripped back still stood in the same spot, covered with old tins and bottles that contained various cacti. A couple of rusty rabbit traps and shears hung on the wall above the table, souvenirs of days gone by. Terracotta pots with large leafy plants were scattered along the wall. At the end stood three large steel wheels from old machinery, which her father had bolted together to close off the verandah.

Tom sighed as he settled himself down in his old spot just left of the door. Reaching for the handle, Izzy called out, 'Hello. Anyone home?' Taking a step inside, she called out again. 'Mum?'

'Izzy, is that you?' A voice came from the cool darkness and her mum appeared. Izzy had inherited her tall, lanky, almost boyish figure from her mum. Jean's curly brown hair, highlighted with soft grey, sat on her shoulders. Her blue eyes shone with excitement and her wide smile emphasised her laughter lines. Small crow's feet in the corners of her eyes made her look wise and beautiful. The plain cream shirt she wore was spotless, and around her neck hung a treasured gold locket that enclosed a small photograph of Izzy's sister, Claire.

'Hi, Mum. I missed you,' said Izzy, stepping into her mother's open arms.

Jean Simpson pulled out of Izzy's embrace, held her daughter at arm's length and gave her a once-over. 'It's so good to see you too, sweetheart. Why didn't you tell me you were coming? How long are you home for?'

'I wanted to surprise you, Mum. But let me get in the door first before you bug me with questions, okay?' Izzy teased.

'Come on, then. Your dad's having a cuppa. I'll make you one too.' Jean placed her arm around Izzy's shoulders and led her into the heart of the house.

Izzy's thick socks muffled her footsteps on the old floorboards as they walked the few steps down the corridor into the open kitchen. Over the sink, light flowed in from a large window, through which the garden was visible. The cupboards in the kitchen were the classic mission brown of their era, with coordinating green benchtops, and they were as tidy as ever. The brown stoneware tea, sugar and coffee bowls sat neatly lined against the wall, and she knew there would be no dust on them or grains of sugar or coffee spilt nearby. Her eyes ran over the empty sink that shone from a recent scrub. Izzy had inherited the cleaning gene. When she worked on a tractor, everything sat in an organised spot and the inside of the cab was always cleaned before she started and again when she'd finished.

The solid frame of her father, Bill Simpson, sitting at the breakfast bar captured Izzy's attention. A faint trail of steam rose up from the mug of tea he held in his wide, deeply lined hand. His dark-blue, almost black, piercing eyes glanced up as he sensed someone's presence.

He nearly knocked his stool over and spilt his tea as he scrambled to his feet. 'Isabelle! My God, what are you doing here? I heard someone pull in, but I thought it was just Will.' He embraced Izzy in a tight bear hug and kissed her cheek, his stubble scratching the surface of her skin. She almost had to stand on tippy-toes to reach her arms up over his burly shoulders. It wasn't that he was taller than Izzy, he just had a much bigger frame and a barrel chest.

Izzy wondered for a moment why he'd be expecting Will, but let the thought slip from her mind as she hugged her dad. Gee, I love this old geezer, even if he does try to run my life, she thought. Bill Simpson smelt just how she remembered him, with a hint of sweat and grease mixed in with his deodorant. His tufted-up short, greying hair had thinned slightly at the front. Deep-set wrinkles stood out on his ruddy skin, and that familiar tiny dimple appeared as he smiled, along with his old set of dentures.

Izzy let go of her dad and pulled out a stool alongside him. Jean placed a cup of tea down in front of Izzy and slid a plate of scones closer.

'Now, tell me, darling, how long are you staying? Did you get time off from work?' Jean asked eagerly.

Izzy couldn't hide the smile that grew large and wide. 'I'm home for good, Mum. If that's okay! Is my old room still up for grabs?'

'Of course it is, sweetheart. It's been waiting here since you left. Oh, I'm so glad you're back to stay, Izzy.' Jean reached over and touched Izzy's hand, a gesture of just how much she had missed her daughter.

'So, what happened to your job over east?' asked Bill, while looking into his tea. 'Didn't get the sack, did ya?'

That's just like him, thought Izzy. Assuming the worst all the time. 'No, Dad. I didn't. The kids are old enough now to take care of themselves and I just wasn't needed any more. Besides, my place is here with you and Mum on Gumlea.' She didn't think he needed to know the truth just yet.

Izzy thought about the Radcliffs. They – well, Rob – had given her a job on their farm, Cliffviews, in New South Wales. It was a good size farm – just over four thousand hectares – and they grew wheat, canola and barley, and ran sheep. It had started out as an 'everything job' – helping with their kids, the housework and the odd farm job when she could manage. But Izzy had told Rob from the start that she loved farm work. She was hoping to learn as much from him as she could – from fencing to tractor maintenance, spraying out chemicals and spreading of fertilisers, more or less anything to do with running a farm. When Rob's farmhand quit, Izzy quickly stepped into the position. She'd worked hard to prove how dedicated she was, and bit by bit Rob taught her more. Then her job had changed to permanent farmhand. He must have believed in her and the skills she had acquired, as they started to take holidays and leave her to run the farm in their absence. Rob even roped her into helping with the farm books, and they'd worked on the crop plan together. Whatever needed doing on a farm, Izzy could do it, and she was damn proud of what she'd achieved in the two and a bit years at Rob's. She was now well and truly ready to help run Gumlea.

She'd never passed this information on to her dad, of course. He'd have a fit if he knew she'd been doing farm work. As far as he knew, she'd simply been the house-hand. Otherwise he never would have let her go.

The Radcliffs had become like an adopted family and Izzy would always remember them for their kindness and love. She sighed heavily. She already missed Alice and the two kids so much. If only Izzy's own dad could be more like Rob; so understanding, and eager to teach her anything she wanted to learn. Rob never held back because she was a girl. It was just a shame he had to go and ruin it all. Everything had been so perfect, but now . . . well . . . every good memory was blurred by his betrayal. She could never go back.

Shaking her head, she tried to throw Rob from her mind. 'So, Dad, what's new on the farm?' Izzy rested her hand on his arm for a brief moment, drawing his attention back to her.

'The farm's the same, love. Not a lot happening. We're counting on this year's crop. It looks like the best we've had in a while. Just as well too. We need it to help pay off the new land and to replace the old header that's on its last legs.' He ruffled her hair. 'But don't worry your pretty little head over it. We have more important things to do. I think your coming home is cause for celebration, don't you, Jean? What say we have a barbie? It's been a while since we've had everyone over.' Bill scrunched up his brow, trying to remember.

'I think that's a great idea,' said Jean. 'I'll do a ring around and let everyone know. How does Thursday night sound, Izzy? That should give you enough time to settle in.'

'Yeah, sounds fine to me, Mum. I don't have a lot to unpack and I already feel settled in. Does anyone need a hand with anything or shall I just go and put my stuff away?' Izzy said, stuffing a large portion of scone into her mouth.

'No, I'm fine, Isabelle,' replied her dad. 'You go do your thing. I'm off to feed the sheep in the side paddock, and then the header needs seeing to.' He swallowed the last of his tea. 'I'm so glad you're home, honey. You've made my day. We'll catch up when you're done.' With a wink, he turned and headed to the back door.

'Come on, Izzy,' said her mum. 'I'll help you get your stuff.' Jean collected up the cups and put them in the sink, then placed the clingwrap back over the remaining scones and popped them in the fridge, which was decorated with the postcards Izzy had sent them from the towns close to Rob's farm near Merriwa. Some were from Dubbo, some from Newcastle, and a couple each from Tamworth and Bathurst. When Rob had given her a weekend off here and there, she'd taken off in her ute and explored New South Wales with Tom.

Walking out of the kitchen, Jean stopped in front of Izzy and smiled before pulling her into another embrace. 'Did I mention that I'm happy you're home?' she said.

'Maybe once or twice.'

2

THE next morning Izzy woke with a warm fuzzy feeling inside. Everything seemed right. She lay motionless for a moment, trying to get her bearings, taking in the smells and sounds of her old room. She blinked as she focused on the wall that held the weight of a large, jarrah frame enclosing a picture of two girls on a motorbike. Both girls had the same blue eyes and oval faces, with similar, striking smiles. Izzy remembered having so much fun with Claire that day. A mischievous twinkle was unmistakable in Claire's eyes, as the wind flicked her golden hair about her face.

They had been young then: Claire was sixteen, three years older than Izzy. Even with the age gap, they still got on like a bonfire. Claire had loved to dink Izzy on the bike, and they'd had their fair share of stacks. She'd been born a daredevil, fearless – something Izzy had tried to aspire to.

Izzy's head swam with memories. Claire had been her best friend as well as her big sister. She had to admit that she'd idolised her, although she'd never confessed it then.

A magpie squawked outside her window, competing with a heap of screeching pink and grey galahs in the distance, and she caught the smell of fresh toast. Mum and Dad must be up already, she thought.

Flinging her arm out of the bed, she checked her watch. 'Bugger.' She sat bolt upright. It was already six a.m. Izzy had planned to be up early to do a tour of the farm with her father. She must have been more tired than she thought after all the driving. Five days it had taken her to get back home, not to mention a lot of petrol money and one flat tyre.

Throwing back the sheets, Izzy swung her slender legs out of bed and planted them on the old wooden floorboards. Stretching out her arms and bending her neck, she stifled a yawn and stood up. It was warming up and high temperatures were expected. The flies were already buzzing around, trying to find a cool spot. Izzy stepped towards a white melamine cupboard and grabbed out a pair of khaki shorts and a dark-blue singlet. Quickly she dressed and put on a pair of thick socks, as well as her boot guards, and strode out of her room.

Mum was in the kitchen alone.

'Where's Dad?' Izzy asked.

'He's just out fuelling up the ute. Here, eat some breakfast first. Your father's already had his.' Jean finished buttering some multigrain toast, then reached for a pan on the stove and transferred two eggs onto the bread. 'There you go, love.'

'Ah, Mum, you're a legend.' Izzy settled herself on a stool at the breakfast bar and began to dig straight in.

As Izzy and Bill drove from one dam to the next, the morning sun sparkled against the golden tips of the wheat and heavy heads leant over in the gentle breeze. An impatient Tom pushed his head out past Izzy to the open window. Little mounds of woollen bodies lay dotted over dry feedless paddocks, trying to conserve energy for the warm day ahead.

The final paddock came around too soon as they checked on the last mob of sheep. A blurry haze had spread out before them as the heat intensified in the late morning.

'It's gonna be a hot one at the clearing sale today,' said her dad suddenly.

Lifting her head from its comfy position on her arm, Izzy turned to her father. 'What clearing sale? You didn't tell me there was a clearing sale on. Whose?' she asked curiously.

'Ray North's. He's retiring early after having too many shitty years back to back.'

Izzy nodded. She knew Ray and his wife. They lived about twenty-five kilometres away. 'Who's interested, Dad?'

'Johnno's already leasing most of the land and Perkins the rest. Ray just has his machinery and sundries to sell. Thought we could go in and have a look. He still has that yellow ten-tonne Volvo truck I wouldn't mind getting, if it's in my price range. Plus there's probably a few other things that might be of interest. Best go give our support as well.'

They settled into silence. Another family was leaving the district while their farm merged with others around it. Towns shrunk, schools closed and local businesses battled. It seemed the way of the world, Izzy thought sadly as she rubbed Tom's ears. She wondered what Pingaring would be like in another ten years. She pictured a derelict town with tumbleweeds rolling past.

It took them most of the morning to drive around the farm checking on sheep and dams. Plus Izzy made her dad detour to other parts of the farm, just so she could see every square inch of it. She had missed it all so much and was happy to find it just how it was before she left. All except the large eucalyptus tree that had fallen over in the rock paddock, which Dad said had happened last year after Cyclone Harry had come down the coast.

When they finally returned to the sheds, Izzy quizzed her dad on his new purchases and checked them over, much to his irritation. She liked the new – well, actually, second-hand – seeder bar he'd got, and the new drill press for the workshop. By then it was almost lunchtime and Jean was calling them on the two-way, telling them to clean up and head to the house.

After a cold meat and salad lunch, they all headed to Ray's farm. Izzy grilled her dad for more details on the way. What other things was he interested in and how much was he willing to pay? She even offered her opinion but knew damn well he wouldn't listen to it.

'I think you'll be lucky to get that truck, Dad. It's gonna go way above your price,' she said, having a go anyway. 'With harvest around the corner it will sell as fast as a carton of cold beer. My bet is it will go for around twenty-five thousand.'

Her dad just 'hmphed' at her.

Crossing her arms, she shook her head. She should have bet a six-pack on it, because she knew the old man was dreaming. Trucks were always in high demand at harvest, especially during a good year.

Her mum was helping the CWA ladies with afternoon tea and drinks, so she was dolled up nicely today. She had on a pair of white shorts, a soft blue shirt and minimal make-up, but that was all she needed. Izzy couldn't believe how graceful her mum could look. Why hadn't she inherited any of that, she wondered. Izzy wouldn't dare wear white. It would never stay clean on her. She was still wearing her work clothes from the morning. She stretched her legs as much as she could. Three adults in a ute was just a bit too cosy. Thankfully, it wasn't going to be a long trip. Lifting up her cap, she scratched her head where the sweat was itching her skin. Clearing-sale days always seemed to be hot.

Soon they were pulling into an open paddock where they found a bare patch of earth and parked among the sea of mostly white utes and dual cabs. Already there was a large gathering of blokes in hats and boots. Dust rose in the air, like when sheep were on the move in the paddocks, but this time it came from the prospective buyers walking up and down the rows of items for sale. In and out of the large machinery they wandered. Even if you weren't there to buy, you still had a look.

Two large red headers sat neatly in a row next to a yellow truck, two green tractors and seeding bars to suit, plus a couple of ploughs and two motorbikes. Ray's work ute, a firefighting unit, and a couple of bits and pieces filled another few rows, and an area in his large shed contained sundry items. That was where the farmers' wives congregated. Izzy tagged along with her dad, looking at various items and stopping to chat to the locals. Everyone was coming up to them wondering who was with Bill and they were surprised to see it was Izzy. The subsequent conversation therefore always lasted that bit longer and they all asked the same questions. Have you been home long? Are you staying for good? How was it in New South Wales? What's the farming situation like over there?

A good hour and a half had passed by the time Izzy glanced over to the shed, where the ladies had set up their tables with an assortment of goodies and an old bathtub filled with ice for the cans of soft drink and beer. Her mum was busily getting the urn organised for those who wanted tea or coffee.

A minute later the auctioneer started up and his voice boomed out erratically as the bids began. He started with the small items first, which took nearly an hour to get through, before starting on the larger items. The truck her dad was interested in was coming up shortly. Izzy stood back from the crowd of men circling around the auctioneer. They were dwarfed by the large black tyre of one of the red headers. Once the auctioneer's hand went down, the men all shuffled on to the next item, raising a dust cloud as they went. They moved together, almost synchronised as if they had an imaginary rope around them all.

Bidding eventually started on the large yellow truck. 'Do I hear fifteen thousand?' bellowed the red-nosed auctioneer. His large gut heaved. He obviously enjoyed the taste of beer, Izzy surmised. Give him a red suit and a white beard and he could easily have been mistaken for Santa Claus. A bloke in front of Izzy raised his hand, clutching a bit of paper with the number thirty on it. In the blink of an eye, hands were rising left, right and centre, and the bids flew upwards. Izzy gave a silent chuckle as the price ran straight over the limit her dad had set himself. She was sure he didn't even get a chance to bid.

'Twenty six and a half thousand, going once . . . going twice . . .' The auctioneer scanned the crowd for a bid. 'Sold,' he yelled after confirming there were no more takers. Izzy saw her dad look across to her and she raised her eyebrows and smiled with an 'I told you so' look.

'What did I tell you, hey?' she teased as she rejoined him, while the rest of the crowd moved on to the next item for sale.

'You had a lucky guess,' he grunted back, avoiding her eyes.

She should have known. Not many blokes out here took a girl seriously, let alone her dad. She was trying to break into a tough market.

'I'm dry as chips,' he said quickly, changing the subject. 'Let's go see Jean.'

Off they strode side by side, both the same height but Izzy half the width, towards the spread of food. Her dad bought a beer. It was only three-thirty but it was a given that it was okay to drink earlier in the day if it was a special occasion – or if there were more than two blokes around. They made all kinds of excuses to crack open a cold can.

'Hi, Bill. Any luck?' Jean asked.

He mumbled his reply.

Jean gave an understanding nod with just a hint of a smile, and winked at Izzy when Bill wasn't looking. 'I'll be finished here in a few minutes, Izzy. Did you want to meet up and go over the sundries?' she asked as she handed Izzy her change. 'Your father will have found a few mates to have a drink with by then, no doubt.'

'Sure, Mum,' replied Izzy, before taking a large mouthful of the lamington she'd just bought.

Izzy headed off to check out one of the motorbikes, which she believed would be very handy on the farm. It would certainly be a lot cheaper to run, as well as being easier to shift sheep with, than the ute, especially with diesel prices what they were. She had seen the blue Yamaha TTR250 earlier, and now she got on it and started the engine. It purred into life. Quickly she shut it off, fearing other bidders would take too much interest. It was only a year old and looked in great nick. The black knobbly tyres still had plenty of tread, and the blue plastic mudguards and bodywork had no scratches or cracks. She guessed it might go for around five thousand and she had that much put aside. Deciding to find Ray and ask him about it, she turned and scanned the crowd.

A tall, lean figure was approaching her. She couldn't tell who it was at first as he had on a hat and sunglasses, and nearly every bloke here was wearing the same with jeans and boots. But she could tell this guy had a body you could bounce rocks off. It wasn't until he raised his tanned, muscular arm in a half wave that she recognised him. Yeah, she remembered his sexy swagger all right and knew if he took off his sunnies that she'd be met with a pair of intense blue eyes. He fitted into the 'tall, dark and handsome' category, and something about him demanded your attention, as if he was magnetised and your eyes were little ball bearings.

Suddenly, Izzy felt rather ill. She had been admiring the fine-looking fella, until she realised it was Will Timmins. Argh! Her skin crawled as the hairs on her arms twitched like little antennas, wary of a predator. Oh, she knew Will all right, had known him all her life. His parents owned the farm next to theirs.

Brian and Sandy Timmins had one of the biggest farms in the area. Her father had told her just that morning there were rumours Brian was going to lease another 2000 hectares off Mike Littlemore next year. Mike was apparently moving to Perth for his kids, where they were booked into school.

Brian and Sandy only had two children, Will and his sister, Jolene. Jolene was older than Will, already married with a couple of kids and living in Perth. Izzy hadn't seen Will for ages, and frankly she'd have been quite happy if she'd never seen him again.

Before she could turn and walk away, he spoke.

'Hey, I thought that was you, Izzy. It's good to see you. How long have you been back?'

Will smiled, wondering what kind of answer he'd get. He had found Izzy by accident, admiring her from afar as she checked out the bike. After watching her for a moment, some of the things she did looked familiar. For a moment, he believed it was Claire standing there and his body almost burst with the thought. When he got his emotions back under control, he twigged that it was Izzy, and felt a moment of disappointment. But now, standing in front of her, he found himself staring at this new grown-up version of the girl he once knew. With Claire momentarily forgotten, he began to remember the little Izzy and took pleasure in noticing the womanly improvements a few years had produced.

Izzy kicked at the dirt, took a step back and planted her arms protectively across her body. Her face was set hard and her reply to his question was short and curt. 'Long enough.'

Will nodded his head. 'Ah, I see you still haven't forgiven me. You know, time is supposed to heal all wounds.' He swung his hands onto his hips as if to reinforce the statement. 'Come on, Izzy,' he pushed. 'It's been years.'

Lifting her head, she glared at him fiercely. 'Why should I forgive you? I don't have to like you, you know.'

The look she was giving him was the same hatred-filled one he'd got the last time he'd seen her, several years ago. It was about the only thing that hadn't altered about Izzy.

Will laughed under his breath. 'You Simpsons are a stubborn lot, you know that?' He knew straightaway that he shouldn't have said it. He noticed her body language change, as if he'd waved a red flag. Her eyes narrowed and were drilling holes into his head.

Izzy couldn't contain the fire brewing up inside her. All the anger and hurt broke free from the knotted ropes she'd used to secure them away and returned in full force. She tilted her head and spat just loud enough for him to hear every word clearly. 'Better than an arrogant, self-centred, using bastard like yourself.'

Izzy couldn't see Will's reaction as his face was partially covered by his hat and sunnies. He just stood quietly. His tall, muscled frame was almost leaning backwards from the force of her words.

Ever so slowly and quietly he replied, 'Why don't you tell me how you really feel? Can't a bloke change?'

Izzy wondered if he had been hoping for a miracle. If he thought she could just forgive him and move on, he was wrong. She wasn't going to give him the satisfaction. 'I'll believe it when I see it. Probably around the same time that all the flies just up and die!' She had already turned and started to leave.

Will watched her walk away. He wasn't angry with the way she'd reacted, just sad. He wanted this whole thing over. 'I'll see you later then,' he called out. 'Don't forget we're neighbours and you can't avoid me forever.'

'Huh! Not if I can help it,' she yelled without looking back.

Izzy's steps were long and forceful, almost stomping. She didn't know where she was headed but soon found herself back at the table where her mum was working. As it turned out, Jean was just finishing up so they headed off together into the large shed to check out the household items. It took Izzy a while to calm down and to stop her heart racing like a mad goanna. Will could send her blood pressure soaring in seconds. How dare he have the hide to talk to her like there was nothing wrong between them.

'Are you all right, sweetheart?' asked Jean, sensing the tension in her daughter.

Izzy forced herself to smile and flapped her arms about freely as if to brush it away. 'No, I'm fine. Just thinking, that's all.'

It wasn't until they got to the end of the shed where some old metal-framed beds and mattresses were stacked that she noticed a small man with slightly hunched shoulders chatting to his wife in the corner. 'Mum, I'll be back in a tick. I just want to have a word with Ray.' She set off to chat with Ray, who was standing with his wife, Louise, after remembering that was what she had originally intended, before Will had made her lose her cool.

'G'day, Ray. How are you going, Louise?' she said, greeting them with hugs.

Ray looked so soft and gentle, like a podgy teddy bear with a floppy hat. What he lacked in height, he made up for in heart size. You didn't need glasses to see that the years on the farm had taken their toll on Ray – he looked older than his sixty-five years. Louise was nearly ten years younger and looked fabulous in her pale cotton dress and straw hat.

Together they had four daughters, all married off with their own kids now. Apparently Ray and Louise were moving to their retirement house to be closer to their family. Izzy hoped that never happened to her. She wanted to live and die on the family farm. With a bit of luck she'd have her own children to pass it on to, regardless of what sex they might turn out to be.

'It's so good to see you, Izzy. It's been a while. Are you home visiting?' Louise asked politely.

'No, I'm home for good. I'm here to help Dad run the farm.'

'Ha, good luck with that, love,' said Ray. He understood the huge wall she had to climb. He turned to head off and leave the girls to it, but Izzy stopped him.

'Actually, Ray, I was wondering if I could ask you a few questions about your motorbike,' she said swiftly.

'Oh, sure thing.' Ray halted and waited until Izzy was by his side again.

Ray's small bow-legged strides led the way through his shed, past large brown cardboard boxes. Some were filled with a collection of new fanbelts protruding out like bows; others held an assortment of old spanners and wrenches – things he wouldn't need in the city. The last couple of smaller boxes held large silver pots and pans with the odd plate set and collection of tea towels. The clearing sale had obviously been a good chance for Louise to clean out her cupboards too.

Ray's well-worn leather Blundstones kicked up a cloud of dust as he stepped off the grey cement floor onto the dry soil, heading in the direction of the motorbikes.

'Which one you interested in, love?' said Ray softly.

'The blue 250. Has it had regular check-ups?' she queried, swatting at the annoying flies that buzzed around her face. It was days like this Izzy wished she had a fly net or a couple of old corks on bits of string hanging off her hat.

'I've only done one as I've hardly used it. Getting too old, you see. It's much more comfortable sitting in the ute. I mainly got it for when the kids came down, but they only used it once.'

Izzy watched him closely for a moment. The deep lines upon his dry tanned skin showed the many years he had worked this land. 'You gonna miss it, Ray? All this?' she asked.

He nodded. 'Hard not to, love. Farming has been my whole life, and my parents', and theirs before them. But Louise is lonely and miserable without the kids and I miss them too. I'm getting too old to be doing this by myself. It becomes dangerous and my back is just not what it used to be. It's going to be a big change, that's for sure.' His face looked tired and his eyes betrayed a deep sadness. 'It's hard to leave something that you've poured all your blood, sweat and tears into. But none of the kids want it.'

'Yeah, well, I'd give my left leg to have our farm.' Izzy felt for Ray. She knew what it meant to him – to give it all up for a small boxed-in yard, squeezed in among thousands of other homes when you were used to the open space with just the bush as your nearest neighbour. Izzy had felt the same at boarding school. There was never any peace and quiet there.

'When are you leaving?' she asked, breaking away from her thoughts.

'Two weeks' time. The kids are coming down to help us shift to Bunbury. Don't you worry. We'll be okay.' He gave Izzy a weak smile, obviously still trying to convince himself. 'We're right next to a nice golf course and we'll be able to play as much as we want. Imagine that, Izzy. A real green golf course. I wonder if my game will improve,' he said, laughing to himself.

Golf was one of the main sports around Pingaring. The fairways were green only after it rained, and then it was usually weeds that grew. Not to mention the greens that were actually sand with oil on them. If you were stuck in the bush off the fairway, you really were stuck in the bush. Many balls were lost every year and occasionally found by another bush goer.

Izzy's dad played golf too. He packed an esky with a few beers to take with him, as did most of the outback golfers. Their buggies resembled rolling pubs, with rattling bottles and cans.

'Yes, I'm going to miss this place. It will always be home,' Ray said, deep in thought.

They merged with a small crowd of men who were already milling around the bikes. Izzy nodded goodbye and left Ray talking to another farmer, while she edged her way into the group.

Digging her hand into her back pocket, she pulled out a small piece of rectangular paper and held it at her waist. She felt like a cowboy ready to draw his guns from his holsters.

The auctioneer started the bidding on the Yamaha, his arms going in all directions, pointing out bids. The action started to slow. 'I have five thousand one hundred, going once,' yelled the auctioneer.

Izzy raised her hand, making her number sixty-eight visible for the first time.

The auctioneer pointed at her. 'Five thousand two hundred. Can I see a three?' He scanned the crowd. There were only two serious bidders left and the man in the black hat was shaking his head as he looked down at his disappointed son.

'Five thousand two hundred, going once . . . going twice . . .' Izzy felt a nervous excitement. 'Sold – to the young lass, number sixty-eight. Congratulations, love,' said the auctioneer before moving on to an oldish red four-wheeler.

Izzy smiled. Her first auction buy. She was stoked she'd managed to get it for just over her estimated price.

Later that afternoon she rode it up a small plank of wood onto the back of her dad's ute. She was deliriously happy, even if her dad had reacted just how she'd expected he would.

'Why waste your money on that? What are you going to do with it? You'd better get a helmet before you go breaking your neck.' Bill ranted on and on.

Izzy wondered what a supportive and encouraging father would be like. Did they even exist? Hell, not in her house.

3

THE day after the clearing sale, Izzy and Bill pulled up near the shed after their morning crop inspection. Tom jumped off the back of the ute and went for a sniff around to familiarise himself with his old stomping ground. Izzy sat in the ute for a while, mulling things over. She had to agree with her dad – the crops were looking good. They were so thick you wanted to lie on top of them, and the heads were huge, packed hopefully with high-protein grains. Izzy was impressed. This was one of their best crops for sure. The weather conditions this year had been perfect for farming. It was about time things started looking up for Gumlea. Dad had been working hard enough by himself all these years. She was glad he was finally being dealt a hand full of aces. He needed it, because, other than Izzy, there was no one else to help.

Bill had a sister, Sarah, who lived in Perth with her family. Being the only son, Bill had inherited the farm from his parents. Nana and Grandad Simpson had retired to a little house in Albany quite a few years back. Grandad used to drive down and help with the harvest and seeding, but he wasn't fit to drive the three-hour trip any more. Instead Bill, Jean and Izzy visited them when they could.

Izzy and her dad had driven around most of the farm checking how far off being ripe the crop was. They both decided to get the header going in the top paddock, as it had been planted first and looked ready to harvest. If they could get a good sample off, then they'd take it into the bin for testing. Dad suggested they let the local contractor know they wouldn't be that far off starting.

Dave Henman had been carting their grain for as long as Izzy could remember. When she was young, she used to catch a ride with Dave into the bin to dump the grain. She loved watching the grain sampling.

Izzy had worked on the bins for some extra money after she'd finished school at the end of year twelve. She smiled, thinking back to that time. It was a great job and she'd loved catching up with all the local farmers as they brought their loads in for sampling. It was Izzy's job to take a sample from the trucks and test for protein and moisture, making sure it passed the standards set by the Australian Wheat Board. She absolutely loved her time there. They'd had some fantastic parties and the friendship among the crew was great. Izzy was looking forward to seeing Dave again and finding out who was working at the bin this year.

The Co-operative Bulk Handling bins situated in Pingaring were opposite a couple of houses, a hall and the local shop. Only the railway line divided them. It was a ten-minute drive from the farmhouse, so they'd be able to drop the sample off that afternoon. If the sample passed, they should be able to start harvesting the next morning.

Mum wanted her to go into town anyway to pick up supplies for the barbecue that night , just some meat packs, nibblies and grog – the standard barbie essentials.

Dad had Swan Draught and a few Emu Bitter cans in the grog fridge, but Izzy felt like something different, something stronger, maybe a bourbon. With this in mind, she headed off towards the house to collect the shopping list from her mum, while her dad jumped in the header to take it up to the top paddock and get a sample off the crop. She wanted to go with him to collect the sample; that first bite into the crop was such a great feeling, but he resisted her efforts. Sometimes she thought it'd be much easier belting her head against the trunk of the gumtree out by the back gate.

*

The late afternoon was still quite warm as Izzy stood in front of the full-length mirror. She tightened the thin straps around her neck and watched the soft blue material swish above her knees. Her hands moved to her flat stomach and began straightening the dress. She smoothed her hair back into an elegant ponytail, and then took one last look in the mirror. Licking her finger, she tried to train her eyebrows into a neater line. Yes, she'd definitely got the Simpson wayward eyebrows, but they looked okay when trained into place. As for her nose, it was purely her mother's – straight, small and almost dainty, which seemed so at odds with Izzy's character. Thankfully her skin looked clear. Izzy took out her standard sleeper earrings and changed them for the small blue drop earrings Aunt Betty had given her for her sixteenth birthday. Satisfied, she headed out of the bathroom, ready to help her mum with the salads and sauces.

Voices floated from the verandah through the afternoon air. Quite a few people had turned up already.

She could see their neighbours who lived south of them, Jim and Betty Cable, who'd retired on the farm while their two sons ran a half each. They'd been like another set of grandparents to Izzy and she loved them dearly. Many times Claire and Izzy had ridden their bikes to Aunt Betty's. Her house was so warm and cosy. Knitted rugs lined the floors and chairs, and thousands of knick-knacks cluttered the shelves. It always smelt of freshly baked cakes. She usually had on hand a big plate of pink-iced biscuits or cake, and some homemade lemon cordial, unless it was the afternoon, when the place would smell of roasting meat that sizzled in the oven. What Izzy loved most were Aunt Betty's hugs hello, when she'd get lost in her flowery apron and ample bosom. Betty was such a special lady, and it was amazing how loved Izzy felt snuggled up in her generous arms.

Izzy made a mental note to grab the little gift off her bed to give to Aunt B before she went and said hello. She hoped she'd like the little crystal frog she'd bought to add to her collection. She noticed friends of her parents from around the district, as well as their other neighbours, Brian and Sandy Timmins.

An outbreak of hellos and g'days occurred in the far corner of the verandah, and as Izzy wandered outside, she caught her dad shaking hands with a young bloke who looked horribly like Will.

'Oh, shit,' Izzy mumbled under her breath. 'What's he doing here?' She'd hoped she'd seen the last of him for a while, but instead she was running into him again. That was the problem with small districts.

Izzy turned back towards the food on the table and surreptitiously glanced across to where they stood. Will's fringe hung across his forehead and she watched him brush it back with a swipe of his hand. Then he smiled at her dad as Bill clapped him on the shoulder. His old cracked and dry hands looked out of place on Will's crisp white shirt. Disgruntled, Izzy turned away.

'Glad you could make it, mate,' said Bill.

'Well, I nearly didn't come,' replied Will.

Bill raised an eyebrow curiously. 'Why?'

'I didn't think Izzy would be too impressed about me turning up.'

'Oh, don't worry about Izzy. She'll have forgotten all about her anger at you for hurting Claire by now, you'll see. It's better she believes you dumped Claire than knows the real truth,' said Bill, dismissing the problem with a wave of his hand.

Will shook his head, looking around to see where she was. 'No, she hasn't forgotten. I bumped into her at the clearing sale, and let's just say that she wasn't too pleased to see me. I'm assuming you still haven't told her?' Will asked quietly.

Bill's eyes became dry and he felt his jaw spasm and his muscles clench.

'No, and she's not going to know either.' His heart began to heave in his chest at the thought of Izzy finding out the secret he and

Will had managed to keep quiet all this time. 'There's no need to go upsetting her. Let's just keep it this way, okay?' Bill knew he sounded gruff. 'Please,' he begged, trying a different tactic.

Will sighed and began playing with the label on his stubbie. 'But I hate it, Bill. She's still so angry. I want to go back . . . back to the way it all was when we used to be good friends. I need all the friends I can get out here. You know how hard it's been. Especially without Claire,' he finished sadly. 'She reminded me so much of Claire at the sale, especially with her "all guns blazing" attitude. Claire always spoke her mind.'

Bill studied his young protégé's freshly shaven face. He saw the pain still buried in his eyes. Will masked it well, but Bill knew him better than most. 'I'm sorry, mate, but please do this for us and for Izzy. She'll come around eventually, you'll see. Who could resist your charm anyway?' Bill joked, trying to lighten the situation.

'I'm damn sure Izzy can.'

Will smiled and Bill knew their secret was safe, for the moment at least. He followed Will's eyes to his daughter. Lifting his arm, he waved and beckoned her over.

For a split second Izzy thought about ignoring him, but it was too late. He knew she'd seen him.

'Isabelle, come say hello to Will. She's home for good now,' he said, turning back to Will. 'All finished over east. We'll have to find her a job closer to home this time,' he concluded, as she reluctantly joined them.

'Hey, Izzy. How are you?' asked Will.

Izzy's eyes ran up his tall, lean frame to his tanned face and all she could muster as a reply was, 'Fine.' He wasn't getting a polite conversation out of her.

She looked down at the ground, anything to avoid eye contact, and became engrossed in his black-and-white, double-plugged thongs with his sock tan standing out like a pink arse on a black baboon. It was common enough when you worked outside a lot. Izzy glanced at her own stylish sock tan, but luckily her legs looked gorgeous and brown against the blue of her dress. Hopefully that was enough to keep the eyes above her ankles.

Bill cleared his throat, trying to cover Izzy's dismissive reply. 'Will's been helping me out a fair bit on the farm lately.'

'Which reminds me, Bill. I have that Honda pump for you. I'll go chuck it on your ute so it's not forgotten,' said Will, cutting in.

That would be right, thought Izzy. Trying to help the charity case no doubt. Dad must be getting old if he was accepting help from the Timminses. He always used to complain that they bragged about their big trucks and headers, rubbing their money in people's faces. She knew they always made her dad feel like he lived in the gutter.

Bill put his arm out, stopping Will. 'Cheers, mate. But you stay here, drink up and enjoy. I'll grab it.' Clearly, he was trying to get them to spend time together. Izzy was having none of that. 'I'd better go and help Mum,' she muttered, as she turned on her heel and left Will standing alone.

'I'll see ya later,' he said into the warm air, but his words never reached her.

Izzy managed to avoid Will for most of the evening, but she noticed how much time her dad spent with him, chatting as if they were best mates. She watched them closely. Will's long, lean arms and large hands moved constantly as he talked to her dad. Every now and then, he ran his hand through his short, mousy-brown hair. Jeez, she thought, he used to do that when he was younger. She had to admit he was pleasant looking. Hell, he was gorgeous and she couldn't deny it, but he knew it too. When he was nineteen, he thought he was so hot with his ute, and all the girls fussing over him. He thought the sun shone out of his arse. But what made it worse was that back then Izzy actually believed it did. She used to follow him and Claire around like a lost lamb. When they had been young kids they'd all played together, but when Will and Claire hit the teenage years, they deemed her too young to join in their fun. Will never teased her though. It was always Claire who'd tell her to go home if they wanted her gone. It wasn't until she had turned sixteen that they really let her hang out with them. Izzy figured it was more for their enjoyment. Watching her get drunk and sending her on little pranks.

Bill started heading towards the beer fridge, so Izzy took the opportunity to corner him on his own. 'Hey, Dad. Havin' a good time?'

'Of course, sweetheart. You?' He paused as he clutched the long metal door handle on the old fridge.

'Yep, but what's going on with Will? How come he's here?'

Bill sighed. 'A lot has changed since you've been gone, Isabelle. Will has been through a lot. Claire's death changed his life too. He was pretty broken up and very lost. He ended up leaving the farm for a while and did some soul-searching. He grew up and came back a different bloke, and since then we've been helping each other to heal. He's really a great guy once you get to know him.'

'Yeah, you think so? I haven't noticed a change yet.' Izzy tucked her loose fringe back firmly behind her ear. 'You must be getting soft in your old age, mixing with Will and taking the Timmins' charity. There's no way I'm letting him sweet talk me around like he's done you. I haven't forgotten about him and Claire.' Izzy gave her dad the look of a stubborn Simpson, then turned on her heel and left.

What would Dad know anyway? she thought. He hadn't been the one left comforting Claire while she'd cried of a broken heart.

It had been a shock seeing Claire like that, as she wasn't one to cry. Not like that anyway. She'd always been strong and carefree, had always looked on the bright side of life. To see her crumpled miserably in a heap on her bed had torn at Izzy and left an image in her mind that she'd never forget – or forgive.

Bill just shook his head as his daughter walked away, then grabbed a cold beer and passed another to Jim.

'Izzy sure is looking great. Whatever she's been doing must have agreed with her,' Jim said, as he screwed off the cap and took a sip. 'Is she still trying to work on the farm?'

Bill growled. 'Yes. But Izzy knows my answer to that. A farm's not a place for a young girl. She could do a whole lot better for herself.'

'Come on, Bill. She's hardly a young girl any more,' said Jim.

'Don't I know it. You know, we took a drive around the place today. She was asking me heaps of questions about the farm and sticking her nose in, like usual. She talked me into taking a sample off in the top paddock. Bugger me if she wasn't right. It turns out that the moisture was just under the limit. So it's all go tomorrow morning.'

'You'd better put that beer back then!' chuckled Jim. 'Or you could always hand it over to me.'

The phone ringing caused them to pause. Jean called out for Izzy, who was somewhere on the crowded verandah.

Izzy walked over to her mum and took the phone from her.

'Hello?' For a moment Izzy listened and then she exploded. 'I told you not to call me!'

A few people in the vicinity looked her way. She took her hand off her hip and waved it about like she was shifting stupid sheep. 'Just piss off, will you? Leave me alone and don't bother calling back.' She punched the end call button with such force that she almost dropped the phone. Now she had everyone's attention. Feeling eyes on her back, she quickly went inside to hide and sat down at the dining table. Izzy wasn't upset this time, just bloody mad.

A hand touched her shoulder, causing her to jump.

'Mum, you scared the crap out of me.'

Jean looked at her daughter carefully. 'Is everything all right?'

Izzy sighed. 'Yeah, I'll be fine.'

'Who was he?'

Izzy glanced at her mum. Why did she have the feeling her mum knew it all anyway? Mums have a sixth sense, Izzy was sure. Sighing again, she answered slowly, 'Rob.'

Jean didn't open her mouth in shock. Instead she remained composed. 'Rob Radcliff, your boss?'

'Ex-boss.' Izzy patted the dining chair next to her. 'You'd better sit down.'

She waited for her mum to sit before she began. 'You know, everything was going great and I loved what I was doing on the farm. Rob was such a great teacher and we worked so well together. That's why this whole thing sucks!' Izzy covered her face with her hands. 'We were fixing the tractor one day, and he leant across and tried to kiss me,' she said through her fingers.

'What did you do?' Jean asked quietly, trying not to let her disappointment and concern show.

Izzy lifted her face out of her hands. 'Slapped him, of course.' Taking a deep breath, Izzy tried to block out the memory that had been haunting her for the last week but it came back with a vengeance.

It had been a normal day, just like any other. They were both in the shed and had been there for two hours even though it was still only seven-thirty in the morning. The air was crisp and her fingers were so cold they'd gone numb. Not that it bothered her. It was just how it went. Rob was not far from her in the shed. His two-day-old stubble, which was starting to go grey, prickled against the cold along his narrow jawline. There was also a hint of grey through his black hair giving him a George Clooney look. He was a bit on the scrawny side, always needing a belt for his pants, but he could do the work of a strong man. On this day they had been looking over the John Deere tractor Rob had just bought, checking everything before they began getting it ready for farm work. Izzy inspected the level and condition of the transmission and hydraulic oil and found it rather low. The oil smelt burnt and was quite discoloured, not to mention the tiny bits of grit that she could feel in it between her thumb and finger.

She wiped the mess off her fingers onto a dirty rag nearby. 'I don't think your new pride and joy is really going to cut the mustard. She's been worked over and neglected a bit. I think you've got a lemon,' she said.

Rob scoffed at her. 'Nah, don't you go knocking my new baby,' he replied, then went to check it himself. She stood behind his tall frame and watched as his shoulders slumped a fraction. He'd seen the evidence too.

'You never know, maybe with some TLC she'll come good.' Izzy tried to cheer him up. Rob then turned around and held up his oily fingers and wiggled them. Laughing, Izzy went to step back away from his threatening hands but he reached out his long arms and wrapped her up unexpectedly.

'No, don't you bloody dare. I'll quit,' she joked, holding her head back as far as it would stretch, while trying to escape his grasp. But with mad glee in his hazel eyes he teasingly pressed an oily finger to her forehead, leaving a smudge the length of his little finger. Izzy thought it had all just been in good fun, until Rob's hand started caressing her cheek. Izzy felt the air around them change. She started to feel nervous, like being cornered in a pen with a charging ram heading straight for you. She tried to yell out a warning, tried to break the weird moment, but it somehow got stuck in her throat. All that came out was a raspy, 'Rob, no.' She tried to scramble backwards, to get feeling to her feet, but she was in a state of shock.

She didn't think he'd heard and began to panic when she saw the swirling emotion in his eyes – something she'd never seen before. In the next instant he kissed her. Izzy's lips remained shut tight, like the lid on a coffin, and her eyes were so wide they were beginning to water. She felt his hold on her relax, and in that moment she leant back and smacked his face. Her hand connected so well that the smack echoed throughout the shed like one of his kids' cap guns.

Rob stumbled, reeling with shock, and held the side of his face. 'Izzy, stop,' he said as she moved away. 'Please listen to me. I'm sorry. I've tried to stop this, but I can't. I really like you.'

Izzy just about died on the spot.

'Don't you feel it too?' he asked.

'No, Rob. I don't. How could you even ask that? Alice . . .' She was too stunned to continue. 'But you still love her, right?'

She could see Rob searching inside himself for the answer. 'Yes, of course, she's the mother of my kids. But you, I can't stop thinking about. I just want to hold you and taste you.'

Izzy cringed at his words. 'Don't be ridiculous, Rob,' she said, trying to sound businesslike. 'It's just lust. You don't really want to wreck your marriage by doing something stupid now. It was just a heat of the moment thing, right? It's not going to happen again.'

Rob looked at her sheepishly. 'I've been trying not to think of you that way for the last month and I just can't take it any more. Being around you every day is driving me mad, Izzy.'

Izzy shuddered at the memory of it all. One minute it'd been great, the next it had all turned to manure, and Izzy knew then that she had no choice but to flee and never look back.

As Izzy glanced at Jean's waiting eyes, she lowered her voice to a whisper and continued. Izzy felt uncomfortable even saying it. 'He was a married man, for God's sake! I trusted him. He was a good friend, as well as . . . I guess . . . a father figure. I looked up to him as a mentor, and in one moment he shattered everything.' Izzy realised her hands were scrunched up into fists and tried to relax. 'I couldn't chance it happening again so I left and came home.'

It had been a hard decision to make – to give up her perfect life on Cliffviews. She'd been in her little cottage chucking clothes into her bags and trying to stop the tears welling in her eyes when Alice appeared at her door.

'Rob's just told me you're leaving, Izzy. I didn't believe him but . . . it's true?'

Luckily, Izzy had already been thinking about what to tell Alice. She knew she couldn't leave without saying a proper goodbye. 'I'm so sorry, Alice. Something has happened at home and I have to go back.'

'Oh, is it your parents? I hope they're okay.' Alice said it with such sincerity that Izzy found it hard to continue with her lie.

'No, they're fine. It's just Dad needs me on the farm right now. He's really struggling and this is what I've been waiting for my whole life. I hope you understand, Ali. I'm really grateful for everything you've done and for embracing me into your family.'

Alice began to cry. Izzy dropped her armful of clothes and held her tightly. She brushed Alice's red curly hair back off her face and smiled. Alice was almost fifteen years older than her but they'd become close friends.

'I'm dreading telling the kids,' said Izzy, grimacing.

'Well, here's your chance.' Alice's blue eyes glistened with fresh tears as she heard a motorbike pull up outside. A few seconds later Emma and Chris came running inside, their cheeks flushed from the ride on the bike.

Emma, the oldest, and the spitting image of her mum with flaming hair and a splattering of cute freckles across her cheeks and nose, got to Izzy first. 'Izzy, you can't go,' she wailed with all the drama a thirteen-year-old could muster. She threw herself into Izzy's arms and whispered into her ear, 'Who will I have to talk to?'

Many times Emma had snuck down to Izzy's cottage for some deep and meaningful conversations on boys and other things she couldn't bring herself to talk to Alice about. 'I'll be fourteen next month and you said you had a surprise planned. Can't you stay till then?'

'I know, and I'm really sorry. My dad needs me for harvest so I have to go now. You can still call me any time or email me. It's not like I'm falling off the face of the earth.'

The realisation that she could still talk to Izzy seemed to satisfy Emma. But now it was Chris's turn. The gangly eleven-year-old, grazed from coming off the bike two days earlier, wrapped his bony arms around Izzy. She scruffed up his hair, as his blue eyes pleaded. 'Who's gonna play pool with me and take me yabbying and fix my bike after I stack it?'

It was so hard leaving them but Izzy had set her mind on leaving. She hadn't really wanted to, but she could see she had no choice. There was no way Rob would forget about her if she was still on the farm and in his face every day. And Izzy had always known that at some point she would return to Gumlea. Her dream of running it wasn't going to happen while she was on the other side of the country. Perhaps this was a sign that it was time, anyway. It was a slap in the face, but it had helped her remember her dream.

Alice had convinced her to stay for dinner that night and had prepared a feast. Rob had been quiet the whole night and Izzy found it very uncomfortable. Luckily they had the distraction of the kids.

The next morning they stood together as a family waving her goodbye. She was sure she was doing the right thing for Alice, Emma and Chris. And for Rob. She didn't hate him. She couldn't, after all he'd given her, but she was very angry and hurt. One day she hoped they could meet on better terms. She'd love to come back and see the kids and Alice again.

Izzy now searched her mother's eyes. Did Jean agree with what she'd done? 'I racked my brain, Mum, and I'm positive I didn't do anything to lead him on or give him the wrong impression. I can't believe I never saw this coming.'

Jean put her hand on her daughter's and gave it a squeeze. 'I know you wouldn't have done anything to encourage him. These things happen. It certainly wasn't your fault.'

'But, Mum, I feel bad for Alice. She doesn't even know. I still feel as if I've betrayed her, even though I haven't. It's not fair. I already miss Alice and the kids so much.' Izzy shook her head. 'I'm hoping that, with me gone, Rob'll realise what a fool he's been and remember that he still loves Alice. But the idiot keeps calling me!'

'He'll stop when he realises you're not going back. He wouldn't leave his farm. One day he'll see how stupid he was and how close he came to losing it all. You were right to leave, Izzy.' Jean said the words she knew her daughter needed to hear.

Izzy turned her head to the crowd outside. 'God, how many heard me out there?'

'Not many,' said Jean reassuringly, but her eyes told another story.

'I might just hide in here for a while,' Izzy said, as her cheeks began to burn.

Jean stood up. 'Well, don't stay for too long. This party was for you, remember.'

'Yeah, a good impression I've made so far,' she said sarcastically, before they both laughed. Izzy watched her leave. Thank God she had her mum to confide in. Sometimes poor old Tom just wasn't enough.

Eventually she made her way back outside and used the moment to give Aunt B her present. She found her sitting tightly packed into a plastic chair on the verandah.

'Hiya, Aunt Betty. I have a little something for you.' Izzy gave her a hug and produced the gift.

'Oh, you shouldn't have, pet.' Aunt Betty's thick fingers opened the present gently. 'My, it's gorgeous. Thank you. I know just where to put it.' She wrapped Izzy up against her bright flowery dress and hugged her again. They chatted for a while and Aunt Betty invited her over for afternoon tea on the weekend. 'I've invited Jess over as well. She's such a lovely girl. You two used to come over all the time for my chocolate slice and sponges. Have you caught up with her since you've been home?'

Izzy smiled as she thought about Jess. She was probably not in the good books with her as they'd lost contact quite soon after Izzy had moved away. But she'd love the chance to catch up with her old friend. She was the daughter of the Painters who lived about twenty kilometres away on their farm, Glencoe. 'No, I haven't yet, so that sounds like a plan. You're a gem. I should have thought to invite her today, but I'm still just getting into the swing of things.'

'Ah, you'll have your roots replanted soon enough.' Aunt Betty waved her away with a wink.

Izzy got herself another drink, then went and said hello to Uncle Jim, Betty's husband. There was no one else close to her age except for Will, as only closest friends and neighbours had been invited. She'd been away for so long she didn't know who'd be left in the district of her age. You could usually count on the blokes hanging around, as they'd work the farms, but most girls would have moved to a bigger town or shifted to the city. At least it sounded like Jess was still around. Izzy couldn't wait to catch up with her.

4

IZZY was up at four-thirty the next day to help her dad get started with harvest. The barbecue had ended early as everyone else was in the same boat with harvest and so they were all in bed by ten o'clock that night.

Today she was going to get the old Honda fire pump going and fill its tank, then help her dad shift the field bins into the paddock. And if she could convince her father to let her, she might get to drive the header.

After a big fry-up breakfast, she headed up to the shed that housed the firefighting gear. It sat on the back of the old yellow Toyota Land Cruiser, the same one Izzy had learnt to drive when she was eight. She did a few checks on the motor, then drove to the standpipe, which was ten minutes down the road, and filled up the tank.

As she drove back into the shed, she saw her dad outside talking to Will. She couldn't believe it. Her guts churned. Maybe her father had adopted him while she was away. He'd always wanted a son.

'Hello,' said Will, as she walked towards them.

A quick nod was all she could muster in acknowledgement, before she turned to her dad.

'The firefighter's all filled up and ready to go and I checked the pump too. She's all good, so I'll run it up to the top paddock if you like. Have you got the new extinguishers?'

'Yep. I'll get you to run me out to the header and I'll make a start. Will, can you take Izzy back on your bike before you head home?' asked Bill.

'Sure, no worries,' said Will, scratching his chin, which was shadowed with light stubble.

'No, Dad. I'm fine,' Izzy said sharply. 'I was hoping to do a few rounds with you anyway to see how the crop goes, then I can just walk back.'

'No, I don't want you hanging around up there with me. Besides, it's a long walk back and Will's here.' Bill leant over to Izzy and lowered his voice. 'It's about time you gave him a break and got to know him. You can't change the past, so move on.' He turned to Will. 'Cheers, mate. I appreciate it. Thanks for bringing over the belt for the header. Let me know how much I owe you.' He nodded to him, then placed a couple of fire extinguishers in the back of the ute. He climbed in and waited for Izzy.

Izzy muttered a few expletives under her breath before climbing in too. They headed off, with Will following behind on his motorbike.

When Izzy got to the paddock, she gave it one last try. 'Come on, Dad, a couple of laps won't hurt. Please,' she begged. Why was it that she always felt as though she was only ten years old around him?

'Maybe later, sweetheart. Just let me get the teething problems sorted out first.'

Yeah right, she thought, angry that he was trying to fob her off. She watched him check over the header and start his first lap around the paddock before she reluctantly headed towards Will, who was waiting patiently on his bike.

He was astride a new-looking Yamaha, his jeans pulled tight across his thighs. He adjusted his hat as she came towards him. His reflective sunglasses made it impossible for her to tell what he was looking at. Her own eyes quickly took in his blue singlet, which fitted tightly over his chest and left his tanned, well-built arms exposed.

'I don't mind walking, if you have better things to do,' she said, as she stopped next to him.

'Come on, get on. I won't bite, I promise.' He gave her a cheeky smile. A tiny dimple appeared on the right side of his cheek, which they used to tease him about when he was a kid but now looked rather sexy. His jaw was lean and narrowed elegantly towards his chin and his skin was the silkiest brown. He would make a great underwear model, she thought suddenly, before shaking it from her mind, annoyed for letting herself get distracted by his good looks. Best get this over sooner rather than later. With a big sigh, she swung her leg over the bike.

'Hang on,' he warned as he kicked the bike into a noisy rumble. Then he reached back, grabbed her hands and drew them around his waist.

Izzy didn't want to touch him. She quickly withdrew her hands and opted to hang onto the back of the bike instead. 'Don't worry,' she told him. 'Claire could never toss me off a bike.' Izzy mentioned Claire deliberately. It worked. Will rode her home in silence.

In front of her house, Will stopped the bike with a small skid and her chest slammed into his back. He shut down the motor as Izzy quickly jumped off, slightly embarrassed that her chest had been embedded into his back. She was about to walk away when Will reached out and grabbed her. His long fingers curled easily around her narrow wrist. He took off his sunnies, as if knowing how the mesmerising blue of his eyes would weaken her.

'All this hostility isn't good, Izzy. How long are you gonna hold a grudge for?'

Will searched her eyes. They were set hard, but they didn't fool him. Behind them was the real Izzy, the girl who would laugh hysterically at a good joke or go out of her way to help anyone in need. He'd forgotten how much time he and Claire used to spend with Izzy. When she came home from boarding school they'd have great times corrupting her. Like the time they dared her to move everyone's cars around outside the hall during a busy function late one night, so when everyone went to go home there was complete confusion. It had been hell funny to watch and was easy to do as almost half the district still left their keys in their cars. They used to sneak Izzy drinks out the back of parties when she was around fifteen or sixteen and laugh when she got pissed, then frantically try to sober her up so they didn't get busted. Izzy had definitely changed since then. She'd hardened, that's for sure. But Will hoped that the carefree, fun-loving side of her was still in there somewhere. He wished she knew the truth about him and Claire. It would be so much easier for them to make amends and move on, but he figured Izzy couldn't fight him forever. No matter how long it took, he would thaw that block of ice she held between them. Claire would have known how to get through to her sister. God, he missed her. And Claire wouldn't want him to give up on Izzy either.

As he looked up, he noticed Izzy had been studying him. Her eyes were fixed and wide as if reading his thoughts. The hairs on his neck prickled. He felt like she'd opened his personal diary, but he'd had enough practice in shutting down his emotional thoughts to know how to handle it.

Izzy glanced at his hand, which he still had gripped around her wrist. 'I'll hold a grudge for as long as it takes. Don't think you can win me over with that smile of yours, Will Timmins, because it won't work on me. Thanks for the ride.' She pulled away and headed towards the house with her head held high.

Will watched her go, a mixture of puzzlement and sadness on his face. He was about to start the motorbike when he heard a car coming down the driveway. Will eyed off the new Toyota Hilux ute as it pulled up and a tall man got out. He walked over to where Will sat upon the bike.

'G'day there. You lost?' Will asked.

'Nah, mate. I'm looking for Izzy, Izzy Simpson. Is this her place?'

Will's ears pricked up and his eyes roamed over the guy – his short black hair and two-day-old stubble. He wore a simple T-shirt and jeans with a pair of workboots, and had a wide stance and his arms crossed. Will would bet a fiver that this bloke was a farmer, and he looked to be in his late thirties. What was he doing here chasing Izzy?

Will was about to reply when Izzy beat him to it. 'What the hell are you doing here?' He felt a gust of air as she stormed past, like a miniature cockeye bob.

'You won't answer my calls. What else was I supposed to do, Izzy? I —'

Izzy threw her hands up in the man's face. 'Don't you start, Rob. I'm not interested. You've come a bloody long way for nothing. Does Alice know you're here?' Her hands were now set firmly on her hips.

Will was listening intently. The other two were so involved in their conversation they'd forgotten he was there. He was uncomfortable on the bike but he didn't dare move in case he made a noise and reminded them of his presence. He was enjoying this little show. It was nice to see Izzy fuming at someone other than himself for a change. But who was this guy, he wondered.

'Of course she knows I came to see you,' said Rob rather sheepishly. 'Look, you left without your pay, and besides, I want you back – I mean, we all do. The kids miss you, Izzy. Chris is following me everywhere like a lost lamb.'

'There is no way I'm going back. Besides, it'd do you and Chris a world of good to spend some more time together.' At the mention of Chris, Izzy felt a pang of sadness in her heart as his cheeky boyish smile came to mind.

'But the farm – I can't run it without you. Look, I'll pay you more. I'll do anything. It will take me forever to find someone I can trust to do your job. I'm so sorry about what happened, but can't we move on? Please, Izzy. It's nearly harvest.'

Izzy shook her head. 'Well, you'd better start looking around because I can't come back, Rob. It just wouldn't be the same. I don't know if I could trust you again.'

Will was about to pipe up and tell the bloke he didn't have a hope in hell of getting a Simpson to change their mind, but he figured it wouldn't go down too well.

With a start Izzy remembered Will was behind her and she really didn't need him listening to this. She grabbed Rob's elbow and led him back around to the other side of his ute. Just seeing the Hilux brought back vivid memories of the hours she'd spent driving it around Rob's farm.

'Who's he?' He jerked his thumb towards Will.

'Our neighbour, that's all. Rob, you must understand that there was nothing between us. What you felt was just lust or attraction, but nothing worth leaving Alice and the kids over. I did you a favour by leaving. Now you can get back to your family and your farm.'

The look on her face confirmed her words; Rob looked dejected. 'Part of me knows you're right, but the other part misses you like crazy. Hell, Izzy, we had some great times.'

'Yes, but it was innocent fun. I care about you a lot, Rob, but as a great friend, nothing more. I'd never ruin what you and Alice have. I know you still love her and you'll soon see that what you felt for me was misguided.'

It was killing Izzy to talk to Rob this way. If only she could turn back the clock. She had been so comfortable at Cliffviews, and Emma and Chris had been like her younger siblings. Every Friday they'd have their movie nights with her at the cottage where they'd share popcorn and copious amounts of chocolate and soft drink. There had been times, too, when Izzy had got together with Alice and a few of her friends and they'd had wild girls' nights with plenty of wine and dancing. The more she thought about all the things they'd done together, the more she missed them all. As she looked at Rob, Emma and Chris came to her mind so easily. Especially Chris, who was Rob all over – same eyes and black hair.

Now Rob pulled a packet from his back pocket and held it out to her.

Izzy took it slowly from his outstretched hand. 'What's this?'

'Your pay, plus a bonus. I didn't want to give this to you; I was hoping you'd change your mind and come back. But I guess you're right. Maybe I'm being foolish. We did spend so much time together. Anyway, please take it, Izzy. It's only small in comparison to what you've done for us. Alice also wanted me to give you this, and to tell you that she misses you heaps.' Rob handed her a tightly sealed envelope, then shuffled his feet and cleared his throat. 'I . . . um . . . really ruined everything, didn't I?' He looked at her with great sadness. 'Don't answer that. Sorry. I tried to stop it, you know, but I couldn't help how I was feeling. You're an amazing woman, Izzy Simpson.'

'Rob —' Izzy went to protest.

He held up both hands. 'I know, I know. I guess this is goodbye.'

'Well, normally I'd invite you in to stay the night, but Mum and Dad would ask questions and it would be too awkward. I hope you understand this is for the best. Where are you staying tonight?'

'At the pub in Lake Grace. Why?'

'How about I meet you there for tea and a few drinks and we can chat some more. But nothing else, okay? I want my good friend back. Can you do that?' Izzy asked.

'Yes, I think enough crap has gone down for me to start putting things into perspective. I would really like to see you later and clear the air,' he replied, the sadness still so evident in his eyes. 'You've been a part of our family for over two years. I hope one day you can forgive me, Izzy, and come to visit us again?'

Izzy nodded in reply, her throat too tight to speak.

Will adjusted his sunnies quietly. He could see the look in Rob's face and the defeated slump of his shoulders. This bloke cared about Izzy a lot. It sounded like Izzy had been working on Rob's farm, and she was a good worker, apparently. He was curious to know more. From what Bill had told him, she'd been looking after kids and keeping house. Well, somebody's been keeping secrets, he thought, smiling. Then he remembered that he had a big secret of his own and his grin dissolved.

'What time will you come, sevenish?'

'Yep, seven's good. Till then,' she said quietly as he climbed into his car, gave one last glimpse behind, and left.

Izzy turned around and headed back towards Will, not daring to watch Rob drive away. Rob wasn't the only one whose emotions were in turmoil.

Will tilted his head like a puppy, waiting for her to say something.

'Oh, just shut up,' Izzy blurted, then stormed off into the house.

Will sat quietly on his bike, his mind churning with questions. Listening to Izzy and Rob's conversation made him realise that he didn't know much about her at all, apart from the bits and pieces Bill had mentioned, and even those seemed wrong now. The last time he'd seen Izzy was a few months after Claire's funeral, before he'd left the farm to seek solitude and find some answers. That was over four years ago, and a lot could change in that time. Will started the motorbike and rode home.

Izzy headed straight to her room and sat on her bed. She glanced at the package with money bulging out of it and placed in on the bedside table. Carefully she examined the envelope from Alice. Izzy's name was written on the front in beautiful sweeping handwriting, with a line and a little heart underneath. Turning it over, Izzy gently opened the back and pulled out the letter.

My dearest Izzy,

When Rob said he was going over to WA to see you, I quickly wrote this letter. I don't have the nerve to call you but hope this will do. I had noticed Rob pulling away from me these last few months. He'd begun to work late and little things started to register. But it wasn't until you up and left that it clicked. The way Rob's been moping around the house, I figured it must be over you. I don't know if anything happened between you, but I assume that you've left to prevent it. I know when women are attracted to Rob and you definitely weren't. Never once did I feel like I had to be watching you two. I haven't mentioned anything to Rob yet as I think it's too soon. I'm sure he'll open up to me later. Fingers crossed he does. But I just want you to know that I still care about you lots and hope this doesn't affect our friendship. Emma and Chris miss you like mad and are seriously hounding me to death.

So thank you for putting us first. I know it must have been hard. I'd love to hear from you. Maybe you could fill me in on the truth.

Love, your friend,
Alice xox

A tear fell from Izzy's nose and landed on the bottom of the page. Alice was such a loving person and Izzy couldn't understand how Rob could do this to her. But the letter had lifted a weight off her mind. Tonight after she'd met with Rob she'd write her a letter back. Smiling, she began to read the letter again.

*

It was exactly five minutes to seven when Izzy opened the glass door to the pub. She had deliberated over what to wear and decided on jeans and a black singlet with a high cut and wide straps. She didn't want anything too nice or revealing. Tonight was not going to get out of hand. Oh, how she hoped Rob was going to behave. She paused inside the door to look around and saw him sitting at the bar with a beer. There were four blokes further down the bar from him, ones she recognised from the local shearing team. Rob, sensing eyes on his back, turned and gestured to her to join him. He was in his usual jeans and T-shirt. As she walked towards the bar she saw Rob order her a beer.

'I'm glad you came, Izzy. I still wasn't sure you'd turn up.' Rob's nervous smile greeted her.

'Yeah, well I said I would. Shall we go and order some food – it might take a while.'

Rob nodded. Izzy grabbed her beer and they headed to the large area to the left of the bar where tables and chairs were set up, stopping by the hole in the wall to order.

Izzy followed Rob to the nearest table and they sat down, both taking sips from their beers as they did so, neither of them really wanting to start the conversation.

Eventually Rob began. 'So is it good to be home, Izzy? Has much changed?'

Izzy smiled, pleased to be able to latch onto a topic that would be easy to talk about. 'It's great to be home. Not much has changed, except the farm looks more run-down. Dad isn't getting any younger so he could really use the extra hands. But I love everything about home – it's where I'm meant to be.'

'It must be. You look great, Izzy. It obviously agrees with you.' Izzy's heart skipped a beat and she looked cautiously at Rob to gauge his mood. Seeing her reaction, he added, 'I'm just speaking the truth – don't stress. You just look healthy and happy. So what else has been happening?'

Izzy began filling him in on last night's barbecue and the day's harvest, and how her dad was still as stubborn as ever. She quizzed Rob on Alice and what stuff the kids were up to as their dinner arrived, both of them keeping the topics of conversation neutral and out of dangerous territory.

'Oh, and Chris stacked the quad bike again on the weekend,' said Rob with a mouth half full of steak.

Squeezing some more tomato sauce over her chips, Izzy's eyes grew large. 'My God. Is he all right? What did he break this time?'

Rob laughed. 'You know him so well. Well, he was lucky this time – just a heap of skin missing from his elbow and his knee. He's had worse.'

Izzy nodded. That boy had nine lives, she was sure of it. As she ate the last of her steak she contemplated telling Rob about Alice's letter. She swallowed her mouthful and cleared her throat.

'Ah, Rob . . . are you going to tell Alice why I really left?' She saw the change in Rob; his body stiffened.

He shrugged. 'I don't know yet. She probably suspects something's going on with me. I haven't been myself lately, but I still love her – I know that. I never stopped. It's just that my feelings for you made it all very hazy, you know?' He pushed his empty plate away from him. 'It's just something that started building up in me. First, it started with me enjoying working with you, your company, our laughs together. And you are gorgeous so it would be hard for any bloke not to want to spend time with you. So anyway, all this just kept growing in me and niggling until I felt like I needed more of you. I couldn't wait to see you or be near you, even if it was just sitting next to you. Do you understand?' He didn't wait for Izzy's reply. 'It became almost an obsession. Like a big carton of cold beer sitting on a table on a hot day, the more you deny yourself a taste the more you want it. I don't know what to call what I feel about you, Izzy – some sort of love or lust – and it still aches sitting close to you but I know I'll get over it. I can see how stupid I've been – taking off and driving all this way thinking I could win you back. I've had some time to think things over this afternoon, and I realise that with you gone, my obsession will fade away and life will go back to the way it was. Alice and I just need to spend time together and I'm sure you will be all forgotten and out of my mind . . . well, you know what I mean.'

'Yeah, I understand. I know you'll be fine once you have time with your family. Hopefully, after a while, I can come and visit and things can be back the way they were?'

Lines creased around Rob's eyes as he smiled. 'I would like that very much. And so would Alice and the kids. Just like old times. So we're good?'

Izzy felt the tension leave her muscles as she nodded. Yep, they were good. And for the first time in the last couple of weeks she could see herself and Rob getting their old platonic relationship back on track.

5

HARVEST was flying along at a rapid pace. Izzy's dad still wasn't letting her get too involved, but at least Dave was happy for her to catch rides with him to the bin every now and then. Bill also let her go for the odd lap in the header here and there, but he wouldn't let her drive. It was so stupid – he got no breaks from the long day's work. She knew she could do so much more. If only he'd just let her.

They were both impressed with some of the crops – they'd gone fourteen to fifteen bags to the acre which was great.

That morning she'd taken a quick look in the silo to check the quality of the grain. 'Dad, you're going to have to adjust the drum a fraction. The white heads are too high,' she'd informed him on the two-way. You got docked at the bin if you had too many white heads, the parts that encased the wheat. 'But on the upside, the rye-grass is much less in this section of paddock. I couldn't even find any wild oats. You're into a good section of crop now.' They also got docked on weeds in the wheat sample, so they liked to keep an eye on things. At least he trusted her ability to sample the grain. Working on the bin sampling the year she'd left school had given her the qualifications necessary to please her dad. It was probably the one thing he actually asked her opinion on.

It was an especially hot day. The radio announcer forecast thirty-nine degrees. But as there was no wind, there was no harvest ban – yet. Only a couple of weeks into harvest and already she was annoyed with the heat, flies and the boredom. It wouldn't be so bad if she had something to do. Instead she was stuck sitting around the house or ferrying Dad's smoko out to him. Big thrill that was.

Izzy sat waiting for Dave in the ute. Bill had already called Dave on the two-way, informing him they had another twenty-five tonnes ready to go. Izzy tapped her fingers on the steering wheel and kept looking out the back window of the ute, which she'd parked next to the field bin and tractor.

A dust trail signalled Dave's approach and quickly she jumped out. His truck made its way into the paddock and headed straight for the silver field bin. Seconds later, golden grains began to flow from the auger into the semitrailer, pinging as they hit the empty metal bin.

'Cheers, Izzy,' Dave called out as his long, scrawny form strolled towards her.

'Hey, Dave. How's it going? Flat out, I presume?'

Dave raised his wide-brimmed hat and scratched his head through his sandy-coloured hair. He was a good bloke: worked hard, never sat still, and would go out of his way to help anyone. Izzy had known Dave her whole life and he always had time for her. He talked to her, not down at her. She used to mix with his two girls, Daisy and Bridgette, until they went on to uni. Now Daisy was training to be a nurse and Bridgette was out teaching at some remote school.

'Sure am. Neville Lane has just had a breakdown with his truck and it won't be fixed till tomorrow. I'm like a dog with a cracker up its arse trying to keep up with the extra work. What pisses me off is that I've a truck sitting at home that could be doing something,' he said, his face contorted with stress.

Izzy brought her hand up to her chin and rubbed it. 'Well, I have my truck licence. If you're desperate, I could drive for you today if it'd help. I have plenty of experience.'

Hope flashed across Dave's face. 'For real?'

Izzy shrugged. 'Why not? Dad won't even know I'm gone. It'd be great to be doing something besides sitting on my arse all day.'

'That sure would help me out of a jam. It's only Neville who will have loads for you. You remember the blue Dodge I've got?'

Izzy smiled and nodded. Sometimes Dave brought the truck out on weekends to make extra storage space, so they could keep harvesting.

'You think you could handle it?'

'Yep. No problems.' She struggled to contain her excitement. Not many people would get excited about having to drive an old truck in this heat, she guessed.

'Great! I'll drop you off and get you sorted out before I take this lot into the bin.' They both nodded in agreement before Dave climbed onto the semitrailer to check the level.

Later that morning the old blue Dodge spewed out black smoke as Izzy clunked it into an idle. After waving his finger and giving her a couple of tips, Dave headed off in his truck to unload. Izzy left Dave's yard and headed south towards Neville's place. The truck rocked along the flat road. It took a few minutes of grating a couple of gears before she got the hang of the difficult gearbox. But soon she relaxed, stuck her elbow out the window and watched the golden crops spread out in the paddocks either side of her, all the way to the horizon, in between a smattering of mallee trees and towering gums. Every now and then, she passed a bare dry paddock that had been left out of the crop-rotation plan and sheep would be visible, usually gathered together under the only bit of scrub bush or gum tree they could find.

Nev was working in his top paddock and, as per Dave's directions, Izzy turned off the gravel road and headed into the bottom corner of the paddock. She bounced in her seat, dust exploding around her as the truck bobbed along the rough plough marks.

With the truck lined up under the field bin, Izzy got out and cranked up the auger. It didn't take long to fill up the trailer, all sixteen tonnes. Goose, Neville's son, had pulled up in their green JD header and unloaded his boxful into the semitrailer as well. Goose was about twenty-eight and well-rounded. Plenty of beer had helped fill out his middle and his neck was solid like a rugby player's. He was heading down the right track to look just like Neville. But what they lacked in the looks department they made up for in character, as never could two funnier blokes be found.

Izzy shut down the tractor and gave Goose a wave, before climbing back into the cab and sliding it into gear. She was tempted to pick up the two-way and say g'day but she couldn't remember their channel number. The truck lurched slowly over the ruts in the paddock, throwing Izzy about before she eased on the brakes near the gate. Quickly, she got out, rolled on the tarp over the wheat that had settled into the trailer and headed back onto the main road.

Five minutes later the truck roared its way around the receival bin at Pingaring and pulled up next to the sampling platform. Izzy jumped out of the cab and tugged her denim shorts down – the jerking of the truck had made them ride up. She shook the bottom of her blue singlet, shaking off the dust and letting the air cool her down. It was dusty and hot but she was enjoying every moment of it. Then she unrolled the tarp back ready for the sample to be taken.

'G'day,' said a girl, fresh out of high school. She looked barely sixteen with her pimply face and puppy fat. Half of the samplers were usually just out of school; Izzy had been. The girl stood above Izzy on the platform while moving the electronic sampling spear into the back of the truck. There was a loud strained noise, like a vacuum cleaner on steroids, as it started to suck up the sample. Izzy began to fill in the delivery form just as another truck pulled up. A cloud of fine gravel dust filled the air, making her choke. She hopped back behind the wheel.

Sitting still in the stationary truck caused more sweat to break out on her forehead and around her hairline. It ran down between her breasts, collecting the dust on her skin and soaking into her bra. The green light came on indicating that the teenager had finished taking the sample. Izzy moved Dave's truck forward, making room for the trucks behind her. Grabbing her paperwork she headed up the metal stairs to the top of the sampling platform.

Laughter exploded as she opened the door. Ducking quickly, she narrowly missed a handful of grain that one of the sampling girls had thrown at a bloke standing by the counter. She swung around quickly and was startled to see it was Will. Well, no surprise really. She should have known the huge shining white Scania road train outside was his.

Luckily, Will was too preoccupied chatting up the female sampler, a girl called Kellie, to notice Izzy enter. Another local guy was leaning on the thin wall next to the door and said g'day as she came in. Travis was a bloke she'd gone to primary school with and hadn't seen in ages. He now had a full head of dreadlocks, making him almost unrecognisable.

'Hey, Izzy. I didn't know you were back in town.'

Will's head snapped around at the mention of her name. Izzy manoeuvred her back to him as she continued her conversation with Travis.

'I haven't had a chance to get out and about much till now. It's great catching up when I can, mind you. How have you been keeping, Trav? Been to Jamaica lately?' She laughed, tugging one of his long brown dreadies.

Travis put on his best West Indian accent and replied, 'Ha, ha, everyone's a comedian, man!' He tucked a few stray dreadies behind his ear. 'Well, we're doing okay. We're having a good harvest this year, which is keeping us all happy for now. Other than that, there's not much time for anything else. What are you up to? Come in for a look around, have ya?'

'Something like that,' Izzy replied, not going into details. She didn't want Will to know she was driving Dave's truck, just in case he blabbed to her dad.

Travis gave a little laugh and punched her gently on the shoulder. 'You know I can still remember when you were sampling here a few years back. I'll never forget pulling up and seeing you out there spearing trucks in this gorgeous little blue dress, made up to the nines!' he said. 'Best sampler I'd ever seen.'

Izzy blushed. 'Oh, God, don't remind me.' She could remember it well. It was after she'd finished high school. Will hadn't been around then, and Izzy had gone a bit wild after losing Claire. She'd kind of become more like Claire in her partying ways. Izzy recalled going to a huge bash at a local pub called the Oasis. It had been such an awesome night – so good she'd passed out in the back of her ute some time around three or four in the morning. When she'd finally woken, she'd only had enough time to drive back to the bin and start work. They'd had the biggest line-up of trucks that morning too. There she'd been at seven o'clock in the morning in her frock and make-up with a throbbing headache. Just to finish the look, her Rossis had quickly replaced her high-heeled shoes. She'd had to get another girl to spear for her as too many blokes were milling around under the platform. Izzy knew her short dress was the reason. Sly buggers. But there were always a few antics at harvest to relieve the stress. Some days the blokes would bring in porn mags, and they'd all clamber around under the platform and discuss the pictures. It was the perfect opportunity to pour water over the unsupecting men, who looked like they needed a cold shower. There was also the standard grease under the door handles and egg on the windscreens of trucks waiting in line. Really mature stuff. Not to mention Johnno's old fire truck that made its rounds, squirting surprised bin crew and blokes through their open truck windows.

'Word must have got around quick that day, because I'd never seen so many header drivers bringing in the next truckload,' Travis said, teasing her.

Izzy rolled her eyes. 'It wasn't till about eleven that there was a break in the trucks and I could go and change. I didn't think I was ever going to live that one down.'

Travis smiled and gave her a wink. 'Come on. That was the best day ever. We had that awesome bin party the next day too,' he continued as he walked up to the counter to take his logbook from a short, young girl.

'Well, I hope to see ya round, Izzy. Be nice to catch up on old times.'

'Yeah, for sure,' she replied.

'I can't wait to tell Jess that I've seen you.' Travis waved and headed outside. The wind caught the door and blew it shut behind him.

Izzy leant against the vibrating wall and watched a machine shaking wheat back and forth, before it eventually came to a stop. She wondered for a minute why Travis would be seeing Jess. She was dying to see her and felt guilty for letting their friendship lapse. It was one of those things where life just got too busy and before you knew it years had passed without any contact. Sad, but she hoped they could pick up where they left off.

Izzy glanced around the white walls of the sample hut as she waited. There were large posters of bugs and weevils, plus lists of grain varieties, and Will leaning against a wall. Bugger, she'd mistakenly caught his stare. She nodded her head when he said, 'Hello.'

Her eyes returned to Kellie as she took the top screen off and put it on the benchtop, before emptying the remaining screenings into a bowl on the scales and weighing them. The sampling process hadn't changed much from when she'd worked at the bin. It looked like they'd finished Will's sample, as a girl with large breasts in a child-size tank top gave Will his book. She leered over the bench at him, smiling sweetly. Will thanked her and turned to leave, but hesitated when he was level with Izzy.

'If you're not doing much, you could always come for a ride in the truck with me instead of Dave?' he suggested.

Not if it was the last truck on earth, she thought, before coming up with a better retort. 'No, thanks. Besides, I'd hate to spoil your chances with your fan club.' And with that she moved up to the bench to wait for her book. Will got the message and headed out the door. Izzy smiled and chalked up a point on her imaginary scoreboard.

Driving the truck all day had been a blast, even if the truck was old and rough and not far off retirement in a metal scrap heap. It had given her a chance to meet the bin crew again and catch up with some of the locals as they waited in line.

Dave gave her a ride back out to the farm at about five-thirty. Her dad was still on the header going round and round, and would be for another couple of hours. The afternoon air was warm as she climbed down from Dave's truck. She was hanging out for a cold beer. Running her tongue over her parched lips, she could almost taste the first frothy white mouthful.

'Hey, Izzy. Two hundred and fifty sound okay for the day's work?' Dave asked as the golden grains of wheat poured into the trailer in front of the pinkish afternoon sky.

'Oh no, Dave. I don't want any money. It was great just to be doing something,' she said, crossing her arms in front of her.

'Are you sure? You helped me out of a tight spot today and it's only right that you get paid.' Dave wiped the sweat from his brow.

'No, I'm sure. Besides, you did me the favour. Please, Dave, keep it. Why don't you take that lovely wife of yours out to tea or something instead?'

Dave shrugged his shoulders and shook his head. 'You were a huge help today, Izzy, and I can't thank you enough, but if you insist.' It was the end of the discussion.

Izzy wasn't fazed. She'd had a great day and was happy to have helped. It was nice to return the favour. Dave's wife Melinda had always been so kind when Izzy had gone to their place to play with Daisy and Bridgette. She'd let the girls do all sorts of fun things, from dressing up in the old dresses she'd kept from the seventies to making cakes but leaving half the batter for them to eat. Izzy and Daisy were nearly the same age, and Claire and Bridgette were close as well, so the four of them often got together. Wandering back to the house, Izzy couldn't help but drift off down memory lane . . .

One time when Izzy was about thirteen they'd been dressing up and they'd persuaded Claire to try a dress on.

'Come on, Claire. Show us what you look like,' Daisy had said, trying to coax Claire out of her bedroom.

They watched the doorknob turn and out strutted Claire with her best cowboy swagger. But try as she might to overshadow the fact that she was in a dress, they all saw her beauty. Claire was wearing one of Melinda's old bridesmaid's dresses. It was a red off-the-shoulder number with a small frill along the neckline and a fitted bodice, and it trailed to the ground with a matching frill at the bottom. It accentuated Claire's long slender body.

'Claire, you look amazing,' said Bridgette, who at sixteen was right into boys and make-up. She ran over to her, pulled out Claire's standard ponytail and let her blonde locks cascade down over her shoulders. It made her cheekbones stand out and the dress showed off her full red lips.

'Wow, sis. I've never seen you in a dress before,' said Izzy. Well, except for when Claire was younger and their mum made her wear one at Christmas. Now she was old enough to wear what she wanted and that was always pants or shorts.

'Yeah, well, take a good look 'cos it won't be staying on for long.'

Claire laughed, did a twirl for them and headed back inside the bedroom to change.

'Doesn't she know how gorgeous she looks?' asked Daisy.

Izzy had shrugged her shoulders. 'I don't think she cares. Claire has never been one to impress people. What you see is what you get. But I like her like that.'

Claire reappeared in her jeans and T-shirt, her hair back up in its ponytail.

'Well, now we've done that, who wants to go cut up on the bikes?' Claire stood with her hands on her hips and a smile that could have melted ice.

'I do,' Izzy jumped in, always keen to do anything Claire would. Izzy thought she was just the best, and at thirteen, one of the perks of hanging around with her was that Will was there too. Oh, how that had changed!

Izzy watched Dave head back to his truck and yelled out, 'But you're welcome to buy me a beer the next time we catch up under the tree if you like.'

Dave swung around and smiled. 'You betcha, Izzy. Thanks again.'

As she headed back to her ute she began dreaming of that cold beer again.

6

THREE small black flies buzzed around outside the kitchen window, trying to find a place out of the heat. Izzy was tempted to take the fly swat and finish them off, but she knew there'd only be plenty more to take their place. Hunched over on a stool, sipping tea from a large mug, Izzy contemplated eating another slice of carrot cake. Jean sat erect beside Izzy, her square shoulders pinned back as she delicately drank from her own cup. She was a vision that wouldn't look out of place in a flash city-style apartment, with a young man catering to her every whim.

Chatting quietly at the breakfast bar, they found themselves, yet again, talking about Bill. Izzy often shared her problems with her mum, hoping that she would get the hint and offer her some support.

'I could do so much on the farm, Mum. Help make ends meet. I have my truck licence now and I could be running in some small loads when Dave can't get back in time.'

'Yes, I know, Izzy, but your father wants more for you than the farm, and I think it scares him too much.'

'Come on, Mum. Everyone knows what happened with Claire was an accident. Even WorkSafe came to the same conclusion. How long is Dad going to hold her death over me? Surely he knows how much this place means to me. It's all I've ever wanted to do.' Izzy bent her head and played with her watch, trying to remain calm.

The day Claire died Izzy had been at high school and, in a way, she'd never forgiven herself for not being there for her. She knew that was stupid because there was nothing she could have done. But it was just one of those situations where 'what if' played constantly on her mind. Izzy had been nearly seventeen and Claire only just twenty. Dad had left Claire fumigating one of the silos while he went to get some more poison. It was very high, older-style silo with a simple metal ladder up the side to the peak at the top. She'd been leaning over the hole at the top when a strong willy-willy had gone through, causing her to lose her balance and fall. Bill found her below, on the concrete slab, soon after it happened. But it was too late. She'd already died from massive internal injuries.

Izzy's whole world had fallen apart that day. It had started as just another uninteresting day at school. She wished her dad had let her go to the ag school just out of town. It would have been so much better to drive farm machinery, put in crops and do other interesting stuff outside. Instead she had to sit inside all day writing, and she just found it all so *boring*! Relieved that another day was over, she'd leisurely strolled back to the hostel where the country kids boarded. Schoolbags swung at their hips, filled with black lever arch files, and thick biology and history books. Their white uniform shirts sat half untucked over their grey skirts and shorts. She remembered catching sight of her parents standing in the car park off to the right, which sat behind the enclosed pool. They'd looked anxious as they watched the kids returning from school, trying to spot Izzy in the sea of grey and white.

At first, surprised by their visit, she'd run to them with delight. But the unexpected vision of their miserable faces soon left her with a wave of goose bumps.

'Hi, Mum, Dad,' she'd greeted them. 'What are you doing here? Is something wrong?'

Her mum's face had never seemed so old. Rings surrounded her red swollen eyes, and her normally perfect postured body was slumped against Bill. She'd never seen her dad so solemn, so ghostly in appearance. Something was seriously wrong. She passed her bag to her friends. Her parents took her hands and walked her away from the flow of rowdy teenagers towards the large green recreation shed.

'Izzy, something so horrible has happened,' her mother whispered quietly, as tears started to fill her eyes.

Izzy couldn't begin to imagine what was making her parents so distraught. 'Mum, you're scaring me.' Nervously, she'd begun to chew at her fingernails. 'Where's Claire, anyway? Why isn't she here?'

She couldn't understand it. If this was so important, why wasn't her sister here? It hadn't even crossed her mind that Claire might have been involved. Not until she'd heard her parents' sharp intake of breath, and seen the hollow look in their eyes.

Dad'd had to support her mum, who by now had started to shake. As the tears broke free, and rolled uncontrollably down her cheeks, she reached out to Izzy for comfort. Clinging to her tightly as she sobbed, it had finally dawned on Izzy.

'Mum, please. What's happened?' She remembered feeling faint and ill. 'Is Claire hurt?' She had to know. What had happened?

The answer had come from the deep but unrecognisably feeble voice of her father. 'I'm so, so sorry, sweetheart. She's . . . she's gone,' he'd choked out.

Everything had been a blur after that – going home to the quiet, empty house and the funeral plans. The truth was almost too painful to bear. She had buried that memory deep within her, squeezed it into a tiny ball that was locked up tight so the pain couldn't keep resurfacing. It had been the hardest time in her life.

She thought back to the funeral. They'd buried Claire in the local cemetery so she'd be close by. It had been an overcast day and as usual a gale was blowing. She remembered seeing Will standing next to her dad, the bottom of his black suit jacket flapping in the wind and his fringe flicking about his face. It had made her seethe, seeing him so close to her dad. How dare he? she'd thought. He'd ruined the last few months of Claire's life, causing her pain – such incredible pain. Izzy would never forget the way Claire had cried. Will wasn't a part of their family, yet there he was, standing alongside them. Was she the only one who'd thought that was wrong? He'd worn sunglasses to hide his eyes and his head hung as low as hers felt. He'd been holding a small box in his hands. She'd watched him carefully, finding it too hard to look at Claire's coffin and cursing the lump that was lodged in her throat. They'd put a large photo of Claire by her grave. It had been taken the previous Christmas and she'd been laughing at a joke. She looked so vibrant, the twinkle in her blue eyes alive with laughter, but Izzy couldn't bear to look at that either. Watching Will, she'd seen his shoulders trembling and her dad's unsteady hand grab Will near his neck. He'd gripped so tightly that Will's suit scrunched up beneath it. She'd wanted to scream, 'Hug me!' *She* needed her dad's embrace. He should have been holding her, not Will. Izzy had put so much energy into her jealousy that she couldn't remember a word the minister had said. She hadn't noticed the tenderness of her mother's hand on her back or the amount of tears that had streamed down her face.

As Claire was lowered into the ground, Izzy had gone over and dropped in the red rose she'd been holding. She would've gazed into that hole for ages had her mum not pulled her back. Moving away, she'd seen Will kneeling beside the grave and heard the sobs coming from his shaking body as they'd mixed with her own. He'd brought the small box to his lips and kissed it gently, leaving a smear of tears on the white lid before dropping it into the deep opening. She'd never given his pain a thought until now. He really had been torn, like half of him was heading down into the earth. It was just how Izzy had felt. Why hadn't she noticed it until that day? And how could he have hurt Claire so much, if he'd obviously cared so deeply? Had he only just realised he did love her? Something didn't sit well in her mind.

In the months that followed she'd almost failed Year Twelve, but the thought of having to repeat had kept her slugging on. Claire would have hated her to wallow in self-pity. She had been a lover of life. And she'd always wanted the best for Izzy. Just for Claire, Izzy was going to try bloody hard to be happy and strive for what she wanted. But that had proven to be easier said than done.

An annoying fly brought Izzy's thoughts back to the quiet kitchen. 'I miss Claire too, Mum, but I have a life to live my way. Why can't Dad see that?'

Jean reached across and held her daughter's hand. 'Why didn't I see before how much being on the farm meant to you?'

'Maybe because you wanted me to go to uni and become a teacher?'

Jean looked to the floor.

'I'm sorry, Mum. I know you wanted more for my life but I never would have been happy. Anyway, who gets to say one job is better than another? I think if you're doing what you love, then it's no one else's business.'

'You're right, love. I guess I just wanted a better life for you than I had. It's not easy living out here, you know that.'

Izzy put her hand on her mum's shoulder. 'I know, Mum, but that's what makes it special. They breed us tough out here.'

Jean got up and took her empty cup to the sink. 'And don't I know it! So when are you heading over to Betty's?'

'About fourish.'

In fact, she headed over at three o'clock to visit Uncle Jim, who was driving a header. When Aunt Betty brought up afternoon tea to them, Izzy took over driving and let Uncle Jim have his cuppa on the back of the ute. They looked a sight, Aunt B in a light cotton dress with plenty of bright pinks and yellows, and Uncle Jim with his knobbly legs sticking out from his blue work shorts and his wide-brimmed hat that flopped over his ears. Eventually, after a short break, Uncle Jim called her up on the two-way and ask her to bring his header back. When she stopped after the next lap, she gave him a hug. 'Cheers for that, but I could have kept going. I don't mind.'

Jim laughed. 'Yes, but I do. Betty had chewed my ear off after ten minutes. This is the only time I get some peace and quiet to myself. Anyway, you'd better head off. If I know Betty, she's cooked you up a feast of cakes and God knows what else for your afternoon tea. You could use some more meat on ya.'

'Uncle Jim!'

Izzy left him to it, ran back to her ute and headed to their place. It was an old house with a high tin roof sticking out from behind the large trees and shrubs that had been planted around it many years ago. She parked out the front next to an old red Ford Falcon, and warned Tom not to chase the numerous cats she knew would be wandering around. Izzy pushed through an old metal gate, which squeaked at the hinges, and followed a little concrete path up to the door. Big bougainvilleas and bottlebrushes hung over the path and large lilac trees covered everything in shade. The lilacs had always been her favourite as a kid. They were so easy to climb, and their little white and purple flowers would cover the ground with colour in spring.

Izzy stepped onto the concrete verandah and tapped on the flywire back door. 'Hel-loo. It's me.'

Aunt B's voice floated to the door. 'Come in, Izzy. I'm just taking some scones out of the oven.'

She slipped off her boots and walked into the house. The ceilings were high, which helped keep the house cool during summer, except the kitchen. Aunt B was usually cooking so the temperature was always ten degrees hotter there. Following her nose, Izzy headed to the kitchen where Aunt B stood with a tray in her gloved hand, transferring scones to a plate. She just about disappeared in the busy-looking kitchen with all its pots hanging from the wall and little ornaments everywhere. Decorative chooks, roosters and cats sat on benchtops, the fridge and the windowsill, and frilly lace curtains hung above the sink. A round dining table in the open kitchen was loaded with cakes and little pots of jam and cream. It was so full that at first Izzy missed seeing Jess sitting at the end of the table. Jess had just taken a bite of sponge cake, had cream on the end of her nose, and was quickly trying to swallow her mouthful so she could say hello.

Jessica Painter had not changed at all. She was still tiny, her thin frame barely visible over the towering cakes. But her hair was different – it used to be long and curly but now she wore it straight and tucked back into a clip. The blonde highlights in her brown hair brought out the light flecks in her hazel eyes. Her face was long and elegant and she looked so delicate that you'd be afraid to play-wrestle her in case you broke her.

'Hey, Jess. Long time no see.'

'You too, Iz,' Jess replied.

Aunt B handed Izzy a plate and pointed to a chair. 'Sit down, love, and grab something to eat. I'll make the cuppas.'

'Thanks, Aunt B. You're a legend.' Izzy pulled out a chair and sat down. Reaching across, she helped herself to the warm scones and jam and cream.

'So I take it you sold your little Datsun?' Izzy asked Jess.

Jess went to laugh and just about choked on her cake. 'I wish. I rolled it a year back. The shire had just re-sheeted the gravel road and it was slippery as anything.'

'Oh, no! What a bugger. The old Dato had seen some good times, hey? You remember when we drove it down to Bremer Bay for the New Year's Eve piss-up?'

Jess slapped her hand on the table. 'Hell, yeah! We'd spent all our money on grog and had to sleep the night in the car. Those were the days, hey, Iz? So, what's your score? Are you really back home to stay?'

'Yep. There's nothing like home. I'd like to help run Gumlea but Dad's not to keen on the idea. What about you? You still living around here?'

'Yeah, but I travel to Lake Grace every day for work. I'm working at the Shire now, doing secretarial stuff. I wanted to move into town but there's nothing to rent. It's too expensive. This way I pay Mum and Dad rent and I get my meals cooked and washing done. It's heaps easier.'

Jess picked up some papers stapled together from a pile of magazines on the table. 'Here – have you read the latest *Gumtree Gazette*? I typed this one up.'

Izzy took the local paper from Jess and read through the three pages of local news and events. 'Wow, Goose is engaged. Who'd he find to marry?'

'Some pommie chick who was working on the bin last harvest. She stayed on and hasn't left. Think they're getting married next September.'

Izzy scanned the birthdays. There were only five names listed. 'It's Jodie's birthday next week. You see much of her?'

Jess shrugged her bony shoulders. 'Here and there. I've been invited to her birthday do, but I don't really want to go. She's turning twenty-six but she's having a big party like it's her thirtieth. Has daddy's money, will spend it. She hasn't changed a bit. Except that she's given up chasing Will.'

'You're kidding. We thought they'd be perfect. Two rich people, perfectly suited.'

'Yeah, well . . .' Jess paused. 'Since Claire's death Will hasn't been the same guy. We never see him out and about, and if he does come to a party, he's pretty quiet. No more drinking games or yahooing. And girls – my God, we think he's gone off them. Seriously, I don't think he's had a girlfriend in the last few years. If he has, he's kept it to himself.'

'Wow, that's not like Will.'

'He has dinner with us every now and then,' Aunt Betty added.

Izzy screwed her face up and swung around to face her. 'True? Really?'

'Yes. I think he's been trying to make up for the time he crashed through the front paddock and took out the fence. Jim spent all morning getting the sheep back off the road.'

'But that was ages ago. I was even around then.'

'I know, but he's really matured up. He's a sweet lad.'

Izzy turned to Jess and rolled her eyes. Time for a change of subject, she thought. 'So, Jess, you got a fella?'

Jess's eyes twinkled.

'Oh, do tell. Who is he? Do I know him?'

'It's Travis.'

'Trav with the dreadies? Sweet. How long you been going out?'

'About a year now. He wants me to move in with him on the farm. But I know he just wants a live-in cook and cleaner.'

Izzy laughed and helped herself to some sponge cake. Aunt B caught her eye and smiled. Izzy was really enjoying catching up with Jess. It was as if they'd never been apart. They had so much to talk about and Izzy soon realised how much town gossip she'd missed. Who'd sold up and who'd bought what, who'd left town and who'd shacked up with whom. They went on well after all the cake and scones had filled their bellies so they looked like over-pregnant ewes. Aunt B had even packed them doggie bags to take home. Izzy promised to call Jess soon. They were both pleased to have picked up their friendship where it had left off.

As Izzy watched Jess drive off in her Ford, she couldn't help feeling less alone in the world of men. It wasn't something she thought about often, but it could get kind of lonely sometimes out here, and it was good to know that she still had some female friends to talk to and have a laugh with. She was so glad Aunt B had invited Jess along.

7

A WEEK later Izzy was still no closer to getting on the header. Sure, she'd sneak off to Uncle Jim's and kick him off his for a while, but it wasn't the same as being on her own. She wanted to be doing the work, not taking rides like a little kid. She found herself inside again, away from the heat and flies, with her mum, having another cuppa. Being a farmer's wife would drive her mad. She didn't understand how her mother handled it. Stuck inside, doing housework, waiting by the two-way in case you were needed to bring out smoko.

'Mum, I'm so bored.'

'There's some washing to hang out if you like?'

'*Muuum.*' Izzy slumped her shoulders.

'I know, love. It'll be better when your father's not so stressed. You know how his blood pressure skyrockets during harvest. We'll work on him when he's not so touchy.'

At that precise moment, the two-way crackled into life and startled them both.

'Jean, Izzy, I have a fire in the header! Get help, quick,' came the anxious voice of Bill.

'Shit.' Izzy jumped up and ran to the back door, shouting orders. 'Mum, call the neighbours. I'll get to the firefighter unit.' She yanked at the flywire door, flinging it open, and was out past the gate before it had even slammed shut.

Jean leapt to the two-way on the wall, quickly flicking to Brian Timmins on channel six. Her hand was shaking as she clutched her chest. 'Be careful, Izzy!' she shouted after her daughter.

Izzy sprinted to her ute. 'No, Tom. You stay here,' she yelled sternly at her faithful companion, before climbing in. Gunning the ute to life, she sped off towards the paddock that her dad had been harvesting. Black smoke billowed into the sky, marking the spot.

'Shit, shit, shit,' slipped out of Izzy's mouth. Flicking the steering wheel, she slid the ute quickly around the corner, spraying dust and gravel out the back, before straightening up. Izzy knew her mum would be trying her best to get as much help as possible. All she had to worry about was getting there fast before anything awful could happen. She hoped it wasn't bad. But the smoke was thick, and it was making her nervous. 'Come on, Dad. Hang in there.'

Judging by the rich blackness of the smoke, it was definitely the header burning. Thank God there was no wind today. A decent wind-driven fire could easily spread out of control for many kilometres, destroying livestock and homes in the process. Hopefully they'd be able to get this one under control quickly, without losing too much crop.

Swerving around a gate and onto the edge of the paddock, she jumped on the brakes and skidded to a halt alongside the old yellow Landy. Without a moment's hesitation she jumped straight in, praying the old girl would start right away. Bouncing up and down, she pumped frantically at the throttle, shouting words of encouragement to the ute, offering promises of new oil and a thorough cleaning. It fired with a bang and a splutter, and groaned when she planted her foot, forcing it into motion and causing a haze of smoke to pour out from the rattly exhaust. She caught a glimpse of the green header through the haze.

Shit. Where was Dad? Maybe he was just to the side, throwing sand or thrashing at the fire with his shirt, she hoped.

Barely able to hold the steering wheel straight, Izzy clamped her jaw shut so she wouldn't bite her tongue. The whole ute was bouncing around like a jackhammer over the ruts in the paddock. Seconds ticked by, but they felt like minutes. Moving back and forth in her seat, she willed the ute to go faster, just another ten metres. Izzy got as close to the header fireball as she thought safe before she jammed on the brakes. She didn't want to get caught up in the flames. In one swift movement, she was out, almost before the ute had stopped, and yanked the old Honda pump into life. With a flick of the lever, the fire hose spurted out like a burst water main.

Izzy ran towards the fire, dragging the long hose behind her. Her ankles twisted and strained as she ran over the ruts in the paddock, her boots kicking their way through the stubble and sandy soil.

The heat and smoke from the fire was so intense that she could only get within a few metres, as the flames reached out trying to lick at her moist skin. Sweat ran down her brow and her back. The smoke made her cough and her eyes water. Oh, what had Dad got himself into? The fire raged. Sucking at the green paint on the header, it circled up as it tried to swallow it completely, like a snake with its prey.

At last Izzy spotted Bill among the flames at the door of the cab. Fire was all around, pinning him in as he fought the blaze with a tiny red fire-extinguisher that dribbled out the last of its white foam.

Aiming the hose, she tried to douse him and his burning pants. His eyes shut and his face relaxed momentarily as the water reached his legs. The drenching didn't take long to put out his trousers. Next, she tried to clear a path down the steps for him to escape the inferno. She watched closely as her dad threw the now empty fire-extinguisher aside and turned to climb cautiously down the narrow steps of the header.

On the other side of the paddock, Will's knuckles whitened as he gripped the steering wheel of their water truck. He was driving way too fast in the old girl and was feeling every bump as his knees smacked into the hard underside of the dash. He wondered how his dad was going bouncing around on the back. He closed his eyes for a split second in a silent prayer. He hoped to God that it wasn't bad. Fires in summer were dreadful, but a header fire during harvest was the pits. Last year Roger Smith lost his whole paddock and some native reserve. Luckily he'd walked away injury-free, but he'd lost a whole lot of money in less than ten minutes.

Will could see the black smoke as he closed in, and his guts churned with fear and adrenaline. His dad was ready to start the pump the moment they got close enough. As the minutes dragged on, he worried about Bill. The man was more than just his neighbour. Over the last couple of years they'd built a close friendship, understanding each other's struggles. Bill had blamed himself for Claire's death. He believed she shouldn't have been working on the farm in the first place. After her death he had lost interest in the property, and his passion for his land had begun to die. Then Will started working on Gumlea to help get it back into shape. At first he'd done it to spend time away from his parents, who didn't understand what he was going through. They let him come and go without question, sensing he needed his space. And for that he was grateful. Little by little Will formed a bond with Bill, and his persistence paid off as Bill started to open up and the two men became close. They both shared the loss of Claire, understood each other's pain and found it comforting just knowing the other was there. Together they'd helped each other without really knowing it. The farm work had brought them closer, and Gumlea had prospered as a result.

No longer did Will cruise the local pubs looking for a good time every weekend. Instead he preferred to share a few beers with Bill in the dying afternoon light. Claire would have called him soft if she'd been around. But Will preferred to think he'd just mellowed and realised what was important.

The smell of smoke wafted through the cab. He was getting close now. Will glanced at his mobile and prayed he wouldn't have to use it. He could see the fierce flames and Izzy with the hose trying to keep them at bay. The header was a goner for sure.

When he was about ten metres away Will turned the big wheel and swung the truck around to give his dad a better vantage point with their hose. It was time for action.

A faint rumbling sound distracted Izzy and a blue truck braked suddenly beside her. Will and his old man, Brian, had arrived with their water truck.

'Oh, thank God!' Their presence gave her more willpower. Brian was on the back of his truck with the pump going, already hosing down the header near Bill. Will had jumped out from behind the steering wheel, opening his mobile and dialling for help as he did. He too had noticed the state of Bill's burnt legs.

Izzy watched anxiously as Bill slowly descended the narrow blackened steps. He was just about at the last step when she saw him slip on the white foam. His arms flailed above his head, and he collapsed backwards, falling into the smoke and flames that were running riot from the core of the header. They seemed to suck him in, engulf him completely, and he vanished completely from Izzy's sight.

'*Daaad!*' Izzy screamed out in horror, before choking on the smoke. Her heart leapt against her chest and a wave of sickness washed over her. A blurry figure passed her and she realised it had to be Will. He disappeared into the thick black smoke and licking red flames, calling for her dad. Desperately, she tried to pinpoint them in the inferno. Precious seconds ticked by. She worried that they would be burnt to a crisp and shuddered at the thought. Wave upon wave of choking black smoke puffed out from around the old header, screening off her view.

Izzy and Brian kept two powerful streams of water on the smoke where the men had disappeared, hoping to keep them from the intense heat. Their faces seemed to appear, then disappear amid the smoke as if it was playing tricks on her, taunting her at this vulnerable moment. Then Will emerged from the smoke like an illusion, dragging a large blackened body along with him. Turning off the hose, Izzy ran towards them. Her heart pounded. Was he dead? At that moment she saw Bill struggle to move one leg, then slowly the other one. Feeling light and dizzy, she gasped for air, not realising she'd been holding her breath all this time. 'He's alive.'

Will easily supported Bill's weight as they stood. Their faces were blackened, and drenched in a mixture of sweat and water. Small reddish burns scarred the top of Will's hands, and his hair looked singed in a few places.

'Isabelle,' her dad said hoarsely as his bloodshot eyes found hers. She reached up and touched his face, wiping off some black soot. Tears started to gather in the corner of her eyes. She'd never felt so overcome with emotion. Her father was okay. Izzy turned to Will and was struck with a powerful feeling of astonishment and deep admiration. It had been the most heroic thing she'd ever seen.

'Look, there's more help coming. Let's leave the firefighting to them. We'd better get Bill back to the house,' Will shouted over the roar of the fire and the churning of the pumps.

Izzy glanced behind her and witnessed the spirit of the bush at its best. A convoy of utes and water trucks carrying firefighters were coming up the track and into the paddock to help another farmer in need. It was a heart-warming sight amid such chaos. Even though they'd been harvesting a few minutes ago, they'd all downed tools, parked their headers and run to a friend's aid without a moment's hesitation. It was just one more reason why she loved this place so much. She'd be sure to put a couple of blocks of beer at the Gumtree, the local watering hole, to show their appreciation.

Glancing down, Izzy saw a close-up of her dad's legs covered in purplish-red burns and white blistery skin. His arms and hands had also sustained burns and looked like they would be causing him severe pain. Izzy looked away. It was all she could do to stop her breakfast from rising up in her throat. With her eyes set ahead, she slipped in under her dad's free arm and helped him carefully into the ute. Sitting next to him on the seat she poured water from her bottle onto his burns to keep them cool. Will ran towards his truck and grabbed his water bottle as well, then ran back to the ute, jumped behind the wheel next to Izzy and Bill, and sped off to the farmhouse.

Grabbing the microphone hand-piece off the two-way with her blackened hand, Izzy called her mum to prepare her for their arrival.

'We're bringing Dad home now. He's got bad burns to his legs, Mum.'

She heard her mum swear, probably unaware that she was holding the button down. 'All right. I'll get the bath filled up with water . . . Izzy, how's he going?'

Izzy could hear the panic in her mum's voice and it began to unnerve her. No – she had to hold it together for Dad's sake. 'He'll be okay. He's a tough old bugger. Will called the ambos, so they can't be too far away.'

'I'll give them a ring and see what's the best thing to do,' her mum replied, still sounding anxious but focused on the need to prepare for Bill's arrival.

'Okay. We'll see you in a few minutes.' Izzy checked on her dad again. He was pale, and probably in shock, but he still managed to give her a wink.

'I'll be okay, love,' were his raspy words of reassurance.

Izzy glimpsed at his burns and tried to get him to have a drink, hoping he was right. Her eyes found Will and silently begged for his assurance that her dad really was going to be all right.

Will found the pleading look in Izzy's eyes unbearable. He knew she needed reassuring but right now he had no idea how things were going to turn out. He could barely look at Bill without feeling sick and the smell of burnt flesh was clinging to the inside of his nostrils. He kept playing the scene over and over in his head – the moment of searching for Bill in the hot blackness, like he was in the middle of hell with a blindfold on. The smoke had been burning his lungs, but that was nowhere near as painful as the thought of not getting to Bill. Then, almost as painful was the look on Izzy's face when she thought her dad was gone. It was the same look she'd worn at Claire's funeral and it ripped at his soul. He couldn't bear the thought of this family going through that again. Looking at her now, he felt just as worried as Izzy. He'd never seen so much emotion in her big blue eyes – the outpouring of strength as she supported Bill amid feelings of terror and helplessness. He couldn't find the words to reassure her so he just nodded and returned to steering the ute down the rough track.

Izzy saw Will's hands grip the wheel. They were black, except where the skin was blistering. She didn't know what she would have done if he hadn't come to their rescue. Will had clearly saved her dad's life. He was a genuine hero, and she could hardly continue to hate him now.

Carefully, she leaned across and poured some water over Will's hands while he was driving. His jeans were black and his checked shirt had countless burnt patches all over it. Will turned and smiled through the black ash smudged across his face. Izzy gave him a rare uncertain smile in return and mouthed a silent, 'Thanks.' He acknowledged it with a quick nod, then brought his eyes back to the road. No, she thought. It's not right to despise a hero.

8

IZZY watched the red lights of the ambulance as they flashed all the way down the driveway. She had managed to stay composed throughout their arrival and assessment of her dad. Now they'd left for the hospital she didn't have to be strong for her mum or her dad, and she started to lose her grip.

Will was standing behind her and saw her shoulders begin to shake. It wasn't until he moved closer that he saw her face. The soft lines around his eyes creased with worry the moment he saw her tears. Then the unexpected happened. Will put his hand around her shoulders and pulled her into a hug. She resisted at first, but the gentle circular movement of his thumb on her neck broke her resistance. That and the fact he'd started whispering, 'He'll be fine,' and, 'Don't worry.'

The ambulance would take her dad to the nearest hospital, which was in Lake Grace, fifty kilometres away. From there they would more than likely transfer him to Perth by Flying Doctor. Jean said she'd call Izzy that night, with an update on Bill's progress.

Izzy felt completely lost after her parents left. She wasn't sure what she should be doing. And she felt awkward and embarrassed about her moment of closeness with Will. She sent him packing by convincing him that he'd done more than enough already, and that he should get back to harvesting, as they were nearly finished.

Sick of twiddling her thumbs and reliving the fire one too many times in her mind, she decided to go into town and put the beer on for everyone who'd helped. She knew they'd all be under the Tree. There was nothing else she could do at home and she wanted to thank everyone personally. Mum would call her on her mobile if she couldn't get her at home.

The Tree, or Gumtree Tavern as it said on her stubbie holder, was their local watering hole, as the town didn't have a pub. It was where they all sat and drank and told a few yarns, under the shade of two huge gum trees. The two trees were out the front of the local shop, which also sold liquor, and it had a huge dirt area for parking. The old CWA building was fifty-odd metres to the left and the kids usually ran around its verandahs on a Tree night. You could easily get twenty cars parked willy-nilly between the shop, the CWA and the gum trees.

On her way out Izzy made a note to ring the insurance company to advise them what had happened, so they could make a time to come and check out the header. With the help they'd received from everyone in the district, there was only a small amount of crop burnt, so in that respect they were doing okay. But the header was well and truly a goner.

Ten minutes later she found herself sitting on the old wooden tree log under the branches of the two gum trees enjoying the chatter. The pink and grey galahs squawked nearby and the Albany Doctor had blown in, cooling off the afternoon. It was the first chance she'd had since arriving home to visit the Tree. She'd missed its atmosphere and the friendly faces.

Utes and cars sat parked at random, wherever there was a free spot. Ladies sat with their wines, while kids happily ran about. The men stood around, beers (donated by Izzy) in hand, swapping jokes, or bragging about how well their crop was going, or how great their new big headers were. If it had been a bad year, there would've been the constant shaking of heads and sighing among the depressed faces.

Izzy was still in her blackened shorts and singlet, as were all the blokes who'd helped put out the fire. Her hands and arms were patched with black soot and she was sure her face was the same. But it didn't matter. No one ever got dressed up for the Tree. It was a come as you are, be yourself kind of place, free from judgement. It made her feel so relaxed just being with all the locals, who in a way were like family – people she'd known her whole life, people who'd help at a second's notice. Yep, there was nothing like a Pingaring crowd.

From a brown paper bag she pulled out a can of beer she'd bought from the shop, revelling in the sound it made as she cracked it open. Putting the can up to her dry lips, she gulped down the first mouthful, which didn't even touch the sides of her throat. Another big guzzle and she'd be over halfway through it.

'Hey, Izzy. How ya going? I've heard all about the fire.'

Izzy looked up to see Jess squeezing her way through the group. She gave Izzy a hug, then pulled up a vacant milk crate and sat down beside her.

'I'm fine, thanks, Jess. Just worried about Dad. It didn't take long for the news to get around.'

Jess's pale skin seemed to glow among the blackened faces. 'Are you kidding? You know what this town's like. Hence the big turnout here tonight,' she replied.

'Mate, how lucky was it that there was no wind? It could have been a bloody big blaze, and right near the reserve too. Could have been really bad,' said Travis, who was standing a metre away, his dreadlocks bouncing as he shook his head.

Old Pete perked up. 'I know. That header was sizzling away like a snag on the barbie!'

'Bloody oath,' Muzza added. 'The smell when the tyres went up – whew!'

Izzy's phone rang. She moved away to a quiet spot among the cars to answer it.

'Hello.'

'Hi, darling. Where are you?' Jean's tired voice was faint over the mobile phone.

'Just at the Tree. I've put on some beer to say thanks. How's Dad?' Izzy asked anxiously.

'Oh, good idea. Your father would have done the same.' Jean sighed loudly. 'Well, they've transferred him to the Royal Perth Hospital. He's settled into the ICU for the moment. They say he has burns to thirty-six per cent of his body. He's on a drip and they've got him on antibiotics and pain medication. They've dressed the burns on his hands as they're not as bad, but his legs are going to need some grafts. Looks like we could be here for a month or more, Izzy, so I've called your Aunt Sarah and I'm going to stay with her.'

'Is there anything I can do?' Izzy's hand was on her forehead as she strained to hear her mum's words.

'No, not really. Just keep the place going until your father's up to sorting stuff out. He's on a lot of meds, so it'll be a day or two before his head will be clear enough to think about the farm. Well, honey, I've gotta go. Sarah has just turned up.'

'Okay, Mum. Take it easy. Tell Dad I love him.'

'Will do. Bye.'

Izzy snapped the phone shut and slipped it into her shirt pocket, then headed back to her seat next to Jess.

'Here,' said Jess, handing Izzy her can.

Izzy's hand was shaking as she took her drink and she quickly had another sip to ease her jitters. 'Thanks, Jess. They're saying Dad'll need skin grafts on his legs.'

Jess's lips went tight and her forehead scrunched. 'Ewww . . . ouch. Your poor dad. But he's tough. He'll be fine, Izzy.'

'Yeah, I know. Better pass on the news, I guess.' Izzy stood up and whistled loudly. The hum of voices died down. 'Hey, guys, I've just had word from Mum that Dad's in the ICU but he'll be okay. Oh, and maybe give it a few days before calling as he'll be a bit spaced out. While I'm at it, we want to thank you for your help today. Can't find a better bunch of fellas to have around when you're stuck. So drink up. The beer's on us.'

A cheer went up and a few blokes nearby slapped Izzy on the shoulder.

Izzy knew the bush telegraph still worked well – those who weren't at the Tree would soon know the latest on her dad and hopefully Izzy would be saved from having to answer lots of phone calls from concerned friends tomorrow.

Izzy spotted Brian and Will through the crowd, their faces lit by the glow of the pink sunset, and decided to go and thank them personally. Brian's thick bushy eyebrows stood out prominently and Will's face looked tired but his eyes were bright, probably still burning with the adrenaline from earlier. He was in jeans and a red and black T-shirt, with his sunnies perched up on his head. He was the cleanest of them all. His mum had probably been fussing over his burnt hands.

'Hey, Mr Timmins,' Izzy said, reaching up into his tall frame and returning his embrace.

'Hi, Izzy. How you holding up, love? And it's Brian, okay,' he added.

'Thanks, Brian. I'm doing all right, I guess.' Izzy stepped back but left her hand on his arm and glanced at Will too. 'I wanted to thank you both again for getting there when you did, and for doing so much. I'd hate to think what would've . . . You know. I really appreciate it,' Izzy croaked as her throat began to tighten.

Will put his hand on her shoulder and gave it a gentle squeeze. 'Just doing what you and Bill would've done, kiddo.'

As Will pulled his hand away, Izzy quickly held it so she could study the burns on his knuckles. 'How are they?' she asked. They looked red and sore even with the white of the cream over them.

'They'll be fine. The cream seems to be working, or it could just be the cold beer,' he laughed.

His hands still looked painful to her, and she bet he'd have trouble using them for a while. Suddenly she realised he was watching her and quickly let go of his hand. 'Anyway, thanks again.'

Brian nodded his head and raised his beer in return. For an old bloke he was still ruggedly handsome. Short stubble covered his strong chin and his hairline wasn't receding like most. Will and his dad made a striking pair. The blue of their eyes kept you mesmerised in such a way that the hairs on the back of your neck would stand on end. Izzy had never seen a blue like it. It was as if their eyes were full of electric currents that gave off little sparks. Silver glittery flecks among a deep sea of blue. As a young kid, those eyes had fascinated her.

'Don't forget, we're just over the fence if you need anything, okay?' Will offered, breaking her train of thought.

'I'll be fine,' she replied, her determination to keep things afloat coming to the fore. 'But if by chance I do get stuck, I'll give you a holler.'

'We could spare one of our headers and Will could help you finish the harvest,' said Brian. 'We're not far from finishing up, and I don't mind jumping on to free Will up. I don't get to do much these days with Will and our new worker running around.'

'Cheers, Brian, but there's no need. Thanks anyway. Mike's offered us his.' Mike Littlemore only had a small amount of crop in this year, so he was already finished. She'd rung him that afternoon and tried to hire his header from him, but Mike wouldn't hear of it. She'd had offers all night from others who'd wanted to help her harvest, but she'd thanked them all and declined. It was something she could handle herself. It was a chance to prove to her dad that she could run the farm.

The crowd's combined voices boomed and echoed in the clear

night air and it was after ten when Izzy finally headed home. Tom ran around barking and trying to get Izzy to play but she was completely bushed. She tapped her waist, indicating that Tom should jump up and rest his front paws on her belly. She scratched his ears and said, 'Not tonight, Tom. Tomorrow we'll go chase some rabbits.'

There were so many messages on the answering machine from people in the district wondering how Bill was and offering their help. Betty had suggested – well, informed her, really – that she was going to make some casseroles in case Izzy didn't feel like cooking. This was wonderful news; Izzy was going to have some late nights until the harvesting was finished.

Just as he'd promised, Mike delivered his header not long after Izzy got up the following morning. Izzy told him she had a contract driver coming later that day. She didn't need it getting back to her dad just yet that she'd be doing the harvesting herself.

Once Mike had left, she fuelled up the header and made a start on the unfinished paddock. It was hard going. Every time she passed the burnt-out header, with the black charcoal ring around it, her stomach gave a lurch and the memories flashed back. Thankfully she finished that particular paddock by nightfall, and wouldn't have to pass it again. But, for the most part, the work gave her an escape from dwelling on her dad. For once, she could relax back into the seat for the long haul. She dug out a box with old tapes in it that must have been Mike's. It contained the likes of Slim Dusty, Kenny Rogers and John Williamson, but the tapes were old and wound too tightly so they wouldn't play. The amount of wheat dust in the tape deck probably didn't help either.

'I guess we won't be listening to that, hey, Tom?' Tom lifted his head from his paws at the sound of his name. 'We'll try the radio.' Izzy flicked onto an old Roxette song, 'It Must Have Been Love', which had been a favourite when she was younger. She joined in with the words, bouncing up and down in her seat. As she sang, she gazed out at the contrast of the bright blue sky and the golden tips of the wheat. She loved the way the wheat heads fell into the comb after being cut and were munched up by the header reel. And the way the stubble that was left behind looked like a crew cut, all straight and short with lines running through it from the header tyres. She loved everything about farming – you got to watch Mother Nature as she moved through the seasons. One day it was gloriously sunny and eucalyptus floated through the air, and the next it could be raining and you could smell the dirt as it got wet. It was pure heaven and she couldn't imagine living without witnessing the changing seasons, experiencing the way of the land. It was definitely her way of life.

The next morning before the birds were awake, Izzy downed her cuppa and placed it in the sink. It was time to start work – the header didn't drive itself.

She made her way to the top paddock, which bordered the Timmins' farm. Izzy loved the morning starts, when the air was still crisp and fresh before the day got too hot. Tom usually loved it too, but he was curled up by her feet and snoozing soundly. He'd spend all day there happily by her side. She was bouncing along in the header listening to Katy Perry's 'Hot and Cold' on her MP3 player when she heard Will's voice across the two-way.

'You on channel, Izzy?'

Tom tilted his head and growled. 'I know how you feel, mate, but we have to cut him a little slack after the other day,' she said, giving Tom a reassuring pat.

Izzy picked up the microphone handpiece. 'Yeah, Will. What's up?'

'Hey, I was just wondering how the harvesting was going. What are you up to at the moment?' his voice crackled back.

'Nothing much,' she replied evasively. 'Why?' This wasn't sounding good.

'I was going to come over and see if anything needed doing,' replied Will.

'Uh . . . you don't have to do that. Um . . . everything's fine, Will. I've got it all under control.' The last thing she needed was Will catching her out and blabbing to her old man, especially now that they were so chummy.

Izzy slowed down the header as she made her way towards the field bin. Reaching beside her chair, she pulled the hydraulic lever to extend the auger and then lined it up with the small opening in the field bin. She'd started to unload the grain into the bin when she heard Will's voice again.

'Ah, it looks to me like someone's telling porkies.'

What the . . . ? Frantically, she looked around and spotted Will's ute parked not far from the header. He stood near the open door with the two-way mic in his hand, and a huge stupid grin on his face as if he'd just caught her skinny-dipping.

Damn it, Izzy thought.

Muscles rippled in his bronzed arms as he jogged over to the header and hauled himself up the steps, letting himself into the small cab. His tanned face made his teeth look extra white as he smiled, and the stubble along his strong narrow jaw held her attention for just a second too long.

'What's going on here, eh?' Izzy could feel his breath as he talked, towering over her in the confined space of the cab. 'I came over to have a stickybeak at this new contractor Mike said you'd hired, just to make sure he knew what he was doing. Must say I'm surprised. He's much better looking than I anticipated.'

'Very funny. So you caught me out.' Izzy rolled her eyes. 'Why pay someone else when I can do it myself? We couldn't afford it anyway.' Quickly she put up her hand. 'And I'm not taking any more handouts.' She sighed. 'Just don't tell my old man, or I'll have your guts for garters!'

Will raised his hand. 'Scouts honour!'

'Yeah, when were you ever a scout?' she scoffed. She wondered how trustworthy he was. It was too hard to tell, looking at his cheeky smile. Izzy now wished she had more on than her blue singlet, especially with him looming over her. Why couldn't he squat down? She resisted the urge to put her hand over the gape of her singlet across her chest, even though he'd be able to see right down it. She wouldn't give him the satisfaction of knowing he could unnerve her. Suddenly the header began to rock slightly, signalling that the box was just about empty. Will turned and stopped the auger for her.

'Well, what are you doing? Leaving or staying? I have a paddock to strip,' said Izzy. Tom looked up, as if to mimic the same thoughts.

'I'll do a boxful with you, seeing as you asked so nicely.' With that, he moved in a bit and slammed the door behind him. With some manoeuvring he squished his narrow butt between the door of the cab and her chair, seating himself on her esky. Izzy was trying to be more tolerant of Will – she thought she owed him that much. What he'd done yesterday was pretty darn amazing in her books. Izzy hadn't forgotten how she'd been rooted to the spot, unable to move as she watched her father falling into the flames. She was a little ashamed and wished she could have been as quick as Will.

'Okay then,' came her reply as he made himself comfortable, although 'Crap!' was what she really wanted to say.

Izzy moved the header forward. Trying hard not to touch Will, she reached across and moved the hydraulic lever that swung the auger back into position. The last thing she needed was him getting any funny ideas – things were awkward enough already.

Putting the long comb into the crop again, she lined it up with the edge of the remaining wheat heads and watched as the comb munched its way through. Staring straight ahead, she tried to concentrate, but it was fairly difficult when she could feel Will's eyes on her, assessing her ability. Half a lap later, Will eventually broke the silence between them.

'You know, I can drive for you if you like. Dad's just finishing the last of ours today.'

'Thanks, but no thanks, Will. Besides, I don't think you could handle this old girl. She's not what you're used to, I'm sure,' said Izzy, teasing him. 'A yellow header is more your style. Say a New Holland TC with a forty-foot comb. Would I be right?' Izzy looked him in the eyes, waiting for a reaction.

'Yeah, you're right,' Will said, nodding with a wry smile. 'Dad loves his New Holland headers. But I'm sure I could still handle this,' he said, as he tried to shift his numb backside in the narrow cabin.

'Ha,' laughed Izzy. 'Mike's header is pure luxury after our old John Deere. Now that was a header! If it hadn't gone up in flames, it would have fallen to bits. At least Dad will be able to upgrade for next year now with the insurance money, and especially with the crops doing so well this year.'

'Bill was telling me about it. It's lucky he never got that bad frost that came through in September. A few in the district lost a fair bit to it.'

'It's depressing – all your hard work can turn to shit and there's not a damn thing you can do about it,' she replied. When farming was your livelihood, you could lose so much from things outside your control like floods, droughts, fire, frost or hail. Farming sure was a hard, stressful way of life. You were always waiting. Waiting for rain or waiting for the wind to stop. It was a game of guessing and more waiting. She sometimes wondered why she longed for it so badly. The need to feel the clean air on her skin. To get up with the sun and follow it through the day till it sets. The thrill of driving for ten minutes and still being on your own land. To know your small community would do anything for you in a heartbeat. It was just in her blood, she guessed.

'How is Bill going, anyway?' Will said, changing the subject. 'I've been meaning to give him a call.'

Izzy thought she detected a note of sincerity. Will actually sounded as if he gave a damn about someone. 'He's doing okay. They gotta take some skin from his back, I think, and use it for grafts on his legs. It's gonna be a while before he can come home. Even then, he's going to have to keep the wounds dressed and clean. Mum said he's being a tough old brute, but he's relying on the painkillers at the moment.' Izzy's voice almost broke. She was finding it hard to talk about. She worried about her dad constantly.

Will could almost feel the lump he knew was building in her throat. Resting his hand on her leg, he gave it a friendly squeeze. Just a quick one – he didn't want to push it. He knew she was grateful that he'd pulled Bill out of the fire. It was funny how, at that moment when Bill fell, Will had just run in after him. No second thought, only the adrenaline pumping and the feeling that he wasn't going to lose another person close to him. He could remember the way he'd almost gone deaf; he couldn't hear the pumps or the crackling of the fire. His legs had just taken off and carried him into the smoke. He remembered his arms flapping about feeling their way through the smoke, banging into the metal steps and then the soft shoulder of Bill as he lay on the ground. Then he was dragging him out and away from the destruction. He remembered the look of relief on Izzy's face.

The emotion he now saw in Izzy's eyes softened him. Her blue eyes had the slightest hint of tears and looked so large and vulnerable. She nibbled on her bottom lip, trying to keep her composure. Will had an urge to put his hand up to her olive skin, caress her face and run his thumb along her high cheekbone. He liked seeing this side of her, the loving and gentle side that showed her femininity. It made a nice change.

'Try not to worry, kiddo.' He watched as his words caused her to regain her composure and shut him out. She really was a breed of her own. He had never known another girl like her. 'I can't imagine Bill sitting down for too long. He's like a fart in a bottle.' Will suppressed a laugh. He could just imagine Bill fighting off the nurses and trying to get out of bed. 'You can't keep a good man down and your dad's an old battler. They broke the mould when they made him.' He smiled as he spoke.

Izzy couldn't help but smile at this either. 'I'd love to go see him, but it takes nearly half a day to get there and, realistically, I can't go until harvest is done. I know he's in good hands and I think I'm needed here more. There's a lot to do. After harvesting we need the shearers, so I'll have to get my act into gear.' Looking back to the rows of straight golden heads, Izzy adjusted the steering wheel slightly.

'You sure you don't want a hand?' said Will, his eyebrows raised.

'Nope. I've managed with this and more. I'm sure I'll cope. Cheers anyway.'

Izzy was no helpless female, that was for sure. She wasn't afraid of hard work. She doubted Will would know what a real day's work was like, especially using old machinery. He couldn't survive without airconditioning and air-cushioned seats.

'Shit, that's nice and thick,' Will commented, gazing out at the crop. 'Don't you wish the whole lot would be like that?' He leaned forward, trying to get a better look through the large front window on the header.

Izzy slowed down the header a fraction as it was struggling to churn through the thickness. 'It's the best bit I've seen yet. This paddock has been going about fifteen bags so far. A lot nicer than the six bags it went last year!'

They were not far from the field bin now. Izzy looked back through the spy-hole, checking how full the header box was. The wheat was about a foot from the top – just enough room to harvest all the way to the field bin.

'What's Bill's old Leyland doing out here?' asked Will, noticing the truck parked near the bin.

'I'm filling it up when Dave can't get back out for a load. I'll run it into the bin when I get a moment. This way I can keep on harvesting. It only holds eight tonnes, but it still helps to get it off quicker.'

'So you've got your truck licence?' asked Will.

'Yes, and don't you worry, it's all legit, and no – I didn't have to bribe anyone to get it,' she said sarcastically. Izzy frowned at him. 'Why look so shocked?'

Realisation dawned on Will's face as he put two and two together. 'Ah, I see, now. You were driving Dave's truck. I guess I don't know that much about you, after all. I don't remember you having much to do with the farm before you went away.'

'By Dad's standards I didn't. But I worked on a farm over east near Merriwa. My boss, Rob, showed and taught me most of what I know.' Izzy shrugged her shoulders and hoped her discomfort at mentioning Rob's name wasn't obvious. 'It's always been my dream to work the farm. The sooner Dad understands that, the better. It's becoming a bit of a mission.' Izzy sighed. This could be her only chance to prove she could do it.

Will stared at Izzy, seeing her in a new light. He ran his gaze over her lean, muscled physique, down to her dry, callused hands. From what he could see all around him, he knew she'd been working hard for some time. He was surprised he hadn't noticed it before now. Maybe it was just too hard to get past how good she'd looked in that blue dress at the barbecue . . .

Will watched her pulling up alongside the field bin. She was a natural with the machine. He could certainly get used to looking at her intense eyes with such focused concentration. Her small singlet was a bonus.

'So, how much you got left to do?' he asked curiously.

'About eight hundred hectares. I should be finished by the end of the week, with a bit of luck. Dad's happy to have me stay home and keep a watchful eye on the contractor.'

'Even if the contractor doesn't exist!' Will laughed.

Izzy gave Will an untrusting look.

'I won't say anything, I promise. So, you'll be free for the bin party on Saturday then. You're gonna come?' said Will, as he pulled the auger lever for Izzy.

'Yeah, wouldn't miss it. There's still so many people I haven't caught up with yet.'

'Cool. Well, if I don't see you before then, I'll catch you there. Thanks for the ride. And remember, if you get stuck, just give me a call.' He grinned when Izzy flashed him a look that said 'not in this lifetime'. 'I'll try and ring Bill tonight. He's in Royal Perth, yeah?' he asked as he opened the door.

'That's right.'

'Thanks. Well, see ya, Izzy.' With that, he gave her his usual knockout smile, shut the door behind him and climbed down the steps.

Izzy watched him walk back to his ute. Such long strides and such long legs. He was very fit. No wonder all the girls swooned over him. With a shake of her head, she prepared to take off for another lap around the paddock.

9

THE week flew by in a haze of wheat and sleep. Exhaustion was beginning to creep into Izzy's body so she was glad to finish the last of the harvesting on Friday at around noon. Proudly, she took the old Leyland truck in with the last load to the bin, thankful it was finished. The crew that worked at the large bin storages checked to make sure she was coming to the party. They liked to round up as many people as they could – the more the merrier.

The next thing on Izzy's mind was to clean up all the machinery and put it away. Not a fun job but at least it was only wheat dust she had to crawl around in and not barley or oat dust – itchy stuff. Izzy knew of a bloke who'd put oat dust in his mate's jocks on his buck's night. The poor fella had scratched himself raw.

By Saturday afternoon the header was clean, and she'd rung Mike to let him know it was ready to take home. Not much was left to do that was important, as she'd already brought the field bins in and cleaned up the truck. That night she was thankful just to sit back and relax while she ate her tea – bangers and mash with a side of vegies – and not have to rush off afterwards. The seven o'clock sleep-in she'd had that morning had been wonderful. The four a.m. starts and then not crawling into bed until eleven p.m. had started to wear thin. Izzy leaned back and rested her legs on the chair opposite.

While sitting there, she thought about what she should wear that night for the end-of-harvest celebration – the bin party. It was usually held as a way for the farmers to thank the bin crew for a good job helping them get their grain off quickly so they could get back in with another load. The drivers would go like the clappers delivering ten or more loads a day. Anyone who spilt grain was fined a carton of beer – and it was at the bin party that debts were cleared.

Izzy swung back on the dining chair, a sausage hanging off the end of her fork. Yes, she thought, this little lady was well overdue to let her hair down. The phone rang, startling her from her thoughts.

'Hello,' she answered brightly.

'Hi, darling. It's Mum.' Her voice sounded tired but happy.

'Hi, Mum. How's things going? Are you at Sarah's?'

'Yeah, we're about to organise dinner but I thought I'd give you a call first. Your dad wants to know how the last couple of loads went.'

'Well, you can tell him we've finished and it's all in the bin now. The last paddock went well, with high protein and bugger-all screenings. Dad should be happy when he sees the money coming in. Tell him Mike's coming to pick up the header and I've paid the contract driver.' Izzy felt a tinge of remorse having to lie to her mum.

They talked for another minute and Jean glossed over Bill's grafting procedure; whether it was to spare Izzy or herself, she wasn't sure.

'I'll try and call you again in a day or so with a better update. But there's not much happening. It's just going to be a long, slow healing process. You take care tonight, love. I don't want you driving home drunk.'

'Don't stress, Mum. I'll pack my swag. I love you. Give my love to Dad. Talk soon.'

'Love you too. Bye, darling.'

An hour later Izzy and Tom drove down the gravel road to the party, singing their hearts out to Lee Kernaghan's 'The Outback Club'. Tom always howled when Izzy sang. She wasn't sure if it was because he liked it or because he was protesting, trying to drown out her voice.

Izzy drove over the railway crossing at the end of town and turned right towards the three large storage bins. Next to them was an open bulkhead, which was a large area of bitumen with small tin walls to hold the grain. When they were full, large blue and green tarps would be pulled over the stacks and tightened into place. Being a good year, the yield was up and the three bins had filled quickly, hence the need for the emergency storage. Izzy pulled into a spot near the accommodation huts and parked next to a large gum tree. She could remember going to bin parties when she worked here. They were always great nights.

There were two large dongas. One was rectangular and filled with individual bedrooms, and the other contained the kitchen and dining area, from which bin staff were coming and going with salads and beer. Outside, a few rusty brown forty-four gallon drums were scattered about the place. Some were rubbish bins. Others were piled high with mallee roots, ready for a fire.

Izzy was well prepared as usual. She had her swag in the back of the ute, along with her esky full of ice and drinks for the night. Turning to Tom she gave him the 'Mum is boss' stare. 'Stay here, Tom.' Tom tilted his head as if he understood and then reluctantly lay down on the seat and put his head on his paws. She was sure that if he was human, he'd be pouting right now. Izzy wound the window down further for him, and then shut the door. 'You just stay near the ute,' she said. Reaching over the back tray, she dipped into her esky, took out a beer and headed off towards the mixed group of farmers, truckies and bin crew.

The sun was close to setting. The beautiful blue sky of the day was giving way to a yellowy red, like a fire dancing on the horizon. Izzy breathed in the evening air with the faint smell of eucalyptus and burning snaggers. God, who was in charge of the barbie?

Izzy's jeans hung low over her thongs, scuffing the ground as she walked. She pulled the low v-neck, deep-red top she wore down over the top of them. It clung just a little too tightly to her breasts for her liking, but it was one her favourites as Claire had given it to her. Surprisingly, she'd gone to the effort of putting on some eyeliner, knowing it picked up the dark specks in her eyes. As she passed a large shrub, she quickly brushed back her hair, which was out of its usual ponytail, checking it wasn't too wayward. She always worried that the slight wave in her hair would get out of hand, but it felt like it was sitting just below her shoulders nicely.

Joining the first group of men, she said a quick hello before cracking open her drink. Travis was in the half-circle next to his dad and he gave her a smile and a nod. It was a mixed crowd of young and old. Fathers and sons usually came, while the wives and mothers stayed at home unless they were up for a drink. But half of the bin crew were females and helped to even out numbers. James, one of the bin crew, came round to greet her, giving her a spare stubbie holder for her drink. He was about twenty, she guessed. Hard to tell because he had such clean fair skin with lots of freckles and looked much younger than he probably was. She'd met James quite a few times on her trips to the bin. He was a nice bloke, always cheerful, full of jokes, and kept his grid clean and tidy.

'Cheers for that, James.' He smiled back at her and tucked his long blond hair behind his ears as he moved on.

The party was starting to hum as there was quite a turnout. There were a couple of fine-looking blokes about, which always made it more interesting. A few she hadn't seen before and she guessed they were blokes from nearby bins who'd heard about the party. There were more than five other bins around Pingaring, all within sixty kilometres.

Will pulled up a little while later in his new red Holden V8 SS ute. Everyone turned their heads towards the low rumble, which had a way of getting under your skin and joining the pulsing of your blood. Not bad, she thought – the ute, that is. Izzy loved the sound of a V8 engine.

As the night wore on, Izzy felt herself relaxing more and more – with the aid of a bourbon or two. She'd run into Jess, who was spending most of the night hanging off Travis. Their love for each other was unmistakeable. They'd already eaten by the time Izzy found them – some sausages and steak dished out on paper plates with plastic utensils. Izzy knew Tom would sneak off early in the morning to clean up the leftovers. Izzy had eaten hers on a wobbly deck chair next to James, Jess and Travis. There was nothing like eating under the stars out in the open with the smell of barbecued meat wafting through the air.

'Hey, you guys wanna come out and catch some gilgies tomorrow?' Izzy asked them as the idea came into her head. They used to have so much fun going from dam to dam.

'Oh, that sounds great, Iz, but Trav and I have to go to a busy bee at the tennis club,' Jess replied.

'I can come, if that's okay,' piped up James.

'Sure, why not. How's after lunch sound?'

'Sounds great,' James replied all too enthusiastically, causing Jess to raise her eyebrows at Izzy. When James left to get another drink, Jess dug her boot in.

'I think he's keen on you,' she teased.

Izzy screwed up her face. 'Please, I hardly know him. Plus I don't need another complication in my life, thank you very much.'

'Come on, Izzy. You could have any bloke here tonight. You look amazing – you should wear you hair out more often.'

'It's very impractical when you're working,' replied Izzy, evading the compliment.

Jess threw Izzy a dark look. 'My God, I'm amazed you've even had boyfriends. Did you have any when you were over in Merriwa?'

'A couple, nothing serious. I was with this one bloke called John, who ran a farm twenty minutes from where I was, but after four months, he found a real nice-looking teacher from the local school. I heard they were engaged before I left. So I haven't had a fella for . . . um . . . it'd be about eleven months now. No great loss. John wasn't that great a kisser.' Izzy laughed and Jess just rolled her eyes towards the Southern Cross.

Leaning back in her unstable deck chair, Izzy watched the young girls vying for Will's attention. Travis and James had made bets on who'd end up with who by the end of the night. If she was being honest with herself, Izzy had to confess that she thought Will was probably the best-looking bloke there. He was quite a sight in his loose-fitting jeans and black shirt with a silver pattern printed on the right shoulder. His hair was gelled just slightly so that his fringe was styled back off his forehead. Ah, who was she kidding? He was the standout without a doubt. James wasn't far behind, although he was the complete opposite to Will, with his fair skin and blond hair. But he was polite, and he had a great work ethic. Already that put him ahead of most of the blokes she knew.

By now darkness had well and truly settled around them. Someone had set up a large floodlight, which kept them in a bright circle away from the moonlit night. From the other side of the party, James caught Izzy's eye and wandered over.

'Hey, Izzy. How's it going? Havin' fun?' James was quite jovial, the contents of the Bundy Rum can in his hand helping to slur his speech.

'Yeah, it's not so bad. You look like you're having a good time, James,' Izzy replied, a slight look of amusement on her face.

James leant close to Izzy's ear – the thud of music blaring out of a nearby car was deafeningly loud. 'So, it doesn't look like you brought anyone with you, Izzy. No boyfriend waiting at home for you?' he asked curiously.

'Gee, you don't waste any time, do you?' Izzy chuckled and wondered how much was the alcohol talking. He was usually quite reserved.

'Just sussing it all out. Don't you worry about me. My bark is worse than my bite.' He attempted a wink, then bumped against her arm as he slurred into her ear. 'Get a load of Angela over there tryin' her hardest to get into Will's pants. That's just *saaad*.' Angela was one of the bin girls and was known for her flirtatious ways.

Will was standing near the white hut, behind a rusty drum that was ablaze with red flames. Out of nowhere, a bolt of fear ran through Izzy's body as orange flames appeared to lick Will's face like large tongues. His icy blue eyes cut a path through the fire. They connected with hers and sent her body into turmoil. Izzy was flooded with unwelcome vivid images of the header fire and felt herself weaken. She wasn't sure why she had reacted so fiercely. It made her uneasy to think she'd been as worried about Will's life as she had about her father's. She should really slow down on her bourbon intake, or maybe she should have stuck to the beers.

Will's eyes were alive and she felt like they could see right into her soul. Was he reading her thoughts? Someone walked in front of him, breaking the connection between them. Will turned and laughed at something one of the blokes said. Angela, who was leaning into Will with her arm resting on his, was trying to join in the conversation. Lucky for some, her small black top was tight, preventing a fallout. It was just about the same at the other end with her tiny denim miniskirt, which didn't leave much to the imagination. Even from a distance, Izzy could see the thick black eyeliner outlining Angela's hazel eyes, combined with too much blue eye shadow, and her vibrant red lipstick looked as if it had been applied with a paint roller. Maybe I'm being harsh, Izzy thought, but there's more to life than trying to get a man's attention.

She felt James's hand on her shoulder before he spoke.

'Angela's had a thing for him all harvest. Been tryin' hard but to no avail.' James knew all the goss. He managed to hear everything while working on the bin with Angela and the others.

Izzy shrugged. 'That surprises me. I thought he'd have jumped at the chance,' she said, genuinely puzzled.

As if sensing he was being talked about, Will glanced Izzy's way. Instantly she felt naked under his gaze. He smiled deviously as if reading her thoughts and she felt his eyes drop. Her body reacted like it would to a feather brushing down her naked skin.

Next to her, James rambled on about a small grain mix they'd had last week and complained about the brainless bloke who did it, who'd left because he couldn't stand the heat. His voice seemed far away and she struggled to pay attention. How could she concentrate? Will's stare was starting to unsettle her. Heat rose to her cheeks. Quickly she broke his eye contact. Feeling inadequate, she leant towards James and spoke, 'To answer your earlier question, no I don't have a boyfriend, but that doesn't mean I want one either.'

James paused mid-speech, raised his eyebrows and gave her a cheeky grin. Without warning, he placed a hand upon her shoulder and pulled her closer, just inches from his Bundy breath. 'I'm relieved to hear it,' he whispered gently, as if sharing a secret.

'Don't think that means you're gonna get lucky,' she warned him.

'Aw, come on. Can't a bloke try?' James shrugged and asked. 'Can I at least get you another drink, then?'

Izzy glanced at Will out of the corner of her eye. He was still watching her. What was his problem? She noticed Will's face was knotted, almost scowling. She wondered what could have possibly aggravated him. Well, whatever it was, it wasn't her problem. She just wished he'd leave her alone. Her gaze flicked back to James.

'Nah, I've got my own back at the ute.'

All of a sudden, a shadow was cast over her. James was so close that he blocked out the light. Panic rose in Izzy's throat. Was he was going to kiss her? Before she could lean back, he began to pull away, reluctantly letting her go. Throwing his empty can into a nearby bin and avoiding Izzy's eyes, James headed off to get himself another refill. Izzy stood for a moment, relieved, and then slyly looked around to see if anyone had seen what happened. Hell, she hoped no one had any bets on her. Maybe James had one to win.

Will had been keeping a watchful eye on Izzy all night, thinking of it as his job to watch over Bill's daughter. He was not at all impressed with James, who was clearly trying to make a move on her. And that moment she and James had just shared, what did that all mean? They'd been looking pretty friendly. The more drinks Will had, the harder he found it to control his eyes. Like a dicky compass they kept wandering back to Izzy. She looked so fresh. It was nice to see her smiling and enjoying herself after what she'd been through. One day he'd like her to laugh and smile like that with him. Maybe there would come a time when they could be great friends. Claire would have loved that. For some reason Will found he needed to be close to Izzy. An unknown force kept pulling him towards her. He watched as she walked off into the darkness to her ute and suddenly found his feet moving. Leaving the crowd, and a stumbling Angela, he followed Izzy, almost transfixed.

She was leaning over the back tray, reaching for another drink, when she felt a hand slide across her shoulder. 'Miss me already?' she said, thinking it was James. She turned around with a naughty smile only to find a pair of electric eyes that did not belong to James. The glow from the moon illuminated Will's strong jawline. Bugger it! Goosebumps had appeared along her arms and she felt slightly dizzy. 'Ah, it's you,' she croaked, not sure why she could suddenly hear her pulse beating in her ears. It must be the alcohol running through her veins. Had she had too much already?

Will raised his eyebrows. 'Expecting someone else, were we? Just as well I came to check up on you.'

'Now, why would you want to check up on me?' said Izzy rapidly, not sure if it was the alcohol getting to her again or Will's intoxicating scent, which was a mixture of soap and aftershave. Closing her eyes for just a moment, she dared to take in another breath. A larrikin smile danced on his face as she met his gaze again, along with a devilish look in his eyes. No wonder women fell at his feet like rabbits with a good dose of mixo.

'Someone has to make sure you get home safely, especially after what I witnessed earlier.' Will reached up to move a strand of her hair that had fallen across her face and was moving in the slight breeze, teasing him. God knows what possessed him to do it but it was dangerous. It was all unscripted territory and he was afraid of what he might do next. Jesus, he had only come over to interrogate her. He felt his body reacting to her eyes, which were full of spark. The heat within him was growing stronger and he had no control.

Izzy slapped his hand away gently. 'Hey, I can take care of myself, mister. I could take you on any day.'

'Oh, I'm sure you could. Come on,' he urged. Will lifted up his hand again and Izzy caught it quickly. For a moment they battled in a war of strength, their muscles raised like the hackles on a dog, neither wanting to give in.

In the midst of it all, Will leant down unexpectedly and brushed her lips with his, ever so gently.

Izzy felt their lips touch and her mind went blank. Slowly the fight leaked out of her arm. *Oh my God* she screamed inside her head. What in hell's name is he doing, besides cheating?

He pushed his hand forward and out of her weakened grasp. Slowly, gently, it moved to the back of her neck, pulling her closer. All she could do was follow like a silly puppy on a lead. All of a sudden, a million things went through her mind – only she couldn't slow down her thoughts enough to understand any of them. She felt confused. But her body felt warm, energised, as if giving away secrets.

She should stop this, she thought, as Will's warm lips pressed even harder. She reached up and put her hand on his chest to push him away. But as she did so, a soft groan escaped from him and all her strength sank faster than a dodgy sponge cake. Gently, his tongue ran across hers, igniting hidden fires. He reached for her free hand and wrapped it around him. Oh, it'd been so long since she'd experienced a kiss like this. Surely she could make an exception. Her insides began to melt from the inferno that had now erupted below her belly, and a tingling sensation crept through her skin.

Unconsciously, she opened her mouth for him as he deepened the kiss. Leaning into her, his warm, hard body pressed her back against the cold steel of her ute. She'd forgotten how wonderful a man's body felt crushed against her own. If he moved away, she was sure she'd flop to the ground like a rag doll. Well, bugger me, she thought. How was she supposed to keep her wits about her at a time like this?

Momentarily she got lost in the kiss and slid her hand down around Will's back to the top of his jeans. *Shit, I can't do this*, her commonsense tried to scream. But his breath intoxicated her, bringing with it the smooth mixture of bourbon and Coke. Her hand found his warm naked skin under his shirt and she felt his body shiver. Was that from her touch? Izzy gripped onto his belt, which she knew was so full of notches. Hell, she didn't want to be another one. This thought was enough to shake her awake. I won't be another Claire, she resolved. No matter how good he smells . . . and kisses. I've only given in so easily because it's been so long, she convinced herself. Gathering all her strength, she pulled away with as much dignity as she could muster.

'Whoa! I'm sorry. That shouldn't have happened.' It was all she could manage to say before covering her mouth in shock. With her eyes on the dark ground she slid from between him and the ute and headed briskly back to the party.

Will couldn't speak. He didn't know what to say. It didn't feel right apologising for something that had felt so amazing. He stood rooted to the spot, waiting for the tightness in his jeans to subside as he watched the way the silvery moonlight shone off her ute. He heard a metallic clang and saw Tom, who had rested his head on the open window.

'Hello, boy,' said Will as he scratched Tom's head. He knew he couldn't hide out here all night. Turning away, he headed back to the party, kicking at the dirt as he walked. He was as confused as Izzy was about what had come over him. Maybe he liked the challenge. Or maybe he just needed to get laid.

Izzy tried to avoid Will for the rest of the night, torn between not liking him and not being sure whether she could trust herself near him in her present state. Will didn't try to talk to her again either, but she did catch him glancing her way a few times.

Luckily, James staggered over for another chat and it took her mind off Will, for a moment anyway. James was way past it. Izzy had a task just trying to keep his hands off her.

'Look, how about you back off a bit, mate? You're smashed. Maybe you should go sleep it off,' said Izzy strongly, but she wasn't really too concerned.

James leant in closer and feigned deafness.

'You heard the lady – back off.' Will appeared from the darkness and his strong arms pulled the offender away.

James threw up his hands like a footballer pleading his innocence after a wayward punch.

'Time to shove off,' said Will, giving him a nudge towards the hut.

James gave a look that said, 'Yeah, I hear ya.' Then with a smirk at Izzy he headed off into the hut.

Izzy waited until James was out of earshot before swinging around to face Will. 'What the hell did you do that for?'

Will shrugged and ran his hand through his hair. 'Just trying to help you out.'

'Well, I'm not a child and I don't need an overprotective big brother. I was quite capable of handling the situation.'

'What – like you did an hour ago?' he said tauntingly, as the taste of her lips came to mind. He tried hard not to smile as he saw the fury in her eyes and the embarrassment on her face. Oh, why did he like to tease her so? He hadn't had this much fun in ages.

Izzy shuffled her feet. She didn't dare open her mouth, afraid of what she'd say. Taking a deep breath, she forced herself to calm down. Instead of yelling, she glared at him and said, 'Why can't people just let me run my own life and fight my own battles?' It almost came out as a plea. She turned and walked away. 'I'm not ten any more. I don't need protecting.'

Will watched her go. He didn't need reminding of her age. You idiot, he thought. That wasn't the best way to get back into her good books. He got the feeling it wasn't just him she was angry at. Well, there was nothing he could do now except have another drink. He felt the cold seeping into his skin and moved towards a crowd around one of the fire drums.

It was well after midnight when Izzy opted for the comfort of her swag, which she headed to alone. The crowd had dispersed. James had crashed earlier with a sore head, and only a few others sat around the dying fire. As Izzy headed to her ute, Travis called out goodbye and she turned, shouting a reply. A movement between a small bush and a parked car caught her eye.

Instantly she recognised Will's form with Angela sprawled all over him, like a spider with many legs wrapped around its prey. But instead of killing her prey Angela was literally kissing it to death. That's what it looked like anyway.

Stumbling on a small rock, Izzy quickly turned back towards her ute. Her ears began to echo with a dull thud, blocking out any other sound. She shouldn't be upset. She knew Will was like that, had been all his life. He couldn't get much from Izzy, so he moved on. Well, that was the Will she knew, and she only had herself to blame.

But why did she feel so angry? 'You're a bloody idiot,' she muttered to herself as she crawled into the back of her ute and into her swag. She should have learnt from Claire's mistake. Wriggling, she snuggled down into her sleeping bag as the fresh night air clung to her face. The stars moved about above as if swinging from a baby's mobile. Trying to block them out, she clamped her eyes shut, only for them to be replaced with a vision of Will and Angela. 'Ugh,' she groaned, before deciding the spinning stars were better.

10

THE cool fresh morning combined with the sound of pink and grey galahs screeching overhead in the large gum tree out the front woke Izzy from her restless sleep. It was early; the sun had only just cracked the horizon, creating a beautiful pinky-red haze, and the few soft white clouds nearby looked as if they were alight. She lifted her head up a bit higher and rested back on her elbows. This was the best part of the day. The air was crisp and it always smelt so good.

It should have been a memorable moment, lying there looking out the back of her ute at the sunrise, with Tom curled up next to her pillow, but the thumping going on in her head was just too much. She also had a horrible 'something just shat in my mouth' feeling and her murky eyes were struggling to stay open.

The camp was quiet. Nobody else was up and about – thank goodness. She could get away without having to see anyone. Besides, with her mouth the way it was she probably couldn't talk just yet anyway.

Throwing open the green canvas cover, then unzipping her sleeping bag, she began to crawl out gingerly. Oh, it was going to be a long morning. She needed to get home and have a shower, and a Berocca to fix her aching head.

Leaving her swag unrolled, she moved to the side of the tray. Like an arthritic old man she climbed slowly over the side of the ute, which was usually a swift, graceful movement on her behalf. After a long guzzle from her water bottle she clambered in behind the steering wheel, resting her head on it for a few seconds while Tom jumped in over her to his side of the ute. She closed the door as quietly as she could, but it still rang in her ears. She fired up the motor and headed back home.

Izzy rested back against the tray of the Land Cruiser and crossed her arms as she waited for James to arrive. She'd invited him over for a feed of gilgies, or yabbies as everyone called them now. She ran her hand down her cargo shorts, felt the bump of her mobile in her pocket. It was on hand in case Mum rang. James had messaged her earlier, letting her know he was on his way, though she still wasn't convinced he'd turn up given the state of him last night. At that thought, she noticed a trail of dust along the main road and could now see him turning up the driveway. His rusty old ute eventually rolled to a stop just metres from her. Lifting her arm, she gave a quick wave of greeting as James got out of the car. She inhaled deeply. His blond hair was now cropped short in an army-style crew cut.

'Love your new do, James,' she said with a slight chuckle.

James ran both his hands over his nearly naked head, trying to get used to the feel of the spiky short hairs. After the initial shock, Izzy had to admit it suited him. It made his face more masculine, more visible, especially with his freckly skin.

'Yes, the gang decided it was time to get rid of it last night, while I was still passed out. Mind you, I should be glad it wasn't an eyebrow or worse.' James moved his head around in elegant poses. 'What do you reckon, eh? I think they used a number one. I guess that'll teach me. I feel naked!' The sunlight picked up red gingery flecks in his hair.

'Don't worry. It suits you, but I hope you've been wearing a hat or you'll end up with a burnt scone.'

James touched his head.

Izzy reached into the Land Cruiser and fished around on the seat. She pulled out an old wide-brimmed hat that looked like the sheep had trampled it to death and threw it at him.

'Here, use this. It'll go nicely with your thongs,' she said, motioning to his white and black thongs, which were worn through on the heels.

'Hey, I hope you're not picking on my double pluggers. These are my favourites!'

They both climbed into the Land Cruiser and Tom jumped in with them, not bothering to get on the back because he knew he was a special dog who rode up front.

'This is Tom. He's my chaperone. You make any move and he'll take your arm off, fair dinkum.'

'Sure, I believe you,' James said mockingly as he rubbed Tom behind his ears, turning the already placid dog to putty in his hands. Flicking the hat back on his head again for the umpteenth time, he said, 'You know, I think it's my colour.'

'James, I don't even think that's a colour. It's more dirt and grease. Personally, I think pink would suit you. You know, bring out your feminine side.' Izzy laughed, as farm boys rarely had a soft side. Even if they did, they would never let anyone know. James took off the hat and threw it at her as they drove off down the track towards the dam.

'You'll keep.' James began fiddling with his hands nervously. 'Hey, Izzy, about last night. I'm sorry if I came on a bit strong. I hope I wasn't too much of a prick. I get that way with a few drinks under my belt. Well, so I've been told.'

Izzy grinned. She could see how uncomfortable he was so she put him out of his misery. 'It's all right. I didn't take it to heart. You're not the first bloke and I'm sure you won't be the last.'

'I was a bit worried I'd overstepped the mark. The look in Will's eye was serious. I was drunk but even I can remember that.'

'Yeah, well, don't worry about him. He had no business stepping in. I don't know where he gets off thinking he can just invite himself into my life.' Izzy gripped the steering wheel so tight her knuckles whitened.

James shrugged. 'He was just being a gentleman and looking out for you.'

Izzy didn't reply. She was sure being a gentleman was the last thing on Will's mind. 'It's gonna be another warm one,' she said, changing the subject.

They joshed about until they reached the first dam where Izzy drove the ute up the hard, dry embankment and parked at the top. Gathering some buckets out of the back of the ute, they carefully descended the slippery bank to the murky water and set the buckets down.

'The water's quite low, but we should still get a good feed. I've had the nets in for a while,' Izzy explained.

James studied his companion's long sleek legs and swift motion as she pulled the first net in. The muscles, obvious in her olive arms, rose to the occasion as she forced the net quickly through the muddy water so the yabbies couldn't escape. Free from the water, she held the net at arm's length to keep her boots from getting wet. She guided it over one of the buckets while James tipped it on its side and shook the yabbies free. Once the last yabby was out Izzy wrapped the rope around the net, threw it onto the bank and bent down to help James collect the ones that had missed the bucket.

'These aren't a bad size, Izzy. Some nice big claws on them too,' said James, carefully picking up another yabby and popping it into the bucket.

'Hmm, yummy! Throw back the ones with eggs and any smaller than this.'

Izzy picked up one that was a fraction longer than her finger and gently threw it back into the dam.

'God, I haven't eaten a yabby in years. Just shows how long I've been away from our farm.' James was at Muresk, an agricultural uni that was about four hundred kilometres away. It was popular with a lot of students from farming backgrounds, who went and did undergraduate courses in Agribusiness and Farm Management.

'How's Muresk going, anyway? What are you studying for?' she asked curiously.

'My plan is to become a farm advisor, if all goes well.'

Izzy's soft voice teased him. 'That's if the B&S balls and drinking don't get in the way.' She threw him a look that said, 'I know what you Muresk boys get up to.'

'Yeah, something like that.' He laughed. 'I'm doing okay so far.'

A sad tone was clear in Izzy's voice as she began to speak. 'I would have loved to have gone to ag school but Dad wouldn't let me.' She took a deep breath. 'He thought it wasn't the place for me . . . for a girl.' Izzy had had her heart set on going to the Narrogin Agricultural College, even for just Years Eleven and Twelve, but Bill had prevented her.

James shook his head in disbelief. 'But lots of girls go. Shit, he's not one of them real olden-days blokes, is he? That's gotta suck,' he said when Izzy nodded solemnly.

'Yeah, tell me about it. That's why I went over east. I got first-hand work experience for a couple of years. It was great and I got paid instead of having to pay schooling fees. The best thing was Dad couldn't stop me.'

'That sounds like the way to do it. Here, I'll pull this one.' James reached down, plucked up the rope, and began to pull the net in.

It didn't feel like it took long to pull up all the nets, but as they were heading for the Land Cruiser James pointed to the sunset.

'Wow, time's just flown.' James held Izzy's shoulder and twisted her around to face the setting sun. 'Izzy, stop and appreciate what's in your own backyard. It just doesn't get any better than this, does it? You miss so much of this when you're in the city.'

'Don't worry. Sometimes you forget to appreciate it out here too. It's nice to have people around to remind you how lucky we are.'

James left his hand on her shoulder and they stood there in silence, watching the orange haze drop from the immense blue sky, as if someone was pulling down a blind very slowly. There was not a cloud in sight and they could see the horizon, all three hundred and sixty degrees of it. It was like being in a snow dome, but with a giant glowing fireball instead of the snow.

She was just about to say something when James leant over so slowly that she saw his baby-blue eyes clearly and almost could have counted the freckles scattered over his nose and cheeks. She knew what was coming but surprise stopped her from moving. His lips were dry, probably from all the drinking last night, as they pressed against hers. There was no spark and neither of them opened their mouths. James pulled away slowly to see her reaction. 'Sorry, I just saw an opportunity and I took it. Hope you don't mind.'

Izzy screwed up her face. She hated moments like these. 'Sorry, James. You're a top bloke but . . . it's just I'm in a bad spot right now and I don't have the time or the headspace to have a relationship. So much is going on here and you'll be going back to Muresk when it starts up. I just don't think it would work. I don't want to stuff you around. I hope you understand.' She could hear herself rambling.

James started laughing. 'It's cool. I thought I was pushing my luck, anyway. Oh well, can't blame a bloke for trying. Don't get too many opportunities like these.' He gave her a gentle shove.

Izzy could tell it didn't bother him that seriously and breathed a sigh of relief. Jerking her head, she motioned in the direction of the ute. 'Come on. We'd better go and cook these suckers. The copper will need stoking by now, too.'

The last of the sun dipped below the horizon as they drove off towards the house in the afterglow.

Izzy walked to the end of the verandah towards the barbecue area with some containers and newspapers balanced neatly in her arms. She laid the items on the outside table while James stoked the fire under a large rusty copper washtub.

'The copper's raring to go, Iz. I only chucked a couple of small mallee roots on it and it's just taken off.'

James lifted the lid off the copper while Izzy dropped the yabbies, still flapping their tails, into the big barrel of boiling hot water. Straightaway, the blue-green shells transformed into a light orange. They stood transfixed, watching the bubbling water slowly push the yabbies to the surface as they cooked.

A little while later they sat at the outside table with a few beers. Two plastic containers, which had hardly any yabby meat left in them, were in the middle. A growing pile of carcasses overflowed from the two scrap buckets and spilled onto the newspaper. Izzy had also made a sauce to dip the yabbies in – her mum's recipe.

'Here, Tom,' said Izzy, throwing him a piece. He'd been waiting patiently at her side for any little scraps. 'You like them too, don't ya, mate? You know, I forgot how much fun this is,' she said, turning to James. 'It's been a great day.' She popped another one in her mouth and then sucked her sticky fingers clean. Now that she'd dismissed any idea of them getting together, she and James had relaxed considerably and were enjoying each other's company. In a way it was a shame he had to leave the district and head back to uni, as Izzy felt they could become good mates. He even liked her taste in music and she applauded when he put Shannon Noll's song 'Lift' on the portable CD player.

'I know, but I'm just about full. I don't know where you're putting it all,' scoffed James, gazing at Izzy's trim figure. Empty shells lay scattered across the table in front of him as well as a few empty beer bottles.

'You're weak as piss. Don't you know they breed us tough out here?' She winked at him before continuing. 'Oh well, more for me. I'm sure I can fit the last couple in.'

With a hint of amusement James watched Izzy lick her lips.

''Allo, 'allo. What's going on here?' A male voice interrupted them from out of the darkness, causing Izzy and James to jump. Will's tall, athletic body appeared in the light from a small lamp that hung over the table. He casually lifted up the bottom of his blue polo shirt as he tucked his hand into the top pocket of his khaki cargo shorts. 'I'm not interrupting anything, am I?' he asked cautiously.

'Bloody hell, Will. Where did you come from? Talk about scaring the shit out of us.' Izzy took her hand away from her beating heart. Then she remembered last night's kiss and felt her face flush with heat, but it passed quickly as the memory of Angela intruded.

Neither of them had heard Will pull up. Not surprising, as they'd been having such a good time and the CD player was now blaring out Jimmy Barnes.

James was the first to answer Will's question. 'No. We've finished our feast. I'd invite you to join us, but I'm afraid Miss Piggy here hasn't left any.' He turned to Izzy and laughed.

Izzy pointed to the pile of claws in front of James. 'Well, I think you better join me in the sty, 'cos you ain't any better.' Her laughter was soft and genuine. She brushed her fingers on her shorts and shook her singlet to remove the little bits of yabby shell. They were both splattered with juices but she had to do a load of washing tomorrow anyway so it didn't worry her.

Will raised his eyebrows and cleared his throat, which sounded rather dry. 'Shall I come back another time? By the way, love your new hairdo, James – what's left of it anyway.'

'Hell, I'm lucky it wasn't anything worse. Come on. You stay,

Will. I'd better be heading off.' James said as he checked his watch. 'Yeah, I really must get going. It's nearly eight and I need to catch up on some sleep after last night's party. I have an early start tomorrow. Bloody Mondays. Boss has me blowing down the bin so I want to get most of it done before the heat of the day. That means a four or five o'clock start. Hopefully I can get out of bed then.' He stood up and started to clear the table.

'No, leave it, James,' said Izzy. 'I'll get it. Besides, you need your beauty sleep. You know, it might even make your hair grow faster.'

'You're a cheeky bitch, Izzy Simpson, you know that? I have had nothing but shit from you all afternoon.' He threw his stubbie holder at her, hitting her in the chest.

'You know you love it. Come on, I'll walk you out.' Izzy came up alongside James and walked him towards his ute.

'I'll catch ya round, Will,' James turned and called back over his shoulder.

'No doubt. See ya, James.' Will hung back for a moment before wandering off to his ute.

The crunching of James's thongs echoed in the still night air as he and Izzy walked towards the shed. James turned to her once they reached his ute, leant over and kissed her on the lips, quite politely.

'I had a great time tonight. We must do it again soon before I go. Thanks for the feed. It's been ages since I've had a taste of yabbies,' he said.

Izzy blushed slightly from yet another unexpected kiss. She was finding it hard not to think he had an agenda.

He must have read her thoughts. 'I don't mean anything by that, I promise. It's just I really did have a good time.'

'I did too,' she replied. 'You're not a bad bloke, James, even without your hair.' Izzy playfully punched him in the arm before he got into his ute.

With one last wave, he was on his way in the dark, crisp night.

She stood there in the blackness watching his red tail-lights reach the end of their driveway before returning to Will.

He was leaning on his ute looking up at the stars when he heard her soft footsteps. He gazed out into the darkness. She appeared slowly, like a graceful ship in the fog, all long legs and beauty.

Copying him, she leant against the cold metal of his ute. It sent shivers over her skin, causing her to rub her arms. She turned towards Will, faint light from the verandah illuminating the outline of his lean face and chiselled features.

'So, what's up?' she asked him, shivering again as she wondered what the hell he was doing here. Hopefully it wasn't about last night. Her stomach churned with the thought.

'Here, it's a bit cold out,' said Will, avoiding her question as he reached into his ute and pulled out a long-sleeved checked shirt for her.

'Cheers.' Izzy slipped on the thick cotton shirt, which was warm and smelled strongly of Will. 'You still haven't told me why you're here.'

'Just thought I'd drop by on my way home from the tennis club to see how you were getting on,' Will said casually, with no hint of a hidden agenda. 'Have you heard any more from Jean?'

'No, nothing new.'

'You and James've got a bit of a thing happening, hey?' Will threw the question into the night air, right out of left field.

'Maybe,' she replied, leaving him guessing. It was none of his business anyway. 'How about you? I'm surprised Angela isn't here with you.'

'Nope, she's heading home today apparently.' Will showed no signs of embarrassment about last night's shenanigans.

'Ah, just a one-nighter then,' said Izzy, trying not to come across too prudish.

Will shook his head when he realised what Izzy had said. 'What?

Hey, I never slept with her. God, whatever gave you that idea?' he spluttered out.

Izzy just raised her eyebrows and shrugged. Surely he didn't want her to spell it out. Will continued, trying to explain. 'I'll admit she did try to maul me last night, but I set her straight. I wasn't interested. I'm not like that.'

Izzy just about choked. 'What? Since when? Surely not since Claire.' She turned to face him, waiting for his reply.

Will sighed. 'I know there was a time when I was a bit reckless and careless, but I've changed.' He paused before going on. 'And what happened between Claire and me was different.'

Izzy tried to study him, to gauge whether he was being sincere, but he was just a murky shape in the dark. 'How? You still slept with her and then left her, just like the others. I saw how upset she was. She was just a good time until the next one came along, right?'

He turned to Izzy, touching her arm ever so slightly. 'It wasn't like that, Izzy,' he said quietly. Will sighed heavily as his fingers ran through his hair. It was almost like a nervous reaction as his mind clouded over with memories. Long ago he had been hurt. It wasn't visible, but he still carried the scars on the inside and he knew it. Taking a deep breath, he tried to explain. He owed Izzy that much.

'It was never like that with Claire. We were great mates. Had been for years. We grew up together, Izzy, you know that.' He paused. The next bit was going to be hard to say. 'We ended up totally smashed one night. Everyone else had paired up and left us alone. Next thing we knew, we were waking up in the same swag with blinding headaches. Neither of us could remember much of it and we laughed it off. To tell you the truth, the bits we could remember weren't that flash and there was no way it would ever happen again. We had never felt that way about each other. We were best mates, and anything else would have been too weird.'

Will didn't feel he could adequately explain it – that it really had always been platonic between them. They were like brother and sister. Never once had either of them thought differently. Claire had understood him so well. In a way, they were the same – two rebels out to enjoy what the world had to offer – so losing her was like losing a part of himself.

'That can't be all that happened,' Izzy said angrily, traces of confusion slipping into her voice. 'I saw Claire when I came home from school and she was completely stuffed up. I figured she was desperately in love with you. You two were *always* together. I mean, everyone thought . . .' she trailed off. It didn't make sense. If they weren't a couple, then what had caused Claire so much grief? Izzy couldn't help feeling that there was more Will wanted to tell her. He kept opening his mouth, like a fish starved of oxygen, and he was cracking his knuckles anxiously. She watched him silently, waiting for him to spit it out.

'We did care for each other, but only as best mates. I would have given my right arm for her,' Will explained.

'So if it wasn't that . . . what then? Claire would never tell me much, but I knew whatever it was that was upsetting her was something to do with you.' Izzy pushed a little more.

Quietly, Will stood deep in thought, debating whether to tell her or not. But hearing the hurt and confusion in Izzy's voice caused him to finally blurt it out.

'Claire ended up pregnant. She was going to have our baby.' There – it was out. It was the first time in ages that he'd discussed it. In a way he had always felt that Izzy had a right to know, but her parents had thought otherwise. Bill had made Will promise to keep it quiet, even if Izzy hated him for it. He hoped Bill would understand that it was time the air was cleared.

Reeling, Izzy felt her jaw drop. This wasn't what she had expected. Surely he was joking. She waited for the laugh to follow, for the mischievous glimmer to appear in Will's eyes, but a quick glance at his face told her it was the truth. Izzy could see real pain sweep across his face. His jaw had tensed as if he was grinding his teeth to powder and his body was rigid.

For once, Izzy was utterly speechless. Not sure how to react at first, she felt herself kind of gawk at Will and then a funny half laugh burst out. But as the shock faded, it didn't take long for the anger to build up. The realisation that she hadn't known about the baby tormented her. Questions bombarded her mind. She felt tears begin to well in her eyes, catching on her lower lashes before tickling her cheek as they fell. Without knowing Will had even moved, she felt his cool, gentle hand on her arm, which caused her to flinch slightly.

'Izzy, say something . . . You're freaking me out.' His voice was soft but broken, almost panicky. 'I just thought you needed to know the truth.'

Jerking her arm away from his touch, she spun around on her heels and briskly walked away. She heard Will start to follow her.

'Izzy, wait. Let's talk about it.' He stopped. 'Izzy!' But she'd broken into a run. With her legs pumping as hard as they could, she ran all the way back to the house and into her bedroom. Sitting on her bed, she grasped at the covers, screwing them up tightly in her hands as silent tears continued to fall. Looking up at the framed picture of her and Claire on the motorbike brought her undone. She flung herself down onto her bed and smothered her face in the pillow as her sobs intensified. Her heart burst with pain. She wasn't sure what hurt more: the fact that her sister hadn't come to her with this secret – she'd thought they shared everything – or that she couldn't talk to her about it. Claire would never get to be a mum or see her child, and Izzy would never meet her little niece or nephew. How different her life would be now if Claire was still alive. It was just so unfair. Life could be so cruel.

Preoccupied, she never heard Will's ute start up a few minutes later as he headed back to his house.

11

IZZY had cried all night. By late morning she'd climbed out of bed and cleared away the mess from the night before. Her puffy red eyes were the only outward sign that something was wrong. But inside, she was churning. Determinedly she headed out to the shed to busy herself with some mechanical work. The less time she had to think, the better.

After the last remaining air escaped the tyre she was trying to fix, she placed the tiny valve in a spot where she wouldn't lose it, grabbed the heavy slide hammer and carried it over to the large-rimmed tyre. Placing the point of the slide hammer under the rim, she lifted the handles up on either side, and crashed it down as hard as she could. The clang echoed throughout the shed and bounced off the walls, making just enough racket to clear her head. Again, she brought it down hard: *clang . . . clang*. Somehow the loud noise was almost peaceful.

Out of the corner of her eye, she caught a reflective flash of Will appearing on his motorbike. Not again! She didn't bother to look up. He switched off his bike a couple of metres from her as she rammed down the rod again, moved it a bit to the left, shifted her feet and then hammered it down again.

She could feel his eyes on her for a few moments before he spoke. 'Izzy, we've gotta talk.'

Izzy glanced his way. Black rings circled his tired eyes and his messy hair showed the signs of a sleepless night, as did the stubble that shadowed across his face. At least she wasn't the only one not sleeping.

'Come on, Izzy. You can't avoid me forever.'

Another deafening clang was her only response and the only one he was likely to get. With a muttered, 'Fine,' he cranked up his bike, pushed it backwards out of the shed and opened the throttle, doing a wheelie as he sped off.

Izzy just kept banging away as if nothing had happened. Eventually, the rubber fell away from the rim. Using the back of her sleeve, she wiped the beads of sweat from her brow.

As she fixed the small hole in the tube, she realised she needed some answers or else she would go stark raving mad. Since she was determined not to talk to Will – perhaps ever again – there was only one other solution. She decided to leave for Perth in the morning to visit her dad. The rest of the farm work was minor and could wait until her return.

'You'll have to stay home this time, mate,' she said to Tom, who was lying on the concrete floor. 'I don't think you'd have any fun in the city. But don't worry, old boy. I'll make sure you have a big bowl of kibbles to eat.'

The next morning Izzy threw her bag into the ute, climbed into the driver's seat and called out a farewell to Tom, who was locked up in the dog yard by the shed. He was giving her the sad puppy-dog look – one that had worked well when he was a pup which he had since continued to use when he wasn't getting his way. But he was safer at home; she wasn't changing her mind, no matter how cute he looked. 'You be a good dog and take care of the place, okay?' It was a long drive to Perth. She plugged in her MP3 player, found the right frequency and cranked up the volume. She'd loaded a few new songs onto it last night so she didn't get too sick of the same ones – a few tracks off Shannon Noll's new album, plus some Coldplay and Rihanna. She was only allowed to play Rihanna when Tom wasn't in the ute. He didn't like modern pop music at all. Lee Kernaghan was his favourite, along with any old Aussie rock songs. Tom was a country dog through and through.

Heading to the big smoke was a good way to avoid Will. Izzy wasn't sure why she was so angry with him – maybe for keeping the truth from her. And she was still a bit confused about her feelings for Will after the bin party. He'd explained that Angela had come on to him and that he hadn't reciprocated, but what worried her was the fact that seeing it had irked her so much. They were weird feelings she didn't have time to think about – and didn't want to think about. Instead she thought about Claire, her baby and Will. Why had no one told her about the baby? Didn't they think she'd cope with it?

She arrived in Corrigin sooner than expected, her mind running away with her thoughts. She had a quick toilet stop and got back on the road towards Brookton.

Two and a half hours later she was on the outskirts of Perth. She stopped and stretched to wake herself up before hitting the Albany Highway again. She needed to be more attentive in the frantic city traffic, not like out in the bush where the road stretched before you with nothing but your car and maybe the odd rabbit or kangaroo. But she'd been to Perth enough times to know her way around and the busy roads didn't bother her. Soon she was pulling into the car park near the hospital. It was the first time she had been to a hospital in the city, let alone the Royal Perth. Apparently, it had a great burns unit. Her dad was in the best of care, so everyone kept telling her.

She locked up the car, ran her hands over her hair and brushed the creases out of her linen pants and light blue cotton top before picking up the bag of papers and magazines she'd brought from home. Feeling nervous, she walked towards the large entry doors of the hospital. She had to admit she was worried about seeing her old man and how he would look. The memory of his burnt legs and the abnormal colour of his charred skin mixed with the horrid smell of singed flesh made her shudder. She was sure it would stay with her for life. It made her wonder how her dad coped with the image of Claire lying on the concrete next to the silos. Had her eyes been open and lifeless when he found her? Were her limbs broken and twisted? She'd never asked, and her dad would probably never tell her anyway. It wasn't something you talked about, but after Claire's funeral Izzy often had nightmares of Claire lying with pools of blood beneath her. They were horrible dreams and hard enough to bear, so she couldn't imagine how her father lived with the real thing. He would have that forever.

After checking where to find Bill, Izzy took the elevator up a few floors and headed left down a long corridor that smelled of disinfectant. From the moment she stepped out of the lift that unmistakeable hospital smell had overwhelmed her. Approaching his room, she peered through the window. There he was, lying in bed with his legs and hands bandaged.

Relief swept over her and she relaxed a little. At least she wouldn't have to try to hide the horrified expression she knew her face would wear if she saw his burns again. He actually looked quite well, all things considered. He was talking to Jean and laughing about something. This cheered Izzy up no end. With renewed enthusiasm she knocked on the door and pushed it open.

'Hiya, Dad. How are you?' she said, entering the room.

'Isabelle, darling. I'm fine. What a surprise. Why didn't you tell us you were coming?'

Leaning over his bed, she planted a kiss on his cheek before turning around to give her mum one too, and a warm tight hug. 'Hi, Mum. So how's he really doing?' she said, glancing back at her dad with a warm grin.

'Oh, you know your father. He's as tough as a Mallee bull and as stubborn as they come. He's started harassing the staff, so he must be doing okay.' Jean looked tenderly towards her husband of twenty-eight years and shrugged. She appeared relaxed, sitting on a simple beige chair and wearing a pink polo shirt and jeans, her legs crossed at the ankles.

Dragging another uncomfortable-looking chair up to the bedside, Izzy placed the papers and magazines on the bed before sitting down.

'Got you some papers, Dad. The last couple of *Elders* are there, and a few issues of *Countryman* for you to catch up on.'

After glancing at the dressings on his burns, Izzy gazed at her dad's tanned but slightly pale face. He blinked slowly, knowing she'd assessed him, and waited for her questions.

'Does it still hurt, Dad?' she asked. 'Are you in much pain? I s'pose you wouldn't tell me if you were, would you? Will you be able to walk again and work the farm?' Izzy shifted in her chair. Her backside was still a bit numb from sitting in the car for over three and a half hours.

'Wow, so many questions. Well, love, it's no walk in the park, that's for sure. But the doc reckons I'm coming along well.' His face lit up at the prospect of getting away from the four walls of the hospital and back to the fresh open spaces of his farm. 'And I'll be back on the farm before you know it. This is just a small setback. A few months, maybe more, and I'll be getting back to normal. I just won't look so flash in a pair of shorts. They said I could be home in five weeks, which is really good.'

Jean smiled as she said, 'They'll be happy to see you go, Bill. I'm sure he's been chatting up the nurses when I'm not here, haven't you?'

'Oh, Dad, that's terrible. You'll have them running in the opposite direction.' Izzy screwed her face up at the thought, and a picture of an old Cecil ram flashed through her mind.

'Have you seen much of Will, sweetheart?' he asked Izzy. 'He probably told you I asked him to take charge of the farm. He's a good lad. Said he'd do it without any hesitation. I suppose it's all going well, as I haven't heard from him in a while.'

Izzy found this baffling. Will had never mentioned anything about being in charge. He'd just been letting her run the farm by herself. Obviously, he hadn't mentioned anything to Bill, otherwise her dad would have been jumping down her throat right now. Funny, she thought Will would have liked to throw his weight around and be in charge.

Carefully, she considered her reply. 'Yes . . . I've seen him around.'

'Did he get the harvesting finished okay? He said you'd organised Mike's header for him to use. I really appreciate that, sweetheart.' Bill lifted his bandaged hand a few inches off the bed and half waved it. It was as close to patting her hand as he could get.

'I've organised the insurance, and the blokes came out and checked the header. They said the fire started because of bearing failure, from what they can gather,' said Izzy.

'Ah, you're a good girl. Can you tell Will that he'll need to get onto the shearers soon? Might need to start in a week or two.'

'Already onto it,' replied Izzy, who was trying not to feel insulted. 'Dad, I can do most of the farm stuff myself, and it would save you having to bother Will. I really don't mind doing it. I can handle it. I've done farm work before.' Izzy pleaded her case but to no avail. She saw the instant change in his mood.

'You know my thoughts on this, Izzy. How many times do I have to spell it out? I'm not going to change my mind – in a hospital bed or out. I don't mind you making a few phone calls, but you're to have nothing to do with the farm work, okay? Just leave it in Will's capable hands.'

Izzy almost pouted as she sighed deeply. Silence descended on the hospital room like a fog. Izzy felt like she was balancing on a powerline as she struggled to control the rage inside. Her dad couldn't even thank her or appreciate what she'd done so far. He didn't know the half of it. Maybe she should tell him she was the one who'd finished the harvesting. He probably wouldn't believe her, anyway. It'd just make his situation worse – and hers. She envied Will. He was to inherit his father's farm, no questions asked, and Izzy had to fight like a stray cat to get even an inch. What was she to do? She knew what she wanted – to work the farm – but she didn't know how to go about getting it. Did she confront her father? She couldn't upset him in his current state, so maybe she'd just wait till he was better, then try it.

Anxious to break the silence, Jean asked after the neighbours and Izzy filled her in on how they were all looking after her. But Izzy was distracted by her thoughts and still a little angry with her dad. The idea that he'd tried to control her life even more by keeping Claire's pregnancy from her festered within her.

Gearing herself up, she sat up straight and fiddled with the hem on her top, nervous about how to start. 'Can I ask you guys a question, and I want the truth?'

Both her parents went quiet, unsure of what was coming, and then they nodded and gave their assurance.

Here goes, she thought. 'D-did you know Claire got p-pregnant?' she stammered.

Both faces hardly changed. There were no sudden looks of shock or gasps of surprise. Right there and then she knew that this was not news to them.

Standing up defiantly, she didn't wait for the answer she knew was coming. She started pacing the tiny room. 'How could you not tell me, even after all these years?' she said, throwing her hands on her hips, her voice slightly elevated.

It was Jean who spoke. 'There seemed no point. We only knew

ourselves for a few months, and then when she and the baby died, it didn't seem worth worrying you with it.'

'But, Mum!' Izzy spluttered as she started getting worked up. 'I am a part of this family too, aren't I? I had a right to know. She was my sister.' She continued to pace. 'I feel so left out.' Her voice was quieter now, broken.

'We're truly sorry, Izzy. We never meant to hurt you. We were just trying to save you from more pain. We thought losing your sister was bad enough. Can't you see that?' Jean said tenderly.

'Is there anything else you've kept from me that I should know about?' she replied, barely able to keep the anger and hurt out of her voice.

'No,' her parents chorused, then Jean continued. 'I assure you, Izzy, we only had your best intentions at heart.'

'I know. I can see that now, but it still doesn't make me feel any better,' she said, almost deflated as the sting began to leave. 'How pregnant was she before she died?'

Jean answered again. 'She was sixteen weeks. We were trying to keep it very quiet. You were away at boarding school and we were going to wait until you came home at the end of term to tell you. Claire thought she felt the baby move the day before her accident.' Jean paused, then laughed softly. 'You should have seen your father when we told him. She told me first and when I got over the shock we told Bill together. Stunned is an understatement.'

'Yeah, give a bloke a moment to gather his thoughts. When I'd calmed down, I was quite excited.' The warmth in his voice was unmistakeable.

'Except you wanted Will to marry Claire before the baby was born,' Jean added. Izzy's eyes widened and Jean continued. 'But Claire didn't want that. They weren't prepared to marry, and in this day and age I guess it's no big deal. How did you find out about the baby? From Will?' her mum asked, already knowing the answer.

'Yeah. We had a bit of a barney and he let it slip,' answered Izzy.

'I hope you weren't too harsh on him, Isabelle,' her dad cut in, all concerned. 'He's been through a lot. You've gotta understand how he felt. He lost his best mate and his unborn child in one afternoon.' He spoke slowly, hoping she would understand. 'He has lost as much as we have.'

Izzy stopped mid-step, slapped her forehead, and groaned. 'Oh, no!'

'What?' they replied in unison.

Slowly she ran her hand down her face, as if trying to wipe the horrible memory from her mind. 'I just remembered. I gave Will a mouthful at Ray's clearing sale,' she said, shaking her head again. 'Oh, and they were some choice words too! Shit, now I feel terrible. Why didn't he tell me then? And what must he have thought of my form?'

'So, that's what went down,' said her father, now understanding. 'Will wanted to tell you at the barbecue – he hated lying to you – but I made him promise not to. I'm sorry, love. He was right all along. We should have had this out after Claire's funeral.' Bill sighed heavily, realising the enormity of his mistake.

'Yeah, well, I second that. Poor Claire,' Izzy said, finally flopping back down in her chair.

Bill cleared his throat and broke the silence. 'You know, Will was looking forward to being a father – once he'd got over the initial shock, of course. But he really has a loving soul, a quality he gets from Sandy, and he was opening up to the idea of a little tacker running around. We talked about it often after Claire died. You know, he's the closest thing to a son that I have, Izzy, and he's come a bloody long way in the last few years. I want you to take it easy on him, okay?'

Bill's comments cut deep. So he wanted Izzy to see Will the way he saw him, yet why the hell couldn't he see her for who she really was!

'But you guys let me believe he'd used Claire, and I absolutely hated him for it. I blamed him for everything and now . . . well, it's going to be bizarre. I've been just horrible to him ever since I got back.'

'He knows it's not your fault, Izzy. It will be all right. He doesn't blame you.' Jean stood up, walked over to Izzy and pulled her up into a tight hug. They stood there, embracing for a long time before Jean eventually whispered into her ear, 'I miss Claire too.'

12

IZZY decided to head home the following day after another visit to the hospital. She'd stayed in a hotel room overnight – she didn't want to put out Aunty Sarah, given her trip had been at such short notice. She was glad to have some time to herself – the peace and quiet was just what she'd needed after the revelations of the last few days.

She got up early, hoping to fit in some shopping after seeing her dad. She needed some more work shorts and another dose of worm treatment for Tom, as well as a big bag of dog treats. When that was done, she did the mandatory KFC stop for lunch on her way out of Perth, then powered home to let Tom out of his yard.

The monotonous driving gave her time to look back on her behaviour towards Will. Her cheeks flushed red with embarrassment at the thought of how cruelly she'd treated him, especially realising it was all unwarranted. She'd used him to vent her anger over Claire's death. He'd been an easy target, and now she sure had some explaining to do. As if things weren't difficult enough between them. She resolved to put their kiss behind her – she couldn't figure out what to make of it and it just complicated matters. Of course, she was attracted to Will – you'd have to be blind not to get all steamed up looking at him – but she still didn't want to be with him. It was just her girlie hormones gone mad. But she liked the idea of being his friend.

Arriving home late afternoon, she decided she'd better get it over and done with and head straight over to Will's place to apologise. Tom barked excitedly, running around in circles as he eagerly awaited her appearance. Izzy stretched out her arms and gave the order: 'Up, Tom.' His large tan paws launched himself up to her chest and into her open arms. A quick cuddle, some running around with a ball and a doggie treat soon saw him contented. If only all relationships were so easy.

Before jumping in her ute, Izzy grabbed the shirt that Will had lent her to wear the other night. It would provide a good excuse for her visit. It was only a two-minute drive along their track around the back paddocks and past the reserve. There was only one fence to open, which separated their farms, then around another paddock to their house. Tom was still excitedly attached to her hip and drooling happily next to her in the ute.

Will's place was an old farmhouse that had been on their land for years. It used to be where his grandparents lived before they built the new house closer to the mail road. The house sat in the corner of a paddock surrounded by scrub bush and tall old mallee trees. When they were kids, they'd used it as their playground and gone through the old clothes and toys left there. They'd pretend to cook and play house. That was when Will and Claire would let her come, mind you. She was ten when they finally let Izzy camp there with them for the night, safe in the hands of the thirteen- and fourteen-year-olds. They would try to scare her with stories by the fire in the old brick fireplace. Smiling, she remembered when they'd nearly burnt the place down. The fire had blown out of control after it caught on a nearby curtain. Luckily, they'd managed to pelt it out with the shirts off their backs. They made her promise not to tell anyone, but the evidence was a bit hard to hide – returning home smelling of smoke, plus the fact that their shirts were singed and sooty didn't help. Especially as Will's had nearly burnt completely. She could laugh about it now, but back then they'd got into a lot of trouble and had been banned from sleepovers at the old place.

In the afternoon glow, the house looked much the same as she remembered it. Pulling up out the front, not far from its wide verandahs, she noticed that the tin roof was new. Izzy tried to recall the last time she visited. She would have been fourteen and she and Claire had gone there with Will to reminisce about the old days.

There was a garden around the house now and it looked well kept, with even a bit of lawn out the side. It was quite formal in design with agapanthus and irises in neat little rows. Further out bottlebrushes and other native trees were scattered about, acting as a native hedge. Will's ute, she noticed, was in the old rickety garage that was off to the left-hand side. At least he's home, she thought.

Carefully, she walked up the bumpy path made out of red and cream paddock rocks. A few weeds sprouted up through the sand in between. Tom, as always, was right behind her. The old wooden verandah creaked slightly under her boots. She was about to knock on the flywire door when Will beat her to it, opening it from the other side. He stood barefoot, wearing blue football shorts and a black shearing singlet.

'Hiya, Will,' she said softly.

'Izzy!' he said, looking shocked. 'I never thought I'd see you here.' He tilted his head slightly to one side as if trying to read her thoughts, before stepping back so she could pass. 'Well, you'd better come in before you change your mind,' he said with a wave of his arm. He thought he noticed a change in her, especially her eyes. They seemed to have lost their daggers. Now he could somehow see so much more of Izzy, and he liked the softness.

'I just got back from Perth. I went to see Dad,' she said, following him along the passageway to the kitchen. Izzy noticed the floors still had the same outdated, flowery brown carpet from years ago.

'Grab a seat. You want a beer?' Will asked as he opened the newish fridge.

Nodding her head, she eagerly replied, 'Would love one, thanks.' Actually, she reckoned she could do with half a dozen. She saw the open *Elders* paper on the table and drew it closer.

'I was just reading it before you pulled up. Not much in it.'

He grabbed two stubbie holders from one of the new cupboards on the wall and slid the stubbies into them before handing one to Izzy.

'Cheers, Will.'

Avoiding his eyes, she scanned the room. The kitchen looked great. Really different from what she remembered. There were the new cupboards, and a large archway had been cut through the wall so it opened up into the lounge room. She loved the restored timber floorboards, which went well with the cupboards and soft blue walls.

'The place looks great, Will. Did you do it yourself?' she asked, breaking the silence between them.

'Yeah. Mum puts her two bob's worth in every now and then, of course. But I'm getting there slowly. All the main rooms are done.'

'I see you finally got rid of the burn marks,' she chuckled, looking at the old fireplace at the other end of the dining room.

'Yeah . . . I'm surprised you remember that,' he said, laughing.

'Oh, I haven't forgotten it, Will,' she replied. 'Claire got busted big time, something about endangering not only herself but me as well. God, I felt *so* bad,' Izzy said, lowering her head as if deep in thought.

They sat there, opposite each other, in total silence except for the soft ticking of a large round clock that hung from the wall behind her. Izzy was playing with the label on her beer when she finally spoke, determined to say sorry properly.

'Will . . . I came to apologise for the other night . . . and the clearing sale . . . and every other time I was horrible. I haven't been very fair on you.' Izzy's cheeks burned. 'I was only thinking of myself.' Will started to shrug it off but she continued. 'No, hear me out. The other night . . . it just took me by surprise – the baby and all that – and I didn't stop to think how hard it must have been for you too. Dad made me realise that I wasn't the only one hurting. Will, I'm really sorry,' she finished.

Reaching across the large wooden table, she put her hand over his. He had endured so much pain, and put up with so much from her as well. 'I've been really awful to you, and I feel like crap for how I've acted towards you over the last few weeks . . . few years.' His hand beneath hers was warm and sent a tingle up her arm.

Will's eyes sparkled as he watched her intently. Rubbing her fingers with his thumb, he replied, 'Thanks, Izzy. I appreciate it, but you have nothing to be sorry for. I totally understand. She was your sister. And you didn't know the truth.'

Izzy reclined on her chair, her hand now back on her beer, insistent on peeling the label.

'That's it?' She shook her head in disbelief. Somehow, she'd been expecting more fireworks.

'There's nothing to forgive, kiddo. You wouldn't have been like that if you'd known the truth,' Will said. 'Well, at least I hope not, anyway.' He raised his eyebrows, teasing.

Izzy just smirked at him and shook her head. She liked the way he'd started calling her kiddo. She wasn't sure why, but it sounded nice when he said it. 'Who knows?' She looked down into the gold liquid and chewed her lower lip. 'I just can't believe Claire didn't tell me something so huge. We never kept secrets from each other,' she said quietly, a sadness creeping into her voice.

Noticing her distress, Will bent across, leaning his elbows on the table, and tried to explain. 'Izzy, she wanted to tell you, I know she did. She was just so scared at first of what everyone would think, including me. It took her a while to even come to me about it, and then we had to figure out what we were going to do.' He took a swig of his beer, thinking back to one of the most difficult times in his life, in a year he'd never forget. 'We were so scared about telling your folks. I thought your dad was going to string me up and skin me alive.'

'Oh, I can just imagine. He would have gone off like a madman.' Izzy's hair swished around her shoulders as she shook her head at the thought of it.

'He was mad at first. He couldn't speak for a while, but surprisingly he got over it really quickly. Turned out, he was happy that we were going to try and make a go of it.'

'I just wish I hadn't been at boarding school while most of this was happening, and I would have loved to have seen more of Claire. I missed out on so much with her, and then she was gone, and I can never get back that time.' Izzy gazed down into her beer once more.

Will looked Izzy straight on with his piercing blue eyes. 'She missed you like mad, you know, when you weren't there. She used to come and hassle me and I'd never get any work done. She was always going on about you and what mischief you'd been up to. Claire was so proud of you, Izzy. She said you were smart and that you could do anything. Claire reckoned she had no drive in life, that there was nothing she felt passionate about. Whereas you, she said, had your future mapped out. Claire did like to live by the seat of her pants. She never planned from one day to the next.' He chuckled at the memory. 'You know, a couple of days before she died I found some little yellow baby boots that used to be mine which Mum had stashed away. So I gave them to Claire and she absolutely loved them. It just made it all so real for us. And as scared as we were, it was a nice thought. It was something to look forward to – being parents. We may not have loved each other like that, but we thought it might come once the baby was born. And if it didn't – well, it still wouldn't have changed how much we'd have loved the baby.' Will's voice was deep with emotion.

'At Claire's funeral I put the yellow boots in there with her . . . for the baby. It was your mum's idea.' Will's eyes began misting up as he spoke and his voice faltered just a fraction.

Izzy swallowed hard. It was moving to see a man wearing so much raw emotion on his sleeve. There weren't many farmers who were good at talking about their feelings or sensitive issues. They all had a strong image to uphold: they were men on the land – the providers and protectors.

'I can remember you doing that, now I think of it. I asked Mum about it but she said she didn't know that's what you'd planned to do. God, I remember thinking you had no right to be there. From that day on, I took some of my anger and grief out on you . . . well, maybe all of it. I blamed you for Claire's death, because the last time I had seen her she was so miserable, and I knew that had something to do with you.' She paused, carried away by her memories. 'She would have made a great mum.' Izzy sought out Will's eyes. 'You would have made a wonderful dad too, and I imagine you still will, some day.' Not wanting to get too serious, she added, 'That's if you can find a woman mad enough to take you on!'

'Oh, if I get that desperate, I can always look you up as a last resort.' He was teasing her but her tender words went to a special place in his heart.

The last of the afternoon sun was glowing through the kitchen window and reaching the corner of the table where they sat.

'Did you want to stay for dinner?' Will asked. 'No point us both eating alone.' He stood up, went to the fridge and peered into it without waiting for her answer.

'Why? Are you gonna cook?' asked Izzy, placing a hand on her hip.

Without moving his head from within the fridge he shot back, 'I *can* cook, you know.' He began sifting through the contents of his half-empty fridge. 'So, what do you feel like? Steak and eggs, steak and chips, or maybe just beer and chips?'

She burst out laughing and moved towards the fridge to see what else was in there. 'It all sounds good. Here, I think you have enough salad stuff for me to whip something up,' she said, grabbing the produce from the fridge and laying it out on the kitchen bench.

'I'll just go and light the barbecue. Hopefully there's enough gas.' With that, Will walked out to the back of the house with a scraper, a pair of tongs, and a roll of paper towel.

Fifteen minutes later, they sat down at the table with their meals ready to eat, and a fresh beer in their stubbie holders.

'Salad looks great, kiddo,' Will said as he filled his plate.

'You didn't do too bad yourself. The steak is great, not burnt like my old man likes it,' she said, pouring tomato sauce all over her meat.

'Speaking of your dad, how's he going?' Will asked.

'He's coming along pretty well, considering. His grafts have taken really well and the physio lady is turning up soon to help get him back into shape.' Izzy's eyebrows knotted together as she prepared to interrogate him about Gumlea. 'He filled me in on a few things, though. Apparently, you're running the farm for him?' Izzy turned her head to the side slightly and gave him a questioning look.

Will sat up straight. 'Ah . . . yeah, I was supposed to mention that.' He shrugged. 'But you seemed to be doing okay by yourself.'

'If only Dad could see it that way. Anyway, he gave me a long list of stuff I'm supposed to give you.'

'So, I'm not going to see that list, am I?' said Will with a cheeky grin. He was beginning to understand Izzy.

'Nope.' She smiled back. 'If I can do it all by myself, then he might just realise that this is what I'm meant to be doing. Eventually he's gotta let me help him run the family farm, hasn't he?' she questioned.

Will had a puzzled look on his face.

'What's that look for?' Izzy asked.

He shrugged his shoulders. 'It's just I've never met a chick who's been so interested in farming or as passionate about it as you, let alone one who's any good at it. Not even Claire was that interested. But you're different. You're not afraid of slugging your guts out, and you're always trying to prove yourself. Most girls just wouldn't be into anything that would break a nail.'

Izzy came across as a tomboy – she liked being outside and getting dirty – but the way she'd looked at the bin party had left Will thinking she was anything but. Claire would never have been seen dead in a dress. But Izzy was different – she just shone out like canola in a field of wheat. She was different from anyone he'd met – she intrigued him.

'Why thanks. I think I'll take that as a compliment.' His comments meant a lot. They would have meant twice as much coming from her father.

'You're definitely not Claire's annoying kid sister any longer. You just keep surprising me, Izzy. It's made me realise how much I don't know about you, and that everything I assumed was wrong.'

'Well, I went away and learnt all this stuff, which will be bloody useless if Dad has his way. He just doesn't understand it, but working this land is the only thing I've ever wanted to do. Since Claire's death he's built a huge brick wall with me on one side and him and our farm on the other. I mean, he has to come around sooner or later, and if he doesn't . . . well, maybe I'll simply have to face facts and work for someone else.' Izzy breathed a huge sigh. The problem had given her many headaches and sleepless nights over the past few years.

'We'll always have work for you, if your old man won't budge. That would piss him off no end, working right next door, hey,' Will said. His smile revealed his perfect white teeth.

'Oh, I'm sure Dad would just love that.'

'I've already spoken to my dad and he agrees that if you ever needed work, we'd put you on.'

Wow, he's been talking about me, she thought, genuinely surprised at this news.

Will winked. 'Then you could stay here with me.'

'Oh, and cramp your style? I don't think so,' she replied with a mouth full of steak. There was a bit of sauce on her top lip, which she managed to lick off eventually. 'The work sounds good, but my first priority is working at home, even if I have to send the old man kicking and screaming into a retirement home to do it.'

'Remind me never to cross your path,' Will said jokingly, before taking another swig of his beer. 'So, what's the go tomorrow? You'd better keep me informed of what you're up to in case Bill rings to see how things are going.'

'Oh, yeah, that's a good idea. Well, tomorrow I've got to feed the sheep and organise the shearing team to come in some time in the next couple of weeks. Then there's a fence on the northern boundary that needs fixing. What are you doing tomorrow?' Izzy asked, while finishing her last mouthful.

'Not much. Dad's taking the day off but he's asked me to move some sheep. It shouldn't take long. I know Bill's been trying to get to that fence for ages. I was going to do it for him but he wouldn't hear of it.' Will pushed his chair back, stood up, collected their empty plates, and carried them off to the nearby sink. 'Your old man sure is stubborn. He's relaxed a bit over the last year, letting me help out more and now entrusting the farm to me . . . well, you, I guess, but he doesn't know that.'

'He told me he thinks of you as a son, so if he's gonna accept help, it's only gonna be from you. Besides, I don't have a set of balls so that counts me out.' Izzy laughed when she saw the look on Will's face. 'Hey, it's the truth.' She picked up the empty stubbies and put them in the bin. 'Thanks for dinner, Will. I guess it will be my turn next.'

'You betcha,' he said, nudging her shoulder. 'Should I put in my order now?'

Izzy picked up the tea towel and flicked it at him before moving over to the sink to wash the dishes. Will quickly stopped her. 'Nah, leave them. I'll do 'em later.'

'Wow, domesticated too,' she said, acting surprised.

They both settled back down at the table and chatted for a while until Izzy looked at her watch. 'Well, I'd better get going. Gotta get up early. Can't have the sheep starving on my watch. Cheers again for the feed, Will.'

'Any time. Hey, give us a bell if you need a hand, all right?' Will led the way back down the passageway and held open the flywire door for her.

Izzy wrung her hands, struggling with the thought of asking for help. 'Umm . . . Actually I wouldn't mind some help with the boundary fence if you're not too busy. I was going to tackle it tomorrow morning. If you're keen?'

Will raised his eyebrows.

She knew what he was thinking. 'See . . . I can ask for help,' Izzy pointed out.

'Yeah, but it nearly killed you,' he mocked.

She laughed gently. He knew her better than she thought. Turning, she watched Tom head for the ute, making sure she wouldn't leave without him.

'Oh, I almost forgot,' Izzy said, running down the path. Reaching through the open window of her ute, she grabbed a small bundle, then carried it back into the light of the verandah.

'Here. You nearly didn't get it back – I was taking a shine to it.' She handed his checked shirt over.

'Thanks. See ya later,' he called out as she headed to the ute. He watched Izzy drive off down the track for a moment, before turning to stroll inside. Raising the shirt to his cheek, he inhaled a sweet fragrance that clung to the material. 'Hmm, Izzy,' he muttered to himself.

13

IZZY loved running the farm without having to worry about her dad finding out. It was how she'd imagined it: the wind blowing in her face as she rode around on her motorbike, Tom running alongside her with his tongue hanging out as the land opened up before them. There was nothing but the big blue sky above and the dry crispy soil below. Just her and Tom, out feeding the sheep and checking dams and fences.

After an early start the next morning, she set off in the ute to the section of fencing that needed repairing. She climbed out and started to undo the sides of the tray. With a creak and screech of metal, the sides gave way and dropped down on their hinges, giving her better access to the tools and roll of fencing wire. Before unloading, she tied up her hair in a loose ponytail, placed her cap on her head, and took off her woollen jumper. Her short-sleeved cotton work shirt would protect her shoulders from the sun, which would be trying its best to burn her skin. Digging her hand into the back pocket of her pants, she pulled out some leather work gloves and slipped them on. As a last-minute thought she reached for her water bottle in the front of the ute, flipped the lid and had a good swig. It was a cool early morning but the forecast was for a hot one.

She put the water bottle on the ground where it would get shade from the tyre, then reached for the long steel pickets. Metal on metal screeched as she grabbed a couple and dragged them off the ute, carrying them a few metres before dropping them next to several old wooden posts that were rotten and broken. She was heading back to grab the wire-cutters out of the toolbox when she noticed Will's ute heading down the fire break.

The sun by now had just cracked the horizon and it sent out a soft golden haze of morning light, which glistened off his ute as it headed towards her.

'Morning, kiddo,' Will said brightly, as he joined her. He was wearing his blue work shirt and shorts with their farm name, Tarramin, embroidered in yellow. He felt great this morning. It was amazing what a good night's sleep could do.

'Good morning to you too, William,' Izzy replied. A faint smile tugged at the corner of her lips.

'I took a punt that this job would be first on your list. Let's get cracking, shall we?' Will put on his gloves and held the fence as Izzy began to cut the last few strands of wire.

An hour later Will threw down the hammer, which hit the dirt with a thud.

'We're just hooning along,' Izzy said, panting. 'I don't think I've seen a fence go up so fast before.'

'I know,' replied Will. 'I'm busting my gut just to keep up with you.' He wiped a line of sweat off his brow with the checked shirt he'd left hanging over the back of Izzy's ute. 'You've gotta admit we work bloody well together, though?' Will looked at their progress in amazement.

'Yeah, we make a good team . . . when you pull your weight, that is!' Taking off her gloves, Izzy stuffed them in her back pocket and picked up her bottle for a swig of water. Sweat was running down her back and along her hairline.

Will unbuttoned his shirt and shook it to circulate the air over his moist body, revealing his hard chest, which had only the finest scattering of curly hairs on his tanned skin. He seemed oblivious to Izzy's admiring gaze. She didn't need super vision to know how taut he was. Will was an athletic guy and he did a lot of shearing – and it showed. Izzy gave her own shirt a shake to cool off too.

'Are you all right?' Will asked, pointing to the underside of her arm.

Izzy screwed up her face, wondering what he was on about. She rolled her arm over and saw a cut, which was now dried shut with blood. Four or five trails of blood had run down her arm to her wrist and were also dry. 'Oh, I must have caught it on some barbed wire,' she said, not bothered by it.

Will just shook his head – she was one tough cookie. 'Hey, you'll never guess who called last night.'

'The Health Department, who found deadly bacteria living in your fridge?'

'Ha ha. No, it was Bill. He rings quite a lot actually. I think he misses the place. He's always on at me to call him at the hospital with any trivial thing.'

'I see.' She waved him on, trying not to let on how much this information hurt. 'And?'

'Oh, I just told him what you told me last night and he seemed happy. He's missing the farm heaps and he warned me to check up on you, make sure you're not doing anything stupid.'

'Gee, he doesn't trust me at all, does he?' said Izzy, wiping the sweat off her brow yet again.

'I wouldn't either,' Will joked.

Instinctively, Izzy threw her water bottle at him. Water spurted out the top and splashed down the front of his shirt, pasting it to his chest like a second skin.

He stood there for a split second and watched the water drip down his pants before a menacing look crossed his face.

Izzy saw it. With a nervous squeal she took off, Will hot on her heels. Her long legs moved quickly around the ute as a fearful chuckle erupted between gasps for air.

'Arrgh,' Will grunted and lunged out his arms, narrowly missing her waist. She could hear his puffing right behind her as she circled the ute again at full speed. Will threw himself forward a second time just as Izzy stumbled on a mound of dirt, which allowed him to catch onto her shirt and drag her towards him. Wrapping his arms around her, he heaved her up over his shoulder, like a rag doll.

'Will, put me down now,' she demanded breathlessly, her lungs crushed against his shoulder.

'Not till I get you back,' he said with glee. Will grabbed his water bottle off the ute, tipped it up and watched as the water ran down her back and splashed over her pants.

With her bum up in the air, Izzy kicked her legs about and pelted him on his backside.

'Careful, I might be enjoying that,' he laughed, carrying her around like a trophy.

'Eew,' she said as she wrestled with him until he put her back down. She pushed him in the chest with both hands. 'That was just pure luck that I slipped, Will Timmins. You run like a girl and never would have caught me otherwise.'

Will bent down, picked Izzy's gloves off the ground and threw them back at her. 'Come on. Move your arse,' he ordered, his full lips spreading into a gorgeous grin.

'You move your skinny little butt, smart alec. You're the one slowing us down.'

'Watch it,' he replied, but the games were over as they were already picking up with their work on the fence from where they had left off.

Will slid his hand into his leather glove. It was a simple task but he was finding it hard to concentrate. He couldn't understand how quickly his body had reacted to her touch, even with her wearing her work gear covered in dust and sweat. This flirting had been so much fun and so completely different from when he used to muck about with Claire.

'Come on, lazy arse,' he said, unable to take his eyes off her.

They worked on in silence, trying to finish the last of the fence. Anyone watching would have been impressed with the smooth way they worked together, like well-oiled machinery. It was only when they were packing up that Izzy spoke again.

'It's James's last day of work today before he heads back to college, so I've invited him over for a barbie lunch tomorrow. Would you like to come too?'

Will was moving about packing up their tools and the remaining wire. 'I wouldn't want to cramp your style now, would I?'

'Come on, Will. He's just a mate. I'm not going there. The last thing I need right now is a long-distance relationship. Especially with a bloke who's at Muresk and attending plenty of parties with lots of single chicks. That isn't something I want to get into. Anyway, it's just nice to have someone to talk to, you know,' she finished.

'Not what you were after, hey,' said Will, engrossed. 'Are you looking for something more serious? Surely you don't feel the biological clock ticking already?' he teased, but still waited eagerly for her reply.

Izzy stopped and leaned against the tray of the ute. 'Yeah, I s'pose I am. I'd like to get married one day and have some kids before I'm too old, preferably around thirtyish. I'm nearly twenty-two now, so I've got a bit of time up my sleeve. What about you? Plan on being a bachelor all your life?' The back tailgate squealed as Will swung it back up on the tray and then joined Izzy around the side of the ute.

'Hell no!' he replied. 'I wouldn't mind my own brood running around and a nice Mrs Timmins at home cooking and cleaning,' he finished with a smirk.

Izzy pulled a face. 'Gee, that sounds romantic.'

'Nah, I was only stirring. I don't mind doing the household chores. I'm used to it now. I had a good mummy who taught me how to clean up after myself.'

'And here I was thinking your poor mum had been keeping it all clean and tidy for you.'

'Fair go! I'm not totally hopeless,' said Will as he began packing away some stray tools.

'So are you going to come tomorrow or not? It's my turn to cook. And I was thinking we could go for a swim in the dam afterwards, so you might want to bring your swimming shorts, unless you wear budgie smugglers?'

'You wish. Yeah, I guess I'll be there. Anything for a free feed.' He winked and threw a pair of pliers at her. 'S'pose I'll catch you tomorrow then, kiddo. I gotta head home now and shift those sheep for Dad. What time tomorrow?'

'I told James around twelve.'

'All right then. Catch ya,' shouted Will, giving her a quick wave before heading towards his ute.

'Yep, see ya, and thanks so much for your help,' Izzy replied and returned the wave.

Izzy climbed into the Land Cruiser and both vehicles headed down the edge of the paddock, then veered off in opposite directions once they got past the gate. Izzy drove straight past the farmhouse and continued on down the driveway. She stopped by a small twenty-litre drum on four legs with 'RMB 273' painted in faded white paint across the top. Getting out, she reached into the rusty tin and pulled out a carton of milk and a handful of mail.

Putting the milk on the passenger seat, she flicked through the mail and came across the *Elders Weekly* magazine.

'Lets see what's in the bible this week, hey, Tom.'

Smiling, she shut the door and drove home, whistling along to the radio while Tom watched her with his head cocked to one side.

14

IZZY spent most of the next morning catching up on the housework. Then she made the caesar salad for the barbecue and put clingwrap over it, placing it into the fridge next to the potato salad she'd made the night before.

Izzy checked her watch – ten minutes to twelve. The boys can't be far away, she thought. Grabbing a cloth out of the sink, she wiped over the bench where she'd been working. When it was spotless, she threw the cloth back into the sink, then got out some plates. A soft hum and a squeal of dusty brakes indicated that someone had just arrived – probably Will, judging by the sound of the ute.

Leaving the plates on the bench, she went out to welcome him. Her arms brushed the soft pink material of the short halter-neck dress she was wearing as she strolled out the back door towards the side gate. James was just pulling up as well.

She stood and watched the guys get out of their respective vehicles. 'You timed it well. Come on in,' she said, beckoning them.

James and Will were both wearing thongs and knee-length board-shorts, but James had on a white tank top, whereas Will was wearing a nice blue polo shirt.

'Good to see you brought the necessities,' said Izzy, nodding towards the small eskies that they both carried, which she knew would be full of beer.

'Hey, Will. How're you doing?' said James, as they all came together and headed to the house.

'Well, thanks, mate.' Will slapped him gently on his shoulder.

'You fellas can put your stubbies in the beer fridge. I'm just gonna go and get the meat out,' she said, before shutting the flywire door and strolling back into the house.

Izzy had planned to cook the meat, but Will ended up taking over, which left her free to set the table inside. The flies were too bad to eat outdoors.

Twenty minutes later, they all sat down at the table and continued to chat, as they dug into their meals. She had to give Will credit for cooking the steak and sausages perfectly.

'You really know how to barbecue, Will,' said James, as if reading Izzy's thoughts. 'The steak is so tender and juicy. What's the secret?' he asked, putting a forkful in his mouth.

Will looked at them both sideways. 'I could tell you, but then I'd have to kill you.' He laughed. 'It's simple – don't over flip. Only cook each side once. If you constantly turn the meat over every few minutes, it becomes boot leather.'

'Well, you can come and cook all my meat from now on,' Izzy replied.

'What varieties of crop have you got this year, Will?' asked James as he put his knife and fork down on his empty plate and wiped up some leftover sauce with his finger.

'We've got in some Westonia and Wyalkatchem – they've been our highest yielding varieties – plus a few others we're trying out.' Izzy listened intently to them discussing the finer points of the varieties. She always tried to pick up what she could. Sometimes to be a good farmer you had to listen to those around you and find out what grows well where.

It wasn't long before Will was picking on James for driving a Ford. They went over the whole Holden versus Ford debate for quite a while, as they were both big fans of the V8 supercars.

'Holdens are always holdin' on. Besides, Peter Brock was one of the best and you can't dispute his history,' said Will.

'Yeah, he's a legend, for sure,' James agreed before turning to Izzy. 'Well, what do you think, Izzy? Where do you stand on this issue?'

Will responded before Izzy could open her mouth, 'She's a Holden girl, of course. No sane person would be anything but.'

James shook his head in disbelief, then turned to Izzy for confirmation.

'Sorry, James. I drive a Holden and my folks do too, so I'm definitely a Holden girl. Fords are for pansies.' Izzy grinned cheekily, then rose from the table and began clearing away their dishes.

'You're so easy to stir,' Izzy said, when she noticed James had dropped his bottom lip. James put his hand under his chin and said to Will, 'She's such a loving girl, with so much compassion.'

Will aimed a bottle top he was playing with at James's head and let fly with it. It flipped end over end and brushed the top of James's cropped hair. 'You're an idiot.'

'Well, you lot, shall we make our way to the dam for a swim?' Izzy interrupted.

'If I drown, are you gonna save me?' James winked at Izzy before shaking his empty beer. 'Hey, Will, do you need a refill?'

'Nah, I'm still right, thanks.'

'Righto. I'll go pack some supplies, then.'

While James went to grab the beer, Will collected the remaining sauce bottle off the table and took it into the kitchen. He placed it on the bench just as Izzy turned around from the sink, almost colliding with him. Luckily, she'd raised her hands to protect herself and they now sat pressed flat against his chest.

'Shit, Will, you nearly gave me a heart attack. Don't you know you shouldn't sneak up on people?' It made her think back to the last time her hands had been there. She shuddered at the memory, quickly moving away and walking around him. 'You coming or not?'

Will didn't move. Not just yet. His mind was also reliving the bin party night, and he was struggling to wipe the smile off his face. She had such a distracting effect on him – another reason why he couldn't let that kiss happen again. Slowly he turned and followed Izzy's heady scent of perfume, which he liked very much.

'We can take my ute. That way we can all fit in,' Izzy said to them both as they walked out the gate.

'I bags driving!' yelled James. 'I have to see what's so good about the Holdens, hey.'

'Be my guest,' Izzy replied. They put their towels and the beer in the back of Izzy's ute, then all got in, sliding along the bench seat. Tom jumped in at the last minute and decided to sit on Izzy's lap. 'Good one, Tom. Now I can't see past your big ears,' she laughed.

'You know, maybe you shouldn't have let James drive your *uuuuute*,' Will half croaked to Izzy, as they were both pressed up against the window when James did a full slide skid.

'Hang on, Tom.' Izzy wrapped her arms tightly around her dog to stop him flying out the window. She was wedged up against Will's large shoulders.

'So, which way am I heading?' James asked with a grin. He'd straightened up and had started to drive properly.

'Just straight down the back track, past the sheds, turn left at the first open gate and it's to our left over the hill.' Her hand bounced up and down in the air as she pointed.

James followed her directions and soon came upon the dam. It was situated in the bottom corner of the paddock filled with wheat stubble. The cloudless blue sky stood out against the pale yellow stretching before them and the whiteness from the loamy dam banks. The dam only had three sides – the fourth was almost flat except for two contour banks to guide the water in on each end. James launched over the first rounded contour bank and then stopped the ute in a sideways skid on the flat part in front of the water.

Falling out of the ute, they all stretched their legs after being squished in so tightly, like a mob of ewes up against a fence. Will grabbed the beer and put it in the shade of the vehicle. Izzy grabbed some fold-up chairs, while James erected a tarp on the side of the ute.

Reaching into the back again, Izzy threw out some empty plastic chemical drums. 'Our floaties. I can't have you drowning.'

Stashing their beers into the holders on their chairs, they began undressing.

'It's bloody hot today. Just as well, 'cos that water is gonna be freezing,' James said, pulling his shirt over his head and flicking off his thongs.

'Oh gee, the glare.' Izzy covered her eyes, pretending she couldn't see for the brightness of his fair skin.

James chucked his shirt at her, ran full pelt at the water with a war-like cry and splashed into it.

Will peeled off his polo shirt. His brown stomach was pulled tight across where his shorts sat low over his hips. Izzy's eyes found their way up to his chest. Hell, she hadn't seen one built like that before. It should be standard on all men, like a steering wheel to a car. Izzy slowly dragged her eyes away, which was such a shame to do so, but she didn't want to get caught staring.

She threw James's shirt onto his chair and took her thongs off as Will did the same. Pulling her dress up over her head, she revealed a black triangle bikini top with shoestring straps and matching briefs. The cut of the top actually made her look like she had a decent bit of cleavage. It was one Alice had helped her buy. Thinking of Alice brought Emma and Chris to mind. She missed them heaps and wondered whether Emma liked the new DVD and shirt she'd sent her for her birthday. Maybe she'd give her a call later.

James had returned and was standing beside Will, water dripping from his shorts. Both men were looking rather strange.

'What's up with you two?' she asked, as she gathered her hair back into a ponytail and placed her hands on her hips. 'Anyone would think you'd never seen a girl in bathers before.'

Will was the first to find his voice. 'We just forgot you were a girl.' Glancing at James, he gave him a wink before the two of them lunged towards her.

'No you don't,' she squealed, jumping backwards.

But it was too late. Two sets of strong arms rounded her up. Will locked his arms under her armpits, while James lifted up her legs and they carried her into the water. She sprayed profanities and kicked at them, but to no avail. Tom barked madly at their ankles trying to defend his boss.

'Put me down, ya mongrels,' Izzy yelled.

'Okay,' they replied, before ditching her into the dam.

The cold water engulfed her olive skin, bringing out goosebumps on impact. Not to be outdone, she reached down under the water and grabbed a handful of slimy mud in each hand. As she stood up, she let fire. 'Take that!'

A pile of sloppy, lumpy mud slid down James's arm, while the other one got Will on the chest, leaving brown splatter marks on his square shoulders.

They tore off after her and a huge water fight erupted between all three. No one could see a thing for the flying water. The commotion sent Tom into a frenzy on the bank, as he barked loudly at them all.

'Truce,' Izzy yelled out, half choking on the water running down her face. When they eventually calmed down, Izzy waded out and grabbed the three chemical drums that were sitting on the bank. She couldn't help noticing both of them watching her. It was a weird feeling – she wasn't used to a lot of male attention. She still felt like one of the boys and found it hard to think of herself as something worth looking at. Being the centre of attention was Claire's thing, not hers.

'Not bad,' teased Will.

'Yeah, I'd give you a ten out of ten,' said James, wolf whistling.

'Bugger off,' Izzy said and pitched a drum at each of them as she jumped back into the water with her own.

'Hey, I've got a great joke. Did you hear about the guy who lost his left arm and leg in a car crash?' said James. 'He's all right now,' he finished.

Will smiled. 'Ha ha. I've got a better one. What's the difference between an oral and a rectal thermometer?'

Izzy and James both shrugged.

'The taste,' Will answered.

'Oh, lovely. I s'pose you'd know,' Izzy said, laughing. Will splashed her, the sexual tension between them well and truly forgotten for now.

'Here, I've got a good one. What do *Star Trek* and toilet paper have in common?' James waited until they both shook their heads before giving them the answer. 'They both circle Uranus looking for black holes.'

Izzy rolled her eyes. 'James, you need better jokes. Where'd you get them from anyway?'

'My *Ralph* magazine!' he replied boastfully.

Eventually they settled down and floated in silence as they thought of more jokes. Izzy had both arms over the plastic drum with her head resting between them and her legs dangled below in the cold, dark water. Every now and then the drum would slip out from under her arms and she'd have to drag it back to her chest and throw her arms around it again.

'Well, I've racked my brain and can't remember any more,' said James. 'I think I'll get out – I'm turning into a prune. Unlike you two, my skin doesn't handle the sun very well. The last thing I need before I head back to college is sunburn.'

Izzy and Will watched James climb out of the dam.

'Come on, I'll race you to the other side,' Izzy said to Will, before ditching her floating drum and breaking into a mad freestyle, trying to get a head start.

Will didn't waste any time. Letting go of his drum, he swam after her. Just before Izzy was about to beat him to the other side, he reached out and grabbed hold of one of her ankles. Quickly, he dragged her back towards him, almost swimming over the top of her. Izzy turned over and tried to grab him around his waist, preventing him from passing her. They struggled together in a whitewash of dam water before Will was momentarily distracted by the brushing of her breasts on his chest. Her bikini did nothing to hide her erect nipples caused by the cold water. Will lost his hold on Izzy and she was able to push him underwater.

When he surfaced, Izzy was already sitting on the bank. She was trying to catch her breath slowly so she'd look like she'd been there for ages. As he climbed out, Will looked down at his chest, half expecting to see burn marks from the contact with Izzy's nipples. He knew he was going to struggle to keep his eyes diverted.

'Not fair. You cheated,' said Will, lying down beside her on the bank. Don't look, he kept telling himself.

'Oh, and you didn't.' Izzy had just about regained her breath. She glanced at Will. 'Come on, then – a rematch, with no cheating this time.'

Together they dived in and swam back to the other side where James was waiting.

Will climbed out from the muddy water and put his hand out for Izzy who was just behind him. She used his arm to help steady her through the slippery mud.

After drying herself, Izzy grabbed a packet of Barbecue Shapes from the ute and handed them around before sitting down with her towel wrapped around her. Tom settled in the shade next to her chair. James had his large black Bundy bear towel over his head and shoulders to shield him from the sun. He slightly resembled a nun, Izzy thought to herself.

Will leant back, putting his hands behind his head and looking relaxed. 'This is the life. Now, I just need me a beer wench to bring me my icy-cold beer,' he said, glancing sideways at Izzy. 'Seeing as there are none around, you'll have to do, kiddo.'

'Hey, that sounds great. I've never had a beer wench before. Can I get one too?' James chimed in.

'James!' exclaimed Izzy, acting shocked. 'See what you've done, Will?' She waved a finger at him. 'You have corrupted a nice young man. Don't you go turning him into a butthead like you.'

James lost it, laughing, and Will just chuckled.

Izzy watched Will through her sunnies as he chatted away, unaware of her gaze. This bloke, who she'd known her whole life, was now the only mate she really had out here. She was beginning to appreciate his friendship, more than he probably knew. And she wasn't going to enlighten him either. She just didn't think Will needed to know how much she'd come to like him and enjoy his company. Besides, his head would probably swell to the size of a large watermelon and ruin his handsome face.

15

A SLIGHT breeze started to pick up, moving about the hot air. It was nearly five-thirty in the afternoon and Izzy had just finished welding a bracket for the new bench she'd made for the workshop. She wiped the sweat off her brow with the bottom of her shirt and then bent backwards with her hands on her hips, stretching her aching back. The breeze felt wonderful against her hot skin, even if it was only slight. After washing her hands in an old basin at the side of the shed, she decided it was beer o'clock. It had been a hard day of work, plus it was Friday and she'd earned it. It was hard to believe another week had flown by. James had left town, along with most of the other bin crew, and nearly all the farmers had finished harvest. She'd found plenty of things to do around the farm to keep her busy enough and she hoped her dad would be impressed with her bench.

'What do you think, Tom? She's a ripper, even if I do say so myself.' Heading for the beer fridge in the corner of the workshop, she pulled out a six-pack. 'What say we find some company, eh, boy? Tom had already guessed her intentions and was heading to the ute.

It didn't take long for Izzy to get through the back tracks and reach Will's quaint house. She pulled up next to his ute. Good, he was home. Grabbing the beers, she headed down the rocky path and up to the old verandah.

'Oi. What ya doing?' Will's voice caught her by surprise.

'Hey, great minds think alike,' she said as she spotted him sitting on a brown sofa out the front. 'Want some company?' The sofa looked as if puppies had chewed on it – the armrests were stripped back to the foam filling and wooden frame. Beside it, a pair of boots sat neatly placed, limp black socks hanging out the top. Will was still in his dirty work clothes, lounging in the seat with a nearly empty beer in his hand.

'Mind if I sit?' Izzy asked, holding out a beer.

'Sure thing.' Will took the fresh coldie she offered, which had beads of moisture running down the glass neck. 'I haven't seen you around for the whole week, Izzy. Busy running a farm, are you? I'm glad you made time for a beer.' Will raised his stubbie and smiled.

Flopping down beside him, Izzy cracked open her own beer. Tom went off sniffing about, frolicking in and out of the scrub bush next to the house, hunting out something long since dead. Izzy took a drink as she idly watched him. 'Oh, now that feels much better.' Her body began to relax.

'What have you been up to? You look like you had a fight with a grease gun,' said Will. He pressed his finger to the marks on her forehead and cheek. 'It's a good look, kiddo.'

Izzy bent over and tried to wipe it off with the bottom of her shirt, then realised that was where the grease had come from in the first place. She gave up caring, leant back and took another swig of her beer. 'Well, at least you know I've been working,' she said, smiling.

Will drained the remaining mouthful from his warm beer and cracked open the cold one.

'Cheers,' they said simultaneously, over the sound of clinking glass.

'Ahh, that's nice. So what you been doing today?' Will asked.

'Just servicing the ute and welding up a new workbench for the workshop, plus a few other running repairs. You?' She stared straight ahead at the view that opened up before them. The evening sun on the wheat stubble made the stalks look golden, and the heat haze blurred the horizon. His place was nestled in such a beautiful spot. He was almost halfway between her house and his parents' house. She wondered if they ever came over for tea, or how often he went to theirs.

'Yeah, a bit here and there. Not as much as you, by the sound of it. It's been warm enough.'

'I was nearly gonna give you a ring and see if you wanted to come over for a swim. But by the time I was free, I couldn't be bothered.'

'Oh gee, thanks,' Will laughed easily.

They sat in quiet companionship for a moment, enjoying the tranquillity.

Will took a mouthful of his beer before speaking. 'So, you're a bit of a welder, then? You know, I'm building a new trailer for the diesel tank and I could do with a bit of help from a handy welder.' He turned expectantly to Izzy and waited for her reply.

She didn't need to think about it. 'Sure,' she replied enthusiastically. 'Just give me the nod when you want me.'

Will raised his eyebrows at her.

Izzy knew what he was thinking and shook her head. 'Get your mind out of the gutter,' she laughed.

'All right. I'll let you know when I need you,' said Will. 'I'm actually taking the weekend off. Well, sort of. Have to go to Perth to pick up a part and thought I'd visit your old man and see how he's doing. Do you want to catch a ride? It'd be nice to have some company.'

Izzy scratched her arm before she answered. 'You know, I might just take you up on that. I talk to Mum nearly every second night but it would be nice to actually see Dad again. His progress is so slow.' She looked at him seriously. 'Thanks, Will. I appreciate that. When are you planning to head off?'

He raised his shoulders in a shrug. 'Was thinking about seven tomorrow morning. We'll stay the night at our city flat, if that's okay with you?'

'Yep. No probs,' she replied as Tom came padding up to her for a pat. 'I'll feed up the animals early and I'll be waiting. Sorry, Tom. You can't come this time either,' she added.

'Tom's very loyal. I can see how much he loves you.' Will tapped his knee and Tom moved his chin across to his leg for a pat.

'I don't know what I'd do without him. He's been my best mate for a long time. What about you? Do you have a dog?'

'I used to have Tess, a border collie, but she was more of a farm dog, and when I moved into this house two years ago she stayed behind at the folks' place as they have the big dog yards. I've been thinking of getting another dog. It can be lonely here. I just seem to sleep, eat and farm most of the time. Have a few people over for drinks every now and then but I've lost touch with most of my old friends.' A sadness came over Will's face. 'There was Shane. You remember him?'

Izzy nodded.

'His old man died from bowel cancer and he sold the farm and moved to Busselton with his fiancée. His heart just wasn't in farming, plus Anne was a city girl.'

'Yeah, Mum told me about all that. What a shame. So you've been in this house two years, hey? I remember coming home from school and you'd already left. What did you do then, if you don't mind me asking?'

Will raised his shoulders as if to say 'whatever'. 'I worked from farm to farm and did a few shearing runs. But no matter what I did, I still couldn't get Claire out of my thoughts. After a year I realised that I'd never forget and that running away wouldn't help. So I came home, and I've been happier for it. Your dad has a lot to do with that.'

Izzy sat up, her attention fixed. 'What do you mean?'

Will leaned forward and rested his elbows on his knees, both his hands on his beer. 'Well, I tried to talk to my dad about how I was feeling, even Mum, but they just didn't get it. I hadn't told them about the baby either. I didn't think Mum could have kept it a secret for long, so I couldn't talk about that. I still haven't got around to mentioning it now. I don't really see the point in disappointing them. Mum doesn't need to know how close she came to having a grandchild, only to lose it. So, anyway, Bill became my sounding board. Don't get me wrong, Izzy – my folks have been wonderful, letting me wander off to see Bill and lend a hand. They have plenty of help around the farm with Keith, so I'm really only needed during the busy times.' Keith was their worker and had been on before harvest. He was in his late thirties and a hard worker. He was reliable, trustworthy and came with plenty of brains, which gave Will reassurance when he wasn't around that things would be getting done.

'Farming's like that. So many have moved to the coast and only come back every month or so to keep the farm ticking over. I don't know how they do it,' said Izzy.

'They probably don't have sheep for a start. But we're lucky that there's plenty of money stashed away.' Izzy nodded her head in agreement. Brian and Sandy weren't tight-lipped when it came to their money – they'd tell people how much this ram cost and how much that truck cost. But no one complained because they supported the local sports clubs well with donations. 'Dad's not too upset that I'm not around much. He's told me to go and run Gumlea full time, but I know you're doing a great job by yourself.'

'Oh, thanks, Will.' Izzy slapped her hand on his thigh in appreciation. 'You must take me around Tarramin one day. It's been ages since I've been on your farm. Not since Claire used to dink me on the bike to go find you. I used to love riding around your canola crops and wished Dad would grow some on Gumlea. Some days I used to sneak over and walk into the sea of yellow and dream. I didn't like the smell much, though.'

'Yeah, canola smells foul, but it's worth its weight in gold if you get a good crop. I reckon I've nearly talked Bill around to trying it soon. Get rid of his bloody Halberd wheat.'

'Oh, come on, Will. Not his trusty Halberd! He loves that variety and it goes the deepest gold when it's ripe. That's one variety of wheat I can pick from the road. You know, growing canola is one of my plans for the place. I have this whole crop rotation worked out. I used to spend my quiet nights on Rob's farm planning it all out. I could remember the soil types in each paddock and had selected the varieties of grain I'd grow to suit. I'd planned the fertiliser and the chemicals I'd spray. Right down to the machinery I'd buy first.'

'True? Can I see it one day? It sounds impressive.' He watched Izzy's face glow from his comment and couldn't help but feel a need to kiss her. She looked so adorable and innocent and her enthusiasm was infectious. His eyes were drawn to her lips as she spoke, and it took all his strength to resist.

'I'd like that. One day I hope Dad is as interested.'

Will glanced at Izzy's empty beer for a distraction and raised his own. 'Want another one?'

'You betcha. Cheers.'

An hour later, six empty stubbies stood upright on the verandah floor.

Will stretched and then rubbed his belly. 'Well, I don't know about you but I'm starving. Did you want to stay for dinner?'

'No, thanks. I'd best be off. Need to get organised for tomorrow before it gets too dark,' she said, rising from the couch.

'Yeah, it gets dark quickly, doesn't it,' said Will, as he reached in behind the door to flick on the verandah light. 'Thanks for the beers, kiddo. It's nice to sit and chat to you these days without you looking like you want to bite my head off.'

Izzy's cheeks flushed. She still felt terrible about the way she'd treated him.

'It's okay. I'm only yankin' ya chain,' he said.

'Yes, it beats drinking with just Tom. Thanks for the company. I'll catch you tomorrow at seven.' Izzy walked down the step and towards the ute, raising her hand in half a wave. 'C'mon, Tom.'

16

TRUE to his word, Will picked up Izzy at seven on the dot. She was waiting by the gate in a pair of denim shorts, which made her legs look like they went on for miles. Her blue long-sleeved checked shirt was unbuttoned and tied at her waist, revealing a tight-fitting blue tank top. Izzy could take his breath away without even trying. Part of her beauty was that she wasn't even aware of it. He'd seen enough girls who flaunted what they had, but not Izzy.

'Is that all you're bringing?' Will said, watching her place her small black carry bag into the back of his ute. When she threw him a strange look, he explained, 'Chicks usually need about ten bags for all their stuff, don't they?'

Izzy gave him a quick wink. 'I'm not your average chick.'

That's for sure, Will thought to himself. He wasn't used to someone like Izzy. He wasn't bored listening to her talk – he enjoyed it. She wasn't afraid to question his ideas or disagree with him. Or give him shit, for that matter. Her views on farming and her plans for Gumlea had made him want to think about his own. He knew his dad would pass the farm on to him when the time came, but he hadn't thought much further than that. Izzy really had it all worked out. She just needed the land.

'So what are your plans, William?' Izzy asked as if reading his thoughts. 'Are you happy to stay on farming or are you thinking of heading off like Shane?'

'No, I'm a lover of the land. You couldn't pay me to move to the city. But I've got it better than most. I feel sorry for the guys – and girls,' he added quickly, 'who have to sell up because they can't afford to continue farming, no matter how much they love it. How I wish we could keep the district together. You remember how many people there used to be around when we were kids? I reckon it's nearly halved.'

'I know. I've noticed the difference just being away for a few years. I can't believe Ray sold up. He loved his place. Me, I hope to live out my life here just like Aunt Betty. She and Jim are in no hurry to leave. She reckons she'd up and die if anyone tried to move her, and that Jim would perish without his little bits of farm work to keep him active.'

'I'm with you on that one too. But you never know what each year will bring. If we get good years like this every now and then to keep us going, it's okay. It's those bad ones that keep coming more frequently that hurt. Like last year. We had the best start to the year. It rained perfectly and the crops took off and everyone started to think you beauty, but then one big frost came in and wiped out three-quarters of it. A whole year's planning gone in one early morning. There were blokes cutting crops into hay just to get something for them. I have never seen so many bales of hay around. It broke my heart.'

Will's comments seemed so genuine and compassionate and she appreciated his words. She realised the two of them were very similar in the way they thought and that he loved his patch of earth just as she did. Little things he said kept surprising her, and begrudgingly she admitted she was really beginning to like him.

As he drove, they chatted easily, and they made it to Corrigin before they knew it. Corrigin was famous for its Dog in a Ute Queue event, which had been held a few times. Izzy's dad had gone to it with their old dog Joe. They stopped at the roadhouse, adorned with a ute on the roof, for a bacon-and-egg toasted sandwich. Will watched Izzy as they sat out the front eating. That was yet another thing that

Will liked about Izzy – she wasn't afraid to eat. 'You put away just as much as I do,' he exclaimed. 'Where does it all go?'

'Same place you put yours,' she replied, oblivious to his admiring gaze.

When it was time to hit the road again, Izzy offered to drive but Will declined. She put on Shannon Noll's new song to try and change his mind but it turned out he was also a fan. It was just before lunch when they arrived at the hospital without any fights erupting over the choice of music. Will never even complained when she put on her mixed CD of old Aussie rock songs from bands like Mental as Anything and Paul Kelly and the Coloured Girls. He even had his finger tapping to the Choirboys' 'Run to Paradise'.

They parked, entered the hospital and walked up a hallway lined with numerous doors.

'Hospitals are kind of freaky, with the smells and all the long corridors,' said Will, feeling out of place.

'I know what you mean' said Izzy, holding out her arm to slow Will down. 'He's in here.'

She peered through the window, checking it was okay to go in, then rapped her knuckles on the door a couple of times before entering.

'G'day, g'day,' said Izzy, as she entered the room.

'Isabelle, what are you doing here?' Bill reached for a remote control attached to a cord. He pressed a button and his bed groaned and creaked as it tilted upwards, putting him in a better sitting position. The whites of his eyes doubled in size as his lids widened and a large smile danced across his tired, pale face when Will approached his bedside.

'Bloody hell. The people you see when you haven't got a gun,' Bill said. He looked as happy as a bobtail with a strawberry.

Will carefully shook Bill's lightly bandaged hand. 'Yeah, it's good to see you too, mate.' He laughed at the sheer pleasure on his face.

'So, what's happening?' Bill had perked up considerably.

'Well, we thought we'd better pay you a visit. Make sure you weren't climbing the walls, trying to get out.' Will gave him an understanding smile. He knew how hard it would be for Bill to have to sit still. 'And I had to pick up some parts as well,' he finished.

Izzy sat down on the bed next to her dad, careful not to knock his heavily bound legs, while Will took the empty chair by his bed.

'What's Mum doing?' she asked.

'Gone back to Sarah's for lunch. Maggie is meeting them there.'

'Oh great. I haven't seen Mags in ages.' Izzy's cousin Maggie was two years older than her. Being a city girl, she'd taught her cousins stuff they'd never known about – like boys, make-up and teenage girl magazines. 'Since we're staying the night, I might be able to catch up with her,' said Izzy, glancing at Will for a split second, seeking his okay. 'Anyway, how's the treatment going, Dad?' Izzy's throat tightened at the thought of those horrific burns and the extreme pain she knew her dad suffered every time they changed his dressings. If it was affecting him, he never let on. She never saw despair cross his face. Instead he was always so bloody cheery and strong. She knew that the one thing killing him most was being stuck in this room.

'Yeah, the doc said they're coming along all right.'

'All right? What do you mean by all right?'

'My hands are doing really well and I might be able to take the bandages off in a week or two,' Bill said, raising his arms, which resembled white clubs. 'Not long now and they might let me go home, maybe another two to three weeks. Jean is learning how to dress my burns so I can get out faster.'

'Ah, that sounds great, Bill. I've certainly missed having you around,' said Will shifting in his chair. The vinyl cover made a sucking sound as it stuck to the exposed skin below his shorts.

'So, what's happening back home? How's Brian coping with you over on Gumlea all the time?' asked Bill.

Will shifted again. Izzy could see he was uneasy about having to lie about the work he wasn't doing on Gumlea.

'Not much. Dad's cool. It's easy running from one to the other. I help Dad and the worker out if they need it and Izzy's been helping me on Gumlea when I need an extra hand.'

'Don't let her do too much. I don't want her getting into trouble. It's easy to get injured on the farm.'

'Dad, as if I'm going to be careless,' Izzy cut in. There it went again – her blood was beginning to boil.

'Bill, don't worry. I wouldn't put Izzy in any dangerous situations.'

Bill sighed heavily as if he realised he'd lost this battle. 'I know you wouldn't, Will. I do trust you, don't get me wrong. But she's the only baby I've got left.'

'*Da-a-d*, I'm twenty-two now,' said Izzy as the hairs on her neck prickled. It was excruciating to hear her dad speak about her like this. 'I'm going to get something to eat. I'll leave you two to gibber on.'

Izzy found herself, and her rumbling belly, wandering the corridors for a vending machine. She couldn't stand listening to her dad talk to Will about the farm as if she wasn't even a part of it, and it was hard to watch them behave like father and son. It was *her* family farm. She couldn't help but envy Will. As much as she appreciated him and realised that he was filling the hole that Claire had left, she would still have given anything to be in his shoes.

A vending machine loomed out from an alcove ahead. She picked up her pace, only to find a white square of paper stuck to it, with the words 'out of order' scribbled in black marker across it. Damn, she thought, she'd have to wait till lunch. She turned on her heel in frustration and headed back to the room. Maybe they'd be finished by now and she and Will could go and get something to eat.

Will caught Izzy's eye as soon as she entered the room. 'Well, we'd better get going,' he said. 'I have to pick up the parts before the shop shuts.'

Thank you, her face seemed to say without words. She had come all this way to see her dad and all he wanted to do was to talk to Will. He'd never asked her how things were going.

Bill nodded his head reluctantly. Life had to go on, even if it did seem to stand still in his little room, which was becoming more of a cell every day. After a round of hand shaking and hugs, they were about to leave when Bill said, 'It's so good to see you happy together.' He smiled at Will.

'Yeah, thanks, Dad. Good to see you too,' Izzy replied, wondering just what he'd been implying with that.

Will gave one last wave, then put his hand in the small of Izzy's back and guided her down the corridor. 'That wasn't so bad.' He gave her a smile, but Izzy was stony-faced.

'For you, maybe. You know, I thought the whole life-and-death moment might have changed his outlook, but he hasn't budged a bit.' She swung around to face Will. 'And why is he so happy to see us together?'

Will didn't know what Bill had meant either so he just shrugged his shoulders and headed to the lift. 'Bill really does have a bee in his bonnet about you doing farm work, hey.'

'You don't say,' Izzy mocked. 'But thanks for helping out back there.'

Will sighed and she watched his shirt pull tight against his chest. 'Don't know what you mean,' he said.

She touched him gently on his arm. 'Well, I appreciate you trying to influence him, Will, even if it didn't work.'

'We'll keep working away at him, Izzy. Eventually he'll come around. He has to.'

It was sweet of Will to say so, but Izzy couldn't imagine it ever happening.

*

A short time later, Will pulled into the driveway of Izzy's Aunt Sarah's house in the suburb of Como. The South Perth Como area was popular with ex-country folk. Sarah's mid-sized red brick house wasn't far from the city centre and close to the zoo. Will parked in the driveway and admired the tidy front yard with its large lawn and frangipanis growing along the fence line.

'You sure you don't want to stay for dinner?' Izzy asked.

'Nah. I'll head back to the flat and grab some takeaway. Mum wants me to put together a new storage cupboard she's left there. So I'll do that and then come to pick you up. What time?'

'Um, they'll probably eat around sevenish, so how about half an hour after that?' Izzy opened the car door and turned back to Will. 'Cheers. I guess I'll see you later tonight, then.'

'Sure will,' he replied, watching her climb out. Izzy gave him a quick wave as he reversed out of the driveway. They had made plans to go to the Ocean Beach Hotel, called the Obie by the locals, for a few drinks and a catch-up with Maggie after dinner. Will knew Maggie from when she'd come to the farm on school holidays. He didn't like hanging around the giggling girls back then.

Carrying her small bag, Izzy walked up the driveway to the front door. It opened before she even had time to knock.

'Well, I'll be a monkey's uncle. How ya been, Izzy?' said a tall, skinny woman dressed in stylish casual pants and a fitted white top. Her blonde hair was pulled back into a ponytail. Izzy couldn't help wondering how her cousin got all the good genes.

'Hiya, cuz,' said Izzy, hugging Maggie tightly.

'Careful. Don't get too close. I have a cold,' Maggie warned.

'Bloody hell, Mags. I'd never have guessed. You're looking fabulous as usual.'

Maggie's red nose was the only thing that gave the game away. Other than that, she looked gorgeous, even though she was in casual clothes. She was one of those people who knew how to dress and carry herself gracefully. More or less the opposite of me, Izzy thought.

'Come on in. It's been ages. I was wondering whose car that was. Was that Will I saw driving?' she asked curiously.

'Yeah, he had to come to Perth so I hitched a ride. We're planning to go to the Obie tonight. You keen?' Izzy asked eagerly. 'You can catch up with him then.'

'Oh, I would've loved to, but I'm feeling like crap. It's half the reason I'm here. Mum's looking after me.' She laughed as she pulled out a tissue from her pocket and began blowing her nose gently. 'Sorry, Izzy. You'll have to go it alone. At least you'll have Will to talk to,' she joked, giving a wink.

Maggie put her arm around Izzy and led her inside. 'Come on. Our mums are in the kitchen.'

After squeals of delight and hugs all round, Aunt Sarah pulled out of Izzy's embrace and studied her at arm's length. 'Izzy, you look so well, all brown and fit. Have you been working out?' Grey hair circled Sarah's long oval face, which was much like Izzy's dad's. They definitely had the same eyes and mouth.

'No, I've just been working. You look great yourself. Not a day older than when I last saw you, and that must have been a good few years ago. I missed the last Christmas get-together. It's a shame I couldn't come home for it.'

'Goodness me. Has it been that long? We must be due for another family get-together on the farm.'

'Yeah, that sounds good.' It was all good in theory, but Izzy knew just how busy everyone's lives seemed to be these days. She turned her attention to her mum and gave her a warm embrace. 'Hi, Mum. How you holding up?'

'I'm missing home lots, love, sick of the city noises and smog, but other than that I'm doing well. It's good you came. Have you seen your dad yet?' Jean asked.

Izzy filled her in and Jean beckoned her to come and sit down. 'We've just put the kettle on,' she finished.

Izzy enjoyed catching up with them all. She had been away from her family for so long. Aunt Sarah had worked as a teacher, where she met Don, the principal of her school. They'd married and moved to Perth, then had Paul and Maggie. Paul was twenty-eight and was working on a mine up north, so he was hardly seen any more. He never used to come out to the farm with Maggie on school holidays as he was so much older, so Izzy wasn't very close to him like she was to Maggie.

The afternoon flew by with constant chatter, most of it about Maggie's new boyfriend, Tim, and how she reckoned this bloke was the one she was going to marry.

'Why? What's so good about him?' asked Izzy, intrigued.

Ever the drama queen, Maggie rested her face in her hands and started to describe him. 'Oh, Izzy, he's tall, strong, half Italian, has loads of money – he works for his father's company in the city. Don't really know what they do, something with the stock market . . . Anyway he lives in Cottesloe not far from the beach. He's so romantic and we've been together for six months now. I'm really in love with this one.' Izzy was spared more on Tim, when he called Maggie on her mobile.

Later, as they sat down for dinner, Izzy turned to her mum and watched her eating her risotto. Did her hair look greyer? She thought perhaps it did, and she looked pale and tired too.

'Hey, Mum. You look knackered. How are you handling things?'

Jean politely finished her mouthful and placed her fork down on her plate. 'I'm okay, Izzy. I just think being stuck in the city is wearing me down. I long for my house and garden, not to mention some fresh air.'

'Why don't you come home for a day or two? I can stay here with Dad.'

Jean gestured with her hands. 'No, darling. I think you and your father would drive each other crazy. Can you really see yourself sitting in a room alone with him for hours on end?' Izzy's grimace said it all. 'And anyway, I don't want to leave him. He's way out of his comfort zone in that hospital, relying on other people. You know how he hates that.'

'As long as you take time out for yourself. Why don't you and Sarah go to the beach and have a break? I'm sure Dad would survive a couple of hours without you.' Izzy put her hand over Jean's. 'Please? You can't look after anyone if you're run down.'

Jean smiled and the wisdom lines around her eyes and mouth crinkled. 'I'll try.'

After they finished their meal, Maggie jumped up off her chair and grabbed Izzy. 'Look at the time. Come on. We'd better get you ready.' She dragged Izzy from the large dining table into her old room.

'What do you mean?' said Izzy, confused. 'I only need ten minutes.' She couldn't understand what all the fuss was about.

'Oh, no. Tonight you're going to catch yourself a man.' Clearly Maggie thought that everyone needed to be as deliriously happy as she was.

'No, I'm fine, Mags. Honest. I was just going to wear some jeans,' pleaded Izzy.

Maggie grabbed her shoulders and pushed her into her old bedroom. From the door, Izzy could see the pink patterned wallpaper and old dolls lining the shelves and windowsill.

'No excuses. You're going to knock some fella's socks off tonight. I don't want you coming home until you find one,' she ordered, shutting the door behind them. 'Luckily I still have half of my clothes here. There should be something worth wearing in this lot.'

At seven-thirty on the dot, Maggie opened the door for Will. 'Howdy, stranger. Long time no see,' she said with a stunning smile.

'You too,' said Will, as he kissed her cheek. 'You're looking as great as ever.' He'd seen Maggie from time to time when she visited Pingaring, but he'd found her city, girlie ways irritating. All she'd ever wanted to do was sit around and watch chick flicks or read teenage magazines with Claire.

'Come in. She's nearly ready.' Maggie beckoned.

Will had noticed Maggie's casual attire. 'Aren't you coming?' he asked. Normally she'd be dressed up to the nines.

'No, sorry. Too sick. I'm living on Panadol, cold and flu tablets and Throaties at the moment. Not a good mix with a drink,' she explained.

'Fair enough,' he said, as she ushered him inside. He spotted the two women sitting in the lounge by the small television. 'Hi, Jean. Hi, Sarah. How's it going?' he asked. Jean looked up and a warm smile broke across her face at the familiar man before her.

'It was so nice of you to visit Bill today. I know it would have meant a lot to him, Will,' she said.

'Come on, Izzy,' Maggie shouted down the hall. 'Will's here.' Maggie gave Will the once-over, and came to the quick conclusion he was still damn hot, if not better. He was wearing a pair of loose-fitting jeans and a nice white collared long-sleeve shirt. His hair flicked out just a bit at the top making him look like he was fresh out of a magazine ad.

'Will, I'm glad that you and Izzy are back to normal again. I'm happy it's all sorted out now,' Jean said quietly, knowing he would understand what she meant.

Maggie's eyes studied Will's handsome face, watching for a reaction to this strange comment.

'You're not the only one,' he replied. 'It's nice to have a friend back.' Will seemed genuinely relaxed and happy, and his eyes were clear and bright.

'I'm ready to go,' whispered a voice from around the corner

as Izzy appeared. She glided into the lounge room on black high-heeled shoes with thin straps that made her legs look even longer than usual.

Maggie watched Will's eyes follow Izzy's legs up to the short free-flowing black skirt, then to her fitted blue silky halter top. She'd insisted on tying up Izzy's hair, leaving a few loose, soft curls falling around her face and neck. Subtle make-up brought out her vivid blue eyes, and a hint of pale-pink lipstick enlarged her lips dramatically. Maggie only had to see the way Will was looking at Izzy to know she'd done a great job.

'See. What did I tell you? You look amazing,' said Maggie proudly.

'Not too over-dressed for the pub?' Izzy squeaked.

'Never!' replied Maggie. But Izzy didn't expect much else from her.

Izzy had noticed Will staring, and felt uncomfortable under his gaze. 'What?' she said worriedly, looking down over herself. 'Is it too much?'

Will, realising that his mouth may have been open and that, quite possibly, he may well have been drooling, managed to gather his senses. 'Ah . . . n-no, you look . . . g-great,' he stammered. 'Let's . . . let's just get going, shall we?' Hell's bells and whistles, he thought. She looked amazing and yet so shy, and fear escaped from her wide eyes. Tonight it was going to be hard for him to control his thoughts. Eager to move and clear his mind, he attempted to steer her out the door. 'See you ladies later,' he called back to Jean and Sarah. 'Catch ya, Mags. Hope you get better soon.' He gave them a smile that would have melted any woman's heart. Izzy's was sure softening.

17

SITTING in the front of Will's ute, Izzy realised that the sequins from her small black handbag were cutting into her hand because she was clutching it so tight. Give me a pair of jeans any day, she thought, feeling way out of her comfort zone. She had told Maggie that she didn't feel comfortable and wanted to change, but Mags had informed her that women who looked good were never comfortable and that she should just 'suck it up'.

For once, there was a slightly strained silence between them, nothing but the commotion of the traffic and the soft voices on the radio floating through the ute. Nervously, her hands pulled at the fabric of her skirt, as Izzy willed it to grow. She tried to breathe deeply to calm her nerves but after a few inhalations decided against it – Will's masculine scent of alluring aftershave and soap was only making the butterflies in her stomach worse.

The trip seemed to take forever. Each set of lights turned red, causing more delay. Izzy tried hard to rack her brain for something to talk about, but her head was just an empty void. In the end she gave up, and shortly they pulled into a parking spot outside the hotel.

'Here we are,' said Will, almost awkwardly as he fumbled with the keys. He seemed to have lost his voice for most of the trip too. Somehow he'd forgotten how to talk to Izzy now. He'd lost his ability to feel comfortable with her.

Quickly Izzy grabbed onto Will's arm after he locked the ute, almost hiding behind him as they headed for the door. She really felt strangely nervous. She sensed him tremble, maybe from the cool breeze. Izzy took a deep breath of the fresh salty air, which was blowing in from the ocean across the road. But that too disappeared once they plunged into the smell of beer and the loud rumble of voices inside the pub. They made their way through the crowd and headed straight to the long wooden bar, both eager for a drink to settle them.

'What can I get you?' Will asked, looking across at Izzy. The high heels she wore brought her almost level to his eyes. He got a whole new perspective on her face from this angle, and for a moment he studied it. Her mouth was so much closer to his and the pink lipstick shimmered on her lips, enticing him even more to see what they tasted like now. He just wanted to take her chin in his hand and tilt her head up so he could study the fear he saw in the depths of her blue eyes. She wasn't afraid of chopping up a snake with a shovel yet here she was scared of how she looked. If only she knew what she was doing to him.

Izzy realised she was still clinging to Will's arm so she let go and tried to look relaxed.

'Um . . . a bourbon and Coke. Thanks.' Something strong, that's what she needed, and fast.

They managed to find a spot near a pool table and before long had bumped into people they knew from school or back home, as the Obie attracted mostly a country crowd.

Izzy had been getting lots of stares from blokes, and one came up and offered to buy her a drink, which she declined. She had never had so much attention before, and she felt like the main act in a freak show.

'Izzy, how can you be worried about what you look like when you're clearly sending the guys here into a frenzy?' Will had half shouted into her ear and was delighted when her face flushed, but then felt bad that he'd teased her. 'Just relax and have a good time. You're still you under all those different clothes, aren't you?' he asked.

'Hell, yeah,' said Izzy, slapping Will on his knee and relaxing a bit.

Will had to admit that he found all the attention Izzy was getting damn annoying. From the moment they'd walked in together, she'd been turning heads, and it didn't sit comfortably with him. Suddenly he felt the need to protect her, to save her from these wayward blokes, who all seemed to resemble the old him. He knew they had one thing on their minds.

Soon they began chatting to an old schoolfriend of Izzy's, Beau Rodgers, and his sister, who happened to be sitting nearby.

'How about a game of pool, then?' asked Izzy after the bourbon had begun to warm her blood.

'Sounds great. How about you and I play Will and Jen?' said Beau, then he leaned over and asked Izzy, 'Are you with this guy on a date?'

'Nah, we're just good friends out for a good time.' As soon as Izzy said it, she noticed the smile on Beau's face and regretted it.

'Sure. You up for it, Jen?' Will asked Beau's sister, who was in the pub for the first time that night, celebrating her eighteenth birthday.

'Bring it on,' she said.

Opposite Jen, Will was trying hard not to stare at Izzy too much. But he found it easier said than done, especially with Beau hanging around flirting with Izzy. He could tell how uncomfortable she was with the attention. But she'd already given him a lecture at the bin party about not stepping in because she could handle herself. Maybe he just needed to see it to believe it. Why did he feel like this?

After they had finished their second game, Will held Izzy's arm as he leant down to her ear. 'Hey, wanna come help me with some drinks?'

Izzy smiled back and nodded.

Will turned to the other two and mimed as he spoke. 'We're going to the bar. Same again?' he asked them.

Both nodded, but Beau looked slightly put out as he watched Izzy and Will head off together.

They made the treacherous path to the bar, among a sea of people squished tightly together. They finally managed to get themselves a tiny piece of bar top and flagged down a harassed barmaid.

'Having a good time?' Will asked, leaning over to shout into Izzy's ear over the rumbling of voices and yahooing.

She gave him a funny look. 'I was . . . but Beau is starting to get a bit much.' She shuddered and continued. 'I'm trying hard not to do anything that's going to give him the wrong impression, you know. I don't want to have to be rude to make my point.' It was getting late, and the more alcohol Beau consumed, the more he was trying to flirt with her. He'd even grabbed her on the bum at one stage.

Will shook his head. 'You want me to rough him up?' he said, acting all tough and putting on a deep voice.

Izzy grabbed his fisted hands and lowered them to his waist. 'Calm down, he-man.' She smiled at him. 'I should have said I was on a date with you when he asked.'

'Don't worry, we can patch that. Come on, you just follow my lead, okay? This will be fun.'

Picking up two drinks each, they headed back to where Beau and Jen were waiting. The crush of bodies was intense and they ended up with more on the floor than in the glasses as they bumped their way through the crowd.

This time Will made sure he was standing next to Izzy, giving her a protective barrier against Beau. But it didn't stop Beau from trying again.

'*Sooo*, Izzy, got any plans tonight?' he slurred as he pushed past Will in her direction.

She went to reply but Will beat her to it. 'Nah. We're just gonna head back to my place and crash. We've got a long drive home.'

Beau was quiet, as if waiting for an invitation, but it didn't come.

They managed to play another game of pool, this time Izzy and Will against Beau and Jen. Will and Izzy won convincingly.

'Played a few games, have we?' Will asked Izzy, impressed with her skills.

'I've played a bit, yes. I don't need to ask you where you learnt to play. From memory you and Claire used to kick butt at the Lake Grace pub, even if you were half pissed.' Izzy smiled at him. She could remember Will driving them to Lake Grace. They'd sneaked her into the pub to play pool, but she never got much of a go as Will and Claire would hog the table.

'So, who taught you? Claire?' asked Will.

Izzy shook her head. 'My ex-boss, Rob, was a bit of a pool shark in his heyday. So he taught me a few things and I spent a lot of my free time playing pool with his young kids. They had a large pool table set up in their games room.' Izzy thought of Emma and Chris with a twinge of pain. She spoke on the phone to Emma now and again. Just hearing her voice almost brought her to tears as she realised how much she missed those kids.

'Izzy, want to help me get the next round of drinks?' Beau interrupted, clearly trying to lure her away.

'No thanks. I think I'll stay here this time. Getting through that crowd is nightmarish.'

He nodded as his face dropped slightly and he went off with his sister instead.

'This is our chance, Izzy. Don't screw it up,' Will said quickly.

'Screw what up?' Izzy asked curiously, as she leant over to hear his reply.

Will found it hard to avert his eyes from the soft curves within the plunging neckline of Izzy's top. He bent over until his lips were just inches from her ear lobe.

'Just play along, kiddo.'

Izzy squinted at Will, then a few minutes later groaned as she watched Beau and Jen push their way back through the crowd. She could see Beau was making a beeline straight for her. Suddenly Izzy felt Will's arm around her back, and his hand on her shoulder pulling her in closer to him.

'What *are* you doing?' she whispered. Will's face was only inches from hers, so close she could see some faint freckles dotted along his tanned cheeks. She'd never noticed them before.

'Just keep talking. He'll think we're into each other,' which, at that moment, Will thought wouldn't be so hard to fake. 'Do you think he'll get the message or will I have to kiss you?' Will watched with glee as Izzy's eyes gaped and her cheeks flushed. Will remembered their last close encounter vividly, even if he had been a little drunk. He wondered if it was crossing Izzy's mind too. He felt himself tense at the memory.

The heat rose up into her cheeks and her head felt a bit giddy. 'I . . . um . . . I'm sure he will,' she fumbled, as Will's mouth was just centimetres from her lips. Every time he breathed, she could feel the warmth caress her face. Her heart was pounding against her chest and everything felt like it was in slow motion. She was glad for the loud pub noise – she was sure everybody would be able to hear her heartbeat. Will was so close she had to keep leaning backwards and was afraid she'd fall off her stool.

His hand moved up and cupped her cheek, then ever so softly, he kissed her cheek just millimetres from her mouth. As quickly as it had happened, he'd let her go and pulled away. She felt a chill run through her despite the hot stuffy pub. Looking up, she saw Beau thrusting a drink in her direction, his eyes boring holes into the side of Will's face. Clearing her throat, she thanked Beau for the drink. As she took a sip she noticed her hand shaking slightly.

Will sat silently watching Izzy for a moment, then just because he knew it would irk Izzy and Beau, he slipped his arm back around her narrow waist. He curled his fingers around her hips, holding her warm skin. A smile danced on the corner of her lips. Darn, he wasn't expecting that. Maybe she was playing along with him now or maybe she liked it. How was he to know?

None of their flirting was wasted on Beau. Eventually he got the hint and gave up. Soon a group of young girls in the back corner attracted his eye and he started to move away. As Beau shook Will's hand goodbye, he said into his ear, 'You're one hell of a lucky bastard, mate.' Giving Izzy a quick kiss on the cheek was as close as he was going to get.

Will and Izzy laughed about it all the way back to Will's parents' flat. He had been the responsible driver sticking to his light beers. It was a fast trip back, with no cars on the road and the lights going their way most of the time.

'Oh, my sides are hurting. Stop it,' said Izzy, clutching at her aching waist, as she staggered in the dark towards a light that was guiding her to the front of the flat.

Will came up behind her and held her by the arm, half guiding, half holding her straight. He felt dizzy himself but not from the grog. He'd only had a few. The click-clack of Izzy's shoes against the paving echoed through the night and began to turn Will on.

Their breathing seemed loud in the quiet stillness. She leaned on Will, not really needing his support, but more for the warmth and scent of his body.

Unlocking the door, Will flicked on a few lights, then guided Izzy through a quick tour of the small flat. It was painted a sandy colour throughout with light terracotta tiles in all rooms except the bedrooms. The furniture was mainly wrought iron, from the light fittings to the black bar stools in the kitchen. There were minimal pictures on the walls.

'Must be nice being able to afford a city house,' said Izzy. She knew quite a few farmers who had coastal properties or city pads for getaways.

'Yeah, I haven't been here in a while. But Mum likes to come up every couple of months.' Will steered her towards the spare bedroom. 'And you can sleep in here. Bathroom's the second door on the left,' he said, as he pointed down a narrow corridor. 'I'll just duck back to the ute and get your bag.'

When he returned, he put her bag in her room and watched as she took her shoes off. 'Do you want a cuppa?'

'No thanks. Think I might hit the hay.' Izzy put the shoes to one side and stood in front of Will, who was looking very alluring with his top two buttons undone. 'Cheers, Will, for being my chaperone,' she said, throwing her hands up on his chest. His hard body felt warm under her tingling fingertips. Their night of games had been fun and she didn't want it to end. Her heart beat wildly for a moment, from the mixture of alcohol and the fact that she was now alone with Will. It was a deadly combination. Electricity was sparking and it wasn't from a stray wire.

Izzy had noticed it building up slowly and had desperately tried to suppress it, knowing that giving in to it now could ruin a great friendship. But she found it difficult to control herself. She was tempted to rip off his shirt and watch the buttons go flying. She ached to touch his bare chest and explore. Her temperature was beginning to rise. Quickly she bit her lip and tried to collect her senses, scolding herself for being weak.

Will, as if grappling with his own thoughts, placed a hand on each of her arms and kissed her forehead. 'My pleasure. I had a great time.' His voice was low and husky. He looked deep into her eyes, testing his resistance, before letting go of her arms. 'Night,' he said, before quickly shutting the door and trying to cut off the flow of energy between them.

Izzy was thankful for his gentlemanly retreat, though her heart continued to race. She flopped down onto the double bed that took up most of the room except for a couple of bedside tables. She wasn't so sure she'd have been able to control herself, if he had tried anything. But a part of her was sad that he didn't try. Thoughts of having a relationship with Will had begun creeping in more and more recently as her attraction to him got stronger. But she knew nothing would ever come of it. It couldn't. Living next door, it would be too hard for him to avoid her. He couldn't dump and run. It had the possibility of destroying not only their friendship now but also his relationship with her dad. And as much as she envied their closeness, she knew Bill needed Will.

Tugging at her hair, Izzy pulled out the clips and let it slowly begin to unravel as it fell to her shoulders. She would seriously have to avoid getting drunk around Will again. She didn't want to do anything stupid.

18

IZZY was still sound asleep the following morning when Will knocked gently on her door before letting himself in. His feet were silent on the grey carpet as he moved up to the side of her bed, carrying a silver tray laden with breakfast. A stack of hairclips and pins lay on the wooden bedside table, next to a couple of blue dangly earrings Izzy had been wearing the previous night. He liked the way she looked in her sleep, so angelic, especially with her brown wavy hair fanned out across the white pillow.

'Izzy? Izzy?' he said softly.

Slowly opening her eyes, she screwed up her face at the morning light that peeked through a gap in the curtains. 'Morning,' she groaned, before shutting her eyes for a moment. 'What time is it?'

'It's eight and I was lonely. Come on, sleepyhead. I brought you some breakfast,' urged Will, amused. It was strange but nice to see this unprepared and disorganised side of her.

Izzy's eyes opened more quickly again as she realised where she was and what Will was saying.

'Oh, cool,' she said, yawning and sitting up. Her hair bounced across her shoulders as the white sheet slid down over her soft, olive skin. Embarrassed, she clutched at the sheet with her hand, remembering she only had on a PJ singlet that sometimes didn't hold much in. The sheet stopped just short of the nipple of one of her wayward breasts, like a ewe darting away from the rest of the mob. She tried to remain calm.

Will, trying hard to move his eyes away from her, cleared his throat and transferred a cup to her bedside table.

'Mmm, something smells good.' Izzy watched the muscles in his arms as he unloaded the tray he was carrying. She realised that he was only wearing a pair of black silk boxers. Bugger. If only her eyes weren't all blurry from make-up and sleep. 'Have you just got up too? You slack arse, making me feel like you've been up for hours.'

Will laughed. 'Now, I'm not sure how your head is this morning, but I brought you some Panadol just in case, as well as some toast and a cuppa.' He held the empty tray in front of him, trying to hide what the silky material of his boxers would not.

Izzy took a quick moment to think. 'You know, I don't feel too bad. I should be okay after something to eat and a shower.' She reached for a piece of toast. 'You're a star, you know that,' Izzy said, before shoving the Vegemite toast into her mouth.

Will laughed. 'I've put a blue towel in the bathroom for you. Just help yourself.' He left her to her breakfast, and padded quietly out of her room and back to the kitchen.

'A girl could get used to this,' she called after him.

When Izzy walked into the kitchen fifteen minutes later, she found Will sitting at the table wearing jeans and a singlet and sipping his tea while reading the daily paper. His hair was sticking up at funny angles, and his suntanned back rippled with smooth muscles as he hunched over the *West Australian*. Izzy shivered slightly.

'Where did you get the paper?' she said as she sat down at the table. She had on her denim shorts and a T-shirt and felt fresh after her shower.

'From the deli down the road. I ducked out while you were in the shower.' Will looked across at Izzy, her hair tied neatly into a plait and her face free from make-up. He liked her like this. Natural. He lifted the white mug up to his lips before draining the contents. 'Well, kiddo, what shall we do today?'

Izzy shrugged. 'I s'pose I should visit Dad again at some stage. Why? What else did you have in mind?' She cocked her head and waited.

Will shrugged. 'Feel like catching a movie before we head home? There's a few I wouldn't mind seeing.' He flicked through the paper to the movie section.

Izzy nodded her head. 'Yeah, that would be cool.' She leaned over his arm to look at the paper. 'What's on?'

Will looked at her sideways. 'Just a warning – I'm not watching any crappy chick flick!' he said sternly.'Let's see what's on at the Carousel at around eleven. See, there's a few good ones.' He pushed the paper over to her. 'Here, you have a look. I'm gonna have a shower and get ready.'

Izzy watched him put his cup back in the sink, then head off to his room. She was glad everything was back to normal. She was also relieved she hadn't acted on impulse last night. He had been so damn irresistible, but she'd done the right thing. Their friendship depended on it.

They stopped off at a newsagent later that morning on the way to visit Bill and picked up a few magazines. They didn't stay with him long because he was about to have his dressings changed. Izzy's mum was there too, so she got to say goodbye to them both.

'Did you have a good time last night?' Jean asked.

'Yeah. It was great,' Izzy grinned and then hugged Jean. 'Now, remember you were going to have some time to yourself too. You really need it, Mum.'

'Okay, I promise I'll try but don't worry about me. You just stay out of trouble at home and call me if you have any problems or you just want to talk. I miss the little chats we'd been having during harvest.'

'Me too.'

Jean looked at them both. 'So what are you two up to now?'

'We're gonna go catch a movie before we head home. Some soppy chick flick that Will's picked out,' Izzy told them before they left.

When they'd gone, Jean turned to Bill and said, 'I'm so happy to see them getting on. It's almost like watching Claire and Will together when they were younger.' Bill had a twinkle in his eyes and nodded his head in agreement. Jean knew he was just happy to see them being civil to each other again, but Jean had the feeling there was something more between them, something perhaps that Izzy and Will didn't even recognise yet.

Izzy and Will managed to pick a film they both enjoyed, *The Dukes of Hazzard*, and they scoffed a large box of popcorn between them.

'That was bloody funny. I've got sore cheeks from laughing so hard,' said Izzy as they walked out of the cinema.

'Shit, yeah. The car chase was awesome. Hey, how about some lunch, Izzy? Does HJ's sound okay? Don't know about you, but I'm starvin' like marvin.' Will rubbed his belly and licked his lips energetically.

Izzy just rolled her eyes. 'You're real mature for a twenty-five-year-old,' she teased.

'Nearly twenty-six,' Will corrected.

Izzy laughed. 'Even worse.'

Hours later they found themselves approaching the familiar sights of Pingaring. Hungry Jack's wrappers lay scrunched up on the floor of Will's ute, among empty water bottles. A bag of jelly babies lay on the seat between them, opened and half empty with a handful of jellies strewn alongside, as if they were making a last-minute run for it.

'I can't believe we're home already. Time's just flown. I can't wait to see Tom,' said Izzy.

Will pulled up next to Izzy's house just as the sun was starting to make its slow descent to the horizon. The hum of the motor and the excited barks from Tom seemed muffled from inside the ute. Slowly, Izzy pushed open her car door and stretched out her cramped legs. Closing her eyes, she breathed in the fresh air that blew into the ute. 'There's nothing like home,' she said, turning towards Will. 'I don't mind the city for a day or two, but it's good to be back in the clean and wide open spaces.'

Izzy didn't need to tell him; her huge smile and the sparkle in her eyes easily expressed how much she belonged in this place. 'I know. I feel exactly the same,' he said, shifting slightly in his seat. His legs were getting numb from sitting too long.

'Hey, thanks for the ride and all . . . you know . . . it was good,' she fumbled.

'Any time, kiddo.' I had a great time too, he thought, as he watched her climb out of the ute. It had been hard at times, resisting the urge to take her in his arms and experience the thrill of kissing her again, but he wasn't ready to rock their new friendship. He had ruined too many when he was younger by rushing in without thinking, and he wasn't going to risk this one. He was sure that, in time, his physical reaction to her would pass. Hopefully sooner rather than later.

He watched her playing energetically with Tom before he backed up the ute and headed home.

19

'SO, we're nearly done, eh? Just about six hundred head to go,' said the burly head shearer. Brad may have looked a little rough around the edges, but Izzy knew he was a softie. He had been working her dad's shed for a bloody long time. His greying hair was scruffy and his hard face unshaven. His bulky arms, emblazoned with tattoos from his youth, stood out against his black shearing singlet bearing the name 'Jackson's Shearing Team' in white.

Brad's shearing team had been going hard for five days and this was their last day. That was if the rain that was predicted didn't turn up. Izzy watched Brad amble back to his stand, pick up his handpiece and continue attaching a new sharpened cutter. Once on, he clicked it back on the down tube, placed it on the floor, and poured oil over the blades, ready for action.

The remaining three shearers got their gear organised, while the rouseabouts organised their music for the day. As AC/DC's 'Dirty Deeds' blared out on the CD player, Izzy took off her checked shirt and threw it into the corner of the old shearing shed. In her black singlet and dark-blue shearing pants, Izzy stood next to the skirting table ready to do her job as wool classer. She was close to the green hydraulic press, which she would use later to bale up the last of the wool. Leaning against the skirting table, which was black and grimy due to the build-up of dirt and oils from the wool, she surveyed the shed through new eyes. She was the boss of this shed, and everyone was coming to her with queries or problems. Hell, she was loving every minute of it.

Sheep were crammed into the catching pens behind the shearers, heavily laden with thick wool, while many more waited in the outside pens. Izzy had penned them up early in the morning before everyone else had arrived. She looked across at the three dividers up against the back wall. They contained different grades of fleeces, and she would have to bale some up when she had time.

Brad threw a glance at the clock, as the shearers each headed off and dragged back their chosen ewes. Holding the sheep between their legs, they picked up their handpieces ready to commence. Spot on seven o'clock a loud mechanical hum filled the shed and reverberated off the corrugated iron, as the shearers took the thick wool off the top of the ewes' heads.

Before long, the first fleece had been gathered up by one of the rouseabouts and thrown across the skirting table. It descended like a dirty white quilt cover. Izzy and another rousie, Todd, whose belly almost sat on the table but who did well for a fifty-year-old, skirted the edges of the fleece, and then rolled it up to the edge of the table before the next fleece landed. Izzy pulled a staple of wool from the fleece and checked its strength to assess its grade, then put the fleece in the relevant section ready for baling.

It didn't take long for the fleeces to build up and soon it was time to press another bale. She grabbed an armful of fleeces, her face buried in the oily wool. She bundled it into the empty bale bag in the wool press, compacting the wool down repeatedly so she could fit more fleeces in, until it met the required weight of the bale. Releasing the bale from the press, Izzy grabbed a fat marker pen and stencilled on the side of the bale the wool grade and farm name, Gumlea.

'Todd, can you give us a hand, please?' she called out to the nearest rousie.

The wooden floorboards groaned and creaked under the weight of the bale as they rolled it towards the mounting collection. Sweat ran down her back as she rejoined the other rouseabouts back at the skirting table. Not much talking went on. The thought of how close they were to finishing had them heads down, bums up and hard at it. Before too long, it was time to fill up the catching pens and the yards out back. Meanwhile the rest of the team had their lunch, which was supplied by the team cook.

Glad to escape the confined smell of wool and sheep poo for some fresh air, Izzy left Todd to press out some bales while she headed down the wooden ramp outside. She could see big, dark clouds brewing in the east and the smell of rain was strong in the breeze. Izzy made her way to the yards with Tom excitedly at her heels. She didn't have to whistle for him – he knew what came next and was ready and eager to do his bit.

Climbing over the wooden fence into the sheep yard, she headed to one of the grey weathered gates, parting the mob of sheep as she went. Tom, in the meantime, was racing around behind her, rounding them up. Opening the gate, she stepped back out of the way so Tom could push them past her through the narrow opening and into the empty pen beyond. The sheep kicked up the dusty soil as they went by and Izzy lifted a hand up to her face, wiping the dirt out of her eyes. She knew she would look a sight. The dust stuck to her sweaty face and exposed arms, which were already greasy from the lanolin in the wool.

With both her and Tom working together, it didn't take long before the last of the sheep were pushed up into the shed. She would have just enough time to get cleaned up and bolt down some lunch. Closing the gate, Izzy jumped when she heard an awful yelp. Panicking, she called out for Tom and then took off towards the agonised-sounding reply. She flew over the fence as fast as she could, her boots sending up a cloud of brown dust as she landed on the other side. Lying nearby was Tom, paralysed with pain.

'Oh, Tom! What have you done, mate?' Izzy's voice trembled. She moved her hand carefully down his back towards his legs, feeling as gently as she could.

He yelped out loudly and tried to snap at her hands to prevent her from touching what felt like broken bones in his spine. Looking around, she saw that he must have landed badly, twisting the lower half of his body on the timber and metal lying next to the yard. Tears welled up as she looked back at Tom, the pain evident in his eyes. Patting his head and rubbing his soft black ears, she tried to calm him down.

'It's okay, Tom. I know what to do. I'll be back in a minute, mate. You just stay here,' she added. He tried to follow her but his broken back caused him to howl in pain.

Izzy knew there was no other choice, as vets were scarce out here. You never left an animal to suffer. It was a rule of the land. Flat out she ran, as fast as her long legs would allow, all the way to the workshop. Nearly slamming into the tall grey cabinet, she quickly unlocked it and grabbed out her father's old .22 rifle and a couple of bullets to suit. Her feet thundered into the earth as hard as her blood beat through her veins. Her mind began to roam over memories of Tom – when she'd got him, the good times, his companionship – but she forced the thoughts away. She would need to concentrate.

She wasted no time in getting back to Tom as quickly as she could. Kneeling down alongside him, she kissed his black nose and gave him an ear rub. Tom whimpered again at her touch.

'Shh, it's okay, boy.' Izzy tried to soothe him. 'I'm sorry to have to do this to you, Tom. You've been the best mate anyone could ever have. I will always treasure our time together.' Her voice wavered as she fought to keep her emotions in control. She didn't want to lose it in front of Tom – he could always sense her moods. 'But I know this is the right thing to do. I can't watch you suffering.'

With one last hug, as gently as she could, she let him go for the last time and rose up to load the gun. 'Goodbye, Tom. I'll see you again one day and we can go round up some stray sheep.' Tears welled in her eyes, as his sad brown ones watched her every move.

Battling to keep her shaking under control, she eventually managed to load the gun, flicked off the safety catch and pointed it close to Tom's head. If he knew his time was up, he was handling it well as he lay patiently waiting for Izzy to save him from his pain. Swiping at the sweat on her brow, she took a deep breath and tried to concentrate on getting a clean shot.

She exhaled and the shot rang out, echoing over the vast land and off the corrugated shearing shed close by. Galahs rose from the nearby gum tree, squawking their protest at the sudden intrusive noise. Izzy stood there, the gun still in her hand, as tears rolled down her cheeks. She was oblivious to the sound of the approaching vehicle or the fact that the activity in the shearing shed had stopped and the shearers were silently watching. No one came to help, but Izzy didn't need it anyway. There was nothing anyone could do.

It seemed like she had stood there for an eternity before she felt a hand caress her shoulder. She didn't need to look to know it was Will.

'I was bringing back the pressure cleaner when I heard the gun shot.' He reached out, took the gun from her, and placed it up against the fence before pulling her into his strong embrace. 'I'm so sorry, Izzy. He was a good dog,' Will whispered tenderly into her hair.

After hearing this, making it seem so real, she couldn't contain herself any longer and she cried into Will's shirt. He just held her tight and kissed the top of her head.

Before long, Izzy noticed the sounds in the shed as the shearers resumed work. She felt miserable. She'd just lost the best mate she'd had. He was like Claire – someone to talk to, someone to back her up, and someone to protect her. He was the only one who understood her. Hard to believe he was just a dog. For a moment, she smiled through her tears. Will was still holding her tight and rubbing her back gently and it made her feel safe.

Pulling a hankie out of his back pocket, Will wiped away her tears before giving it to her to use. If Izzy hadn't been so heartbroken, she might have laughed. What bloke carries around a hankie these days! Nonetheless, she was grateful for it.

'I've gotta take care of Tom and get back to work, as I'm classing,' said Izzy, before sneaking a glance at Tom. She wanted to be with him, lay him to rest, but she needed to keep working so they could be finished before the rain came.

Will put his hand on her chin and tilted it up until she was looking him in the eyes. 'Don't worry. Leave Tom to me. I'll put him next to where we buried Jo last year. Bill was pretty cut up about losing his best sheepdog to a bloody snakebite. So I gave him a hand – I know where to go. You've got a shed to run. Off you go.' Will gave her another kiss on the top of her head and then gently pushed her off towards the noisy shearing shed, watching her until she disappeared.

She didn't feel like eating her lunch any more, plus she had a few fleeces of wool already piled up to be assessed. Nobody in the shed said anything to Izzy as she went back to work. There wasn't much they could say, plus they had a job to do. Todd did put his hand on her shoulder and gave it a squeeze, but that was the way it was out here. The sheep still had to be shorn.

Will arrived back nearly an hour later, and he gave her an encouraging wink as he touched her arm on his way past to help Todd load up the pile of wool into the press. She pushed herself extra hard throughout the afternoon, trying to put Tom to the back of her mind. As the last few ewes were dragged from their pen, she saw his dirty bale bag sitting in the corner of the shearing shed – empty. It had been a long time since her heart had felt so heavy.

Will had been helping out all afternoon and came to her now. 'How about leaving this for Todd and the others to finish up and I'll take you up to Tom.'

Izzy looked into Will's tender eyes and said, 'I'd like that.' She went up to Todd who was skirting a fleece on the table. 'Todd, would you mind holding the fort while I duck off for a bit. I'll be back to help bale the rest later.'

Todd scratched his grey whiskery chin. 'No sweat, boss. You take your time.'

Izzy followed Will to his ute and they sat in silence as he drove to the pet patch where Tom had been buried. A minute later, they arrived via the two-wheeled track in a section of bush with large mallee trees, smaller shrubs and Guangdong trees. There were little mounds of dirt in between the trees and scrub where previous loved pets had been buried. When they stopped, Izzy got out and paused at a section of dirt with an old wooden cross pegged into it. 'Joey' was engraved into the flaking wood, but only Izzy knew what it said – she'd carved it when she was fifteen. Joey had been her pet kangaroo and he was two years old when they found him dead, unsure of what had killed him. She followed Will towards Tom's resting place and knelt down to pick up his dog collar, which Will had left on top. Her fingers caressed the old leather with its blue and green ear tags. The blue one said Gumlea and the others had Rob's farm name, Cliffviews, on them. Tom's round metal name tag dangled from the middle. Instantly, Izzy's eyes misted up as she fingered the cold disc. She heard Will's feet shuffle backwards as he gave her some time alone. Seizing the moment, she placed her hand on the freshly turned soil and whispered her last goodbye.

'Farewell, my mate. I'm gonna miss ya, Tom.' She stood up and scrunched her hand, feeling the coarse grains of sand rub against her skin. Then reluctantly she brushed her hand on her pants, feeling like she was brushing away the last of Tom. Izzy gripped Tom's collar tightly and turned to Will. 'Let's go.'

Obligingly he wrapped his arm around her shoulders and squeezed her as they walked back to the ute in silence.

*

Cut-outs were a commonplace thing after finishing a shed and were normally noisy drunken affairs. Not tonight. Izzy sat next to Will on the solid bales and chatted quietly, drinking cold beers slowly as the stormy humidity circled around them.

Brad Jackson had to get home early because they were taking the kids away for the weekend, and the rest of the crew had wanted to head off. The Lake Grace pub had 'chase the ace' on. It was a game where one person got the chance to pick a card out of the pack and if it was the ace they won; if not, the money stacked up till the next game night. The pot was now up to five grand. It was guaranteed to be packed out with plenty of fun on offer, and that's where the shearing crew wanted to be tonight.

Giving the crew a final wave as they headed off in their little white bus, Izzy and Will found themselves alone on the floorboards near the large sliding door of the shed.

'Well, that's gotta be the cheapest cut-out we've had yet. Dad will be pleased to know Brad and his lot didn't drink all his piss!' Izzy laughed.

'Thank God for the pub, hey.' Will's extraordinary blue eyes fixed upon her, exuding warmth and sympathy. She felt caressed and melted into their depth.

'Will, thank you . . . for everything.' She reached out her hand and held his arm lightly for a moment before letting go. 'It means a lot.' She wouldn't have trusted the job to anyone else.

'It's okay, kiddo. You'll be all right.' He brushed some stray strands of hair from her face, before resting his hand on her shoulder, giving it a squeeze. He wasn't sure how long he could handle seeing her this way. It was indescribable the way the sadness in her eyes worried him. She looked so vulnerable he just wanted to wrap his arms around her and make it all better.

'Yeah, I'll be okay, I'm sure.' She gave him a reassuring, half-hearted smile.

'By the way, I came to drop off the pressure cleaner and to tell you that your folks are coming home tomorrow. Sorry it's taken me so long. They couldn't get hold of you so they rang me,' said Will, remembering why he had visited in the first place.

'Oh, great . . . not. So they finally got sick of Dad and sent him home early. There goes my freedom. Just kidding,' she added quickly, seeing Will's raised eyebrow. 'I knew they'd be home some time this week.' They both stepped out into the night sky. 'I've had my mobile with me but the reception is crap here at the shed, so I'm not surprised Mum rang you. Did she sound excited?'

'Yeah, she sounded like she couldn't wait to get off the phone and get home.'

Izzy felt her belly flip in anticipation of having her parents home again. 'Wow, look at those black clouds. Hmm, and smell that rain. God, I love that smell,' said Izzy, soaking up the fresh, moist air as it drifted past her nose.

No sooner had she said that than the heavens opened up and large drops came pelting out of the dark sky, landing on her hot skin in the warm night.

Will opened his mouth to the rain, tasting it. 'Now, that's refreshing.' He nodded towards his ute. 'You want a ride back to the house?'

Izzy watched the rain drip from his wet hair down his face to his soaked shirt. 'Nah, she's right. I think I might walk home in the wet. Thanks again, Will.' She leant over and gave him a hug. 'Catch ya later.'

She watched his tail-lights disappear into the evening, then began her walk to the house. The rain was heavy now but she didn't care. She clutched Tom's collar tightly as the drops soaked through to her skin and fresh tears mixed with the rain dribbling down her face.

20

IT rained most of the night. Izzy had enjoyed going to sleep with the pitter-patter on the tin roof, and it was still going steady into the afternoon when her folks arrived home. They'd had nearly two inches already. Good February rain.

Eagerly, Izzy opened the door into the car shed and welcomed her mum, before kissing her dad and aiding him into a waiting wheelchair.

'So, how long you gonna need this for, Dad?' said Izzy, tapping on the steel frame.

'For a while I think, sweetheart. There's still a long way to go yet. Your mum's stuck changing my dressings, the poor woman. You know she picked it up just like that, put them out of a job,' he said proudly, looking at Jean. 'She's been amazing. She's giving me the courage I need to get through this.'

Jean blushed at her husband's words of praise. She wasn't used to it, especially from him. 'I love you too, honey,' she said as she caressed Bill's face.

'Oh, get a room, you two,' Izzy said, laughing at them happily.

Jean looked seriously at Bill. 'Never mind that! He still has to take it easy. It's added a lot of stress to his body and he's not allowed to lift a finger.'

Bill rolled his eyes. 'I can't even do that,' he said, lifting his lightly bandaged hand. Soon he'd be able to take the dressings off his hands – they were only so the wounds wouldn't get infected.

Izzy began to push her dad's wheelchair through the open door of the garage. It was probably the newest thing they had around here. The old timber-framed asbestos one had blown down a few years ago on a day they'd had gale-force winds. It had been like watching a wrecking ball demolish a building, but without the ball. Luckily, the insurance had covered a new one. It even had a matching green roller door, manual operation of course – nothing too fancy out here.

Izzy spun Bill around on the spot, then tilted the wheelchair back, and slowly, carefully pulled him up the small rise to the concrete floor of the verandah. At the same time, she made a mental note to rig up some wooden ramps in the next couple of days.

'So, how was shearing? Did they get it all finished before this rain?' Bill asked.

'Yes, luckily they did. The wool . . .' Izzy was about to continue but realised what she was about to say and decided to change it slightly. 'Er . . . Will said the wool wasn't bad this year – the micron was down a bit. It's definitely an improvement on last year. It must be all Clyde's handiwork.' Clyde was their prize merino ram. Her father had splurged on him two years ago with the hope of just this result.

'That's some good news. How was Brad and his shearing team? Drink much of my grog?'

Izzy laughed. 'No, it was a quiet cut-out.' She remembered why she had felt so horrible last night and her heart sank as she thought of Tom.

'What's wrong?' Jean asked, searching her eyes for answers.

Bill quickly glanced up at his daughter, trying to see what was going on between his two girls.

'Bugger-all misses you, does it, Mum?' Izzy inhaled deeply and let it all out in a rushed blur of words. 'I had to put Tom down yesterday.' She saw their instant alarm and then their questioning expressions. 'He jumped a fence and . . . busted his back on some timber. Will buried him up near Jo in the pet patch,' she explained sadly.

The pet patch was the area where all their pets had come to rest over the years. They had been through six working dogs, four cats, a couple of pink and grey galahs and two kangaroos. And that was just in Izzy's lifetime.

'Oh, sweetheart. I'm so sorry,' said Jean. She put her arm around Izzy and gave her a squeeze.

'I thought something was missing when we arrived. He was a bloody good dog. I'm sorry you had to put him down, love.' Bill held her hand and gently squeezed her fingers as best he could. He was thankful he had taught his girls how to use a gun properly, and how to respect them as well. You never knew when you might need to kill a snake or an animal in pain. Also, there were kangaroos, foxes and rabbits that needed culling. Mind you, he didn't like Izzy using them at all now – only for emergencies. She'd first learnt with the .22 rifle on empty beer cans, and then progressed to his Winchester under and over shotgun. She was quite a good shot on a moving target. Even when she was hanging on for dear life on the back of the ute. But that was back when days were more carefree. Bill had already lost one daughter through being too blasé and he wasn't about to lose another.

Jean and Izzy collected the two black travel bags from the car and returned them to the bedroom. Izzy put her dad's on the floor and sat her mum's on the floral double bed. The room had soft blue carpet and cream walls with several blue-framed pictures: one of their wedding, ones of Claire and Izzy, and a family shot they'd had done together at Izzy's sixteenth birthday of them all piled together on a hay bale. Izzy watched as her mum began unzipping her suitcase.

'How was the trip home?' she asked.

Jean pulled out the neatly folded clothes and placed them back into the drawer in her old jarrah wardrobe. 'Long. I couldn't wait to get home. It's been ages since I've driven the car. Normally your father takes us everywhere, so you could imagine how bad my nerves were heading out of Perth. But once we hit the open road I was fine. The house is clean, Izzy. Thanks for keeping everything on track.' Jean emptied the case, then lifted the cream flounce and pushed it under the bed.

Izzy waited until she'd sat down next to her. 'No worries, but I think I lost the daylily in the pot out the front.'

'Oh, it'll come back with a bit of water. How have you been, and Will?' Jean asked with an expression of interest. 'Did I detect something between you two when I last saw you in Perth?'

'Mum!' Izzy's heart flipped and then she felt embarrassed that her mum had noticed. Was it obvious that she liked Will? She'd only just acknowledged it to herself. Izzy liked him a lot but was adult enough to deal with it, or so she told herself. But if her mum could tell . . . could Will?

Jean must have been reading her thoughts as she said, 'No one else has noticed. Your father couldn't tell. He's just happy to see the two of you at peace at last. It's given him so much strength and he's been itching to get home to see you both again.'

Izzy spoke truthfully. 'I do like him, Mum, but I'm only just figuring it out. Nothing will come of it as he might not feel the same. Besides, it's probably just a crush that will disappear in time.'

'You used to say that to me when you were fifteen and you thought he was the duck's bum. Maybe it's never left?' Jean asked.

'I don't know. He's just a great guy to be around and he's changed. I see that now so clearly. It's made him a better man.'

'And I'm sure he sees the change in you also. You've done a lot of growing yourself in the last few years.'

'You think so?'

Jean cupped Izzy's face. 'I do. You're even more beautiful than I could have hoped for and you've grown into a strong, determined young woman with the world at her feet.'

Izzy hugged her mum and held her for a minute before pulling away. 'Thanks, Ma. But do you think Dad's seen the change? I feel like he still sees me as a teenager.'

'Your father's a tough one, Izzy. He doesn't *want* to see the change, but I'm sure he knows it's happened. Speaking of your dad, we'd better go check on him. I have to watch him like a hawk now. He'll be wanting to do things he's not yet capable of.'

Bill had slowly, awkwardly and a little painfully wheeled his chair around so he was facing the sliding glass doors. Rain continued to pelt down outside, making small splashes as it hit the flat puddles on the waterlogged ground, and whooshing down the gutters full force.

'So, are we gonna need to build an ark?' Izzy's voice floated through the air with a hint of humour.

'This rain is a worry,' Bill said. 'I was watching the weather forecast this morning, and due to the cyclone up north it looks like it's going to be hanging around for a while.' His frown lines deepened. Cyclones never reached them but they always brought some wild weather.

'I was thinking of heading out to check that the sheep are on high ground, Dad,' Izzy said, trying to relax him.

Bill squinted at his daughter. 'You make sure Will is with you. I don't want you getting stuck out there in that crap. You'll probably end up bogged somewhere and it'll be dark in a few hours.'

Gee, talk about getting shot down in flames. 'Don't worry, Dad. I can manage.'

Bill stared at her hard, as if to say, '*You do as you're told or else,*' and it got the results he was after. She caved in and nodded her head obediently.

'Better still, give Will a ring and get him to come over and pick you up if he's not busy. That way I can catch up with him before you head out.'

'Sure – whatever,' Izzy said under her breath. Instead of heading out the back door she swung around and stormed off towards the phone near the kitchen, her shoulders slumped in frustration. She didn't need chauffeuring around. It was embarrassing. She felt sorry for Will too, always being dragged into their family stuff.

An hour later Bill sat propped in his wheelchair opposite Will at the dining table, the pair of them waffling on like two old women at a CWA meeting. Izzy slouched in a chair next to her dad. Her joints were rusting up and the dust was starting to settle while she waited for them to finish jabbering. She wanted to check the sheep and see the water damage. It beat listening to her dad praise Will for his efforts in keeping the farm going.

'Like I said, Bill, I didn't do that much. Izzy kept most of it going herself. She's the one who needs thanking.' Will had tried to explain things to Bill but every time he broached the subject, Bill shut him down.

'Well, it's nice that you kept her involved but you were the decision man, so thanks.' Will looked to Izzy and she nodded her head as if to say 'don't waste your breath'. His chest felt tight, like it was knotted up. How could she just sit there and let him take all the praise? If their positions were reversed, he reckoned he'd be having a fit. But Izzy was just sitting with a bored expression. She caught his stare and rolled her eyes.

Will raised his head slightly. 'What?' His tantalising mouth questioned her.

Izzy sat up and leant forward. 'You're going on like a bloody old woman. Yada, yada, yada.' Izzy snapped her fingers open and shut like an imaginary talking mouth. 'And they think women are bad,' she huffed.

Before she could finish her sentence, Will pitched the small top of his stubbie at her, causing her to smile, which lifted his spirits.

Bill intervened. 'All right, you two. Go on, get outta here. And take care. It'll be dark out soon. *But* make sure you fill me in on everything, okay. It gets bloody boring sitting in this all day.'

Izzy could see the longing in his feeble blue eyes, like an animal held in captivity.

Will went over and clapped his hand on Bill's shoulder. 'I bet it's driving you mad. Don't worry, Bill. Once the rain's finished, I plan on taking you out for a drive around the farm.'

Bill's face lit up like a kid with a fist full of lollies. 'That would be bloody lovely,' he said happily. 'Catch you two kids later then.'

With a quick wave, they were heading towards the door. Izzy was doing a great impersonation of an old lady hobbling along with a pretend walking stick. 'I'm just going to tell Ethel that the CWA meeting's over,' she teased.

Will grabbed her around the head in an armlock and ruffled up her hair with his knuckles. She squirmed beneath him, trying to land soft blows to his tight belly.

'Go and put your big gumboots on. There is a shitload of water out there already.' He gently pushed her through the doorway and onto the verandah.

The sound of the huge raindrops on the tin roof was so loud that Izzy struggled to hear the last few words he said.

21

LARGE heavy raindrops pelted the cold windscreen moments before the arm of the wipers drained it away. Izzy leant forward in the Land Cruiser and peered through the rain-splattered window. Her nose almost touched the glass and caused two little clouds of fog to appear under her nostrils. Already the water had cut through the dirt road. Endless puddles lay everywhere and were starting to gather, forming little rivers that rushed into each other. Small ripples that mimicked miniature rapids rolled on the top of the pooling water. It would be one hell of a ride for an ant, she thought. The movement and flow of the rain had cut the gravel in the road, so badly in spots that it left gaping valleys. The Land Cruiser hit one and lurched, flinging Izzy's body and slamming it against the door. She rubbed her arm slowly, not really registering the pain. The awesome sight before her was mesmerising.

'Oh, Will, look at that.' She pointed to the left of them. The fence line hung suspended in mid-air as the water churned below it, cutting away the dirt that once held the fence posts rigid. The only thing holding it up was the wire, like a spider's web, sagging slightly under the weight of the exposed wooden posts. Further up in front of them on the road lay two heavy steel gates, about two metres from where they once belonged. They lay apart as if a giant had pushed them aside. The water rushed by, unforgiving. Large slabs of grey concrete, which once were buried deep down in the earth, were now lying exposed on their sides, still tightly anchored to the gates.

Izzy shook her head. Already she was counting the days of work needed to repair the damage. They drove on in silence, too shocked to speak. Dams once nearly dry were now overflowing. They came across one dam that had a small leak through a side bank. They knew that if this rain kept up, it would blow out to a massive hole and take most of the dam bank with it. Izzy guessed the costs involved to fix it would be huge – bulldozers were not cheap.

They decided all of the sheep would be best in the paddock they were currently in, which was the closest one to the shearing shed where they'd come from yesterday. It was also the highest-lying area on the farm and close to the house, which meant it should be safe too. Luckily they didn't have to get out of the ute and drag some poor sheep out of a watery trap.

Izzy's heart went out to the lambs and ewes as they looked for protection. Their small figures stood trembling against the fence or under the trees. 'I hope it's not too much of a shock after just being shorn. Do you think they'll be okay?' Izzy asked Will.

'We'll soon find out.'

Izzy looked at him sarcastically. 'Ever the optimist, you are. How's it looking on Tarramin? Is your house okay?'

'Dad and I went out earlier and it was much the same situation as here: a few fences down, dams overflowing, gates and sheep missing. We found a heap of stubborn ewes stuck in the bottom paddock. Silly bitches wouldn't move. Here we were, soaking wet, trying to get just one of them to go the right way to get out and they wouldn't budge. And they weren't the lightest waterlogged sheep either.'

'Did you get them out?'

'Yeah. We were about to give up on them and leave 'em for dead when one just decided to grow a brain and headed out to the higher ground. The others began to follow it as if it was the Pied Piper. Weirdest thing we'd ever seen.'

'Lucky for you. Clever sheep don't come around too often,' Izzy replied.

'Tell me about it. We were that close to losing the lot.'

After checking that all the sheep were fine they headed home. It was getting late in the afternoon and already it was dark, making driving even more risky in the wet weather.

'I wonder how Dave and Melinda's house is holding up? Do you remember what it was like the last flood we had ten years ago?' Izzy said, thinking back to the devastation. Claire and Izzy had been on the back of their parents' ute when they'd headed over to Dave's place to give him a hand with some sandbags. They were amazed at the sight of the little house. It looked like it had been dumped in the middle of a small lake. Izzy had laughed at the sight of Dave's legs under water riding his motorbike, but could still remember the wet squelch of the carpet that was beyond saving. As a kid, witnessing a flood had been exciting, and they'd loved all the water. But this time was different. Izzy could see the loss and devastation through the eyes of an adult.

When they got back to her house, Izzy put on her hat and lifted up the collar on her wet weather jacket before turning to Will. 'Catch you tomorrow some time. Thanks for the ride.'

He gave her a wink in reply and watched her run towards the house, the muddy water splashing up her legs.

That night Izzy relayed all she had seen to her parents as Jean fossicked about making dinner, relishing the freedom of her own kitchen. Izzy had been prepared for their arrival and had put a roast in the oven after lunch. Jean was happily getting some vegetables together to go with it, even humming from time to time as the pots clanged and cupboards banged shut.

Her dad kept probing for every little detail. What had been damaged and had anything needed saving? He had her silently worried when he asked whether they'd seen Clyde, their randy and very expensive ram.

She'd forgotten all about him and so had Will. They'd been too preoccupied with the destruction. Dad kept Clyde and the other rams in a paddock down near the back boundary fence, which was very low lying. 'No, Dad, I'm sorry. I forgot. I'll go look for him in the morning.' She tried hard to mask the concern in her voice. The last thing she needed was Dad getting upset over this.

After dropping off Izzy, Will had driven straight to his parents' place to check in and see what was the go work-wise for tomorrow. He pulled up in front of the large sprawling homestead with its cream bricks and almost black tin roof. He walked into the backyard, a large green manicured lawn and neat rows of garden beds full of healthy roses. Walking along the paved path towards him came Brian.

'Hey, Will. I was just going to pen up the dogs. Want to join me?' Will nodded and spun around to walk with his dad. They both had on their matching blue work shorts and shirts with Tarramin embroidered on the chest. Will knew he'd be lucky if he could age as well as his father. Brian still had all his hair, though it was slightly grey now, and the lines on his face made him wise and distinguished looking. The twinkle in his eyes was his strength. Brian always said you could never pull a good bull down without a fight.

'How's it looking over on Bill's? Is he happy to be home?' Brian asked.

'Yeah, he's rapt, except he still can't get out and about much. Thought I'd take him for a drive around the place. Gumlea's looking a bit worse for wear. We're lucky we have some higher land. Even though it's not much it's still making a hell of a difference.'

'The rain is supposed to hang around for a day or two yet, so it could get worse. I must go over and see Bill. He'd probably like some farm talk.'

Will and Brian came to a large wire enclosure with an old metal water tank in the middle. It had a door cut out of it and inside were the dogs' beds, tucker bowls and self feeders.

'I reckon he'd love to see you, Dad.'

Brian scratched his head. 'I can't believe how Izzy's gone and grown up so fast – and to think she's coping over there just fine.'

'Yeah, well, Bill doesn't know the half of it.'

Brian whistled for his dogs and two kelpies and one border collie came running towards them. Jess, the collie, stopped and panted excitedly at Will's feet. He gave her an ear rub before she followed the others into the pen.

'A father doesn't like to see his little girl growing up. It was hard for me to let your sister go, but it was what she wanted. Then she got married not long after and I lost my little girl for good. It's that bit harder for Bill because he's already lost one.'

'I guess,' said Will as he watched his father slide the pin across on the gate.

'Come inside and see your mother. I'm sure she'd love you to stay for dinner.' Brian clapped Will on his shoulder. 'Looks like we might be having a quiet day tomorrow, buddy. I might send Keith off to check the stock again so you can do whatever.'

'Cheers, Dad.' As they walked back to the house in the fading light, Will couldn't help but feel lucky he had an understanding father. When the pressure was on or your back was up against the wall, Brian was always there. You couldn't ask for more.

Morning came, and with it soft showers of rain still fell intermittently. Izzy walked to the kitchen in her jeans and checked shirt, sniffing the air as she went. 'You beauty. Bacon and eggs. I'm so glad you're back. Nothing ever beats Mum's cooking.' Hungrily she leant over the breakfast bar.

'How did you manage without me?' Jean asked.

'I can cook, Mum. I just don't have the time to cook anything great. But Aunt Betty would drop over a casserole from time to time.'

'Well, go and sit down and I'll bring this over. Do you want a cuppa as well?' Jean asked her.

Izzy quickly sat in her chair. 'Sounds great. Thanks, Mum. Dad not up yet?'

'No, he's just resting in bed,' said Jean as she carried over Izzy's plate and placed it in front of her before heading back to make the tea.

Izzy was relieved to think she could get away and check on Clyde without Bill poking his nose about.

'I can't believe it rained all night as well. But it looks like it's slowed down a bit this morning,' Jean commented as she sat opposite Izzy at the table, passing Izzy her cuppa and then sipping her own.

'I know. I don't know how much more we can take,' Izzy said, and stuffed a large chunk of bacon into her mouth with relish.

Jean shook her head silently at her daughter. 'So, how has it been here all by yourself – really?' She raised her eyebrows curiously.

'It was brilliant. I could do whatever I wanted without having to fight about it with anyone,' Izzy replied softly, just in case her father could hear.

'So, just how much did Will actually do on the farm?'

Izzy looked at her mum's knowing eyes and laughed. God, she was good. 'Not much at all,' she replied with a smirk. 'Don't worry, though. I was careful. We couldn't afford to be putting anyone else on and it's not fair to keep Will busy. He has his own farm to run,' she said by way of explanation.

Jean's eyes widened before she spoke. 'Looking out for Will's best interests now, are we?' Carefully she studied her daughter's face.

'Mum!' Izzy protested in mock indignation. 'He's just a good mate, that's all.'

'Who happens to be a top bloke, owns a large farm and is gorgeous.' Jean smiled and Izzy laughed. 'You realise how wrong you were about him now, don't you? Bill has such a soft spot for him.'

'Like I hadn't noticed,' Izzy sighed heavily. 'He probably wishes he had him as a son, instead of me making his life hard.'

'Your father loves you very much, Izzy. That's why he's so protective.'

'I know, I know. It just sucks, that's all.' Putting the last bit of bacon in her mouth, Izzy rose and took her plate to the sink. 'Well, I'm off to find Clyde. Let Dad know I went to Will's first okay. Ta.'

'No worries. Take care,' replied Jean, but her daughter had already left.

22

WILL had been sitting at the table staring out of the window at the muddy ground outside, eating his breakfast, when the phone rang. He wiped his hands on his jeans and headed over to the phone, 'Hello.'

'G'day, Will. What's happening?'

'Hey, Bill. Not much. Why? What's up?' Will shifted his weight to his other leg and leant back against the wall.

'Just thought I better check up on Izzy and make sure she did actually come and see you. Knowing Izzy, she's likely to go gallivanting off looking for Clyde on her own.'

Will's house was cold and quiet, and his half-eaten piece of toast sat all alone on the large table. 'Yeah, she's here. We're just having a chat while I finish my breakfast. Did you want to talk to her?'

'No, just as long as she's with you I'll know she's in good hands. Did you have any luck with Clyde?'

'No, haven't headed out yet, sorry, Bill. We're just about to.'

'All right. I'll leave you to it then. I'll catch you later, mate.'

Will mumbled back his goodbye before hanging up the phone. Shit! What was that girl up to now? He forgot about the last of his breakfast and hurried outside. Putting on his coat and boots, he headed to his ute. Luckily he'd brought home his dad's Rodeo; being a higher ute it was the safest option. The last thing he needed was to get bogged or to ruin the motor in his ute by driving through unpredictably deep water.

A misty raincloud still hung low over the land. It felt like he had skipped a few seasons and landed in winter. For a moment, he enjoyed the feeling of the moist air on his face and the gorgeous view. It made a nice change from the dry windy heat they'd had at harvest.

He drove off towards the paddock where Bill usually kept Clyde, and soon spotted the Land Cruiser parked near the gully. He pulled up alongside and at once spotted Izzy and began laughing out loud. Her coat was off and she was desperately trying to get a rope around Clyde. With sloppy mud splattered all over her clothes and smudged on her face, she was a sight to behold.

He wasn't laughing for long, though, as he realised the predicament they were both in. Clyde was on the other side of the gully, which was normally dry but was now alive with roaring foamy water. He wasn't sure how Izzy had made it across in the first place because it was about four or five metres in width and running quite deep.

The rain had started up again and he watched as she just managed to get the rope tied around the large ram. Izzy was a mad bugger, too bloody stubborn for her own good. No doubt she was trying to prove something out here by herself.

Will got out of the ute and waved to her. 'Hi,' he yelled out. The sound of the water rushing past in the gully was quite loud so he wasn't sure if she could hear him.

Izzy lifted her head towards the faint sound and spotted Will. She waved back before kneeling next to the large merino ram and checking that the rope she'd just fastened on him wasn't too tight. It had been quite a fight, convincing Clyde that she was only trying to help. Eventually, she had managed to get him to higher ground and put the rope over his head and front legs. But now he was stuck on this small island with the rising flood waters all around. She was sure he knew he was in trouble – the fight had gone out of his eerie brown eyes.

The smell of his wet coat hung in the air as she squatted beside him. She was completely buggered and really glad to see Will. He seemed to hesitate for a moment, then threw his coat back into the ute before walking up to the edge of the gully, which was now more like a river.

Will watched the water churn past rapidly and knew that if this rain kept up, it would swallow the island that was keeping Clyde alive in just a few hours. They had to get him out. 'What's the best way across?' he yelled out to Izzy.

'Where you are is where I went through. It's about chest height at its deepest point,' she replied.

Will nodded and slowly started to walk into the rushing path of the water. He inhaled deeply as the icy water poured into his boots. At least his feet were protected from the unknown things that could be lurking below. Lots of old rusty tins and glass bottles would be swept from clumps of bush, which were used as farmers' rubbish tips. The water rose up past his knees and goosebumps made the hairs on his arms stand up. Further in he walked, fighting the force of the water that pushed against him. The bottom of the gully was rough under foot, making it hard work. The deepest part of the gully rose up and he had to stretch to keep his head above water. So much for it being shoulder height! How long had it been since Izzy had waded through? The water level began to drop as he moved up the bank to the other side.

'That wasn't as bad as I thought it would be,' he said, his wet boots squelching towards Izzy and the flinching ram.

'Yeah, but imagine doing that on the way back with a frantic ram. Not my idea of a cuppa tea.' Izzy looked up at Will curiously. 'What are you doing here, anyway?'

'Ah . . . well, you see . . . your Dad rang me up just to check that you got to my place okay,' answered Will.

'Oh, okay . . . and . . .'

'And I covered your arse, yet again. You seriously didn't think you could do this on your own, did you?' he said frankly.

'Why not? You would have done the same. Why is it when a woman does something like this it's called stupid, but if a bloke does it it's heroic?' she asked. Water dripped from Will's clothes as he stood still. No comment came from him, and she knew it wouldn't. Yes, she was well used to this male-dominated world. Izzy raised one shoulder in a half shrug. 'Well, I thought it was worth a try. We can't afford to lose this ram, Will. Besides, I can't have you babysitting me all the time now, can I? You've probably got better things to do than hold my hand.'

'Hanging out with you sure beats spending time with my dad any day. Plus, taking the piss out of you is much more fun,' Will said with a chuckle, holding out his hand to help her up.

Izzy grabbed a handful of mud before reaching up to take his hand and squishing the mud into it. Will pulled away from her, shook off the excess mud, and planted his now dirty palm right on her backside. It left a perfect brown muddy print.

Raising her eyebrows, hands on hips and a teasing smile on her lips, she said, 'Have you finished? Can we get on with what we're here for and work out how to get this stupid ram to the other side of the gully?'

Will just shook his head and smirked before checking out Clyde. 'How's he holding up?'

'Okay, I think. He's calmed down a bit,' Izzy said, as she steadied the rope, keeping Clyde still. 'When I got here there were three of them. I tried to get to Clyde first but he was being a right prick about it. The other two were easy enough. They were more than willing for me to drag them through the water in a headlock. As for Clyde, I think he's only just realised his predicament and begun to let me close.'

'I see.'

'Personally, I'd like nothing better than to see the stubborn idiot drown.'

Will patted the flinching ram on his head. 'Don't listen to her, Clyde. She's a sweet, caring girl, really.'

Together, one on either side of the ram, they walked him to the edge of the gully. They paused and watched the hypnotising water rushing past.

'So, you're the hotshot. How do you think we go about this rescue mission?' she asked, glancing up at Will.

He thought for a moment as he watched the salty foam collect on the bank. The rain was stirring up the salt from the salt lakes and land, causing the water to froth. 'I think if you go back to the other side and pull from there as I guide him through the creek, we should manage. Sound all right?'

'Yep.' Izzy handed over the rope to Will, then slowly half waded, half swam through to the other side again. After threading her end of the rope through the bull bar, using it as a pulley, she secured it around her waist so it wouldn't slip out of her wet hands.

Slowly and carefully, they guided Clyde into the water. Even larger drops began to fall as the rain got heavier. 'Bugger. That's all we need,' said Izzy, trying to blink away the rain.

Will stepped into the muddy water, pushing the uncooperative ram along with him, as Izzy tightened the rope on the other side. Inch by inch they started the slow process of getting the ram across the flooded gully.

'How ya coping?' Izzy bellowed out. Water lashed around Will's shoulders and splashed in his face. He was at the gully's deepest point. Clyde would be depending on Will to keep him afloat.

'It . . . would be . . . a shitload easier . . . if Clyde . . . would keep his friggin' legs . . . out of my . . . guts,' Will spluttered, in between gasping for air and spitting out water.

Izzy watched intently as his head bobbed just inches above the water amid the foam. The water level in the gully was rising fast. Being a natural watercourse, it was flowing in from everywhere. A panicked look came into Clyde's eyes – the hum of the water and the fact he couldn't touch the bottom were obviously freaking him out.

'You're over halfway now, Will,' Izzy shouted with encouragement.

Coarse fibres from the brown twisted rope ripped at her palms as she struggled with the combined weight of Will and Clyde. Her soaked body leant back and her boots dug deeper into the muddy earth, leaving marks as she heaved on the rope and battled to keep a good solid grip. Quickly she swiped at the rain that was streaming into her eyes before readjusting her grip. Clyde was going ballistic, making so much whitewash it was impossible to see Will. Jumping to the side with a jolt of dread, she tried to see if he was hidden behind the ram. But there was nothing above the water except for the large chunks of foam floating downstream. Will was gone!

Thudding began in her ears as her body started to react, fearing the worst. Quickly, she pulled hard on the rope, dragging Clyde towards the end of the gully. His head bobbed under water a few times, then finally he rose from the turbulent water as he found his footing. Not wanting to waste any more time, Izzy tied the rope off so Clyde wouldn't get sucked back in. She ran to the edge of the gully and her body froze with fear. Will's head had become visible, but it was floating just under the surface of the water.

'*W-i-i-i-ll*,' she screamed, lunging into the water, her eyes fixed on the back of his head.

There was nothing graceful about the way she splashed past Clyde, whose legs thrashed about like deadly swords as he struggled to climb the steep bank. A quick sting to the back of her shoulder signalled a direct hit from one of his wayward legs. But it was the least of her problems. Her waterlogged boots felt like concrete clogs as she forced her way through the rushing water. She finally reached Will and grabbed his shoulders. She tried to pull him up above the water, but he slipped out of her hands. Something held him under.

Luckily, whatever was holding him had stopped him being swept downstream. Taking a deep breath, Izzy dived below the murky water, her heart pounding out of her chest. Feeling her way down his legs to his feet, she found that his left foot was stuck below a large slimy tree root and wedged into the mud. She grabbed a handful of his jeans and yanked on his leg, trying to pull his foot free from his boot. Bubbles escaped from her mouth as she screamed with her last bit of effort. At last she felt it pull free, as if someone had let go of the other end. With his foot released, she kicked off from the bottom of the gully, pushing Will's body along with her.

The moment they broke the surface she pulled him across to the edge of the gully. It took all her strength to drag his heavy sodden body up the muddy bank. It took a few goes, as traction was impossible in the sloppy mud.

She didn't even notice that Clyde had climbed out of the gully to safety. Pushing her wet hair off her face, she leant down and checked if Will was breathing. No breath came out from his blue lips. She felt dizzy. Her numb fingers struggled to find a pulse in his neck, but finally beneath them she could feel blood pump weakly. He was still with her. Thank God.

Fumbling, she checked his airway and then carefully tilted his head back. Pressing her lips to his cold mouth, she started to breathe for him.

Oblivious to the turmoil, the rain kept falling down. It ran along the muddy drag marks, which stretched from Will's motionless body to the water's edge.

Izzy's frozen blotchy fingers shook slightly as they held Will's nose shut and she breathed for him again and again.

'Come on, damn you. Don't you bloody die on me, you bastard,' she shrieked, finally finding her voice as she pelted him in the chest. 'Will, get up,' she yelled again between breaths. 'I'm not losing you too.'

Tears rolled down her face uncontrollably, irritating her. This was not the time to be weak. Her hand on his chest felt the movement first. He began to cough and splutter into life. Relief overcame her as she helped him onto his side so the water could escape from his mouth. He coughed and groaned as she sat him up. Finally she leant him back on her chest with her legs either side of him, and he gasped for air.

To see his eyes blinking out the rain filled her with indescribable delight. Will held her hand on his chest and laid his head on her shoulder, shutting his eyes. His wet hair stuck in clumps across his face, but he still looked breathtakingly handsome.

'You're a bloody idiot, Will Timmins. You know you scared me half to death,' she said, beginning to cry without warning.

For what felt like hours, they sat in the mud and pouring rain, as water continued to rush past in the gully. Clyde stood quietly nearby, recuperating after crawling his way out, still attached to the rope.

Izzy held Will tight and muttered softly to him. 'Don't you *ever* do that to me again? You hear me?' She had never felt so scared and so out of control. Hell, to think she'd nearly lost him for good. Izzy wasn't one for praying, but she had never prayed so hard. She'd asked, 'Please bring him back, please bring him back,' over and over. And that moment, when he'd coughed . . . Oh, she'd never felt so thankful.

Slowly Izzy felt the coldness seep through her body, as the adrenaline died down and she was forced to her senses. 'Come on. Let's get you warmed up before hypothermia sets in.'

She helped him up and put his arm over her shoulder to guide him to her ute, but he had recovered well and was supporting most of his weight. Once Will was in the ute she untied Clyde, who seemed quite happy watching all the commotion, and made sure he was safe from any further danger. Leaving the ram and Will's ute behind, she drove to his house in silence, too shocked by the events to say anything. There was no way she was going to take him to her place. Her dad would have a fit. Besides, Will just needed a rest from the shock of it all. He'd be fine.

At his house, they pulled off their wet and heavy jumpers, boots and socks, leaving them on the verandah before heading inside. Izzy kept her arm around Will's waist, half trying to support him and the other half being too afraid to let him go. He pointed Izzy towards the bathroom, then pulled out a towel for her and placed it on a chair by the bath before turning around to face her.

'How are you feeling?' she asked.

'Not too bad, just cold and tired.' Will began to unbutton his shirt, normally a simple task, but too hard with his shaky hands. 'God, I can't stop sh-shaking,' he stammered. Izzy put her hands over his and gently pushed them aside.

'Here, let me.'

He just watched, exhausted, as one by one she slowly undid his buttons, her fingers cold and sluggish, but at least steady. As she finished, he gingerly pulled off his shirt, revealing a large, reddish mark on his chest below his shoulder. It just happened to resemble a ram's hoof.

'Ouch,' said Izzy, screwing up her face. She raised her hand and touched him gently just under the point of the mark, which was already beginning to bruise.

Will lifted his hands, instinctively holding her hand to his chest. The thud of his heart pulsed through her palm. His skin was tight and hard from the cold.

Will waited until Izzy lifted her head, so he knew he had her full attention. 'Thank you for saving my life, Izzy. I owe you one, big time.' He said it softly and sincerely, hoping she understood how grateful he was.

'You don't owe me anything. You saved my dad, don't forget. If anything, we're square,' Izzy said firmly. Drawing her hand away, she looked down at her feet. Her wet clothes were dripping and the water was pooling in the grooves of the tiles. 'I couldn't stand it if I lost you too,' she mumbled.

Will put his hand on her shoulder and pulled her in close against his body. Izzy nestled into his arms and rested her head against his naked chest. It felt so safe and comfortable.

'Izzy, you're bleeding.' Will brought his bloodied hand away from her shoulder. Tugging at her collar, he tried to see the cut but her shirt was too tight.

Izzy unbuttoned her shirt and gently peeled it away. 'Is it bad? I can't see a thing,' she said, craning her neck around as far as it would go. 'Here, use this.' Izzy gave Will her wet shirt.

Carefully he wiped away the blood on her shoulder to reveal a nasty gash. It was only then that Will realised that she was standing there in nothing but her wet jeans and a black bra. The water dripped from her hair, down her neck and between her breasts. He cleared his throat and tried to bring his attention back to the cut. 'It's a bit deep, but I think I have some butterfly clips left,' he said with a gravelly voice.

With that, he strode from the bathroom to where he kept the first aid kit and returned with three bandaids in his hand. His strength had come back to him in his concern for Izzy. Using a damp towel, he cleared away as much blood as he could. He hooked his little finger under the strap of her bra, moved it across her shoulder, and began to stick on the butterfly clips. It took all his effort to do the job right, especially with her so close.

'These should work a treat. They're just as good as stitches,' he mumbled.

'Cheers.' Izzy tried to get a look at his handiwork.

Leaning over her shoulder he stuck the last bandaid on and made sure the wound was closed tightly to minimise scarring. He realised how close his lips were to her smooth skin. Impulsively he leant down and kissed her shoulder just near the cut.

Will watched as Izzy's head moved towards him slightly. It was all the enticement he needed. Dragging his lips across her damp skin, he left another gentle kiss further up at the base of her neck. Slowly he breathed out, before kissing her on the soft spot below her ear. His hands, with a mind of their own, moved to her waist and pulled her closer. He nibbled on her ear before moving his full mouth across her cheek to her mouth. Briefly, he kissed her cool lips before placing a hand on her neck and raising her chin with the other. Staring into her crystal blue eyes, he waited, wondering and watching.

Then he saw it.

A smile had crept from the corner of her mouth, and her hands moved across his body. He couldn't think any more as he exploded within. Kissing her again, he was calm and gentle until she deepened it and blew his mind in the process.

Feverishly, they clung to one another. Will pulled her in tight, and ran his long fingers through her wet muddy hair. This is what he had been aching to do since the bin party. From then on he had wanted so much more. He had been holding back and now he was quickly losing any chance he had of controlling himself.

The sharp intake of air whistled through Izzy's lips. Her body was motionless, except for the radiating heat that started flowing through her skin from the spots where Will's mouth had been. They burned like the marks from a branding iron. Soon she didn't feel cold or wet any more. Those sensations were being replaced by warmth and a longing to be touched by Will again.

Izzy, throwing caution to the wind, returned Will's kisses with yearning and obsession. Her heart pounded madly against his, like the beating of drums. Reaching back, with one quick flick, she released her bra. Shrugging it off, she sent it falling to the floor.

A groan escaped Will as her soft rounded breasts pressed against his upper body. He could barely contain himself as he felt her fingers find the small trail of hair at his waist and follow it to down to the top of his jeans, where she began to unbuckle his belt.

Breaking loose from her lips, he gave her a devilish look. Hell, she was sending him totally nuts. Leaning across to the shower, he turned on the taps and soon warm misty water sprayed down into the base. He felt so tired and exhausted, but at the same time, a fire in his belly was egging him on for more. The pain in his lungs from coughing up water was soon forgotten as the desire to have Izzy increased.

Meanwhile, Izzy had already unbuttoned her jeans and shaken them off. She flicked off her wet knickers onto the pile of wet clothes on the floor and jumped under the warm water, watching and smiling as Will struggled to peel off his jeans. She took pity on his tired state, leaned out of the water and pulled them down for him, as well as his boxer shorts.

Joining her in the shower, his excitement was unmistakeable. Izzy reached up on her toes and kissed him passionately, drawing him under the water. With his renewed strength, Will pushed her against the tiles and groaned as his body melted into hers. Slowly he ravished her with his tongue. Down from her neck to her breasts, where he stopped and took delight in exploring and tasting one silky bud then the other. His tongue sent shivers down her back and she clung to his wide shoulders for support. The warm water stung their cold skin as they explored and devoured each other until the last of the mud drained away.

Will pulled Izzy away from the wall of the shower, but staggered dizzily. The warm water was forgotten – he had his own burning desires. He groaned, feeling the closeness of her whole body next to his and shuddered with pleasure as she worked her way down, exploring his body with her mouth. Then suddenly he smacked his elbow on the taps. The shower was just too small. As if reading his thoughts, Izzy turned off the water. Will wanted to pick her up and carry her out, but knew he did not have that much strength. So he held her hand and guided her towards his room.

Izzy followed him blindly to the room with dark blue walls that made his tidy room feel small, and the queen-sized bed, with its masculine stripy doona cover, very large.

Will gently laid her down and rolled her across the soft fluffy covers, still dripping wet. Then he started slowly kissing her from her bellybutton, up between her breasts to her silky neckline.

Izzy traced her fingers along his rigid muscles down his back to his narrow hips. She moaned from the sheer delight. Pulling him close, she begged him to continue.

As he moved in between her, he gazed into her eyes. She looked so sweet and delicate trapped under him – a look he wasn't used to from her. After this, there would be no turning back for him. Beads of water glistened on her smooth skin, and he itched to lick them off. He studied her, giving her the option to stop. But there was no hesitation – just a burning in her eyes as she pulled him inside her.

23

MOVING quietly, so she didn't disturb Will, Izzy slipped off the bed. She'd rested there next to him for what seemed like ages, watching the rise and dip of his chest and the way his hair fell across his forehead just above his eyes. The large bruise, which had darkened considerably, seemed out of place on his perfectly tanned skin. She wanted to run her hands over his arms and rest her head on his chest, but she didn't dare wake him. He seemed so different, so quiet and peaceful, as he slept, and she wanted the moment to last forever. She wasn't sure if she just saw him differently now, after all that had happened.

There was no denying how she felt – she was falling for him. From the moment he gasped for life after being dragged out of the gully yesterday, she knew she could no longer lie to herself. It made leaving him so much harder. What she really wanted was to wake him with her lips. Oh, but she couldn't – he needed his sleep. She knew a part of her had always loved Will, right from when she was young, but her childhood crush had grown into something more the moment she'd got to know the real Will. Claire was no longer around to dominate all his spare time, and Izzy was no longer the kid he'd done his best to avoid.

She couldn't deny the fact that Will was an amazing bloke, but what if it wasn't meant to happen? What if it was a mistake, like it had been with Claire? Now that her feelings ran so deep, she didn't know whether she could handle the rejection. How could they be friends again after that?

Reluctantly, she opened his wardrobe and pulled out one of his warm checked shirts to wear. Izzy knew it would probably be best if she wasn't here when he woke up. It would hurt too much if she had to watch him make his excuses and say that it had been a heat of the moment thing. She couldn't put herself through that, not now. Will Timmins feeling as strongly about her as she did about him? She doubted it. Izzy wasn't going to embarrass herself. It would be best to move on with a bit of dignity. If she snuck out now, it would give them enough space so that the next time they met, things would be back to normal. They could pretend it hadn't happened.

Izzy quickly pulled on a pair of track pants, which she found folded neatly on a chair, then quietly snuck out, glancing back at Will lying sprawled out on his bed. Taking a deep breath, she moved on to the bathroom to pick up her wet clothes before rushing out of his house and trying to erase the feelings the last few hours had aroused.

Tiptoeing back into her house, she hoped to avoid her parents. At least until she was in her own clothes. To her dismay, they were both sitting by the sliding door with a cup of tea and a plate of scones. They stopped chatting and looked up, their eyes full of questions.

'Izzy, you've been gone for ages. Is everything all right?' Jean probed.

'Have you been with Will all this time? What were you doing?' said Bill, twisting his body around in his wheelchair to face her.

'Yes, I have. We . . . ah . . . had a big rescue mission to save Clyde,' said Izzy, itching to get to her room and be by herself.

'What happened to your clothes?' Those hawk-like eyes of her mother never missed a thing. She watched her dad's eyes open in awareness; he'd only just realised she wasn't wearing her own clothes. Think quickly. 'Um . . . we got drenched saving Clyde and I got changed back at Will's.' She tried to make it sound light, like it was no big deal.

'Why didn't he drop you off home to change? What's going on with you two?' No doubt Jean's mind was ticking over, so the last thing Izzy needed was her face to start heating up. Luckily, her dad seemed to be struggling to understand the implications.

'I had to drive Will home. He was completely buggered. It was really serious – he nearly drowned. We were soaked to the bone after crawling through the creek.'

'What do you mean, nearly drowned? What in blue blazes were you doing?' Bill barked, fuming as he waited for answers. His complexion had changed to a brighter shade of red.

Izzy sighed. She'd hoped to avoid this.

'Clyde was stranded and we had to get him out – the gully was filling up fast. Will slipped and got stuck under the water. Not before Clyde had belted him, mind you. I managed to drag him out and got him breathing again,' Izzy rattled off quickly before taking a deep breath.

'What? Bloody hell! Is he okay?' It was all her dad could say, as he was still seething.

'Yeah, he's fine now. It was just a bit of a shock, that's all. Clyde got out okay, too. We saved him, Dad.'

'Forget the bloody ram. You could have killed yourself by the sound of it, and Will too. How many times have I told you not to get mixed up with farm work? It's too friggin' dangerous.' His voice was doubling in volume.

'Dad, I have a bigger chance of being hit by a bus than being killed doing farm work. You have to let me live my life at some stage. Being here on the family farm is what I want to do. If I do die here, at least it's where I want to be.'

'Over my dead body,' he screamed, waving his arms about. Bill had never felt so cross in all his life. To think it could have been her lying at the bottom of the gully. How could he bear to see another daughter of his dead? His little girls, both gone. It'd kill him. No, he was tough on Izzy for a reason. It was for her own good.

'Urgh.' Izzy threw up her hands and began to plead her case. 'What do you think I was doing at Rob's place? He taught me everything he knew about farming. He didn't care that I was a girl – he just treated me like any other worker. I just wish it were you, my own father, who'd have been proud enough to give me a go. If only you gave a damn about what I wanted,' Izzy finished, her cheeks flushed with anger.

Bill shook his head violently. 'Well, you don't seem to give a damn about what *I* want! I don't care what you know. There is no way in hell that you are working this farm, and that's final.'

'Well, just so you know, I have been. The last couple of months it's been all me, not Will. Me! I did it all and I bloody loved it. Can't you see that's what I want? I want to be a farmer, just like you. I bet if I had balls, you'd be there patting my back, like you do with Will.'

Bill shook his head again and Izzy thought she saw a vein pop in the side of his neck. 'Well you don't, so that's that,' Bill replied, but she knew she'd hit him hard and he'd been offended.

Izzy stared at him in disbelief. 'When Claire died you only lost one daughter, not two. I'm standing right here in front of you and you still don't see me.' Her eyes set firm on her dad's enraged face. 'Seeing as I'm not wanted here, I'll go work on another farm somewhere else, somewhere I'm valued and appreciated.'

Jean moved forward and took a protective stance in front of Izzy. 'Bill, can't you see how important this is to her? She's going to do it whether you like it or not. Bill, please, I've only just got Izzy back and you're not going to drive her away . . .' She stopped herself from adding the word 'again', just in time.

'She's not working on this farm, or anywhere else around here if I can help it,' Bill spat.

Fury erupted inside Izzy's head. She couldn't believe that he still wouldn't budge. Damn it. Well, if that's the way he was going to be, he left her with no choice. 'Fine. I'm outta here. Enjoy running the farm from your chair, Dad. You've made it crystal clear that you don't want a daughter like me.' She was already heading to her room to pack.

Randomly she threw things into her bag, still bubbling with rage, as she listened to her parents' argument continue. She'd never be able to change his mind. She must have been dreaming to think the old fart would welcome her back with open arms. Now she knew once and for all that she'd have to move on and leave this dream behind.

Storming out past her parents, she said, 'Goodbye, Mum.'

'Izzy, wait,' pleaded Jean.

Izzy stopped, standing in Will's clothes and bare feet as her mum came rushing up to hug her.

'Please don't go, love. Give him time to cool down,' she begged as she used her finger to put Izzy's loose hair back behind her ear. It was not quite dry and was starting to curl.

'It's no use, Mum. How much longer do I have to wait? I need to be out there working. I have a life to live. Men like him can't change. I was deluding myself to ever think he might.' Sighing, Izzy said, 'I'll call you when I get settled . . . somewhere.'

Tears welled up in Jean's eyes and threatened to spill. She stood with slumped shoulders in her blue fleece jumper, track pants and slippers. The pained expression on her face pulled at Izzy's heart. 'I love you, Mum. This isn't your fault, and I know you tried. But this is something I have to do,' said Izzy, giving her one last hug before turning away and heading out the back door.

Bill's wheelchair didn't move.

The rain had finally stopped as Izzy tugged on her boots and stepped outside with her bag. The clouds were still dark and gloomy, mirroring how she felt. Negotiating the muddy ground, she made her way to her faithful ute, scanning the land she so loved as she went. She made a mental picture and took a long deep breath to steel herself.

Her foot was on the pedal hard as she sped down the driveway, through the gum trees, and finally past the Gumlea sign. Izzy felt as though she was leaving some part of her heart behind, and that she wouldn't be whole again. Mud flicked off the wheels and hit the mud flaps as the ute slid over the slimy road. As she pulled out of the driveway for the final time, her mind flashed to Will. She pictured him asleep on his belly with his hair hanging over his face and the doona cover skewed at his waist exposing his taut brown back. Should she call and tell him? Would he even care? Perhaps, after everything that had happened between them, it was too soon. He didn't need to be burdened with this. He was probably still asleep anyway, the lucky bastard. She needed to talk to someone else. Automatically she turned towards her passenger seat, which was cold and empty. Tears streamed down her face. She realised she was facing this new journey on her own – without Tom, without her family, without Will, and without a clue where she was headed.

24

WILL felt like he had springs on his feet as he headed towards the Simpson house. He'd held off for a whole day before visiting Izzy. All the excitement of the day before – the ordeal at the gully, as well as his incredible afternoon with Izzy – had left him with a lot to think about. He'd woken up late that night, and after fixing himself a quick sandwich had gone straight back to bed, really wiped out. It had been strange waking and instantly feeling for Izzy, but the bed had been long cold. He could still picture her lying on her side, his cover pulled up under her arms and her hair framing her face. He realised she'd gone home, but that hadn't worried him. He knew where to find her. He just didn't want to seem too eager.

Opening the flywire door, he called out, '*Hellooo*.' Jean's voice beckoned him in.

'Oh, Will. We were going to call you,' she said, somewhat anxiously.

'Why? What's up?' Maybe he was going to get the third degree for keeping their daughter out for most of yesterday. He wondered if Izzy had said anything to Jean. Did she know already? Would she be happy?

'Have you heard from Izzy?' Jean asked.

'What?' He must have looked as confused as he felt.

'Izzy and Bill had a huge fight yesterday and now she's gone. I've tried everyone I can think of and I tried you a few times but you didn't answer. Brian hadn't seen you either.'

'Oh, I was probably out getting the ute. But she'll be back . . . won't she?' he said optimistically. As he floated down off his big white cloud, he began to notice the terror on Jean's face and the teary glaze that had crept across her eyes. It was clear that Jean had been pinning her hopes on Izzy being with him. A weird panicked sensation spread through his body and his muscles tensed. His hands balled up into fists as he tried to control himself. This was bad.

'After what happened at the gully yesterday, I assumed she'd be with you – that's why I wasn't worrying too much. I figured maybe she just didn't want you to answer your phone.' When Will shook his head, Jean continued, 'I'm sorry Will, I've been so worried about Izzy, but I must ask how you're doing? Izzy said you nearly drowned?'

'Nearly, but not quite. I'm fine now. I was just a bit tired, that's all.' Will tried to hide the anxiety in his voice.

Jean nodded in an absent-minded way, only half taking it in. 'Bill's gone and done it this time. I've no idea where she's gone and I don't think she'll be back any time soon. She was so angry. You have to talk to him, Will. He won't listen to me.' Jean's hand shook as it went to her mouth.

Will placed his hand on her shoulder and squeezed gently, trying to give her some comfort. 'Where is he?' he asked.

She pointed to the dining room. 'He's been there all day, just staring out the window.'

Leaving her behind, he headed towards Bill, his walk broken and uneven. Anger began building up inside, filling every crevice like gas before an explosion.

He got straight to the point. 'Bill, what did you say to Izzy?' he said accusingly.

'Hey, Will. How are you? I hear you saved our ram yesterday. Much appreciated, mate,' Bill said in a kind of a daze. His face was set hard like a concrete slab, avoiding the main issue.

'Don't thank me. Thank your daughter. She's the one who did

most of the work. Not to mention saved my life,' he said, putting his hand to his chest. It set off a vision of Izzy's wet mouth working its way up to his neck. He trembled momentarily. 'Bloody hell, Bill. What have you gone and done?'

Bill's battered body sat slumped in his wheelchair as if nothing had happened, but he looked as if he'd aged ten years.

'She's even left her mobile behind,' Jean volunteered, clutching the tiny silver mobile as if it was the last thing Izzy had touched.

Taking hold of the metal frame of Bill's wheelchair, Will spun him around to face them, then he went off like a pyrotechnics display. 'I never thought you'd take it this far, Bill. You're telling me you'd rather lose another daughter than spend the rest of your life working beside her? God, you're an idiot!' He took a deep breath to calm himself down before continuing.

'The way you lost Claire was just a freak accident. Nothing you could have done would've prevented it. We've talked about this before. It was her time to go. And that's life, Bill. But Izzy, she's got her whole life ahead of her, and she wants to share that with you. What the bloody hell's wrong with you?'

Bill was about to speak, his eyes wide with shock, but Will jumped in again.

'No. Just shut up and listen. You're so hell bent on trying to keep her off the farm that you haven't noticed how much it's a part of her. I've seen it first hand. Who do you think ran this place while you were in hospital? It sure wasn't me. You'll never be able to take that away from Izzy.'

Bill resembled one of the open-mouthed clowns at the fair as he shook his head in disbelief.

'And let me tell you, she's one hell of a worker. Dad and I would have her work for us any day. Any farmer in this district would. You should be bloody proud of who she is and what she's become.' Will paused for a breath. 'Don't you see? You could have it all, but you're pushing her away, hurting her and everyone else in the process.' Even me, he thought, as his body ached at the emptiness she'd left. Trying to get through to the old man was hard work. Now he understood how much Izzy had endured.

'I just couldn't stand to go through it again.' Bill finally spoke.

It was barely a whisper, but Will heard him. Bill looked small and weak slumped in his chair. For a moment, Will even felt sorry for him. He ran his hand through his hair, hoping this was a breakthrough.

'Well, what other options do you have? What if something happens to her on someone else's farm and then she's gone for good? I don't know about you, but I'd never forgive myself. I'd rather spend every moment possible with her while I could. If you would just open your eyes, you'd see how remarkable she is. Claire's gone – but you still have one incredible, smart and beautiful daughter.' Will stopped, Izzy's image plainly visible in his mind. 'You don't know what you're missing out on,' he finished passionately.

'My God, Will. You're in love with her.' Jean shocked herself with her own words. Quickly she clamped her hand over her mouth and blushed at her indiscretion.

Two pairs of eyes watched Will carefully, waiting for his reaction.

He stared out through the sliding door and felt a wave wash over him. It was as if it had cleaned away the sand in his mind and left something clearly visible. Silently, he laughed at himself as the realisation dawned. 'Maybe I am,' he replied quietly. Saying it out loud made him feel like he'd finally grown up.

All three stood quietly absorbing this new information.

Will realised he had to tell Izzy, but not knowing where she was hurt like hell.

Bill just sat there wearing a grin from ear to ear.

'What's so funny?' Will asked, anger still rippling inside him.

'You know, I always hoped that you'd marry one of my girls,

but I never thought of my little Izzy. Will, you're the closest thing I have to a son. Nothing would make me happier than to see you two together.'

Will rolled his eyes. 'Yeah, well, we still have to find her. And let's get one thing straight,' he said, pointing to Bill. 'If Izzy will have me, she can do as much farming as she wants. It's who she is, and I don't want her to change for anyone.'

Bill nodded vigorously. A sparkle had returned to his eyes. The old man suddenly looked alive again.

'You might be right, Will. I know I've shut myself off from Izzy.' He thought for a moment. 'I guess in the process I've missed out on seeing my girl grow up.'

'Let's just hope it's not too late,' Jean said. 'Hopefully she'll be back after she's calmed down a bit. Till then, all we can do is wait.'

Part Two

25

'WHICH way now?' Izzy said to herself. Closing her eyes, she felt the rumble of the ute pulse through her body as she waited for a sign. 'Come on, Claire. Help me out.'

Her hand fell off the steering wheel in her relaxed state and accidentally hit the indicator lever. When she opened her eyes, the right arrow flicked wildly as if saying 'pick me, pick me'. She didn't know if that was a sign or not, but it was as good an indication as any. 'I guess it's north, then,' she said aloud and laughed. People would think her strange if they could see her talking to herself, but she'd always talked to Tom. He'd bark back every so often just to let her know he was listening. A part of her liked to think he was still listening.

The landscape before her was wide open with stubble paddocks that met the sky, and the odd mallee tree and lots of dead weeds lining the road. Turning right, she left the road that she'd always thought of as the road home. She couldn't bear to look back. Who knew if she would ever return? The thought filled her guts with a sickness mixed with great sadness. Would she ever be happy? No beloved farm, no happy family, and especially no Will. For a short moment there, she'd dared to dream of the perfect life, but who was she trying to kid? This wasn't a fairytale. The farm would never be handed to her on a silver plate. It would've been bloody nice, though.

No, it was her life, and it was up to her to go and grab her own happy ending. It would take time, but she was sure there'd be another bit of land somewhere to keep her happy. And as for Will, well, there were always plenty more snags on the barbie – or that's what she tried to tell herself. It was up to Izzy now to turn her life around. Never say die – that's what Claire had always said. Never say die.

Throwing open the country road map on the seat beside her, she tried to figure out how far north to go. She'd slept her first night just out of town at the local tourist spot called Buckley's Breakaway. Jean used to take them to play when they were kids and they would often have their birthday parties there. It was a special place where erosion had formed spectacular white cliffs. Izzy had sat at the top among the cypress pine, blue mallet and box poison bushes, her legs hanging over the ledge, looking down into the white gullies completely lost in thought. She'd replayed the fight over and over again, remembered the anger in her dad's face, and dreamed of a different outcome. She'd decided to keep driving through the towns asking for work until she found something. Let fate run its course. But she wouldn't stop until she was far enough from home. She didn't need her dad ruining her chances of finding work. Then, last of all, when she was finally snuggled up under the canvas of her swag, she thought of Will. His vivid blue eyes and the way his whole face radiated when he smiled. She couldn't imagine a better man, one more caring but also so much fun to be around. Well, she couldn't be around him any more so she'd just have to get used to it. She wasn't sure how, but with the distance between them, it was going to make it a damn sight easier. She knew she should try to forget him – he'd probably forgotten about her – but she decided to allow herself one last night to dream of him and the feel of his strong arms around her.

The following day she turned up the volume on the Triple J CD, pulled down the sun visor, and settled back into some long-distance driving. Only this time she felt very alone.

She drove over two hours until she got to Merredin and then

spent another two hours asking around for work. After no luck, she headed further north into the heat towards Morawa. She stopped at Dowerin for the night and staked out the pub, thinking she'd ask the locals if anyone needed a farmhand. Izzy sat at the end of the long bar with her beer and saw a tall bloke wearing boots, jeans and a checked shirt approaching. She noticed his hands were stained and rough. He looked like the right sort to ask.

'G'day, mate. You a local farmer, by any chance?' she asked as he pulled out a stool.

'Yep. Name's Paul. Haven't seen you around these parts before.' Paul held out his hand and Izzy shook it.

'I'm actually looking for work. Don't know anyone chasing a farmhand, do you?'

She felt Paul's brown eyes give her the once-over as he scratched his stubbly chin and thought. 'I can't say I've heard of anyone needing a worker. But I'll go ask around for you.' Izzy watched as he headed over to another bloke and slapped him on the shoulder. They exchanged words, and even asked a few others standing by, before Paul returned. He shook his head, 'Sorry, mate. Not a job anywhere at the moment.'

Izzy hung around for a bit longer, but by ten-thirty she'd parked her ute just out of town in a parking bay and crawled back into her swag. As she lay snuggled up under the umbrella of night, looking at the Milky Way and the Southern Cross, she wondered whether she'd ever find work. Would there be any farmers out there like Rob, willing to give her a go? What would she do if she couldn't find a job? Would she end up being a barmaid or a checkout chick? Izzy shuddered at the image before rolling over in her swag.

In the morning she rose to the early squawking of magpies in nearby trees and the heat already filling the day. The land was flat around her, paddock upon paddock of leftover stubble from harvest and bare ones with sheep already moving for shade.

Izzy checked her map and decided to skip breakfast and keep going towards Morawa. It was another three and a half hours in the saddle before she got there, five if you counted the stops at the towns to inquire about work. After hunting out the local information boards and the pub for employment information, she was knackered. Morawa was a big town and Izzy felt out of place, so in the warmth of the afternoon sun, she decided to press on and soon came to a small town called Mullawoon, about four hundred and thirty kilometres from Perth. Instantly she liked its small-town feel. It had a general store, a couple of banks, some small clothes shops, a sports oval and pavilion – and most importantly a local pub. As she walked towards the red-brick two-storey pub, she could almost taste the yeasty cold beer. Izzy smiled at an old bloke with scruffy orange hair as he held the large wooden door open for her.

'G'day,' he said cheerfully.

She nodded her head in reply before entering. 'Thanks.' No wonder he's happy, she thought. He's leaving the pub with a belly full of beer. Lucky bastard.

She walked the short distance to the bar and sat on a vacant stool. It seemed pretty quiet for a late afternoon. There were a couple of young guys playing pool over in the far corner and an elderly man with a floppy cream hat just a few stools up from her. By the look of him he was settled in for the night. Pulling her wallet out from her back pocket, she fished out a ten-dollar note and laid it on the bar top.

'Hiya, love. How ya going? What can I get ya?' asked a busty barmaid, who was wearing a small white top with the words 'I like it hot' in big letters on the front. She looked about Izzy's age, had a mane of straight blonde hair, a high, almost pointed nose and a figure that wouldn't look out of place in a *Ralph* magazine.

'Just a middy, thanks,' said Izzy, as she watched the barmaid push her hair back behind her ear with a perfectly manicured nail. Izzy noticed the guys at the pool table eyeing her off. They definitely weren't here just for the beer. 'Friends of yours?' she asked. The barmaid plonked the beer in front of her, causing the white foamy head to spill over the glass.

'Don't mind them. They're harmless. Bit too young for me, but that doesn't stop them trying,' she said, winking as she placed her hand on her hip. It was a simple move that almost looked seductive. 'So, haven't seen you around these parts before. You just passing through?'

Izzy sipped the top off her beer before answering. 'Maybe. It all depends on whether I can find a job.'

'What kind of work you after? There's plenty going here. We could always use bar staff, and they need cleaners out the back in the hotel rooms.'

'Nah. Sorry, not my kind of thing. I'm actually after farm work. Know anyone who needs a farmhand? I'm Izzy, by the way.'

'Hi, Izzy. I'm Simone. Nice to meet you,' she said, shaking Izzy's outstretched hand. Simone turned and dragged over a stool, then sat down across from Izzy. 'Hey, Ned, give me a holler when you want another one,' she yelled, giving the old bloke a wave. 'Ned's one of our regulars. He's here every day, same time, on the dot.' Leaning on her elbow, she took in Izzy's short dirty nails and rough hands. 'Farm work, hey? Let me think. I know one farmer looking for a worker, but . . .' She finished by screwing up her nose.

'But what? Look, I'll take anything at the moment.'

'Well, you can try. I'll give you his number.' Simone paused, as the cogs ticked over in her brain. 'No, better yet, I'll take you out to see him if you like. It might be harder for him to knock you back if he meets you face to face. Do you think you could hang around for a bit until my shift finishes?' she asked, raising one of her perfectly sculpted eyebrows. She was a girl who took extra effort in her appearance but underneath she was still a country girl at heart.

'Hell, yeah. Especially if it could get me a job. Hey, thanks. I really appreciate it.'

'Don't thank me yet. You haven't met the guy,' Simone replied cryptically.

'You seem to know a lot about him,' Izzy said, already halfway through her beer.

'Well, I should do. He's my father.'

'Oh, I see.' This could help, Izzy thought, wondering just what she could have done to be any luckier. 'How much land does he have? Does he run sheep or cattle?'

'Buggered if I know how big it is. It's biggish, that's for sure, and he has sheep. I don't know too much about the farm. That's my brother Blake's thing, not mine. I'm quite happy to stay well away from it all,' she said, wriggling her nose as if smelling fresh sheep poo.

'Well, luckily I love it! So, what makes you think your dad won't hire me?' Izzy asked frankly.

'The fact that you're a girl would be the main thing. I've probably set a bad example. He reckons I'm useless, but the fact is I just gave up. I got sick of being told off 'cos I was stuffing it up or I was pushing the sheep the wrong way. I didn't really like it much. Anyway, a girl has better things to do,' said Simone, as she whipped out a nail file from thin air and began fiddling with her already perfect nails.

The doors behind Izzy flung open suddenly and three rowdy blokes strode in as if they owned the place. All were in shorts and thongs and had moved their sunnies to the tops of their heads. Young farmers from around the district, she figured.

'I guess the footy meeting's over. Excuse me. I'd better get ready. You might want to sit over by the window – we're about to be inundated with testosterone.' Simone nodded to the little tables and stools by the window as four more fellas burst through the door.

Grabbing her cash and her beer, Izzy retreated to the back tables and settled in just as more rowdy males entered. It was a meat market.

Izzy saw Simone talking to a tall bloke, who was in great shape, and then nodding in Izzy's direction. Ducking her head, she pretended she hadn't noticed they were talking about her, but when she lifted her head, she saw the guy was coming her way.

'Oh, no,' she groaned. The last thing she needed was male attention, especially from one as well-dressed as him. His Billabong surf shorts hugged his toned behind to perfection, his white dress shirt with silver detailed writing on the back brought out his deep tan, and every hair on his head was in its right spot. This guy definitely liked to look good.

'G'day. How you going?' he asked, before nodding towards the bar. 'Simone told me you might need some company for a few hours.' He smiled and the room just about radiated with light, but not even this fetching man could interest her heart now. It would take an eternity to forget Will, and maybe then some. She thought it was best to set this poor bloke straight and save them both the embarrassment later.

'I'm sorry, but I'm really not interested. Feel free to sit if you just want someone to talk to,' she said, half expecting him to turn away, but he just stood there with a funny expression on his face, which caused her to bumble on. 'It's not like you're not good-looking or anything. I mean, you're probably a great guy, but I've just hit a bad patch in my life right now . . .' Izzy could feel the blood rising in her cheeks as words spewed from her mouth. She really was making a mess of it.

'It's just as well that I'm not interested in you either,' he replied matter-of-factly, ignoring the flustered look on her face. 'Do you mind if I sit?'

His smooth brown chest was exposed by his unbuttoned shirt, and Izzy couldn't help but be reminded of Will. The thought held her preoccupied for a moment as the man sat down. To think just days ago she'd been nestled against Will, breathing in his scent and enjoying his warmth.

Eventually the stranger's words sank in and she looked up, startled and a little relieved. 'No, go ahead. Actually I'd enjoy some company. I'm Izzy.'

'Most people call me Mac. Nice to meet you, Izzy,' he said, shaking her hand firmly. His eyes went to her brown and callused hands. 'So, Simo said you're new in town. Where've you come from?'

'A small town south of here by about seven hundred kilometres called Pingaring.' She knew he probably wouldn't have heard of it. 'It's just past Wave Rock, near Hyden,' she added.

'Oh, yeah. I'm with you now. That's a bloody long way away. What brings you here?'

Izzy sighed and told him the truth. She'd been without company for the last couple of days and was longing to talk. 'Family problems. I'm cursed with an old-fashioned father who won't let me work on our farm. It's a long story.'

Mac watched her closely. Her eyes held so much pain and he could tell she was holding back. When Simone had asked him to keep her company, he hadn't minded helping out. Besides, he'd just spent two hours with the boys, supposedly talking about their footy club, but he'd ended up hearing more about their weekend exploits, in graphic detail. He'd had about enough of that lot. And this newcomer looked intriguing. She wasn't dressed for the pub like the girls he knew. She wore jeans, a pair of work boots and no make-up, but the most amazing thing was that the moment he'd started talking to her, he'd felt the weirdest pull and knew he'd like her straight off. Already he was entranced.

'Well, I have a couple of hours to spare. Will that be long enough? Come on, I'm all ears,' he prompted. 'It's not every day you get to meet a new person in this town.'

Mac seemed so genuine and not a bit like the blokes at the bar who were talking loudly and spilling beer on the floor already. 'You sure you wouldn't rather be with your mates?' she said as she watched the large crowd of beefy males clowning around.

Mac slowly shook his head. 'No. Believe me, I need a break from them. It gets a bit boring talking about chicks and footy all the time.' Rolling his hand he motioned for her to begin her story.

For the first time in a while, or maybe ever, Izzy completely spilled her guts. She started right back with Claire's death and ended with her hasty departure from the farm. She left nothing out. There was something about Mac that kept her talking, or maybe she just needed someone to open up to so badly and he was as good as any. He gently encouraged her with the right nods and expressions just when she needed them. Normally she wasn't one to share her problems, especially with a stranger, but he was the perfect listener. Maybe a stranger was what she needed – everyone else was too close to the problems.

'No wonder you don't want any male attention. Will sounds interesting,' he said at last with a heart-warming smile.

Almost an hour had passed and the noise level had increased dramatically. The pub was now bursting with patrons, and occasionally the boys from the bar wandered over to Mac and tried to get him to join them or hounded him about being with a girl.

'Come on, Macca. You gonna join us? Our fearless team captain.'

Mac just smiled. 'Nah, Jacko. I'm gonna see enough of you blokes during footy season. Count me out tonight.' Jacko shrugged his wide shoulders and headed back to the bar, but not before giving Izzy the once-over.

'Hey, you wanna come and sit outside, get some fresh air?' Mac asked.

'Sounds like a great idea,' Izzy replied, downing her third beer. But suddenly she began to question his motives again. After all, she hardly knew the bloke.

As they squished their way to the door, a cheer went up and the rowdy males began chanting 'Mac, Mac, Mac' as he headed outside with a gorgeous girl by his side.

'Taking her to ya ute, hey, Macca!' said one as he grinded away on an imaginary girl. 'Gunna give her a bit of this?'

Izzy turned to the bloke at the bar and pointed. 'Your fly's undone and from what I can see it's just not all there,' she said, wriggling her little finger. She saw him look down and then heard a roar of laughter as she followed Mac into the cool breeze outside.

'Burn!' said Mac laughing. 'Hell, I like you even more now.' He draped his arm over her shoulder.

Turning to Mac, still not entirely sure of him, she asked, 'Hey, you sure you're not trying to get me in the sack?'

He guided her around the corner of the pub to a seat near the back wall, and motioned for her to sit. 'No, I'm not. I'm afraid you're just not my type,' he said in almost a whisper.

'And why not?' she asked in mock indignation.

'Let's just say I think your Will sounds pretty hot.'

'Oh, I see,' answered Izzy, the penny finally dropping. 'But the blokes in there thought we were . . . so . . . They don't know, do they?' she asked.

'Hell, no, and I'd rather it stayed that way. Could you imagine if they found out their team captain was gay? You know what these guys are like. I probably wouldn't live to tell anyone.'

Mac shook his head with resignation and Izzy said, 'Maybe it's time you told me your story.'

Mac shrugged. Izzy touched his arm and said, 'It doesn't worry me one bit,' she said, giving his arm a squeeze. 'It takes a lot of guts to live with a secret, and even bigger guts to share it with someone. I'm a stranger in town who's not about to judge. Is that why you told me?'

Mac just raised his eyebrows. 'I don't really know. Maybe it's because you're an out-of-towner, but I guess I feel comfortable with you. I haven't even told my own sister. It's just nice to have a conversation with a girl who isn't trying to flirt with me. And I can already sense similarities between us. We both want things that aren't considered "normal",' Mac said, making inverted commas with his fingers in the air.

'Yeah, I guess,' said Izzy, deep in thought.

The fact that Izzy didn't appear shocked by his revelation set him at ease, given that he'd just blurted it out without thinking. He'd never seriously contemplated sharing his secret before. Not out here where blokes were blokes. It'd be lambs to the slaughter for sure. 'I hope you're planning to hang around a while, Izzy.'

'Well, I hope I can. I'm looking for a job at the moment.' Izzy thought for a second, reflecting on what Mac's life must be like. 'How do you handle it, really?' she asked.

Mac leaned back into the hard wooden seat and stretched out his long legs. He was a few inches taller than Izzy.

'I have my bad days, for sure. But I go to Perth a lot and I stay in touch with people through the Internet. It's just enough to keep me sane. I have thought about leaving once or twice, but I love the farm life and this town. I keep trying to pluck up the courage to tell my folks, but that's a scary thought. In the city homosexuality is okay, but out here I'd be looked at like I had mad cow disease or something.'

'They'd have to get used to it eventually, and those that don't aren't worth caring about,' Izzy said matter-of-factly.

'I wish everyone would be as accepting as you.' Mac leaned forward and pulled out his mobile phone from his back pocket. 'Hey, give me your number so we can keep in touch.'

Rolling her eyes, Izzy laughed. 'I'd love to, but I left my mobile at home. I kinda left in a whirlwind. But in a way it was good – I think I need some space from my family for the moment. Maybe later, when I'm happy and settled somewhere, I might give them a call, but until then, Dad can stew.'

'Well, you can always use my phone.'

Mac handed her his phone and she realised a part of her was itching to call Will. Her eyes sought out the numbers on his phone that made up Will's number. Had she not slept with him she would've called in a second, but now it felt too bizarre. She didn't know where she stood and it's not like she could go back to him with her father right next door. Maybe she should just try to forget him, her brain thought, but her heart leapt in disagreement. She closed the phone and handed it back to Mac. 'I can't do it. If I call or text Mum, then she'll probably hound you with calls so I best leave it. Maybe I'll send her a letter when I get settled.' She watched, conflicted, as Mac pocketed his mobile.

It was getting dark when Simone came out of the pub looking for her. The sun had begun to set and a vivid orange streak spread across the horizon like the stroke from a paintbrush.

'You finished already, Simone?' Izzy exclaimed. 'Crikey, time has flown,' she said to Mac.

'I didn't know if you'd still be here,' Simone said as she stopped before them. 'I see my brother has taken good care of you. At least, I hope he has!'

Izzy looked at them confused. 'Your brother? Isn't he called Blake?'

Simone nodded and Mac held out his hand. 'Blake MacDougall at your service. Sorry I didn't properly introduce myself. Didn't realise you knew my sister that well.'

'I'm taking her home. Is it all right if I travel with you?' Simone asked Izzy. 'Blake can take my car home – he got a lift into town with Jacko. Is that all right, bro?' Blake nodded in agreement.

'Okay. Well, my ute is the blue one just over there.' Izzy pointed it out.

Simone gave her a wink. 'Lucky you paced your beers, hey? I take note of all my drinkers in the pub – I'm a responsible bartender.' She brushed her hair with her fingers and smiled. 'Well, I just gotta get my wallet out of my car and then we can hit the road. All right. Be back in a tick.' Simone headed off around the corner to the staff parking area, while Izzy looked back at Blake.

'So, after all that, you're the one I need to suck up to for a job,' she said.

He scrunched his eyebrows up in confusion. 'What do you mean?'

'Simone said your dad was looking for a worker and I'm hoping it will be me. She's taking me home to meet him. I asked her for some info about the farm, but she didn't seem to know too much.'

'That's Simo for you,' laughed Blake. They were still chuckling when Simone returned.

'You ready? See ya at home, bro.'

'Yeah, thanks, Mac, or should I call you Blake? Hope to see you around,' Izzy said.

Blake leaned over and gave her a hug. 'Either one's fine, and don't worry, I'll put in a good word with Dad. Can't have my new friend leaving town now, can I? You know too many of my secrets,' he said, winking at her.

26

'CHUCK a left here,' said Simone, pointing to yet another narrow gravel road. 'So, you and Blake seemed to be getting on well.' Simone turned in her seat to face Izzy.

'Yeah. Maybe it's because we're both nuts,' Izzy joked. 'Either way, I think he's a great bloke. I still can't believe he's your brother, though.' Simone smiled warmly. She looked strikingly beautiful in the golden glow of the sun as it began to sink below the horizon. The love in her eyes for Blake brought out a serious expression, and showed Izzy another side of Simone.

'Seriously, you didn't think I would leave you alone with all those unruly footy heads, did you? I'm not that cruel. I knew Blake would look after you. He's good like that. He gets on well with all my friends.'

Izzy took her eyes off the road for a moment. 'I really appreciate all of this, Simone. I can't thank you enough.'

'It's nothing. I just hope you get the job. It would be so nice to have someone new around town.' Simone sat up straight and pointed out the window towards a house and a collection of sheds in a far paddock. It was only just visible in the fading light. 'That's Mickey's place over there. He and Blake have been best mates since they were kids. Our farm's just five k's further up the road.' Simone stared in the direction of his farm until it disappeared from view. 'But don't go left because that's old Mr Smith's place and he doesn't take kindly to new people. He's the old dotty sort that comes running out of his house firing the shot gun over your head, telling you to "piss orf".'

Izzy laughed at Simone's description as she began to slow down. A small road appeared and a farm sign stood next to the cattle grid. The paddock to her right had sheep in it; the lights from her ute picked up their eerie eyes in the dark.

'A. J. and D. L. MacDougall, Erindale, Prime SAMM stud.' Simone read it aloud. 'That's us.'

'The sign looks fairly new,' Izzy commented.

'It was made up a couple of years ago when Dad and Blake set up the SAMM stud. They hold a sale day each year,' she said proudly.

'Sounds great. I'd love to see how it all works.'

Simone pulled a face at Izzy. 'Please tell me you're kidding. Jesus, I can't believe you're actually interested in that stuff. It's just sheep.'

Izzy shrugged. 'What things do you do, then? What do you enjoy?' She was curious. What else could be better than farming, especially when you lived in a farming community?

'Well, when I'm not working at the pub, I'm at the primary school as an aide for three days a week. I love working with the kids. We have the pre-primary to year three kids all in the same room so it keeps us busy. Then I just hang out with a few friends or find a party and the odd B&S. Don't you worry. I manage to fill in my days.'

'So, a party girl, hey? Have any plans?' Izzy asked, as she saw a large homestead coming into view.

'For sure. I'd like to find a nice fella and get married. I'm twenty-three now, so soon I'd like to get off this farm and have a few kids. Don't you want that?'

'Yeah, but I'd just like to get on a farm first, then think about the rest later. Where's the best place to park?' she asked as she followed the gravel road. It was a big house – transportable, Izzy guessed, as it was raised on blocks a fraction, and had cream cladding on the outside. A warm glow showed through the windows and three sensor lights switched on when Izzy drove closer. There was no fence around the house, just a row of shrubs acting as a hedge.

Simone pointed to an empty spot in the large open shed next to the house. 'Just park in there, next to Dad's ute.'

Izzy looked to Simone after turning off the engine. 'So, is there anything I need to know about your dad before I meet him? What's he like?'

The sweet sound of Simone's laugh wasn't reassuring. 'He's usually pretty good. But like a lot of farmers, he loses his head with uncooperative sheep. His snarl is worse than his bite. Don't let him fool you. He's a softie really. He turns to mush just thinking about grandkids.'

'Great,' said Izzy, hoping he didn't mind women workers. Both girls climbed out and headed for the back verandah, past the shrubs and along a concrete slab path.

'Let's go get this over with. I still have to get back into town for tea and bed.'

'No, you don't. Either way you can stay with me.'

'What? Here?'

'No, I live in our old house with Blake. It's just up the back by the sheds. We both like our space. It beats having to answer to Mum and Dad, and they leave us alone most of the time.'

'I must admit it sounds better than another night in the back of the ute. I like sleeping under the stars as much as the next person, but it gets bloody cold at night. A nice hot shower and a bed sound great. Cheers, Simone.'

Clasping her hands together tightly, Izzy followed Simone into the house. She was trying hard not to get her hopes up, but this would be a great place to work, and she'd love to get to know Blake and Simone better. They both seemed like such lovely people and she could sense the beginnings of a special friendship between them all. It looked like a decent-sized farm, which grew similar crops to back home, and the stud was just the icing on the cake. She'd love the chance to learn more about the South African Merino Mutton.

Simone stopped by the pale brick wall and took off her shoes. A large kelpie came bounding along the paved verandah and nearly knocked Izzy from her feet.

'Down, Suzie. Sit,' growled Simone. 'Sorry, Izzy. She gets a bit excited.'

Izzy gave Suzie a pat and glanced around at the large patio. It had a big built-in barbecue up the end next to a huge wooden outdoor setting. She couldn't make out much of the garden in the dark but from the patio lights she could see lawn and garden beds edging it. 'It's a beautiful home your folks have.'

'Yeah. Dad finally gave in a few years back and built Mum a new house. She thought it was about time the farm did something for her, plus we got to move into the old one.' Simone opened the door. 'Come on in.'

She led Izzy through a large open lounge room to the kitchen and dining room at the other end. The timber-look vinyl flooring gave the house a feeling of space, and an ivory colour throughout was accented by different colours in each room. Izzy particularly liked the kitchen with its jarrah cupboards and cream benchtops. The furniture looked newish and well looked-after. The eight-seater timber dining setting was stunning. Izzy could see a woman in the kitchen stirring a pot on the stove and a large man leaning against the wall next to the fridge.

Simone started with the introductions. 'Hi, Mum. Hi, Dad. I've brought someone home to meet you. Izzy, this is my dad, Alan, and my mum, Di. This is my new friend, Izzy.' Alan was half a foot taller than Izzy and his shoulders were wide and strong. This was a man who liked to work his farm and not sit back and let his son take over, Izzy thought. His expression was gruff, helped by his rather bushy eyebrows and leathery skin.

'Hi. Isabelle Simpson. It's nice to meet you.' Izzy took hold of Alan's hand and gave it a firm shake and nodded to Di. She was short and petite and must have felt it, with her children and husband towering over her, but Izzy could tell by the strength in her blue eyes that she could handle them all easily.

'Hi, Isabelle.' She felt Alan's eyes looking over her. 'Friend of Simone's, hey? How do you two know each other?'

'Met at the pub, Dad.' Simone rolled her eyes, expecting an interrogation to follow.

She opened the fridge, helped herself to a couple of cans of beer, and then held one out for Izzy. 'So, Dad, have you found a worker yet?'

Izzy said thanks as she took the beer Simone offered and cracked it, while observing Alan. Izzy could see Blake was the spitting image of his father with the same height, eyes and strong body shape. But Alan's jaw was more firm and his brow looked as if it was set in a permanent scowl. When he spoke, it was in a low rumble, like the sound of distant thunder rolling through the sky.

'Not yet, love. I think I'll ring the agency again. I might be able to get a rent-a-Pom or a stray Kiwi, hopefully before we've started getting the tractors ready to rip up.'

Simone smiled and her eyes flashed brightly at Izzy. 'Well, look no more, Dad. Izzy here has been looking for some farm work, so I told her you might be interested.'

Alan's eyes almost squinted as he checked her out again. She could see him trying to think of a way to say no. She'd encountered that look many times before. The best way to combat it was to get in first.

'Look, I know I'm a girl, but I'm a hard worker. I've got plenty of experience both here and over east. Worked sheep most of my life and I'd love to pick your brain about your stud.' She could tell he still wasn't convinced. 'How about a week's trial? I can start straightaway, and if by the end of the week you don't think I'm good enough, we'll call it quits. What do you have to lose? It'll probably take a week or two before they can get you a lackey out here, anyway.'

She could see he was starting to come around.

'I don't know. I'll have to check with my son.'

'Check what with me?' said Blake, surprising everyone with his quiet entry.

Simone piped up. 'Whether or not to give Izzy a job.'

'Yep. I say it's a great idea. Welcome aboard.' Blake clapped Izzy on her shoulder and gave her a smile.

'But . . .' Alan looked at his son with unease.

Blake laughed. 'It's okay, Dad. Izzy and I are already like old friends, and from what I can see, I'm sure she'll be great.'

'What do you say, Mr MacDougall? Do we have a deal – please?' Izzy stood strong but her heart was in her throat. It had been a while since she'd been this nervous.

Alan scratched his stubbly chin. 'Please call me Alan, and yes, we have a deal. Welcome to Erindale.' Alan knew when he was beaten, and he really didn't have anything to lose. He took another glance at Izzy. Her work clothes, tanned skin and rough hands all indicated that she was definitely a different breed from his daughter. And he liked her determination.

They shook hands and Di asked, 'Would you all like to stay for tea?'

Simone gave Di a hug. 'No, thanks, Mum. We'll whip something up at home. We'll get Izzy settled in first.'

A wave of sadness slapped Izzy as she watched them embrace. She saw a kindness in Di's eyes that made her miss her own mum even more. 'Thanks, anyway. It was nice of you to offer. I can't believe how generous you've all been. Thank you so much, once again.' Izzy added.

Alan motioned to the dining table and Izzy pulled out a chair. 'I'll pay you what I was going to pay the rent-a-workers, and you can stay with the kids at their place. That'll be included in your wage.' Izzy listened as Alan rattled off the terms. 'I'll ask Di to get together the paperwork and pass it on to you some time this week. See you tomorrow at seven.'

'No worries.'

'Come on. We'll show you our place,' said Blake after Alan had finished his spiel.

'Nice to meet you, Izzy. We'll see you tomorrow,' said Di with a smile.

'You too. Bye.'

Two minutes later, Blake was carrying her bag as they followed Simone towards their house. It was too dark for her to see much but she could feel the closeness of trees and smell the native bushes nearby. A couple of sensor lights came on and lit up the pathway and backyard. 'I take it you don't get much time to garden,' said Izzy, as she walked past weeds that came to her knees and a lawn that was nearly a foot in height. They either didn't spend much time at home or weren't into gardening.

'No, but you must admit we're bloody great at growing weeds. Blake manages to mow the lawn every now and then, so that's a plus,' Simone said as she opened the flywire door.

'Simo does have the time. But she doesn't want to break a nail,' jeered Blake.

'That's not true! It's just that there's so much there and it would take forever. Ignore him, Izzy. Come on, I'll show you to your room.' They walked into the kitchen with its mint-coloured walls. The stove looked older than Izzy, and grease was splattered up the tiles that covered the wall behind it. The country-style kitchen also had a round dining table in the centre. Blake gave Izzy her bag as Simone took her arm and led her past the lounge room, with its worn brown carpet and old vinyl rocking chairs, down a narrow passageway with mission-brown doorways and architraves.

'This one's mine, that one's Blake's, and this can be yours. It used to be Blake's, but he's moved into Mum and Dad's old room now 'cos it's bigger. Anyway, I'll leave you to unpack. I'll just go grab you some bed sheets and a towel.'

'Thanks, Simone.' Izzy walked into a cream-coloured room. It was bare except for a double bed and a chest of drawers. She sank down onto the mattress and looked out a small window above the bed.

'I know it's not home, but I'm glad you're here, anyway,' said Blake from the doorway. 'Go on, get unpacked and we'll start dinner. I'm not a bad cook, if I may say so myself.' He sauntered off and left her to it.

Izzy unzipped her bag and placed her remaining clean clothes in the top drawer, leaving the rest in her bag. Thank God she'd found a place – she really needed to do some washing. With the unpacking done, she laid back on the bed and stared up at the ceiling. She could see a few star stickers stuck up there and smiled as she remembered the ones that had adorned Claire's old room. Tonight she'd enjoy seeing them glow. Izzy closed her eyes and began to relax. She wondered what her parents were doing. Her mum would be worrying, probably trying to find Izzy or waiting for her to call. But her dad? Well, somehow she couldn't imagine him being too upset. He was probably still fuming. Then she thought of Will. His image came to mind easily. She pictured him shirtless, his track pants hanging low off his waist, as he shuffled around his house. Would he be eating or watching TV? Or maybe he'd be lying in bed trying to picture her too? She could only hope.

27

WILL went to Bill and Jean's for a roast dinner and spent the whole time filling Bill in on the things Izzy had accomplished while he was away. Bill wanted Will to take him up to the shed at some time and show him the workbench she'd built. He found it hard to picture Izzy welding. It had come as a shock, but he was impressed. Will also passed on Izzy's dreams and plans for Gumlea that she'd shared with him over the past few months – the canola and new varieties of wheat she had it in mind to try, and the idea of introducing some better stud rams.

By the end of the night, Bill really did seem to have heard what Will was saying. In fact, he almost seemed in awe of his daughter. He'd underestimated her so much. This should have been a thrill for Will to see, but he just felt sad that Izzy had never been able to get this through to Bill herself. After a big bowl of apple pie and ice-cream, Will said as much to Bill.

'I know, Will. I see that now and you can't imagine how much it pains me. I knew she had stuff to say but I was too scared to listen. I thought all would be okay if I just stuck to my guns. I guess it just made things worse. I'm hoping she'll ring you, mate. If she'll call anyone, it'll be you.'

Will nodded, but inside he wasn't so certain. Their relationship was complicated now. He didn't know where he stood any more.

Needing time to ponder, to clear his head, he headed to his thinking spot. It was a small granite rock in the reserve between their place and Bill's, where the views were stunning. All around was the fresh smell of the scrub bush and the wet scent from the moss that clung to the rock. Long ago, it had been his and Claire's spot. Many a time they'd met up there, with a six-pack of beers each, to watch the sunset and talk. When they were under-age, they used to sneak out and drink the grog they'd pinched from their parents' beer fridge. Then they'd try and creep back home and pretend they were stone-cold sober. He was surprised that they'd never ended up lost getting back through the bush.

Will sat back in the old deck chair with its fraying canvas, and sipped his beer. There was an empty chair beside him, Claire's chair, and it sat protected from the weather by the large boulder that was half hollowed out, almost like a cave. It had a protruding lip that stuck out like a mini verandah. Over the years they'd decked the area out with a few milk crates for storage of their playing cards. They also doubled as a table when the time called. They had an old esky to keep the beers cold and some rugs and jackets to throw on when the night chill came in after the sun went down.

Will ran his hand over the inside wall of the rock and traced his finger over the question mark engraved into it. Claire's voice came to him as if he'd been talking to her yesterday.

'You know what I don't get, Will, is why everyone thinks I need to be doing something.' Claire had been sitting in his chair attacking the rock face with a pen knife they'd kept in a special hiding place.

'I don't think you need to do anything,' he'd replied.

'I know, but that's you. Dad keeps harping on about me going to uni and doing teaching or something. Says I can't just hang around the farm helping him out between my shifts at the shop.' She'd sighed and tucked her blonde hair back behind her ear. It was something she did a lot when she was deep in thought. 'What to do . . . what to do? That's the question.' She'd dug the knife in harder as she dotted the question mark.

'Well, what do you want to do, Claire Bear?'

She'd swung around to face him, knife in hand, and pulled a face that resembled someone who'd just eaten a handful of nuts, then remembered they were allergic. 'Buggered if I bloody know. Izzy's younger than me and she's already got her mind set. She's got this drive that I seem to be lacking. I'm just happy enjoying life at the moment. I'll be an old fart soon enough. May as well have fun while I can.'

'Hear, hear. I'll second that.' Will had taken a swig from his beer.

Little did they know it, but that afternoon had marked the last of their carefree life. Nearly eight weeks later, they'd met back at the rock, their friendship strained to breaking point. They'd had their share of spats over the years, but they'd always been able to mend them over a beer. This problem Will hadn't been able to fix, even with a carton of beer. Hell, he hadn't even known what the problem was.

'Are you going to explain any of this to me?' he'd demanded.

Claire had sat with her knees pulled in to her chest, her arms wrapped around them with her head resting on top. Her hair had fallen across her face like a protective blind.

'You're the one who wanted to meet, Claire.' He'd brushed her hair back from her face, exposing big blue eyes on the verge of tears. Her face had paled over the last few weeks and she looked so fragile. It worried him to see her like this. Claire was the guts and wit in their friendship, and he'd been missing that more than he could say. 'Tell me what's wrong. You haven't talked to me for weeks. That's never happened to us before, Claire. Come on. I've never told anyone about your crush on Linda's boyfriend,' he finished, trying to guess what this mood stemmed from.

'It's not that, Will,' Claire had sighed. 'If only.'

Her voice had been a whisper.

'Is this because of what happened after the party . . . where . . . you know. I thought we'd agreed it was a big mistake? I mean, even you said it was like doing it with your brother.' Claire smiled at his comment, and for a moment he'd thought she was back, until the flood of tears had followed.

'Shit, Claire. Is it really that bad?'

Once she had sniffed back her tears and wiped the rest away with her sleeve, she'd taken a big breath. 'Will . . . you're my best mate and I can't bear the thought of things changing between us. But we've stuffed things up big time. I know I've been giving you the cold shoulder —'

'You mean the large ice glacier? That's nothing I can't handle! Give me an ice pick the size of a crowbar and I'll chip it away,' he replied, trying to lighten the mood.

Claire's sweet laughter had echoed around the rock and he held on to that memory. 'I'm sorry, Will. I didn't mean to shut you out, but I couldn't come running to you this time.'

'Come on, Claire. Get it off your chest.'

And she had. She'd told him straight out and it had left him numb. 'I'm pregnant.'

Sometimes that moment seemed like so long ago, like a faded dream he'd nearly forgotten. But being back here brought the memories alive again. And now here he was again, in a different predicament with another Simpson girl. He was finding it hard to go about life without Izzy. Everything seemed so mundane – like she'd left and taken the sunlight with her. Every day he welcomed the long hours of work he did between both farms, keeping his mind busy. But some days just weren't busy enough, and he was tormented by the questions that wouldn't leave him alone. Where was she? And why hadn't she called? Did he really mean that little to her?

Leaning back in his chair, he let memories of Claire flood back. He wondered what she'd have to say about her sister. She'd always given it to him directly.

The evening air was cooling rapidly and he was nearly out of beer. It was time to head home and check the answering machine, again.

28

IZZY slept like a dead dog and woke re-energised. She now had a job and was eager to start. Not wanting to be late on her first day, she was up at five. She managed to find herself some breakfast – she'd been told to help herself to anything, as it was all included in her wage. After eating, she tidied up the kitchen and then went for a walk around the sheds. When she got back, Blake was in the kitchen with just his work pants on, making himself a cuppa.

'Morning, sunshine. What'd you do? Wet the bed?' he asked.

'Nah, just wanted to be organised. I've checked out the machinery and am getting myself familiar with everything. Simone not awake yet?'

'No, she won't be up for another hour or so. She needs her beauty sleep and I've found it best not to disturb her. Do you want a cuppa?' he asked.

'No, thanks. I had one earlier.' Izzy tapped her fingers on the kitchen bench. 'So, what's the plan for today?'

'Well . . . we're just getting the tractors ready so we can start working back tomorrow. Make the most of the moist soil from the rain we had.' Blake raised his eyebrows. 'You're an eager bloody beaver, aren't you?'

'Just want to impress your dad so he doesn't let me go at the end of the week. Plus it'll be nice to have something else to occupy my thoughts. How long you gonna be?' Izzy placed her hands on her hips.

Blake was still jiggling his tea bag in his cup. 'Ten minutes. I'll meet you up at the workshop if you like. We're working on the Case tractor that's parked there.'

'Righto, I'll see you there then.' Izzy put on her cap and headed out the door. She felt good. Nothing frustrated her more than sitting around twiddling her thumbs. She'd done enough of that these last few days.

As it turned out, Izzy ended up seeing Alan before she saw Blake. So much for him only being ten minutes. Alan had a walk that went from side to side, almost like a gorilla, and she smiled when she realised Blake did exactly the same thing. His workboots scuffed the ground as he approached. The jeans and short-sleeved shirt he wore were clean and ironed to perfection. The MacDougalls clearly took great pride in their appearance. Maybe she could take a leaf out of their book.

Alan rumbled as he walked towards her. 'An early bird, are you? Where's Blake?'

Izzy stopped sweeping the concrete and rested an elbow on the broom she'd commandeered. 'He'll be here shortly. He said we'd be working on the Case today, so I thought I'd clean up the workshop before we got started.'

Alan nodded and continued past her, but it didn't mean that her eagerness or the thorough job she'd done had escaped his eye.

Izzy bent down and patted the dog that had bounded up to her. 'Hi, Suzie.' Quickly she gave the dog a scratch before getting back to work.

Alan started a red truck that was parked in the corner of the shed, fiddled around for a bit before finally coming back to speak to Izzy.

'I can't wait around for Blake any longer. Let him know I'm taking the truck into town to get the gearbox seen to. I'll probably be gone most of the day. Can you tell him that I want the Case serviced and I'd like the bar hooked up and the points checked?' He gestured towards the wall. 'There are new points in that box – that's if you get that far. Think you can remember that?'

Izzy nodded but she felt like rolling her eyes. She could finish his list by herself before he was back with the truck. It wasn't the first time she'd prepared for seeding. But she didn't tell Alan in case he misinterpreted it as arrogance. This job meant too much. 'Sure. It won't be a problem.'

Alan climbed up into the truck without another word, backed out of the shed and roared up the driveway towards town. Black smoke trailed behind as he put his foot down.

Izzy checked her watch and then continued. She'd managed to find the oil and the right tools that they'd need by the time Blake eventually turned up.

'Ten minutes, my arse,' Izzy said as he strolled in.

'Hey, I was on the phone. My mate Mickey rang. He was chasing some welding rods. Anyway, he was just telling me he has a huge bonfire ready to light up for a party on Saturday night. And you're coming with me.'

'Why? Do you want me to shepherd off the young ladies for you?' Izzy half joked.

Blake's eyes gleamed. 'That sounds like a bloody great idea. You know, there is this one girl, Kelly, who's been trying to get her claws into me for ages. Bet my left butt cheek she'll be there. I seriously could use you.'

'Just use and abuse, don't you,' she laughed.

'Come on, Izzy. I want you to come so I can introduce you to Mickey. You'll love him. Everyone does!'

'You can stop trying to convince me. You had me at the words "bonfire" and "party".' She needed a good time out with a few ales.

'Great!' Blake looked around, noticing for the first time that things appeared different. It was tidy. 'Looks like you've been keeping busy. Where's the old man?'

Izzy pointed to the empty spot in the shed. 'He's taken the truck in to get fixed. He left us some instructions.'

Blake nodded and together they went about servicing the tractor.

Three hours later Izzy spotted Di coming towards the shed carrying a tray. She was wearing denim capri pants and a black shirt, which suited her slender frame. It was easy to see where Simone got her looks.

'You two ready for morning tea?' she asked, as she carried a freshly baked cake to the tiny table that was pushed up against the back wall of the shed.

'You bet. Is that carrot cake? Yum! Thanks, Mum,' Blake said, switching on the old white kettle while Di unloaded the cake.

Izzy watched them joking together. Di only came up to Blake's shoulders. Izzy chuckled at the thought of Di trying to tell him off while he towered over her.

Di glanced over her shoulder at Izzy. 'What would you like – tea or coffee?'

Cleaning her hands, she joined them both at the small table. 'I'll have a tea, thanks. White with one.'

'Pull up a chair, Izzy,' said Blake as he sat down. 'I'm going to try some of this cake. It looks great.' Blake handed a piece to Izzy first. 'You look like you could do with some fattening. Here, eat up.'

'Gee, thanks,' Izzy said sarcastically, but she took the cake with a smile.

Di handed out the cups and then sat down. 'So, you're settled in okay? I hope the house wasn't too messy. They're not the cleanest housemates around.'

'Ma,' Blake whined.

'No, it's great, thanks. I think I'll enjoy living with them both. It'll be nice to have some company for a change.' Izzy licked the icing off her fingers as Blake gave her a wink.

Di didn't miss it. 'You know, my Blake's an amazing man. He's sensitive and he's single.'

Blake's hands flew up in the air. 'Jesus, Mum. Give Izzy a break. She only just got here. Don't go scaring her off with that. For your info we're just friends. Besides, Izzy's in love with someone else, so give it a rest.' He turned to Izzy. 'You know, the number of times Mum has tried to set me up lately is amazing. She could start her own introduction agency.'

Di butted in. 'I'm just looking out for your best interests. I want grandchildren one day, and preferably before I'm too old to hold them.'

Izzy caught the glimmer of something sad in Blake's eyes but he hid it quickly. She knew the comment would have hurt him and it would only get worse over time. She decided to change the topic. 'Living with Blake and Simone will be like having a brother and a sister. They've already made me feel so welcome. I'm incredibly lucky to have met your family,' Izzy said to Di.

Di gave her a caring smile as she brushed back her golden hair with her fingers. 'Do you have any brothers and sisters, Izzy?' she asked.

Izzy shook her head. 'I had an older sister called Claire, but she died in an accident on the farm when I was seventeen. Nearly five years ago now.'

'Oh, I'm sorry,' Di said sincerely, reaching across to her.

Izzy held up her hand. 'It's okay.'

'That must've been hard, and you were so young. I couldn't imagine losing one of my kids.' Di looked lovingly at her son.

'Yeah, my dad didn't take it too well. He's tried to keep me in a cocoon ever since. He won't let me work our farm in case I get hurt like Claire did. That's why I'm here working for someone else.' Izzy moved the cup around in her hands before taking another sip.

'I can understand his worry. It's hard being a parent, you know. Your children never stop being your babies, no matter how old they get. I hope you don't hate him for it?' Di had sensed Izzy's resentment towards her father.

Izzy sighed as she shook her head. 'No, I don't. I know he's only trying to protect me, but it doesn't make it any easier to accept.' She drained the last of her tea and placed the cup back on the table.

'He'll come round one day,' Di reassured her.

'I hope so.'

'Well, I hope he doesn't,' said Blake, butting in. 'I want to keep you here with us. Call me selfish, but I don't care.'

Di got up and started to pack up. It wasn't until she was almost back at the house that Izzy felt free to talk.

'You should tell you parents, Blake. They're gorgeous people and they clearly love you. It might take a while for them to accept it, or it might not, but you have to give them that chance.' She held his arm to stop him walking away. 'You can't avoid it forever, you know. It will only eat you up.' She spoke from personal experience and wished that someone could have told her the same thing years ago.

'I know. But I'd just hate to see the disappointment in their eyes – or worse, disgust.' His face clouded over and creased with lines.

'Well, I'm here for support, and I'm not going anywhere, hopefully. Maybe you could start by telling Simone?' She watched the terror spread its way through his body at her suggestion. 'She probably already knows, or at least suspects,' said Izzy.

'What makes you say that? Has she said something?' said Blake quickly.

'Keep ya tits on. What I mean is you don't grow up that close to someone and not notice things. I think you'll find she won't be shocked. I mean, you've been living together for a while now. She would put things together.' Izzy could tell he was worried. 'Just carry on as normal and when you feel the time is right, sit down and have a chat with her.'

'What if she hasn't guessed and she goes ape shit?'

Izzy smiled. 'What if she doesn't? All I can say is be thankful you still have a sister.'

Blake smiled and rested his hand on her shoulder fondly. 'You know it's strange talking about it here. In Perth it doesn't bother me, but out here . . . it's like I'm in a different world. I feel like I have two lives, like I'm two different people.'

'And that's not going to change until you can start combining the two.' Izzy wiped the sweat from her forehead. 'Come on. Let's get these points changed. I don't want to be in the bad books with the boss.'

Blake laughed. 'Yeah, well, I don't want to get too much done, just in case he expects it to be like this all the time.'

'Slack arse!'

By late afternoon, the sun was sinking fast, causing long grey shadows to crawl along the land and off the nearby sheds. A cool breeze picked up, bringing with it the soft rustle of the gum leaves and the flapping of loose tin on the old shed next door.

When Alan brought the truck back, the five-in-one bin sat parked in its spot. He came and stood by Izzy, who'd been working on it. His large hands rested on his hips.

'What are you doing, and where's the tractor . . . and Blake for that matter?' Alan asked rather gruffly.

Izzy smiled, grease smudged on her brow and all over her hands. 'He's taken it down to the bottom paddock, ready for tomorrow.' She felt like laughing at the look on his face. 'We ended up having to change most of the points. He told me this motor had been playing up, so I said I'd take a look at it while he made a start in the paddock.'

'Oh.'

Izzy pointed her greasy finger at the outdated motor. 'I think I found the problem. I replaced a seal and cleaned it. I've just about got it back together to see how it goes.'

Alan watched her quietly as she went about putting the small motor back together. He didn't miss anything. He could tell from her technique that this wasn't her first time working on motors. She held a screwdriver with precision and instinctively reached for the right parts without looking. Alan hadn't seen a girl so keen or so knowledgeable. He knew of girls who liked to help move sheep and drive a tractor every now and then, but he could tell Izzy was well beyond that. He smiled, thinking what a handy wife she'd make for Blake. She could have kids *and* drive the header.

Putting down the spanner, Izzy wiped her hands on a rag and gave the rope a pull. The motor screamed into life, then soon settled down to a constant, normal rhythmic thudding. Izzy raised her eyebrows at Alan as if asking him what he thought.

'Music to my ears,' he shouted over the motor.

Izzy turned it off and began to put away the tools she'd used.

'Izzy.' When he had her full attention, he continued, 'The job's yours.' He saw the puzzled look on her face and laughed. 'I know the week's not up – hell, the day's not even up – but you've shown more nous than half the blokes I've had working for me over the years. And I want to apologise because it wasn't fair putting you on a trial. I'm man enough to admit that I didn't think a girl would be capable. So, I'm sorry.' Alan held out his hand.

Izzy grinned and shook it. 'Thank you. I appreciate it.'

'I'm just bloody impressed with what you've achieved today. You might give Blake something to aspire to, and I might actually get some work done around here!'

Izzy laughed as she watched Alan head to his truck.

Turning back, he yelled out, 'There's a beer fridge near the table. Help yourself before you head home. I'll see you in the morning.'

With a quick wave he left, leaving Izzy in high spirits. Grabbing a beer, she made her way back to Blake's place. As she walked, she breathed in the fresh evening air that swirled around her. Galahs squawked overhead in the trees and a bunch of them eating spilt grain nearby flew away. Despite feeling so happy, there was still a deep longing to be home on her own land, and closer to Will.

29

THE rest of the week flew by as Izzy got used to the MacDougalls' routines and machinery. By Saturday night, she was ready to have a good time.

'Simone, get out of the bathroom. We need to use it too.' Blake banged on the door once again.

'Yeah, all right. Hold ya flippin' horses,' came her reply.

A minute later Simone opened the door, her hair neatly styled up on top of her head and her face glowing with fresh make-up. 'He's just as bad as I am,' she said as she walked to her bedroom, passing Izzy on the way. 'God knows why a bloke needs to take so long.'

Izzy laughed. Watching their banter made her wonder what life would be like if she still had her sister around.

Simone popped her head back out of her room. 'Are you getting ready?' she asked, scrutinising what Izzy was wearing.

She ran a hand over her jeans and pulled some fluff off her long-sleeved fitted shirt. 'I am ready. I'll have you know these are my good jeans.' She saw the disapproval in Simone's eyes. 'What's it matter anyway? It'll be that bloody cold we'll all end up with jackets on!'

'You're all class, Izzy. Me – well, I'm out to impress.' Simone strutted out of her room wearing tight jeans and a gorgeous silver top with thin straps.

'So, is this for anyone in particular?'

Simone shook her head far too quickly. 'No, it's just in case. You never know when Mr Right might pop up.' With flushed cheeks she disappeared into her room again.

Izzy had been ready for a while. She'd been looking forward to the party all week. It was a great way to meet some of the locals and to help her forget things for the night.

Blake came waltzing out of the bathroom looking very handsome in jeans and a white open-necked shirt.

Izzy joined him in the small lounge room and sat down in an old rocker recliner with worn brown vinyl armrests.

Blake stood in front of her while he did up his cuffs. 'You know, Dad can't stop praising you and talking about how quickly you found that oil leak yesterday. He reckons you saved a shitload of hydraulic oil. Not to mention the damage it could have done.'

Izzy shrugged as she rocked gently. 'It's not that big a deal.'

'He doesn't think so. If you keep this up, he'll end up turfing me off the farm and handing it to you.'

'Yeah well, I like your dad. At least he acknowledges me and what I can do. It's more than I can say for my old man. Maybe we could swap farms. I'll work here and you can go help my dad.' Izzy thought of Bill and pictured him back at Gumlea stuck in his wheelchair, gazing helplessly out the window. 'I wonder how he's coping. Will must be helping him, unless he's hired a worker.' Izzy's voice faded away.

Blake squatted down, put his hands on her knees, and waited until she stopped rocking. 'If you're worried about him or the farm, why don't you give him a call, or your mum? She must be beside herself wondering where you are.'

Izzy shook her head defiantly. 'No, no, no. It's too soon. I don't want him to know how much I miss the place or how much he hurt me.'

'Sure. But why not call Will then?' Blake said, giving her a devious smile.

'*No!* How could I call him? I wouldn't know what to say.'

'Well, maybe you should think about it.' Blake stood up and held out his hand. 'Come on. Let's go. If Simo's not ready by now, we'll just leave without her.'

Simone yelled from her bedroom. 'I heard that. I'm just getting my jacket.'

Blake picked up the large esky full of drinks and headed to the door with Izzy, who paused to grab her jacket from the kitchen bench.

Simone heard the front door slam and came running from her room. 'Wait. I'm comin', I'm comin'.'

Blake got into his Hilux and started it up as Izzy and Simone both squished into the passenger seat. They sat in silence, all deep in thought.

Darkness had fallen early and it brought with it cold, moist air and the smell of freshly turned dirt from the paddock next to the house. Izzy loved that about seeding time – driving the tractor through the night, stopping for a break and being engulfed with the smell of the earth. It was a heavenly scent, one of nature's purest, and she always felt grateful to experience it. People in the city missed out on so much. The smells from restaurants and takeaway shops and pollution would never have that effect on her.

Blake interrupted her train of thought. 'I can't wait to introduce you to Mickey, Izzy. He's a top bloke and I know you'll like him. Then there's the rest of the guys from town, not to mention Mickey's brother Jacko.'

'You'll like Mickey. He's the oldest of four – two sisters and Jacko,' Simone added. 'He's down to earth, like you.'

Izzy could see the red glow of the bonfire as they followed the narrow gravel road into the farm. They swung past the farmhouse and headed towards a clearing in front of one of their machinery sheds. Light danced off the tin shed, which helped illuminate the area. Utes were parked around the bonfire a safe distance away, and dark shadowed bodies stood before the red arching flames. Izzy reckoned there were about twenty people or more.

'That's a ripper bonfire. They must've been stockpiling it for ages,' Simone said, bouncing on her seat.

Blake parked and they climbed out and headed to the fire with stubbies in hand.

Smoke was thick in the air. A couple of large gum trees near the shed towered over them. They gave the feeling that something was watching, lurking in the dark. Izzy watched the flames rise up and paused for a moment, transfixed by the twirling smoke.

'What's up?' Simone asked, when she noticed Izzy had stopped walking.

'Izzy?' Blake rested his hand on her shoulder. 'You okay?'

'What's the problem?' asked Simone.

Assuming Izzy was remembering the header fire, Blake told Simone about Bill's accident, and saw Simone's eyes bulge in shock. 'He's okay, but still badly burnt,' he explained.

'Will you be all right?' Simone asked Izzy tenderly.

'Thanks, I'll be fine. Don't worry about me.' She didn't want to tell them that she hadn't been thinking of her dad. Instead she'd been remembering the sight of Will's face through the flames at the bin party night. The events of that night had been the first telltale sign she had feelings for Will, not that she'd admitted it then. But that kiss had been something else. Her knees had lost all strength and her body had quivered. She'd been trying to savour the picture of him while it was still clear. With the memory lost, Izzy asked, 'Did anyone think to bring marshmallows?'

Blake laughed. 'No. Simo would have just eaten them all.'

'Hey, Macca, Simo. Over here,' someone shouted from over by the fire.

Blake and Simone grabbed an arm each and led Izzy over. 'Come on. That's Mickey.'

They approached a well-built man who was a fraction shorter than Izzy. He wore a blue beanie and had short black stubble across his narrow jaw. His black pearl eyes reflected the red flames dancing in front of him.

'Mickey, this is Izzy, our new recruit,' Blake said.

Izzy held out her hand. 'Nice to meet you, Mickey. I've heard a lot about you.'

Mickey laughed. 'Good things, I hope. One never knows with Blake. Simo I'd probably trust.'

'What do you mean *probably*?' Simone asked defensively.

Mickey gave her a cheeky smile before introducing Izzy to one of his sisters, Julie, who was short and solid and had a smile that made you want to hug her, and his brother, Jacko. Jacko was stocky and strong, like a roo dog – all solid and muscle.

'Gee, is the whole football club here too?' Blake asked.

Mickey shrugged. 'Who knows? Jules did most of the ringing around. I'm just here to make sure things don't get out of hand.'

Talk soon turned to the weather and farming, Izzy's favourite topics of conversation. She instantly liked Mickey. The way he greeted her as an equal and spoke to her about farming instead of assuming she wouldn't be interested. His eye contact was strong but kind. Simone was right – he seemed much older than twenty-five. Blake was the same age and appeared younger by comparison.

'So, Izzy, what do you think about GM crops? Are you for or against?' asked Mickey, shooting a question straight at her.

'Personally, I'm against genetically modified anything. Yes, it has its bonuses, like herbicide-resistant plants and crops, but I just can't get past the fact that you're messing with Mother Nature. It's like playing God. Who knows what outcomes or side effects there will be that can't be foreseen.' Mickey scratched his forehead, moving his beanie back and forth as he listened intently. 'Why? What's your take?'

Mickey smiled. 'I'm totally with you on this one. I know there have been trials of GM canola in Victoria and New South Wales, but I don't want it on my farm or even in WA.'

Jacko stood next to his brother and nodded his head. His shoulders resembled a length of four by two but the smile on his face was that of a cheeky twenty-year-old. 'Farming's turning to shit, unless you've got the big bucks to make it work. And there's not many of us that well-off. I think I'll stick to shearing,' said Jacko.

'If you like having your feet stuck up sheep arses and standing in their shit all day, then good for you, Jacko.' Blake raised his beer in a salute. 'Someone's gotta breed the sheep for you to shear and it might as well be me.'

'Good to know you'll keep me in work, MacDougall,' Jacko added cheekily. Izzy noticed Simone yawn before sculling her drink.

The temperature began to drop and everyone gradually moved closer to the fire. People were wrapped in bulky jackets and beanies, with one hand holding their drink and the other hovering towards the heat.

Simone had wandered off, bored of farm talk, and made her way around the fire catching up with friends. Blake and Izzy just stayed in the one spot, warming rotisserie-style by the flames.

Blake had his arm around Izzy's shoulder. It worked wonders in keeping the girls away, especially Kelly – plus it had the added advantage of keeping them warm. Blake was telling Izzy what a special friend Mickey had always been to him. His breath turned to fog in the cold night air. 'There was this one time when Dad got a new ute and I wasn't allowed to drive it. I was only ten at the time. Anyway, Dad was away so I took it for a test drive to check the sheep. I ended up getting bogged and it was Mickey who borrowed his dad's ute to help. It took us half the day to get it out and to clean the mud off. We laughed about it for ages. Mickey's always been the one bailing me out of trouble. He has a strong right hook too.'

Izzy studied Blake's attractive face closely. His eyebrows were full but not too bushy, and his jaw was strong with a faint dimple in his chin. Looking at his strong features made her want to touch his face and run her hand through his perfect soft hair. 'Yeah, I liked him straight off,' Izzy said, then paused in thought for a second, wondering if she dared ask the question on her mind. She decided to bite the bullet. 'Have you ever liked him as more than a mate?' she asked curiously. Mickey was good-looking and obviously a really popular guy.

Blake looked into Izzy's eyes. 'I can't believe how well you read me,' he said, then continued slowly. 'I did, long ago. There was a time when I found it hard to be around him, when I'd get insanely jealous of the girls who liked him. But I soon figured out that I had to get over it. The hardest thing was keeping it a secret. It took a lot of effort, let me tell you.'

The light from the fire flickered over his face. Izzy could only guess how difficult it must have been for him, especially with no one to share his feelings with. She leaned in and gave him a hug. Resting her head on his shoulder, she couldn't help but feel tormented. Having a firm, male body to hold made her think of Will and how much she longed for his touch.

'Hey, you two, get a room,' shouted Jacko as he staggered towards them.

'Piss off,' said Blake, laughing.

Jacko, unlike his brother, was a real shit-stirrer. He had the same black eyes and dark hair as Mickey, but a devilish look to his face.

'So, what's it like working for Blake?' Jacko asked Izzy, curiously.

Izzy smiled. 'Great. I can't wait to learn some more about the stud, though.'

Jacko looked at her oddly, then back at Blake. 'That's one weird chick you found, mate, but I bet she looks better in a work singlet than you do. If you get sick of working with Macca, you can always come and work for us.'

Blake looked at him sternly, then tried to change the subject. 'Our Jacko's a bit of a gun shearer, when he's not out pissing his talent away.'

'Hey, I'm still young and I'm enjoying it while I can. So, Izzy, if you want a real good time, you just call me. I'm right down the road.'

Blake put his hand on Jacko's chest and pushed him backwards gently. 'Piss off. This one's mine,' he said, trying to sound tough without laughing. Jacko gave them a thumbs up and headed over to a crowd of young girls.

Izzy just smiled and shook her head.

The night went quickly. The black sky was twinkling with stars and the moon was only a sliver. The air had cooled and become crisper. Even the fire had died down, and you could see over to the other side.

'Yo, bro. *Hooow's* it *haaanging*?' slurred Simone as she tottered up to them.

'Simo, you look plastered. How 'bout you take it easy?' said Blake, shaking his head.

Simone saluted. '*Suuurre* thing, boss.' She tried to give him a wink but it looked more like she was constipated.

'Hey, Mickey. I've got a *booone* to pick with *yooou*,' she yelled out before heading off in his direction.

'She'd get there five minutes faster if she could walk in a straight line,' Izzy laughed. 'Will she be okay?'

'Who knows? But she's old enough and ugly enough to look after herself.'

Izzy thought back to the last time she'd partied with her sister. Izzy had just turned sixteen and it was the first time that she'd finally been old enough to go to a party with her parents' consent. So of course she'd sneaked more drinks than she was allowed and ended up blotto. Luckily, Claire had found her passed out in a ditch and cleaned her up before any great harm was done. If she remembered correctly, it was Will who'd carried her to the car. The things siblings did and the secrets they kept for each other – any parent would be astonished to know the half of it.

'Hey, look at Kelly, Mac. D'you think she's trying to get your attention?' Izzy nodded towards a girl gyrating on the other side of the fire with her top above her head and her jugs jumping around for all to see. She laughed. 'If only she knew you'd rather see a wang.'

Blake kicked her up the bum with his boot and spilt his drink in the process. 'Now look what you made me do,' he laughed.

'Hey, looks like Reggie's ready to have her.'

Blake turned to see the evidence for himself. Trying not to laugh, he put his hands over her eyes. 'That's too disgusting for your innocent eyes.'

'No different to watching a randy old ram.' She laughed and choked, causing beer to come out her nose.

Izzy had met quite a few of the locals and it was clear that Mullawoon was just like any small town. Everyone seemed to get on and everyone knew everything about everyone else – or at least they thought they did. Most of the blokes she'd talked to had nearly finished ripping up or had started seeding by now. The talk of rain was always the hot topic at this time of year. If you could get a dollar every time the weather was mentioned, you'd sure be rich. As the evening wore on, the more the topic changed to dirty jokes and stories, usually involving pranks or nudity. Finally, most of the older locals headed home, leaving just a few stragglers around the hot coals.

'I don't know about you, Mac, but I was ready for bed ages ago. We've still got work tomorrow. Any chance we can head home?' Izzy asked as she stifled a yawn.

Blake had his beanie stretched down over his head to cover his cold ears. He rubbed his hands together, holding them over the remaining embers and trying to bring back some feeling in them. 'I'm with you there. See if you can spot Simo.'

The walked in opposite directions around the fire, saying a few goodbyes, as they tried to find Simone. Izzy was so tired she could hardly keep her eyes open. The smoke had dried them out and her bones were aching from the cold. After coming up empty, she went and joined Blake, who was talking to Mickey. 'I didn't see her. Did you, Blake?'

'Nup. Mickey, have you seen Simo?'

Mickey's face glowed like a spotlight. 'Yeah, she's passed out in the back of my ute.' He turned and led them in that direction.

Simone lay buried under a sleeping bag. It almost seemed a shame to wake her.

Mickey must have been reading their thoughts. 'How 'bout you just take my ute home and we'll swap them over later?' he said. 'Then if she wakes up, she can crawl into her own bed.'

Blake slapped Mickey on his back. 'Shit, you're not just a pretty face after all. Cheers, Mickey. I'll catch up with you later. Night.'

'Nice t'meet you, Mickey. No doubt I'll see you around,' said Izzy as she waved goodbye.

It was lucky they didn't have far to drive, otherwise Izzy was sure they both would have fallen asleep and probably ended upside down in a ditch. Blake wasn't too drunk and managed to keep the ute on the road, and no kangaroos jumped out at them in the dark.

When they got home safely, Izzy managed to strip off her jacket and jeans before crawling under the covers. She was fast asleep seconds later.

30

IZZY barely heard the alarm at five o'clock. She felt like she'd only been asleep for ten minutes. But she had to take over from Alan, who'd been driving the tractor all night. She was going to do a shift until lunchtime, then Blake would work the afternoon, giving them both half a day off – it was Sunday after all. Izzy had volunteered to do the early shift. There'd been plenty of times when they'd all shared late nights and had to show up for work the next morning. It was nothing new out here. Work hard, play hard or go home. Something like that, anyway.

As she headed out to the paddock, Izzy checked on Simone and found her still curled up in the swag on the back of Mickey's ute. Light misty dew coated everything, including her sleeping bag which was pulled up over her head. There was no way Simone would be venturing out any time soon.

Izzy drove to the paddock Alan was working in. After a moment, she spotted him and headed out over the soft mounds of freshly turned soil. He was in the middle of the paddock and he stopped the tractor when he saw her approaching.

'Morning, Izzy. How was last night?' Alan asked as he climbed down from the tractor. 'It must have been a good bonfire. I could see it from here.'

'Yeah, it was okay. I got to meet the locals and the famous Mickey – though some more sleep would have been nice.' Izzy stifled a yawn.

'I know how you feel. I struggled last night. Must be getting too old. There were a few times when I nearly nodded off, but the thought of waking up in another paddock or taking out fences kinda kept me awake. Blake would have a field day with that, not to mention the rest of the town.'

Izzy figured she must look pretty bad, and reading between the lines, she knew Alan was warning her. 'Don't worry, Alan. I'll take it easy.'

He laughed. 'There's not too much fuel left but it should see you through until Blake's session. I'll get him to fill her up when he comes over. Di might have some morning tea ready for you later, too.'

'Sounds great.' Izzy's belly gurgled at the mention of food.

Alan got in Izzy's ute and headed back to the sheds while she climbed up into the tractor. The inside of the cab was warm and the radio was blaring away. Izzy reached for a black, padded case that was sitting behind the seat and flipped open the lid. She ran her finger down the spine of Blake's collection of old tapes and picked one out. It was a compilation from the early eighties.

She popped it into the tape deck above her head and Kylie Minogue broke out in song, drowning out the thumping of the engine. She couldn't help but laugh.

Slowly she worked her way up a couple of gears to cruising speed, and then checked the plough line behind her. Just six hours to go, she thought. Sitting back, she relaxed a little. As usual when driving the tractor there wasn't much else but for her mind to wander off. Izzy soon found herself thinking of Claire. She could almost remember the smell of wattle flowers that floated in the warm spring air as she'd walked towards her big sister one day, seven years ago. Claire sat upon a large motorbike, her blonde hair draped around her open, smiling face. Her blue eyes twinkled with delight as she revved the throttle back on the motorbike.

'Come on, Izzy. We've got fuel to burn.'

Izzy laughed at her eighteen-year-old sister, whose free spirit and infectious sense of humour was intoxicating. At fifteen, Izzy looked up to Claire with awe. She never seemed to worry or get stressed about anything and what you saw was what you got. Claire was big on life and was open about everything, whereas Izzy kept her feelings close to her chest and wasn't a big risk-taker.

Izzy brushed away her brown wavy hair, threw a long leg over the back of the motorbike and put an arm around Claire's narrow waist.

'Girls, just wait there a tick.' Their mother Jean came running out through the gate from the house with a camera in her hand. Her thongs slapped as she ran and her hair bobbed at her shoulders. Her daughters had inherited her oval face, clear skin and her eyes. Their bright smiles and their stubbornness they'd got from their father – something Jean was constantly telling them.

'Smile, you two,' she said as she took aim.

Izzy leant towards Claire and hugged her tight. Her hair smelt of frangipani and was soft against her cheek. She closed her eyes for a moment and enjoyed the closeness. Soon she'd have to go back to boarding school. Izzy always missed her like mad. The motorbike rumbled impatiently underneath them as she opened her eyes and smiled.

'Say cheese,' their mother prompted.

'Cheese,' said Izzy while Claire shouted, 'Sex.'

Jean took the photo and then shook her head at Claire. 'What am I going to do with you?' she laughed. 'Okay, you can go. But take care and come back before it gets too dark. Dinner will be at six. Love you both.'

'Love you too, Mum,' they shouted back.

Izzy put her feet on the footrests and shimmied closer to Claire. She held on tightly with both arms now. She knew this would be one hell of a ride, but she trusted Claire with her life.

'Where we going, sis?' she asked.

Claire craned her head back and Izzy counted seven little freckles scattered over her nose. 'How 'bout up to the top paddock? You hanging on?' Claire reached down and gripped Izzy's hands.

Izzy rested her head on Claire's shoulder and breathed in the warm afternoon air. 'You betcha, Claire Bear!'

Izzy took a hand off the tractor's steering wheel and rubbed at her eyes, which were beginning to blur with tears. She wondered how long it would be before her memories of Claire would begin to fade. How long until she struggled to remember their times together? It scared her. She always felt bad when she realised she'd gone a few weeks without thinking of her. This year she'd planned to go to the cemetery where she was buried to sit and talk to her. She reckoned Claire would be there listening. But her body lay in the tiny Pingaring cemetery with only five other graves among the shrubs and a little gazebo, and Izzy was miles away once again. She should've made the effort to go sooner, while she was at home, but she hadn't expected to be off again so soon.

Towards the end of her shift, Izzy noticed Blake pull into the paddock and watch her finish off the corners. She swung the tractor around easily, sending the seeder bar over the last patch of unturned earth, and then headed for the gate, stopping just short of Blake. He gave her a hand getting through the gate into the next paddock.

'I think it's about time you put some new music in the tractor!' she teased.

'No way,' Blake replied with a chuckle. 'Come on, you know you loved it.'

He looked bright and well rested, which was the opposite of how she felt. 'Did Simone pull up okay?'

'Better than I thought she would. But she can't remember a thing about last night. She's a worry, that girl.' His lips parted in a wide smile. 'So we're onto the last paddock. Hopefully, it's not too dry.

There's supposed to be a front coming through some time next week if we're lucky.'

Izzy brushed a fly away from her face. 'Fingers crossed,' she nodded.

'Did Dad say if he'd ordered some more fuel? We're all out,' Blake said, raising his eyebrows.

'Yup. Truck should be here by tomorrow arvo.' Izzy held up her hand and waved. 'Anyway, I'm wasting precious relaxation time, not to mention missing the chance to stuff my face with lunch. I'll leave you and Kylie Minogue to finish the last paddock in peace.'

Blake gave her a thumbs up and climbed up into the tractor as Izzy headed to his ute.

When she got home, she found Simone busy in the kitchen. 'Wow. Are you actually making lunch?' Izzy asked in disbelief.

'Don't get too excited. It's only ham-and-cheese toasties,' said Simone as she buttered another piece of bread.

Izzy threw her jumper on her bed before joining Simone in the kitchen. 'So how are you feeling? Can't be doing too badly if you're up to making food.'

Simone's wet hair sat tied up on top of her head and she was wearing a fresh pair of jeans and a shirt. 'No, I'm feeling better. Killer headache, though. I was going to make bacon and eggs but we don't have either, so I thought I'd try a toastie. Do you want one?'

'Please. I could eat a horse.'

Simone screwed up her face. 'You look like you could do with some sleep. Have you seen the bags under your eyes? God, you look how I feel.'

'Cheers. You're so thoughtful.' Izzy threw a tea towel at her. 'I'm gonna have some lunch, do some chores, which quite frankly I have to do or else I'm gonna have to turn my knickers inside out and back to front —'

'Eew.'

'And then I might tackle the garden. If I get all that done, then I'll definitely be up for a nanna nap.'

Simone rolled her eyes. 'That sounds like a shit way to spend a Sunday.'

Izzy shrugged her shoulders. 'Not much else to do. Hey, Blake tells me you wiped out big time last night. Is it true you can't remember anything?'

Simone laughed and then stopped quickly. She held her hands to her head, a look of pain on her face. 'Oh, that hurt. Yes, if you must know. I can remember telling Dougie the time at eleven and that's about it. The rest is a mystery. Hopefully everyone else won't remember much either. I wasn't too stupid, was I?' said Simone, as doubt started to creep into her voice.

Izzy quickly took out the hot pressed toasties while Simone replaced them with two more she'd prepared.

'No, nothing out of the norm. I barely saw you all night to be honest,' Izzy said, laughing.

'Gee, thanks.'

'You did go chasing after Mickey at one stage.'

Simone looked horrified. 'Oh, God. What did I do?'

'Don't stress. I don't think you were too bad. And I reckon I caught Mickey checking you out a few times anyway.' Izzy knew that would get her full attention.

'Really? You sure?'

'Ha! I knew you liked him,' Izzy said after seeing Simone's reaction. 'Don't go pretending you don't. It's too late now,' Izzy teased between bites. 'Besides, what's wrong with liking Mickey?'

Simone stopped what she was doing and sighed heavily. 'I don't know. When I was young, I had a huge crush on him. But when Blake found out, he went ballistic and told me in no uncertain terms that I was to stay away from his best mate. He said if we got together and then broke up, it could cause all sorts of problems for everyone.

I wouldn't want to affect their friendship. Plus he told me Mickey wasn't even remotely interested.' Simone handed Izzy the tomato sauce and shrugged. 'So I gave up. It's only been in the last year that those feelings have come back, or maybe I've just realised I still like him. It's hard not to, Izzy. Mickey's not like most of the blokes around here. He's more grounded. He's looking to his future instead of pissing it up against a tree like the rest of them. He could be the one to give me a reason to bring myself into line, you know – give me something to better myself for, maybe even settle down and marry.'

'Shit, that serious, hey?' Izzy knew what she meant. She'd thought Will was wasting away his youth too. It had taken her a while to realise he'd changed. He'd turned a corner, and had become a man she could see herself with for the rest of her life. Even now she surprised herself thinking that.

So often since she'd left Pingaring she found herself with a head full of romantic thoughts about Will. She could just see him teaching young kids to ride his motorbike or drive the tractor. With Will, she saw a future, and she'd never felt that with anyone else – ever. Izzy shook her head. This was no time to dwell on it.

She rested her hand on Simone's arm. 'You're a big girl now. Why don't you go and ask him out?'

'You've got to be kidding,' she laughed. 'There's no way. I don't think Blake would be very happy about me moving in on his best mate.'

'Stuff Blake. A lot of time has passed since he warned you off. You might find he's changed since then.'

Simone's hand went to her mouth. 'I just don't think I could go and ask Mickey out.'

'Said the girl who normally waltzes up to any guy,' Izzy replied.

'But he's different. This is Mickey we're talking about. It would be too weird. I don't want to lose our friendship. That would suck, big time.'

'Sometimes these chances are worth taking.' Izzy listened to her own words and realised how ironic they were coming from her mouth. She'd tried hard to hide her feelings – not wanting to be hurt, not wanting to ruin a friendship. But, maybe what she was saying was the truth. Perhaps if she could take a risk, she might find her own happy ending?

'I suppose you're right. But I don't want to rush anything.'

Simo looked gorgeous standing there in her anxious state. Her eyes were wide with nervous energy as her fingers twirled the tips of her long blonde hair. Izzy smiled before giving her a hug for encouragement. Her figure was slender like Izzy's but Simone had the curves where it counted – a beautiful hourglass shape. Izzy pulled away and looked into her deep hazel eyes. 'Well, you know where to find me if you ever need to talk.'

Simone gave Izzy another hug and whispered out the words, 'Thanks, Izzy. Claire was so lucky to have you as a sister.'

Izzy cleared her throat. 'Come on. Let's finish lunch before it gets cold, then we can plan your strategy.'

31

JEAN sat slumped in an armchair, as sad and worn out as Will had ever seen her.

'We've called everyone we can think of and no one's heard from her. It's like she's just disappeared,' Bill said quietly. 'It's been nearly three weeks now.'

'Don't stress too much, Bill. She's a big girl who can take care of herself. You just concentrate on getting yourself better. She'll be back when she's cooled off.' Will clapped his hand on Bill's shoulder to reassure him.

'And what do we do till then?'

Will ran his fingers through his hair, which stood up for a moment before flopping back into position. He could hear the despair in Bill's voice. 'You rest and I'll get the truck fixed.' Will could see he was going to protest and stopped him. 'I've told you not to worry, Bill. I've already had a talk with Dad and he said between him and our worker, they've got Tarramin covered. He knows that without me Gumlea won't run. Dad's going to come over tomorrow to catch up and see if there is anything else we can do to help out.' Bill's hand started to rise and there was a stubborn look in his eyes. 'No buts, Bill. You just tell me what needs doing, and when it comes time to start seeding, we can sit down and go over your programs as well. We'll work together to keep things going. All right?'

Bill nodded. 'Thanks, Will. I don't know how to repay you.'

The way Bill was squirming in his wheelchair Will saw that all this didn't rest well with him. 'I know it's hard for you to sit back and watch. But if you don't let us help, who else is there?'

After clearing his throat, Bill said, 'Well, once you've got the truck up to scratch, there is the fence down by the main road to repair and maybe you could start checking over the tractor. I've got a map in the office and when you have a free day I'll mark up what's going where and which paddocks I don't want cropped.'

'Sounds like a great idea,' Jean jumped in. 'Will, does roast beef tickle your fancy? Care to join us for dinner tonight?' she asked.

Will sighed and smiled. 'Who could refuse? Thanks, that'd be great.' He bid them farewell and headed for the door.

Outside he felt the humidity thicken the air and his legs grow heavier. It had been a while since the floods but the heat kept drawing the moisture up out of the soil. That wasn't worrying him – what was worrying him was the wedding dinner he had to attend the following week for his cousin, John. It was in the city and sounded like fun, but the last thing Will felt like being was the wet mop at what should be a joyful celebratory party.

Putting it out of his mind for now, Will reached the shed and went straight for the truck. It had been having problems with the alternator and needed a really good service. The alternator turned out to be stuffed and he had a new one organised to arrive through the local mechanic in the next day or two. Until then, the truck would sit unfinished, but he completed the service of new oil and filters. His jeans were covered with smudges of grease and dust and he smelt like a diesel spill.

He saw Izzy's motorbike sitting in the corner of the shed and went over and touched the seat, wanting to be near something of hers. Sitting on it, he backed it out of the shed and kicked it into life. He rode it past his own bike parked at the front of the shed and headed home for a quick shower and a change of clothes. He pulled the throttle back hard, blowing the cobwebs from the motor and clearing his head at the same time. The rush of the wind pushed at his eyes, forcing out the moisture. It made him feel like he was shedding tears. He didn't dare take his hand off the handlebars to wipe them away as he flogged the bike along the gravel track. He pushed it to its limit – over the bumps, around the holes and past the fence posts at breakneck speed. He kept pushing till the adrenaline filled his veins and, for the first time in weeks, he began to feel alive.

He pulled up with a sideways skid near his house, dismounted and bounded inside. Instinctively he headed to the phone. Four messages flashed before him. He hit the play button and listened to two hang-ups, a message from John about the dinner, and then, finally, the call he'd been waiting for. The voice caught him mid-breath.

'Hi, Will. It's Izzy. Can you let Mum know I'm fine? I'm settled at a place and have work, so she's not to worry. Hope all's okay. Um . . . thanks . . . bye.' Damn. He hit the tabletop with his fist. He was pissed that he'd missed answering it. He pressed the play button and listened to her voice again. She didn't give any indication of where she was, and didn't leave a number. No doubt on purpose, he thought. He picked up the phone to call Jean immediately.

'Oh, thank God,' she replied when he told her the news. 'Finally. Thanks, Will. I'll go tell Bill. Let me know if you hear from her again, won't you.' The relief in Jean's voice soothed Will's own anxiety. At least Izzy was okay. That was the main thing.

After talking to Jean he went into the lounge room and sat in his favourite leather recliner and pulled the TV remote out of the side pouch on the chair. He flicked through the channels but couldn't find anything to hold his interest. He picked up the book he'd been reading from the table next to his chair, but took one look at the tiny words and knew he didn't have the concentration. Maybe he'd go and get his dog Tess and take her for a run with the motorbike. More fresh air would do him good. As he got off his chair he detoured past the answering machine and listened to Izzy's voice one more time before heading to the door where his boots were waiting.

He really needed a release. For the last two weeks or more he'd been so tightly bound up with tension. Where was Izzy? How was she? Did she miss him? Why didn't she call him? – all these thoughts and more constantly circled around in his head. Surely hearing her message should have put some of them to rest but it had only created more unanswered questions. Who was she working with and where? Why had she called him? Was it because she wanted to talk to him or was it just so she didn't have to call home in case her dad answered? Hell, he felt like his head was going to explode.

Lately the days had been coming and going and he'd flitted through them in a joyless way. Life on the farm just didn't seem so great any more without Izzy. He realised now how much he'd looked forward to seeing her, how his weeks weren't complete unless he'd spent some time with her. How was he going to survive if she never came home? Angrily he threw the boot he'd been trying to put on and it landed with a thud in a clump of agapanthus. He walked with one boot to the edge of the verandah and leaned against the post in defeat. He didn't want to think about Izzy never coming home. Without her it was as if the air was tainted – he struggled to breathe because each breath seemed to hurt. Izzy was his clean air; he needed her more than he had realised. Gumlea wouldn't be the same without her. He wouldn't be the same without her.

32

IZZY pressed the redial button again. The phone rang, then clicked as a machine answered.

'Hi. You've reached Will's place. I'm either at work or outside havin' a beer. You can leave a message and I'll get back to you when I can. Cheers.'

The sound of Will's voice had her hanging on his every word, so much so that the beep at the end of his message made her jump. You idiot, she thought as she bumbled out a quick message before hanging up. Her heart was racing. She'd decided yesterday that she'd call Will and leave a message for her mum. She knew he wouldn't be at home during the day and she could safely leave a message, whereas her mum was home all day. She wanted to avoid the questions she knew they'd be dying to ask.

Izzy turned around and surveyed the kitchen and dining area. It was Wednesday afternoon. Blake was on the tractor, she was having an early break and Simone would be just about home from school. Dishes sat piled up in the sink, and Simone's leftover bits of toast still lay on a crumb-filled plate next to the toaster, alongside the butter and Vegemite that had been left on the bench. It annoyed her that Simone was such a slob. And it was her turn on dishes today.

Grumbling under her breath, Izzy began to clear up. As she put the butter back in the fridge, she heard Simone's little hatchback pull up. Moments later, she burst into the kitchen, dumped another armload of stuff on the already full table, went straight to the fridge and pulled out a can of Coke. Izzy went to say hello but Simone silenced her with her hand as she gulped down her drink. Finally Simone stopped, pulled out a chair and sat down.

'Sorry. So knackered. Who would have thought running around after fifteen little kids could be so bloody tiring?'

'That good, hey?' Izzy turned her back to her and began running dishwashing water in the sink.

'Leave them, Izzy. I just didn't get time this morning. I was running late.'

'How can you run late when you don't start work till eight-thirty? Blake and I get up at five-thirty so we can get our jobs done before we go to work at six-thirty.' Izzy tried to keep the gruffness out of her voice.

'Yeah, but you two are weird. No one should have to get up that early. It's not normal.'

'Don't forget it's your turn to cook.'

Simone slapped her forehead. 'Ah, shit. I forgot to take out the sausages this morning. Oh well, that's why we have microwaves. I'm just gonna make a sausage casserole. Sound okay?'

'Yep. Well, I'll leave you to your chores then. I've got a load of washing to put through. Oh and I've added washing powder to the shopping list.'

'Oh, my washing's still in there from this morning. Would you mind hanging it up for me while I do the dishes . . . please?' she begged, flashing a winning smile.

'Sure,' said Izzy sighing as she headed to the small laundry. She liked Simone a lot but gee, was she disorganised.

March had been and gone and they were into April already as Izzy settled into life on Erindale. She couldn't believe she'd been there a month and a half already. She now knew all the paddocks from boundary to boundary and was impressed with the red sandy loam soils. She wondered if she'd still be there at harvest. They had finished ripping up and now Alan wanted them to concentrate on his stud rams for their on-farm sale in two weeks.

'So, chook, you coming into the pub for a Saturday night drink?' Simone asked Izzy, as she sat next to her on the couch. 'Come on. You promised you'd have a drink with me. I had a hard week at school, what with Janice leaving to have her baby, and we've been through three different relief teachers all with their own routines. I tell ya, I don't know whether I'm Arthur or Martha.'

Izzy sank back into the couch and half listened to Simone's ramblings. She put up her feet on the coffee table. 'Yeah, I did promise, didn't I? Well, then, I guess we are. Shall we stay for dinner?'

'Sounds like a plan. I don't think I could handle another one of Blake's specialty meals. One can only eat spag bol so many times. Now, seeing as that's sorted, I'd better jump in the shower.' She gave Izzy a smile before skipping off to her bedroom.

Izzy heard the water hitting the tiles as she headed to Blake's room. She knocked on his door and then carefully opened it.

'Hey, Blake, you wanna come to the pub tonight with us for a drink and a feed?' Blake was sitting in front of his computer screen. For a moment, she wasn't sure whether he had heard her. 'Blake?'

'What's Simo doing?' he asked, without taking his eyes off the screen.

'She's in the shower.'

'Good. Come in and shut the door,' he said, finally turning around.

'What ya doin'?'

'Don't tell Simo, but I've been messaging this guy I met in a chat room.'

Izzy saw the excitement on his face and raised her eyebrows. 'How long's this been going on?'

Blake smiled. 'We started talking a couple of months ago and now we talk nearly every night.'

'So, you like this fella, then? What's he like? Come on, tell me all about him.'

Blake breathed slowly. He wasn't even remotely fazed about talking openly to Izzy. 'Well, he's also a country boy. He works on a farm near Katanning with his two brothers. Izzy, we have so much in common, it's amazing.'

Izzy couldn't help smiling at the joy radiating from Blake as he spoke. 'Do you have a picture?'

Blake clicked a few buttons and brought up a photo of a bloke standing in front of a large tractor. 'His name's Dean. He's a good-looker, even if he is shorter than me by an inch or two. But check out his muscles. I'd love to see him without the shirt.'

'So would I,' Izzy added, then laughed as Blake shot her a dirty look.

Blake clicked back to his messages. 'He wants to meet me in Perth next weekend – it's almost the halfway point for both of us. What do you think?'

'I don't know, Mac. It's up to you. Do you think he's for real?' she asked. She didn't want Blake to be disappointed.

'Oh, yeah. I feel like I know him well enough to trust him.'

Izzy rubbed his shoulder, trying to loosen his clenched muscles. 'Well, maybe you should go and meet him, then.'

'But how would it work, Izzy? If we did start a relationship, I'd be driving over four hours to Perth just to catch up, and I'd be leading a double life.' Blake sighed heavily and his shoulders sagged.

'Just take one step at a time. Go and meet him, then deal with the rest later.'

Blake looked up at her, like a puppy begging for a treat. 'Will you come with me?'

'For company or to hold your hand and protect you in case he's a loony?'

'Both.' He winked before turning back to reply to Dean. 'I'll see if he's free next weekend. I don't think Dad would mind us taking the weekend off. We haven't had much of a break since we've been ripping up.'

'Sounds good. Well, I'll leave you to it. I'd better go and get ready or Simone will be waiting for me, for a change.'

'I'll bet you ten bucks you're ready before she is,' said Blake, holding out his hand to shake on it.

Izzy smiled and shook her head. 'I'm not that stupid.' Turning for the door, she said, 'Let me know how things go with Dean. Oh, and I take it you don't want to come out with us tonight?'

'No thanks. Might just have some two-minute noodles,' came his distant reply. He was already busy tapping at the keyboard again.

The road into town was narrow, hardly a car's width, and it was a well-worn path. Large potholes dotted the bitumen, some filled for the hundredth time, while others just spewed out gravel from deep below when run over. They readjusted the wheel alignment and rattled your teeth.

Simone pulled off onto the gravel when they passed a ute coming the other way. A shower of gravel stones and loose blue metal pelted the windscreen, which was already scarred with chips and a lightning-shaped crack.

'You know, Mullawoon's way out bush and I complain about it enough, but it's home and I do love it,' said Simone, turning to Izzy. 'I suppose you feel the same about your place?'

A smile spread across Izzy's face. 'Yep. It will always be home, that's for sure. There's no other place I'd rather be.' She cleared her throat. 'I mean, I love it here – especially living with you and Blake. You guys are great. But the family farm is where I belong . . . where my heart belongs.'

'You really love the land, hey? I don't think I'd ever feel that passionate about our farm – a bloke maybe, but not a slab of dirt with a bit of grass on it. You and I are so different. It's funny that we get on so well.'

'Only 'cos I put up with your shit.' Izzy laughed. 'Nah. Maybe we're just opposites who complement each other.'

'Yeah, extreme opposites.'

Simone turned into the Mullawoon pub car park and carefully negotiated the assortment of utes. 'Wow, looks like a good crowd.'

'Sure is. Hey, I recognise that ute.' Izzy pointed to a white Holden Rodeo with a brown bull horn sticker across the back window. 'I distinctly remember you asleep in the back of it,' she said, laughing. Straightaway, she noticed Simone's posture straighten up at the reference to Mickey. When they had parked, Izzy noticed Simone checking herself in the rear-vision mirror nervously.

'Yes, you're still beautiful,' Izzy smirked.

Simone threw her a dark look. 'Don't you do anything to embarrass me tonight or you'll be in deep shit.'

'As if I would,' Izzy replied. Simone ran a hand down over her tight velvet top as they approached the pub doors. Izzy reached out and held her arm. 'How about you take a deep breath and relax? You're beginning to make me jumpy.'

'Sorry.'

Inside they walked across the black-and-white chequered floor to the bar and ordered some drinks. There were about twenty people in the pub tonight and Simone knew every one of them. Izzy was familiar with about half. They were mostly the ones she'd met at the bonfire and through their trips to the pub on Sunday nights. She recognised Jacko with a few of his mates leaning against the red-brick wall next to the numerous footy premiership flags and team photos. Izzy and Simone took their beers and found an empty table by the wall, not far from the pool table.

'How 'bout we have a drink or two, then head into the bistro?' Simone shouted over the thumping Cold Chisel music coming from the jukebox in the corner.

Izzy nodded in reply, but her eyes were scanning the room. It didn't take long to spot Mickey. He was holding up the bar with Reggie and a few others she'd seen before. By the look of it, he'd already spotted Simone. Izzy caught him sneaking a quick glance in their direction. She smiled to herself. It was so obvious when you were watching from the outside. Poor Simone just couldn't see what she was doing to Mickey.

'Who're you waving at?' asked Simone, peering around Izzy's shoulder.

'Just saying hi to Mickey.'

Simone ducked back, hiding behind the safety of Izzy's frame. 'My God. I think I've forgotten how to act around him. I'm so nervous just knowing he's over there. Now I've admitted my feelings to you, I suddenly feel like it's written on my forehead for all to see.' Izzy watched Mickey walking towards them. He wore his workboots with loose-fitting jeans and an olive and white shirt, which suited his brown skin. His dark eyes never once left Simone's face.

'Just be cool. He already knows you're a dork,' said Izzy.

Simone was still glaring at Izzy as Mickey dragged over a bar stool and sat down.

'So, what's new?' Mickey said loudly, brushing back his dark unruly hair.

'Not a lot. We've just come in for a feed,' Izzy said.

Simone added, 'Yeah, we're sick of eating Blake's crap and he won't let either of us cook. He seems to think he's actually good at it.' Mickey smiled, then took a sip of his beer.

'Would you like to join us for dinner?' Izzy asked.

His eyes darted from Izzy to Simone. 'I wouldn't want to impose.'

'You kidding? Come on, the more the merrier,' Simone said all too quickly, before turning slightly pink.

'Yeah, it's fine with us, as long as we're not taking you away from your mates,' Izzy added.

Mickey looked across to the bar at his mates who were laughing and spilling beer on the floor. 'I'm sure they'll survive without me. Besides, if a bloke had to choose between a couple of noisy blokes and two gorgeous girls, there'd be no contest,' he said. 'So, Izzy, have they worn you out yet? Still liking it here?'

'Yeah, I do, thanks, Mickey. It's a great place and it's just the best staying with Simone and Blake. And we've got the stud sale coming up to look forward to.'

Mickey nodded. 'I'll be there. I bought six rams off them last year. Averaged about a thousand dollars each and they were worth every cent. When Alan and Blake started up the stud farm a few years back, they converted me.'

'Really? Why?' asked Simone.

Izzy was amazed to see Simone's sudden interest in sheep. She even looked quite genuine. Hell, she must like Mickey a lot. Even he looked slightly taken aback.

Mickey spoke first. 'I didn't think you were interested in this sort of stuff.'

Simone shrugged. 'I'm not normally, but I guess some of Izzy's enthusiasm has rubbed off on me.'

Mickey held Simone's gaze for a while. Izzy could tell he was just as besotted as she was. The smile on his face said it all.

'You'd better answer her question before she changes her mind,' Izzy said laughing.

Slowly he began to speak. 'Well, we run merinos and have done for years, and they've been great, especially wool-wise. But Blake kept nagging me about some Prime SAMMs he wanted to start breeding.'

'South African Merino Mutton,' Simone piped in.

'The girl's getting good.' Izzy applauded.

Simone blushed as Mickey gave her a dazzling smile.

'Anyway, he said that an excellent product can be produced using a Prime SAMM over a merino ewe. So, I trusted his judgement and tried it out. Needless to say, he was right and I haven't looked back.'

'Wow. I think I might even have to go to this sale. It could be interesting,' responded Simone.

Izzy smiled. 'You should, Simone, especially as it's in your own backyard.'

'You can stick with me for the day and I'll teach you a few things if you're interested,' Mickey said.

Izzy was sure Simone would've walked to town and back in her underwear just to have Mickey show her a few things.

'I'd like that a lot,' she said eagerly.

Izzy could feel the sexual tension buzzing between the two of them – her hair must have been standing on end from the static. 'Well, I've gotta duck off to the loo. I'll bring back the next round of beers. Same again?'

'Cheers, Izzy,' Mickey and Simone replied together.

At the bar she handed over some cash and said g'day to Jacko.

'So, Izzy, what's new? You haven't come to visit me yet.'

'Haven't had time, sorry. Don't know what you've been doing, but we've had our arses glued to the tractor seat.'

'So, Macca's keeping you all to himself, hey?'

Izzy put her wallet away in her back pocket and picked up the three beers with a precision that came from plenty of practice. 'Maybe,' she replied. 'Catch ya later.'

When Izzy got back with the drinks, they were still deep in discussion about Mickey's farm and his plans. Simone was coming up with some great questions and Izzy couldn't help but feel proud.

Ten minutes later, they headed into the meals area to get a table. After paying for their steaks, they went and stood by the large indoor barbecue. A few other people stood round watching their steaks sizzle away as the smoke sailed up to the large overhead fan.

'Wow, this is pretty cool. Cook your own meat, hey?' Izzy said, impressed.

'Yeah, it's all right if you like that kind of thing.' Simone handed Mickey the tongs. 'Here, seeing as you're the man, you can be our cook. I never was too good at barbecuing, unless you like your meat burnt and tough . . .'

Mickey snatched the tongs off Simone. 'No, I don't,' he laughed.

Izzy left her slab of porterhouse in Mickey's capable hands and went for a look-see. She'd never been in this part of the pub before. It was made with lots of exposed timber beams and logs – very country-looking. She ventured out through two large French doors into the beer garden. A couple of girls sat in the corner chatting not far from a wide fire circle filled with sticks and mallee roots. Izzy heard a wolf whistle and felt a body brush past her.

'Waitin' for me, are ya?' laughed Jacko as he walked towards the circle. He held a container from which he squirted fluid over the wood before taking out some matches. With a 'whoof' the stumps were ablaze. 'Now, that's how you start a fire.'

Izzy gave Jacko a smile of approval. She felt the warmth touching her skin and smelt diesel in the air. A large salmon gum grew in the corner against the bricked enclosure, and the closer she got to it, the more clearly she could see where people had engraved their names into the bark. There was also a wall plastered with photos of the locals. She found one of Simone with the words 'barmaid of the year' scribbled underneath. There was also one of the local footy team, with Blake right in the centre, but the one that really had her laughing was a picture of Jacko parked at the bar with a funnel in his mouth and a couple of blokes pouring beer into the top. 'Jacko's 20th piss-up' it said underneath. No doubt that had been a blinder.

'That was a great night. At least I think it was. The bits I remember were good.'

Izzy felt Jacko's breath on her neck and turned to see his dark eyes behind her. He was shorter than Izzy with arms like an AFL player and he had a cheeky grin and a twinkle in his eye. He would easily get his pick of the girls, she guessed. 'You eating here?' she asked him.

'Nah, I've eaten already. The boys are just having one beer before we go out shooting later on. I thought I'd come and light this for Paula.' Izzy had met Paula once. She worked behind the bar some nights and was also the owner of the pub. She had wiry red hair and the look of a fifty-year-old smoker.

'Well, I've got Mickey cooking my steak so I should see how he's going.'

Jacko walked inside with her. 'You're game. Mick likes his still mooing.'

Izzy screwed up her face as Jacko waved her goodbye and went to put the diesel away in a back room. Izzy went to save her steak.

'Hope you like it medium to well done,' said Mickey as he handed Izzy her plate.

She took a bite to see if it bled. Cooked through, thank Christ, she thought. 'Cheers for that, Mickey.'

'I think my brother's got a thing for you,' said Mickey, pointing a pair of greasy tongs in Jacko's direction.

Izzy laughed. 'Nah, he just wants a root!' She reached for the large spoon on the salad table and filled up her plate. 'God, I'm famished.' And they were practically the only words she managed to get out for the rest of the meal. She didn't have much of a chance, with Mickey and Simone reliving the good old days. She wasn't bothered. It was just nice to sit and listen. She could feel a current running between them and caught them watching each other. It was nice to witness the beginnings of something. When she'd finished her steak, she excused herself once more.

Simone was glad when Izzy went to the toilet. She'd been dying to have some time alone with Mickey. As she watched Izzy leave with her hands stuffed in her jeans pockets, she turned to him and asked whether he'd enjoyed his night. He smiled back at her, his full lips enticing her as they moved.

'Absolutely. We should do this again some time, if you're keen?' he added.

Simone felt her face flush with his comments. 'Really?' She was sure she could read something in his eyes and had felt a spark between them tonight. But was that just because she wanted it? 'Do you mean with me and Izzy?' She watched his hand slide across the table to hers and grab hold.

'I meant just us. Would you like that?'

Mickey's voice was husky and sent shivers up her spine. She couldn't take her eyes away from the blackness of his own, and his hand was still on hers, gently massaging it with his thumb.

'Yes, I would.' Their eyes stayed locked until she caught a glimpse of Izzy's figure coming back and felt the coolness on her hand as Mickey pulled his away. At first she felt abandoned, until she glanced at Mickey, who smiled and gave her a sly wink. Her heart soared again.

When the leftover juices from their steaks had set on their plates and the table sat littered with a few empty glasses, they decided it was time to go home. Izzy said her goodbyes first and headed out to the car, leaving the two of them alone.

Her breath began to fog up the windows as she waited patiently for Simone. She used her finger to write on the window: IS ♥ WT. Rubbing her hands together, she tried to stop the cold from seeping in. She shuddered as her numb fingers reminded her of the time she'd tried unbuttoning Will's shirt that fateful afternoon. For a moment she let her mind roam, enjoying the memory and the sensation it brought. Just as she was getting to the good bit, to the point where she could almost taste him, the door opened and she was blasted with cold air. Tonight, with the cold, she could see Will so clearly in her mind and her heart had been racing at the memory. 'Holy shit, Simo. You scared the living crap out of me.'

'Sorry, Iz. What were you doing? Sleeping?' Simone didn't bother starting the car. Instead, she faced Izzy.

Even though the interior light was on, Izzy was sure the energy in Simone's eyes would have lit it up anyway. 'All right. Do tell. What happened? I could feel a vibe.'

'Well, there was a vibe,' Simone prattled on excitedly. 'We talked about us. He asked me if I'd like to go out with him some time soon, and I'm like, "Yeah, sure." You know, I think we both just want to take things slow. We really don't want to stuff this up. Oh, Izzy. He gave me the sweetest hug and kissed me on my forehead. I nearly melted then and there.'

'So, you had a great time then?'

'Hell, yeah. We could've talked all night.'

'Tell me about it. Next time I'm staying home,' said Izzy. But, she wasn't offended. Instead she reached out and slapped Simone's leg. 'I'm really pleased for you, Simone.'

Simone sighed heavily. 'Tonight was great. I'm so glad you came with me, and for giving us time alone. You're the queen of tact.' Turning, she fired up the car and drove out of the car park. 'I feel so alive, like I could just fly. God, I hope this is the start of something good. I so want this one to work. When I was eighteen, I used to dream about us getting together in a house down the road from Mum and Dad. I'd better get my act together,' she said, realising she was jumping the gun. 'I might scare him off with talk like that.' She looked quickly back at Izzy. 'And you can't mention any of this to

Blake. Not yet anyway. It might go nowhere and I don't want him yappin' in my ear.'

'No worries. But I think you'll find he'll be okay with it.'

As the night lights in town flashed past, Izzy could see the happiness all over Simone's face. Izzy felt so pleased for her. It was hard not to get caught up in her enthusiasm, and she let it wash over her. They giggled like lovesick teenagers all the way home.

33

'IZZY, wake up. It's an emergency,' whispered Blake as he shook her shoulders gently.

Quick as a flash she sat up, her eyes wide. 'What's wrong? What's happening?' Her hair, crinkled from sleep, hung around her face and her eyes felt like they were clogged up with glue. She was wearing Will's trackpants and shirt, which she hadn't been able to part with. They'd long since lost any scent of Will but she still found comfort in wearing them, if only to feel closer to him.

'It's Simo. She's up already and she's cooking breakfast. Do you think she's lost the plot? What the hell happened last night?'

'Oh, is that all? I can't believe you woke me up for that.' Izzy groaned and flung herself back into bed, pulling the covers up over her face.

Blake tilted his head, like a dog would when it was trying to listen. 'What's with you, anyway? Normally you're up and running around by now, picking on us for missing the best part of the day.'

She yawned. 'I didn't get much sleep last night, that's all.'

'What's bugging your arse?' demanded Blake, prodding her through her blankets. He sat back and waited for her to explain. He picked up the little framed picture on the bedside table, ran his hand over the engraved words 'Tom' before putting it back down. 'Come on – spill.'

Izzy flopped back the covers as she watched Blake putting her picture back. She reached out and moved it a fraction to the right so she could see Tom more clearly. It was the only personal thing she'd managed to grab in her rushed exit from home. There were times when she wished she could have taken a minute longer and got the family one with Claire in it too, and her favourite soft pillow with her name sewed into the corner in blue cotton that her mum had made when she was eight. But she couldn't turn back time, no matter how much she wanted to. 'I couldn't get Will off my mind. Playing things over in my head, doing things differently, dreaming of the way I wished it could be. You know – the same old stuff.'

'One of those nights, hey? Well, get up and we'll have some brekkie. It'll make you feel better – I know how much you like to eat. Simo's fried up some bacon too.'

'Bloody hell. She's gone all out.' Izzy smiled before another yawn overtook her. She hauled herself out of bed as Blake left the room. The smell of bacon and eggs wafted through her door, making her dress quickly. Soon she'd discarded her blue shorts and tank top and was crawling into a pair of jeans and a work shirt.

'Good morning, sunshine,' said Simone on seeing Izzy. 'Gee, you don't look so flash.' Her brow knitted in worry when she saw Izzy's tired face.

'I don't feel so flash either. But I'll be okay after a feed.' Izzy pulled her wayward hair back into a ponytail.

'Righto. Here, sit down. I'm just about to serve it up.'

'So, what has put you in such a good mood this morning?' Blake asked curiously. 'Did you get a bit last night?' He looked to Izzy, searching for the answer. 'Please tell me someone has offered to take her off our hands.'

Simone pointed her fork at him. 'Don't be mean. Anyway, you know you'd miss me. Besides, it's none of your concern. Is it, Izzy?'

'Leave me out of it. Can't I just enjoy this meal in peace?'

'No, you bloody well can't. You're part of our family now, and you live in our house, so whatever concerns us concerns you. Okay?'

Izzy shrugged, but smiled. 'All right.' Turning to Blake she said, 'It's none of your business.'

Simone gave her a knowing glance before cutting into her bacon. 'So, what's everyone got planned today?'

'Well,' said Izzy, 'I thought I'd mow the lawn – after I fix the mower, that is. I think the blades are out of whack. Starting to think Blake ran over something.'

'Sorry, I can't help. I'm going to Mum's this morning. She wants to clean out my old room and turn it into a sewing room,' replied Simone.

'I can help you, if you like. It might be fun – sort of,' he said, screwing up his face.

Just then the phone rang and Simone jumped up to answer it.

'Is she expecting a call?' Blake asked.

'Maybe, maybe not. I'm not telling you anything. My life depends on my mouth staying shut. So . . . um . . . . how did it go with Dean last night? Did you make any plans?' Izzy asked.

'Great. I'll fill you in later. I'm so nervous just thinking about it.' Blake jumped as Simone ran back into the room, her face drained of all colour.

'That was Mickey. Jacko was out shooting with some mates last night and got shot.' Simone said it so fast that it took a few seconds for them to catch on.

Blake bolted upright. 'What? How the hell did that happen? Shit. Is he okay?'

Izzy looked from one to the other. 'But I was only talking to him last night at the pub.'

'I know. Mickey said he left early, not long after we'd seen him. Apparently, he was on the back of the ute when one of the others jumped down to finish off a wounded fox. As he landed on the ground his gun hit his knee and discharged. Mickey said it blew a couple of Jacko's fingers away. He's at the hospital with Jacko now.'

Simone put down her cutlery and picked up her bag from the table. 'I'm going to head in right away.'

'Shit.' Blake swore again, completely shocked and bewildered. 'Okay. Well, tell Mickey if they need anything, just to give us a call. I wonder which hand. Bugger it! That could stuff up his shearing.' He ran his fingers through his hair.

'Hope not,' Simone replied, then added for Izzy's benefit, 'He's one of the best shearers around. Jacko's been to the Royal Show a few times to shear in comps, and he's won heaps of prizes. Dad reckons he's one of the cleanest and quickest he's seen in years.' Simone sighed, then turned and headed for the door, waving as she went.

'We'll come soon,' Izzy called after her, then turned to Blake. 'Don't worry too much, Mac. Not until we hear all the details. He's bloody lucky it didn't get him in the chest or worse.'

'When you put it like that, yeah, I guess he is,' he said, sighing loudly, but Izzy could see the tension in his body.

Blake forced his fork towards his mouth, taking the bacon that had been waiting, but his appetite was long gone. 'You know, they rang me and asked if I wanted to go with them, seeing as Mickey didn't want to, but as you know, I had better things to do.'

'Yeah, well life's like that, you know. But how was it with Dean, anyway?' she asked, distracting him from his concern for Jacko. 'Was he keen to meet up?' She watched the eagerness spread over his face, as he could finally fill her in on the details.

'Yup, we've planned to catch up at the Obie this weekend. Izzy, he sounds just as excited as I am, but it's a big deal meeting for the first time. I hope everything he's told me is true. I couldn't handle being disappointed.'

'You'll be fine. You just have to relax and take it easy. I'll be there, until you give me the secret nod to head off.' She smiled encouragingly.

'There won't be any secret nod.' Blake said, laughing. 'I'll just tell you to piss off and leave us to it.'

Izzy shook her head as she collected their plates. 'So, when are we heading up?'

'Early Saturday morning. I've already booked us a room. My shout.'

'You don't have to do that, Blake. You're not twisting my arm to come, you know.'

'I know,' he said, getting up and following her to the kitchen.

Izzy put their plates into the sink and began filling it with warm water. 'Is it okay to have the weekend off?'

Blake nodded. 'Dad's fine with it as long as we get the tractors cleaned up and fix that broken pump. He also wants the sheep pampered a bit more with the sale coming up.' Izzy smiled and it struck him just how beautiful she was – and what a good friend she was too.

'I think we can manage that.'

It wasn't until some time after lunch that Simone came home. For someone who'd been to see a bloke with missing fingers, she was looking and sounding rather chipper. Izzy couldn't help but laugh.

'Is Blake home?' Simone said, as she looked around the room.

'No, he's gone into town to see Jacko and then he's going back to Mickey's place.'

'You didn't want to go?'

'Nah. I've had my share of hospitals lately. Besides he'll have his family and friends there. Don't want to intrude.'

'Fair enough,' Simone replied as she put her mobile phone on the table and sat down next to Izzy, who was relaxing in front of the TV. 'What ya watching?'

'Just the midday movie. I wore myself out this morning hacking back that jungle of a garden.'

'Yeah, I nearly didn't recognise the place. The yard looks great.'

'Well, you'd be amazed at how many nice plants and shrubs there were under those weeds. My back's buggered, though. Anyway, what's news at the hospital?' Izzy asked.

'Yeah, Jacko'll be fine, but they can't put his fingers back on – there wasn't enough of them left. Apparently they were quite mangled. They operated on his hand and neatened it up. He'll have two little stubs left, but he was lucky – it was only his pinkie and his ring finger.'

'I suppose he won't know how it will affect his shearing until he picks up a handpiece.'

'Yeah, and that won't be for ages. The doc reckons it will be sore and tender for quite a while. In typical male fashion, Jacko was laughing and joking about it. Mickey will have to keep a close eye on him, I think.'

'Speaking of Mickey, Blake and I are going to Perth next weekend, so you'll have the house to yourself,' Izzy said. 'Oh, but just one word of advice – don't cook him dinner.'

'Ha ha, funny. Well, seeing as you've worked so hard I suppose dinner's on me, then. I think I can throw something nice together to say thanks for a job well done.'

Izzy gave Simone a smile as she put her feet up on the coffee table. 'Just don't make that tuna mornay dish again. Not even the dog would eat it,' Izzy chuckled.

Simone rolled her eyes. 'Yeah, it really sucked, didn't it?'

34

WHEN Will pulled up outside Bill's house, the afternoon air was starting to cool and the sun was commencing its descent. He gave a couple of knocks on the flywire door and then let himself in, calling, 'Hello.'

Jean popped her head out from the kitchen. 'G'day, Will. He's just about ready.' She lowered her voice when he got closer. 'Cheers for this. I can tell he's excited to be going out. I think he really needs it.'

Will could sense that she was worried. He had been so busy between both farms that he'd neglected Bill a bit of late. To make up for it, he'd offered to take Bill to the Tree for a few drinks to catch up with the lads. Bill had jumped at the chance.

'Don't worry, Jean. I'll look after him.'

She answered him with a smile before motioning to a chair. 'Course you will. I know that. Grab a seat. I'm sure he won't be long.' Jean sat down next to Will and studied his face like she was trying to decipher a code. 'Will, can I ask you something?' She paused. 'What happened between you and Izzy before she left?'

Will's blue eyes flinched, his mouth moved but no words escaped.

'It's just that before the fight that started it all erupted I noticed she was wearing your clothes.'

Now Will smiled. 'Really? I didn't know. So that's where my favourite pair of trackies went.'

'You still didn't answer my question.'

'Izzy told me how quickly you pick up on things! Yes, something did happen between us, although she didn't hang around long enough for us to figure out what.'

Jean put her hand on his for a moment. Her nails were short but neat and tidy. 'But you know how you feel about her.'

Will's dimple appeared as he smiled and replied, 'Yes.'

'Well, I know for a fact that she was affected by what happened too. She had feelings for you, Will, but she was still trying to understand them. Does she feel the same as you, do you think?'

He took a deep breath. 'I really don't know.' Looking at Jean reminded him of Izzy, her eyes and the way she moved. It made his heart ache more. 'I wish I did, Jean. I just wish I could be home next time she calls so I can talk to her.'

Just as Jean was about to speak, Bill's voice came from the passageway. 'Will, is that you?'

'Yeah.'

'Mate, you'll have to help me with this contraption. I still can't seem to get it going on this carpet.'

Bill came slowly down the passageway towards them. Will got up and took position behind the wheelchair.

Bill motioned to Jean. 'Catch ya, love. Don't wait up.'

It took Will a bit of manoeuvring to get him outside and then into the ute. He stashed the chair on the back and jumped in the front. 'Ready to go?'

'Ready when you are, boss,' replied Bill.

Will pulled out a beer from his small esky, took the top off and handed it to Bill before driving away. 'I'm glad we're doing this. You've looked a bit down lately.'

'I know. I've been dark on myself. It pains me whenever I think back to all the times I put Izzy down and shut her out. I feel bad that I can't tell her how sorry I am.'

Will winced at the hurt he saw in Bill's pale sunken face. He still looked sickly white and his anger at himself would not help his recovery. 'Try not to worry too much. Izzy's tough and she loves you, you know. When she's back you'll have all the time in the world to make it up to her.'

Bill looked out the window and mumbled, 'God, I hope you're right.'

Ten minutes later they arrived at the Tree to the usual crowd of utes and blokes from around the district. Will made sure to pull up behind a few vehicles so they couldn't see him lift Bill into his chair. Then somehow Bill found the strength to wheel himself the ten metres to join the nearest circle of men. Will handed him his beer, pulled up a milk crate and sat beside him. It felt good to be out and about, but there was just one thing missing – Izzy.

The blokes all politely asked Bill how he was going, and then with that out of the way it was straight on to farming.

A little later Frankie, who lived two farms down from Bill, handed him another beer and asked, 'Hey, Bill, if you're interested, I can have Paul bring over the Case and help turn some dirt for you after it rains.'

The offers came thick and fast, but Bill shook his head. 'Cheers, fellas. I'll keep it in mind. Will reckons he's got it covered, but if we get snowed under, I'll let you know.'

Will knew how much it was killing Bill to have even him on his farm. He doubted he could handle half the district helping him.

They'd begun discussing a new variety of wheat when Muzza came bursting into the huddle with a box. 'Hey, any of you fellas want a good working dog?' He put the box on the ground and scanned their faces for interest. Will leant over and could see three little kelpie pups. Two were snuggled in the corner asleep on each other and the other one was trying to get out. Will picked up the active pup – a girl, he discovered – and held her in front of his face. The pup sat relaxed in his big hands, eyes glued on Will, and attempted to lick his face.

'You're just a bit too cute, aren't ya?' Will laughed and snuggled the pup into his neck.

'She's a go-getter, that one. Never sits still. You want her?' asked Muzza.

Will thought of Izzy, and of Tom. And how alone he'd been feeling. This pup definitely had Izzy's zest for life. Maybe he'd get her as a present for Izzy, for when she returned to the farm. In the meantime he'd have some company.

'How much, Muzza? She looks great.'

'Yeah, both parents are fantastic working dogs. But for you, Will, she's free.'

Will turned his head and questioned with his eyebrows.

'Mate, I still owe you for that day's work when my shearer took sick. If you're happy with a swap, it's a done deal.'

'Sounds good to me, Muzza. I kinda got the feeling I wouldn't be seeing any money for that anyway. I know how good you are at misplacing your chequebook.'

Muzza laughed as he picked up the box and took the other pups back to his ute.

Will scratched the top of the pup's head. She had settled on his lap, curled up but with her eyes still wide open, taking everything in.

Bill reached over and gave her a rough pat. 'Didn't know you wanted a new dog, Will?'

'I didn't really. But I thought Izzy might.'

Bill's face stayed rigid but Will saw the smile that radiated from his eyes in the dying light.

'Yeah, I reckon you're right.' The old fella had given his approval.

'What are we gonna call ya, girl?' Not wanting to disturb the happy little thing, Will reluctantly got up and headed to the shop, twenty-five metres behind the Tree, with her tucked in his arms. He walked through to the hardware section to see whether they had any puppy food. He found a bag and carried it back to the counter.

'Can you bung this on the account for us please, Jane?'

'Sure, no probs, Will,' she replied. 'Is that one of Muzza's?'

Will handed the pup over for Jane to cuddle and inspect.

'Ya gonna give her a girlie name?' Jane asked.

'Don't know. I was thinking of Gully. Yeah, I like Gully.' Like the gully that had nearly cost him his life and also brought Izzy closer to him. He took the pup back and held her up to his face. 'What do you say? Do you like it?' The pup just yelped and play chewed on his finger. 'That'll do, then.' Grabbing the bag of pup food, Will nodded goodbye.

'Hey, if I don't see ya, have fun at the wedding wearing ya monkey suit!'

'Sure will. Cheers, Jane.'

'Can ya give the fellas a holler and tell them final drinks before I close up?'

Outside, the darkness had dropped around them and the large storage bins blocked off the last of the setting sun. Will found his ute and chucked the food on the back. He thought about leaving Gully in the ute but decided against it. Already he was too attached. He wandered back to where Bill was chatting, and sat listening quietly, patting Gully and thinking of Izzy, wondering whether she might be looking up at this same sky somewhere out there.

35

'WHAT are you doing out here?' Blake asked Izzy, who was standing at the end of the verandah. It was Friday night and tomorrow they'd be on the road to Perth for his hot date. The week couldn't have finished any quicker for him. He'd been counting down the days and hours.

Izzy's chest rose as she took a deep breath. 'Can't you smell it? The rain's not far away.'

'I know. I saw the forecast on the Internet,' said Blake, in a matter-of-fact tone.

Izzy looked at the sky and pursed her lips. 'Well, I like to tell by looking at the sky and smelling the air. I reckon it's only a few minutes away and I can hear some thunder in the distance. It should be a good rain.'

'You like to do things the old way, don't you?'

She shrugged her shoulders. 'Some things I do. Some of the old ways are best but not all. I like the future and change too. I can be flexible.'

Blake slung his arm around her shoulder and together they stood, watching the black clouds rolling overhead.

'Isn't it beautiful, nature doing its thing?' Izzy said. 'I love watching the seasons come and go. And to think nobody would probably have started ripping up at home yet.'

Blake squeezed her tightly. 'You're a remarkable woman, Izzy Simpson. I've never met a woman like you. You're really at one with the land. You kinda stand out – especially compared to Simone – but in a good way.'

Izzy took another deep breath as the rain started to fall in large drops, which pinged off the iron roof. A bright flash of lightning ripped its way through the dark sky. A thunderous boom followed five seconds later. Izzy leant on Blake's shoulder. 'You know, I could stay here all night and watch this. Maybe I should drag my mattress out here.'

'Yeah, you could. But the mozzies would carry you away, and I need you ready for tomorrow.'

'Gee, you're a hard man, Mac. You'd make a good boss one day.'

Twelve hours later they were on the road to Perth.

Izzy looked at the land through the rain-splattered window as they drove out of town. 'You know, you have great soil up here. Back home we struggle with salinity. Almost a quarter of our farm is unusable because it's salt affected. We have heaps of salt lakes dotted throughout the district.'

'Any you can waterski on?'

'Yeah, there is one. Usually after a flood we can go skiing on it for a while. But it's pretty disgusting when it gets low. If you come off the skis and get a nose or mouth full of the salty water, you just about puke.'

'Is there much you can do to stop the salt?' asked Blake.

'No, not really. We just plant a heap of salt bush and trees, and some people have drains. We need big pumps to lower the underground water level and stop the salt rising. It's just one of those environmental problems that's hard to reverse. Hindsight's a wonderful thing.'

'Tell me about it. You know, one day I'd love to see your farm,

Izzy. You paint such a vivid picture of it. I feel as if I know it so well.'

'You will see it, one day.' Izzy just wished she could believe her own words.

When they arrived at the motel, they unloaded their bags and stretched out on the beds. The large window in their room overlooked a few rooftops. Nothing special, but over them you could just glimpse the ocean. Most of the swimmers had headed home; the afternoon had come in cold, leaving the diehards in their wetsuits to brave the small barrelling waves.

'We'll have to go for a walk along the beach tomorrow. It's been a while since I've had sand between my toes,' said Izzy.

Blake smiled as he walked to the window. 'It's a pity we didn't get a chance today. It would've been perfect earlier on. We'll just have to get up at dawn and go for a stroll, hey.'

'That's if Dawn doesn't mind! It might be a bit cosy with the two of us,' Izzy said, smirking.

Blake picked up the neatly folded towel from the end of the bed and threw it at Izzy, not finding her joke very funny. Then he held up two shirts, which he'd pulled out from his overnight bag. 'What do you think?'

'Hmmm, I'd go with the black one. It really suits you.'

'Does it bring out my eyes?' he asked sarcastically. 'Okay, now which jeans? Dark or light?'

Izzy sighed. 'Definitely the light ones. Don't tell me I have to pick out your shoes next, or worse, your jocks?'

'I'm sure I can manage that by myself. Well, I best get ready,' said Blake nervously, as he walked towards the bathroom. Izzy went to her bag and pulled out a pair of jeans, not ironed, of course. She had this theory that once you wore them for ten minutes all the creases came out anyway, so what was the point of ironing. Her mum would be horrified to hear that. Izzy also pulled out a long-sleeved, low V-necked blue top and a black jacket in case it was cold out.

Nearly an hour later they parked outside the Obie and headed inside towards the noise. Izzy felt the ocean breeze on her face and breathed in the salty air with relish. Last time she'd been here she'd been holding Will's arm, not Blake's. That had been a great night, and she remembered their fun with delight.

'You know, I'm glad you didn't get too glammed up,' said Blake, patting her on the shoulder.

'Why's that?'

'Because I want his eyes only on me tonight,' he laughed.

Izzy wrapped her arm around his waist as they pushed through the doors and into the crowd. 'I wouldn't worry about that. You really do look a million bucks. I'll have to fend off the ladies you're going to attract. But seriously, if you guys do want to nick off to be alone without interruption, go to his room, not ours.'

'Will you be all right by yourself if we do?' he asked her.

'Of course. Don't stress about me. I'll be fine. I'll head back to the motel and see what's on the idiot box.' She grabbed his arm supportively.

Blake looked down at her and gave her a warm smile that came from his heart, then they both collided with a group of blokes heading out the door.

'Sorry,' said Izzy automatically, and turned to apologise properly. Her words almost stuck in her throat as a pair of bright, electric-blue eyes pierced through her. Suddenly everything seemed to slow down. People around her began to blur. It was as if someone had hit the slow-motion button and time itself had almost come to a standstill.

Blake felt Izzy's hands tighten around his arm, cutting off his circulation. She looked startled and mesmerised at the same time. He followed her gaze and connected with a pair of eyes that made him catch his breath. He knew straightaway that it was Will. Izzy's description of him had been perfect. Blake knew he would have trouble getting those electric eyes out of his mind. He felt as if they had stripped him bare. 'Are you okay, Izzy?' he whispered.

She could only nod her reply.

Izzy found herself face to face with Will amid the bustling crowd. 'Izzy, what are you doing here?' said Will, his eyes following her arm, which was wrapped around a man who was tall, athletic and, he had to admit, very handsome. It instantly grated on his nerves. How could he compete with that?

'Hi, Will. This is Blake. Blake, this is Will, from back home.'

Blake took great pleasure in shaking Will's hand, but he knew it wasn't reciprocated. He stretched his fingers out afterwards, trying to get some feeling back. You don't wring a man's hand like that unless you're trying to tell him something. 'Here, why don't you two catch up? I'll go get us a drink. Bourbon and Coke?' he asked. Izzy nodded, and he watched the nervous panic race across her eyes as he pulled away from her. Blake gave her a look of encouragement.

Izzy felt weak. She wasn't sure she could muster up any words. Then she leant her head to one side and, keeping her voice light, asked, 'What are you doing here, Will? Fancy bloody running into you, hey?'

'I asked you that first.'

'Oh,' she said, trying to get a hold on her mind. 'We just got the weekend off after seeding. We've got a big ram auction coming up and so we came down for a well-earned break before we get busy again with the preparations. You?' Will ran his hand through his hair slowly, and damn if it didn't rack her body with goosebumps.

'It's John's wedding tomorrow and we're just having a few drinks to celebrate.' He nodded to a bloke standing nearby with a few mates. 'I'm in the bridal party.' Izzy recognised John from home and another one of his mates, Chris. They were much older than she was so she'd never had much to do with them. A picture of Will in a tux flashed in Izzy's mind. Was she seeing her own wedding? Will broke into her thoughts with a question she didn't quite catch.

'Pardon? What was that?' she asked.

'I said when are you coming home? Don't you think you've been away long enough? You know your dad wants you back.'

'Yeah, sure. I could just see him begging me to come back,' she laughed, trying to hide her anxiety. 'Besides, I've just got settled into a great job and I don't want to lose it. They have the stud sale coming up and they need me.'

'You know your parents have been trying to find you? We all have,' Will said with an edge to his voice.

'Well, I left a message on your phone so they wouldn't worry. I'm a big girl now, Will. I can take care of myself.' She folded her arms across her chest, starting to feel angry that Will was being so abrupt and wasn't happier to see her. 'Besides, it's probably much more peaceful there without me. I s'pose you're doing most of the work – or has he managed to hire someone?'

Will's eyes sparkled. Oh, he knew she was fishing for information about how the farm was going. Tough luck, he thought. 'Why don't you come home and find out, Izzy? We've got so much to talk about – and you know exactly what I mean.' His tone softened. He watched her carefully for any hint of how she was feeling.

'Oh.' Izzy's heart skipped a beat. She couldn't think clearly. Running into Will so suddenly had thrown her for six. As they stood there, people kept pushing past her, shoving her into Will. He grabbed her arm and pulled her to the side of the door. The touch of his hand sent her mind blank. Looking into his eyes, she began to feel like chocolate left out in the sun.

Will wanted to ask her if she'd felt anything for him but now he was scared of her answer. Especially seeing her with that guy Blake. The happiness and laughter he'd seen in her eyes when she'd been looking at Blake before he'd bumped into her told him a lot. 'So you've moved on? You're happy?' he asked, holding her gaze.

She realised he was waiting for her answer. Hurriedly she blurted out, 'Yes, I'm happy.' As happy as I can get without being home on Gumlea and without you, she thought.

'Come on, Will. You comin'?' yelled Chris, who was waiting just outside with John and two others. Chris walked up to Will and recognised Izzy. 'Hiya, Izzy. Long time no see. Sorry, but we need him. Come on.' Chris grabbed Will's arm and gave it a tug.

'Yep, okay. Just give us a sec, will you?' replied Will.

'Well, I'd better get going too,' said Izzy. Leaning over, she gave Will a hug, desperately trying to avoid eye contact. His blue shirt was soft against her skin and as she breathed in, she closed her eyes. It seemed to last an eternity, then it took all her effort to peel herself off him, like a sticky pair of latex gloves. His aftershave clung to her skin, making her head dizzy. 'It was good to see you, Will. Take care of yourself and have fun at the wedding.' Turning, she walked away as quickly as her jelly legs could take her.

Will watched her leave. He tried to talk, tried to get her to stop, but the words stuck in his throat. The way her hair swung from its ponytail and her manly swagger had him strangely hooked. His heart sank to the bottom of his chest. She had already moved on. She looked happy, yet he felt like crap. It didn't seem fair. He knew it sounded like an old Mills and Boon novel but he'd dreamed of this moment so many times. He'd imagined meeting her at last and them running into each other's arms, him telling her how much he loved and missed her. Then he would get to kiss her warm lips, which had taunted him in his sleep nearly every night, and feel the way her body fitted neatly against his own. He was so shocked to think that some other bloke had taken his place. He stood there saying barely a word. Nothing had gone the way it was supposed to.

Will took another glance at Blake through the glass doors, as his cousin pulled him towards the car. He'd never envied a bloke this much or felt so jealous. He was a very good-looking guy and Will had nothing over him. He could feel envy pulsing through his veins like poison. As he headed to the car with the lads, he felt the first pangs of pain begin in his chest, and he knew his heart was breaking.

36

'ARE you okay? You look a bit pale?' Blake moved a strand of hair off Izzy's forehead.

After a few deep breaths, she found her voice. 'I think so. God, I wasn't prepared for that. Look at me. I'm still shaking.' The bourbon in her glass resembled rough seas as it splashed up the sides.

'Take a few more sips. It will help calm you down,' said Blake, as he guided the glass to her mouth. 'But I'm not surprised. He's a hell of a catch. Damn, you weren't exaggerating at all. He is gorgeous, and those eyes are truly remarkable. My hair stood on end just looking at them.'

Izzy's despair was clear on her face.

'Don't worry. I think he still likes you.'

Izzy pulled at her top, stretching it down over her jeans. 'What makes you say that?'

Blake rubbed his hands together. 'The death grip handshake for one thing, and the disapproving looks for another.' He saw her confusion. 'A straight man usually struggles to spot a gay guy. Izzy, he thought we were together.'

Izzy's hand flew to her mouth, her eyes wide. She didn't know whether to laugh or to cry. Now she understood why Will had asked whether she was happy. He meant happy with Blake. She felt awful. 'Maybe there's hope yet, Blake, if what you reckon is true.'

Blake smiled. 'Oh, yeah. I'd bet my life on it.'

Did she dare to believe that Will cared for her as more than a friend? And even if he did, would it work when she wasn't welcome at home? Her head screamed with a million thoughts. Could they really be together one day? Should she call to explain?

Izzy, remembering that Blake was anxious enough himself, turned her attention to his situation and tried to give her mind a break. She had a quick look around the bar. 'Have you spotted Dean yet?' she asked.

Blake didn't move. 'He's sitting in the corner to your left.'

'You're kidding! Why didn't you tell me sooner?' Izzy stood on her toes and craned her neck over the sea of heads.

Blake pulled her down quickly. 'Shit, Izzy. Don't make it bloody obvious.'

'Well, if you know where he is, why are you still here?'

He drained the beer from his glass before turning to her. 'Just finding some Dutch courage. Besides, I wanted to wait for you.'

'Well, I'm here now, so let's go.' Grabbing his shirt, she dragged him through the compacted bodies.

Izzy recognised Dean from his picture and made a beeline to where he sat by himself. He had that horrible, nervous look of someone on a first date: his hair was overstyled and his aftershave was too strong. He was trying hard and Izzy had to give him points for that. Dean had large green eyes, which were almost hidden by his long black fringe, and his lips tugged in a nervous smile. He wiped the sweat from his hand before shaking Izzy's. Dean was as filled with anticipation as Blake was. She could see it clearly, and began to relax, knowing that Blake would be all right. 'G'day. I'm Izzy.'

Dean shook her hand but he only had eyes for Blake, and after shaking his hand too, he finally looked back to Izzy and responded. 'Hi, Izzy. I've heard so much about you. It's nice to meet you.'

Izzy looked at Blake and smiled. 'You mentioned me? I hope it was all good,' she said as she glanced back at Dean. They each pulled up a stool and sat down. Izzy thought she'd break the ice and get the conversation going, so she did it the only way she knew how. 'So, Dean, what kind of farm do you run? Blake tells me it's down near Katanning. That's not far from my family's farm in Pingaring.'

'Yeah, we have about two thousand hectares which we crop and run sheep on,' replied Dean, easily moving into farming talk.

Izzy turned to Blake and laughed. 'Not still worried he's a weirdo?'

Blake went red and explained. 'Sorry, Dean. It's just I've never done this before. I mean, I've talked to people on the Net but I've never met anyone before. You hear so many bad stories.' Blake felt better getting that off his chest and even more pleased when Dean agreed with him.

'Don't stress. I felt the same, but I think we're doing okay. I came up with my brother, Nic. He's staying back at our hotel but he's near the phone in case I call for help.'

Izzy watched Blake laugh and enjoyed seeing the spark in his eyes and the way he got all coy when talking to Dean.

Within minutes, the guys were talking away like two old crows. Izzy attempted to pay attention but found her thoughts drifting back to Will, over and over again. She tried to remember all his words, memorising them and recalling how he ran his hand through his hair, and the way his eyes kept her from breathing normally. She wished she could've had better responses to his questions instead of standing there blankly, surprised and confused. Only now that the moment had passed could she think of the right things to say. She wondered whether he wanted her to come home. Would he have said more if Chris hadn't hurried him away?

Dean noticed Izzy's glazed expression and a faraway look in her eyes. 'Is she okay?' he asked Blake.

Blake smiled. 'She's just had a blast from her past. I daresay it's shaken her up a bit.' Turning to Izzy, he put his hand on her shoulder and gave it a gentle squeeze.

She looked across at him, startled by his touch. They were watching her as if expecting her to fall in a heap and cry.

'What did you say?' She saw their smiles and realised they'd caught her out. 'Sorry. I'm not really with it at the moment.'

'We can see that. Anything we can help you with?' Blake offered.

Izzy shook her head. 'No. I'm not the best of company, am I? I think I'll head back to the hotel and maybe stop in at the bottle shop on my way.'

'You sure? Don't leave on our account,' said Dean. 'I'd like to hear more about your farm. We probably know some of the same people, given we're only a few hours away from you.'

'I reckon we probably would but I'm afraid we'll have to leave that discussion for another day.' Izzy got up off her stool. 'I'm pretty knackered. Blake had me drive all the way here. Besides, three's a crowd,' she said with a wink. 'Don't worry about me. You just enjoy yourselves.'

Blake hugged Izzy and handed over the keys to his ute. 'I'm sure we will. Just as well you only had one drink. You take care of my ute now.'

'It's not me you have to worry about. It's the other loonies on the road,' she laughed. 'It was nice to meet you, Dean. Hopefully I'll see you around.'

'Likewise, Izzy,' said Dean, as he drained the last of his beer.

'Thanks,' Blake mouthed to her before she headed out of the pub.

Izzy climbed back into Blake's ute and sat there for a while. She'd hoped to see Will again outside – maybe he was still close by – but there was no sign of anyone in the dimly lit car park and she couldn't spot his ute. They'd probably taken taxis anyway.

She drove back to the motel and headed towards her room, a paper bag containing a bottle of bourbon in her hand. The whole time she was looking out for him. Maybe, just maybe, he was staying here too, she thought. She would've given anything to catch another glance.

She unlocked the door and headed inside, knowing she'd have trouble sleeping. She could still feel the warmth of his body and the enticing scent of his aftershave, which lingered on her clothes. Grabbing a glass from the mini fridge, she poured herself a large sleeping pill and then went out onto the balcony. It was so tiny Izzy could only just fit a chair there. She sat, quietly drinking and overlooking the city lights, wondering which room was Will's or which taxi he was in. When that started to make her feel too claustrophobic, she gazed up to the sparse blackness of the sky and to the ever familiar stars that brought her closer to home.

37

WILL had enjoyed John and Paula's wedding. They couldn't have asked for more – clear blue skies, no wind and a happy bride. But Will had to admit his heart hadn't been in it. Sure, he'd smiled and played his part, but inside his emotions were in turmoil. Seeing Izzy again had shaken him, to say the least. They were back at the Broadwater Pagoda in Como for the reception, which was a cocktail-style event. He hung out with Chris for a while but he was busy with his girlfriend, who looked stunning in a long yellow strapless bridesmaid number. He'd also had to contend with Tiffany, another of Paula's bridesmaids and friend from the city who'd taken a shine to him. She was nice-looking, tall and elegant with high cheekbones and lovely cleavage, shown to full effect by her dress. Five years ago he'd have encouraged her, and probably taken her back to his room before the speeches had even started. But today he avoided Tiffany's eye contact and headed to the far wall where his mum and dad sat talking. His mum was chatting with his Aunty Jen, no doubt talking about how great everything was and how stunning the bride looked, and his dad sat beside her in his black tux, staring into space as if following a fly with his eyes.

'Hey, Dad,' he said, sitting in the empty chair next to Brian, which was decorated with a white chair cover and tied with a yellow sash.

'Hi, William. Why aren't you over there with the younger ones enjoying yourself? You look like you've attended a funeral, not a wedding.' This brought a smile to Will's lips until his dad added, 'Here comes one of them young beauties now.'

Will looked up to see Tiffany walking towards him with a beer in one hand and a glass of champagne in the other. Her hands looked soft, with nails that were long and painted bright red. They looked like they'd never seen a day of physical labour. He remembered John saying she was a secretary in a law firm.

'Hi, Tiff,' he said politely and thanked her for the beer.

'A few of us are going up to their room to shortsheet the bed, among other things. Would you like to come?' Tiffany took a sip from her glass, then licked her freshly applied dusky pink-lipsticked lips.

'I think I'll pass, thanks. I'm just gonna chat to my dad for a bit and maybe go over my speech,' he said as an excuse. She looked startled, but he was sure she'd find someone else soon enough. Besides, he was not great company at the moment.

'Oh . . . okay. I'll catch you later, then.'

As she turned, Will admired her slim shoulders and bare back. 'Thanks again for the beer,' he yelled out. She glanced around and gave him a smile that said, 'If you change your mind, come and find me.'

Brian slapped Will's knee and turned to see his son's curious expression.

'What's up, my son?'

Will wondered what to say. He hadn't told his parents about his feelings for Izzy yet. It just hadn't felt right up until now. 'I saw Izzy last night at the Obie.'

'Well, that's good, isn't it?' Brian said, trying to coax more out of him.

Brian yanked the bow tie around his neck, then groaned in discomfort. His father hated getting dressed up.

'Yes, it was good, except she was with another bloke.'

Brian rubbed at his clean-shaven chin. 'I see. So that's why you gave Tiffany the flick. Not many would give up a chance with her. You must feel a lot for Izzy.'

'I do, Dad. I should have said something, maybe, but I was afraid of getting hurt. Anyway, now it's too late and I forgot to ask her where she's staying or where she's living. I don't know when I'll see her again.'

Brian put his hand on his son's shoulder, but as for words, they didn't come easily to him. He didn't know what he could say to help. He'd never seen his boy so uptight, and it explained why he'd been distant over the past few months since Izzy had left. He thought it was the pressure of trying to help Bill on his farm without neglecting their own place. Now he saw that it was Bill's daughter who'd had his son tied up in knots. Sandy was better at talking about stuff like this. Maybe when she'd finished talking to Jen he'd tell her about Will. Until then he said the only thing he could think of. 'She'll work out, Will. Don't worry.'

'What do you mean you saw Izzy? Is she coming home? Did you tell her we want her back?' Jean said, throwing out the questions in rapid fire.

Will shook his head slowly. 'I told her to come home and said that everything was okay, but she didn't believe me. She said she wasn't ready.'

'You should have dragged her home.' Jean sat down on a stool at the breakfast bar and put her head in her hands.

'I'm sorry, Jean. Seeing her there took me by surprise. I wasn't thinking straight.' Annoyed with himself, he ran his fingers over his stubble roughly.

'There's something you're not telling me, isn't there, Will? What's going on?' Jean stood up and approached him, forcing him to look at her.

'Izzy was there with another bloke, so I kind of lost all train of thought.'

'Oh. Well, maybe he was just a good friend?' she said, sounding optimistic.

'I'm pretty sure of what I saw. They had a connection. What if she's so happy she doesn't want to come back?'

'It won't come to that. I know Izzy, and this farm is her life. She'll come back. It's beyond her control. And I know when she left she had real feelings for you.'

'Yeah, but maybe they weren't strong enough. Maybe she had a better offer. Who knows?' Will sighed. Jean was right. This farm was Izzy's life. He could always take comfort in that. Sooner or later she would return.

'Did she say who she was working for, or anything else that might give us a clue to where she is?' Jean asked. Will could hear the desperation in her voice.

Will had been over their conversation in his head a million times. Izzy hadn't mentioned anything or given any clues. Slowly he shook his head.

'Where is Bill now?' Will asked.

'He's gone up to the shed. He wouldn't let me help. He's withdrawing into himself and I can't seem to reach him.'

Will nodded. He understood exactly. 'Maybe I'll go and tell him I saw Izzy. It might be just the cheer-up he needs, knowing she's well and happy.' I wish I felt the same, he thought to himself, then gave Jean a quick hug and headed towards the door.

Bill's arms were sore. The sand on the pathway was too much for the thin tyres of his wheelchair. He bent over and reached down further to give him more leverage. Holding on tight to the cold metal, he pulled with all his might. His only chance was to go backwards out of the sand and find harder ground. Jean had told him not to attempt it, but he was sick of feeling like an invalid, sick of being inside, and sick of having his wife do everything for him. He wanted to do something by himself for once. For Christ's sake, he couldn't even crap on his own.

Izzy was always in his thoughts. The longer she stayed away, the more it affected him, and he could see the spark had gone out of Will's eyes too. He'd caused that pain. Why was he such an idiot? He should have let her work the farm – at least she'd have been happy and near him.

The wheelchair was still going nowhere and he was running out of steam, but giving up was not an option. Reaching down, he tried again. He could feel his face reddening and felt the tear of his raw skin over his burnt knuckles. Pain ripped up his arm. At first he thought it was just from splitting open his burns but then he came over faint. He felt more pain in his chest as he struggled to breathe. He collapsed in his chair and the light started to fade. He wasn't sure, but he thought he heard Will's voice calling out to him as he fell into blackness.

38

IT took two minutes of Blake knocking on the hotel room door before Izzy let him in.

'Geez, you look lovely,' he joked as he walked in. Izzy's hair resembled a knotted-up ball of yarn. Her eyes were barely open as she tried to read her watch.

'I'll save you the effort. It's one o'clock.' Blake smiled when she groaned. He pulled his wallet out of his jeans and placed it on the tacky melamine bedside table, right next to the half empty bottle of bourbon. 'No wonder you look like shit.'

Izzy flopped back onto her bed and buried her head in her pillow. Blake laughed at the sight of her drooping PJ pants revealing her undies and the way her arm hung limply down the side of the bed.

'Tried to drown your sorrows, hey?'

Izzy turned her head slightly to face him and mumbled, 'Something like that.' She rolled onto her side as Blake sat on the edge of his bed. 'So how'd it go? By the annoyingly stupid grin on your face I take it things went well?'

Blake started unbuttoning his black shirt. 'Izzy, it was great. Dean's amazing. We talked about everything – family, work, his plans for the farm and mine. You name it. It's going to be so much easier emailing him now we've met.'

'So, is it fair to say you're "an item"?'

'I guess you could say that.' Not that he really had anyone else to share the news with. That took some of the excitement away. Dean was in the same boat, to a degree. His family knew he was gay, but come hell or high water they wouldn't tell anyone in their district. They'd had a hard enough time dealing with it themselves, let alone worrying about what others would say and how they'd treat Dean. But Dean could escape to Albany. His cousins, aunts and uncles and one of his brothers lived there, and he was able to be completely open there. He'd even had a few serious relationships.

'I just don't know how we'll last living seven hundred kilometres away from each other.' Blake sounded nervous but you couldn't mistake the excitement on his face.

'Just take it one day at a time,' she said, looking at him through bloodshot eyes.

'Such words of wisdom at this hour,' Blake teased, before remembering some of the things Dean told him. 'You know Dean was in the state hockey team for a few years but gave it away to stay on the farm . . .' Blake paused when he saw Izzy waving her hand at him.

'Can we save the rest for the trip home? I'm really interested, just not at one in the morning.'

Blake stood up, took off his shirt and leant down to kiss Izzy on the forehead. 'Sure thing, Sleeping Beauty. I'm gonna have a quick shower first. I'll be as quiet as I can.'

'Ta.'

He watched Izzy sleepily climb back under the covers before heading to the bathroom. Blessed was the day she drove into town. He lifted his shirt and breathed in the faint scent of Dean's aftershave. It had been hard to say goodbye but they'd agreed to meet again, soon. Blake knew he was going to have trouble keeping the smile off his face.

Simone looked at the white box. She turned it over in her hands and read the information on the back for the third time today. She'd bought the pregnancy test on Friday after work. Not that she really believed she could be pregnant. But it was over six weeks since her last period, and she just wanted to be sure. Mickey was due over for dinner any minute so she stashed the box back in her top drawer among her lacy knickers and G-strings. She'd already decided to do the test on Sunday. She didn't want to ruin her night with Mickey. But she just had a niggling feeling. She put it to one side and concentrated on getting ready.

She stood up and looked at herself in the full-length mirror. She smoothed out her grey knitted jumper, then turned to see how her bum looked in the skinny-fit jeans. She'd decided not to get overdressed and opted for just the slightest hint of make-up. She wanted Mickey to see the real Simone. Besides, she'd known him as long as she could remember and he'd already seen her at her worst. Like the time when she was thirteen and she'd stacked her bather top with tissues to impress the boys at the local pool. It was all good fun until she jumped into the water and surfaced to find soggy tissues floating around. Mickey and Blake had helped her collect them, amid fits of laughter.

She heard Mickey knock on the kitchen door, then let himself in, just as he'd done many times before. He put a bottle of red wine on the table. 'Hey, Simone. You look great,' he said as he awkwardly gave her a hug. They were still overcome by a strange initial shyness each time they met up.

Simone felt just as weird and nervy, and didn't know whether to hug or kiss him. Mickey was wearing a rusty red jumper, which made his eyes look vibrant. Normally he'd have stubble or a good three-day growth, but tonight he was clean shaven. She'd rarely seen him looking so tidy. She pointed to the kitchen table, which was laid out ready for dinner, and asked him to grab a seat. She poured them some wine while she added the last-minute parmesan to the chicken risotto, and then served it.

'So, have you heard if Janice has had her baby yet?' Mickey asked, to break the ice.

Simone put down her fork. 'No, but it could be any day now.' The excitement in her voice was unmistakeable. And then they were off chatting, as the stiff nervousness eased out of them.

An hour later, their plates lay empty at the sink and the bottle of wine sat almost empty at the table.

'You're telling me that tough Mickey likes to watch chick flicks?' Simone laughed at his selection of movies – all ones she liked: *How To Lose a Guy in 10 Days*, *The Devil Wears Prada*, *Made of Honor*. Perhaps he was just trying to be nice. Mickey held her hand and she revelled in the heat his touch brought.

'Swear on your life you won't tell anyone I chose these movies!' he demanded jokingly.

'Don't worry, Mick. Just so you know, Blake watches these too. You guys all act tough on the outside.' Simone found herself playing with his fingers and liked it. She was really beginning to feel at ease in his company.

'Maybe we all want happy endings too.'

Mickey's intense gaze had her heart racing like ants to a dropped ice-cream. Then he reached up and held her face and she knew he was going to kiss her. Mickey's lips found hers, gently at first, and she savoured the taste of sweet wine. She wanted more. Her hands climbed up his jumper to his neck, and she buried her fingers in his thick hair. Then her mind went blank, as she was consumed by her passion for the guy with the gentle heart.

Late the next day Izzy and Blake walked into the house together, bags swung over their shoulders and smiles upon their faces.

'Hello there. You two look like you had a great time,' Simone greeted them from the kitchen.

'We sure did. How was your weekend, Simone? You seem tired.' It was easy to spot the black rings under her eyes, and the large shirt and track pants she was wearing made her appear like she'd just crawled out of bed. Well, that wouldn't be unusual for Simone, except that it was five in the afternoon.

'Yeah, it was fine. Had a late night watching movies . . .' She didn't finish but Izzy gave her a quick knowing smile. She knew Mickey had been here.

Blake showed no indication of noticing. 'Well, I'll leave you girls to it,' he said as he went and threw his bag into his room. When he came back, he waved to them both. 'I'm just gonna catch up with Dad and see what he wants us to start on tomorrow. I should be back soon to help with dinner. Catch yas.'

When he was far enough away, Simone grabbed Izzy's arm, dragged her over to the couch and sat her down.

'Whoa! What's wrong?' Izzy watched her pacing back and forth in front of her, anxiously biting her nails.

'I need your help,' she said, glancing at Izzy from the corner of her eyes.

'Come on. Sit down and tell me what's got you so worked up.' Izzy patted the couch next to her. Simone sat down with a slump.

Covering her face in her hands, she began to cry and laugh at the same time. 'I've got myself in a right mess, and I'm buggered as to how it happened. I mean I know how it happens . . . just not how this happened.'

'How what happened?'

'I'm pregnant,' Simone said in a whisper.

Izzy took a few seconds to register what she'd just heard, then sat stunned for a few seconds in shock, before finally breaking out in a big smile. 'You sure?'

'Hell, Izzy. I did both tests and my period was due nearly three weeks ago. I can't pretend it's not happening. I've tried all morning.'

'Well I guess congratulations. That's great.' Izzy gave her a hug, and then pulled back so she could see her face. 'It is, isn't it?'

Simone wiped away a loose tear. 'No. It's terrible.'

'Why? I thought Mickey was the one anyway. You're just moving things along faster than normal, hey.'

'That's what makes this so hard. It's not his baby.' Simone saw Izzy's confusion and explained further. 'Mickey and I haven't slept together yet. We're taking things slowly. Last night was the first time we even kissed, and I mean kissed. We just don't want to rush things – we both want this to work. Now this news is going to ruin our relationship before it's even had a chance.'

'Well, if it ain't Mickster's, whose is it, then?'

Simone gave a funny little snort. 'That's the problem. I don't know. I haven't slept with anyone in bloody ages. The only thing I can think of is whether something happened that night at the bonfire. The timing's right and I was blind. Anything could have happened.' Simone tried to keep a straight face but suddenly the absurdity of it all struck her and made her laugh uncontrollably. It didn't take long before Izzy joined in and they were rolling around on the couch.

'Well, at least we can narrow down the field a bit, as we know who was there that night,' Izzy managed to say between fits of laughter.

Simone sighed after one last half-hearted giggle. 'Yeah, I s'pose you're right.' Turning to Izzy, she grabbed her hand. 'Oh my God, what a mess I've got myself into, Izzy. It's either laugh or cry and I've done enough crying this morning. There's nothing I can do about it now. But this is where I need your help. Any chance you could quietly sniff around to see if anyone saw me with someone? It will need a lot of tact on your behalf. Do you think you could do it, please?'

Izzy leaned back on the couch. 'Yeah, I think I can do some snooping without being found out. You just leave it to me. I wish I could help you myself, but I spent the whole night with Blake. You did go missing for a while there . . .'

'Someone out there must know, unless they were totally drunk as well. God, then I really am stuffed, aren't I?'

'Hey, don't be so hard on yourself. There's nothing you can do to change it, so all you can do is start looking on the bright side. Just think, a little Simone!'

Simone wiped her nose on the sleeve of her shirt. 'Thank God you're here, Izzy. Imagine if I had to confide in Blake or, worse, the girls at the pub. They're the town's gossip lines. None of them can keep secrets.'

'Well, I'm glad I could be here for you too. Now, how 'bout a cuppa before Blake gets back?' Izzy stood up and waited for Simone's answer.

'Cheers. That sounds great. But make mine a hot chocolate, please.'

Izzy headed to the kitchen, flicked on the kettle and collected some cups. 'So, have you been feeling sick?'

'No, not at all. But I know Mum never had any morning sickness with us. I have been feeling weird and more hormonal, though. I keep bursting into tears over absolutely nothing.'

'Have you thought about what you'll do?' Izzy asked, then added, 'Just so you know, I'm behind you a hundred per cent, whatever you choose. Okay?'

'Thanks, Izzy. I appreciate it,' Simone replied as Izzy spooned chocolate into the cups. 'Well, I've been thinking about it – in fact, that's all I've bloody done all day – and quite frankly it's driving me nuts. I can't make a decision until the father knows. He has a say in it too. But if I find out who it is and I really don't like him, well, I think I'm better off deciding on my own. God, it all just gets so complicated. Hell, I hope it's not Reggie's.' Simone pulled a face.

Izzy handed Simone her drink. 'Here ya go, chook. This might help. Chocolate always does.' Simone gave her a weak smile as she sat down. 'Would you like me to go into town tonight? Most of them will probably be in the pub for the Sunday Session.'

'Izzy, I'm going spare. I'd love you to, if you're sure you're not too knackered after your long trip. I got out of my shifts for this weekend so I can't go in myself, but I can't stand not knowing.'

'It's all right. I'll go before dinner, but don't get your hopes up, okay?'

'Yes, ma'am.' Simone saluted her. 'Thanks, Izzy,' she added in a more serious tone. 'I'll put your dinner in the oven, if Blake comes up with something edible.'

'Maybe I'll get some chips at the bar instead.' Izzy gave her a conspiratorial grin.

The last thing she felt like doing was going out again after a long trip back from Perth, but she knew how anxious Simone was and she couldn't let her down.

As soon as Izzy walked inside the pub later that evening, she felt confident of success; most of the blokes from the bonfire night were propped at the bar. Where else would they be on a Sunday night? She headed towards Jacko, who was there with one of his mates, Paul. A good place to start, she thought. She nudged her shoulder in between them and pulled up a stool.

Jacko moved over a bit, giving her more room. 'Hiya, Izzy. How ya going?'

'All right, Jacko. Yourself? G'day, Paul.' Paul said a quick hello before turning to continue his conversation with a bloke on his other side.

'Weren't you supposed to be in Perth? Mickey said you and Blake were going up together. A romantic weekend away, hey?' Jacko asked.

Izzy frowned. 'Yes we went to Perth together, but no, it wasn't a romantic weekend away. Blake's not my type.'

'Am I your type?' Jacko asked with feeling. 'You don't even have to take me to Perth.'

'Jacko, you'd take anyone who looked at you sideways. How many rousies have you been through?' She knew she'd got him thinking. A gun shearer like him would attract a fair amount of attention. He was eye-catching in a musclebound, hard-working kind of way. 'Anyway, how're those missing fingers of yours? I'm surprised even to see you here.'

Jacko held up his bandaged hand and shrugged. 'I'm not dying. It's only a few fingers. It can't stop me from having a drink in my pub.' He saw the concern in Izzy's eyes. 'Don't worry about it, Izzy. I'm trying not to. You need a drink. Fancy sitting at the bar without one. What's your poison?'

'Just a beer, thanks, Jacko.'

Jacko waved his good hand at the barmaid and handed over a ten-dollar note. 'A middy, cheers.'

'Hey, I've been meaning to ask you about the bonfire night.' The barmaid plonked the beer in front of them and dropped the change near Jacko. They both took a guzzle before Jacko turned to face her.

'Bloody good night that one, except for Blake being a bit protective of you.' Jacko was openly flirting with her.

Izzy laughed. 'It was a good night. Do you remember seeing much of Simone?'

Jacko scratched his very stubbly chin. Obviously shaving was impossible with his injured hand. A few more days and it'd be classed as a beard. 'Nearly thought I was in with a chance but she wandered off looking for Mickey.'

'When was that? You know she wiped herself out.'

'We're all prone to a bit of that occasionally.' He smiled and Izzy couldn't help but smile too. He had an infectious nature about him. Almost like a clown, he poured out happiness and fun. 'That was the last time I remember seeing her. Maybe you should ask Mickey. He's been keeping his eye on her for a while.'

Izzy felt a hand on her shoulder. 'Ask me what? Hi, Izzy. You here alone?'

'Hey, Mickey. Yeah, thought I'd pop down for a cold brew after the trip from Perth.'

Mickey's unruly black hair had been trimmed, his face recently shaved and he smelt of soap and aftershave. Not the normal greasy dirt mixed with sweat smell. Had he been hoping to see Simone tonight?

'Oh, how'd it go? Have a good time?'

Jacko got off his stool and waved it to Mickey. 'Here you go, bro. I can see fillies waiting for some help.' He pointed to the jukebox where two young girls fought over which song to pick next. 'Leave yas to it. Catch ya round, Izzy.'

'Yep, see ya, Jacko. Thanks for the beer,' she said, but he was already gone.

Mickey ordered a beer as he parked on the stool. 'So it was good?' he asked again.

'Oh, yeah, it was great. We got to the beach this morning, but it was too cold for a swim.'

'I'm itching to get to the coast myself for a spot of fishing some time soon. My cousin's got a flash fishing boat I'm yet to set foot on.'

'Sounds nice. I haven't been for years. The last time was when I was fifteen, I think. We went down to Hopetoun and did some fishing off the beach. My dad was pissed because my sister and I caught bigger skippy than him.'

The barmaid handed Mickey his drink and he quickly skimmed off the overflowing head of beer. 'Ah, that's better.'

'Hey, Mickey, at the bonfire, you remember how drunk Simone was?'

'Yeah, she was pretty plastered. But hell funny.'

'She can't remember a thing, and Jacko reckons you might have seen her towards the end of the night.'

Mickey's black eyes were watching her intently. 'I did, yes.'

'Well, she can't remember a whole lot about that night.'

A smile broke out on Mickey's face and his eyes danced with laughter. 'Ha. I didn't think she remembered anything.'

Izzy turned her head towards him, highly interested.

'Remembered what, exactly? Is there something she should know?' She watched him think for a minute.

'Well, it *was* my ute she was sleeping in.' He raised his eyebrows, meaning that Izzy would have to guess the rest. 'When she never mentioned anything about it, I figured she either didn't want to remember or she couldn't. I must say I'm happy to know it's the latter.'

Well, this was a turn-up! Izzy felt her bottom lip land with a clunk on the bar top. I bet Simone never even thought about Mickey being the father! 'Why didn't you tell her?' Izzy continued.

'I guess I was a little embarrassed. I knew what state she was in and I was too weak to knock her back. I've liked Simone for as long as I can remember. Part of me thought it might be my only chance. Sad, isn't it? Please don't tell her. We're just getting it together now. I'm the happiest I've been in a long time.'

'Well, you aren't the only one! Anyway, it's bound to come out in the open one day. I know from experience that secrets never stay secrets. It's best to be up-front. You know, Simone really wants it to work between you both too, and I think you'll last.'

Mickey smiled warmly at her words. 'Well, I hope you're right.'

'Hey, why don't you come around for tea Tuesday night? It might be a good time to tell Blake about you and Simone.'

Mickey screwed up his face in caution. 'You reckon? I always had images of Blake pounding the crap out of me for dating his little sister. He's been very protective of her over the years. Mind you, I'm the same with my sisters. If I found out that Blake was with one of them, I might freak too. At first, anyway.'

Izzy finished off her beer, then tucked a loose bit of hair behind her ear. 'Well, we'll expect you around six on Tuesday evening. And no weaselling out of it, okay?' She looked at Mickey and saw the anxiety in his eyes. 'It'll be a good thing. Just you wait and see.'

'All right, but if he gives me a black eye, then you owe me a block of beer. Deal?'

'Deal.'

'You want another drink?'

Now that Izzy was at the pub she was enjoying herself. 'Why not?' She figured Simone could hold on another half hour. She couldn't wait to see the look on her face when she told her who the father of her child was.

39

WILL sat in the soft leather chair, but it may as well have been a wooden church pew. He was waiting by the phone at his parents' place, hoping to hear from Jean. His parents stood in their kitchen surrounded by modern white cupboards and stainless steel appliances, having a cuppa and talking quietly. His mum had stayed home from a golf meeting and his dad had work waiting to be done, but it was all forgotten as they waited for news of Bill. Will leaned forward and put his head in his hands as he listened to the tick of the hallway grandfather clock and the murmur of concerned chatter from his parents. He felt so churned up with concern for Bill and anger at him too. The bloody idiot! He should have known better than to push himself. Will told himself he was just venting because he was so worried. It was hell waiting for the phone to ring.

The events of yesterday played over in his head. He'd left Bill's house after talking to Jean, walked out through the gate and seen him slumped in his wheelchair. He'd called out Bill's name, thinking he was just resting, but when he didn't answer he'd yelled out again and then begun to run. Will's heartbeat quickened at the memory. If only he'd found him sooner. If only he'd come in the rear entrance he might have seen Bill sooner and stopped him heading to the shed. Will had picked up Bill and carried him to their car, all the while yelling out for Jean. She'd heard him and come running. He'd never forget her look of horror, the way her hands went to her mouth, and her eyes so frightened at the sight of Bill being carried like a child.

Will had to scream at her to open the car door to shake her from the shock. When he had Bill in the back they'd both jumped in and Jean had begun to drive the fifty kilometres to Lake Grace, the nearest hospital, while Will phoned for help. They met the ambulance on the road thirty kilometres out of town and transferred him. Will had followed behind in the car and didn't leave until Bill had been organised on a flight to Perth. It had all happened in a blur. He worried that Bill might die and Izzy was . . . God knows where.

He jumped when he heard a ding, but it was just the sound of his dad dropping his cup into the sink. 'Sorry, son.' At that very moment the phone rang.

Will practically launched himself across the chair and pounced on the receiver.

'Hello,' he said quickly.

'Will? It's Jean.' He voice was weak and faint.

'Oh, Jean. How is he? What's happening?' Will was gripping the phone so tight his palms began to sweat.

'He's had a stroke, Will. They're doing blood tests and he's been for a CT scan. I should hear more about it soon. They say he'll be okay but the extent of the stroke is still unknown. I just thought you'd like to know. Thanks for your help. I don't know what I'd have done had I found him myself. He probably wouldn't be here.'

Will heard Jean choke up with tears and his heart went out to her. She had dealt with so much and now this. She really was a trouper. Will could see where Izzy got her strength from. 'He'll come through, Jean. I know he will.' He didn't know what else to say, but his mum was standing by and he knew she'd have more encouraging words. He said goodbye and gave the phone to Sandy, who took off her apron and held the phone gently like she was holding Jean herself.

Will got up and moved through the large French doors that opened onto a glassed sunroom. He felt he was barely keeping things together. What's more, he was hurting for Izzy. She had no idea that this had even happened.

'You all right, son?' Brian put his arm over Will's shoulder and half hugged him close. 'Come on, there's not much we can do for him now. Let's go get those sheep shifted.'

Will nodded and let his dad escort him from the house, like a dog on an invisible lead. Maybe work would take his mind off Bill. Why couldn't Izzy call? It'd make him feel so much better, even just to hear her voice.

40

SIMONE jumped closer to Izzy on the bed as she half screeched, '*Whaaat?* What do you mean, I should already know who the father is?'

The bedroom door was shut to keep away prying ears, but Blake had already fired up his computer and wouldn't be bothering them.

'Well, we know you slept with someone, right, and that you passed out in the back of Mickey's ute. That should tell you something.' Izzy couldn't resist letting Simone figure it out by herself.

'Tell me what? Izzy, what did you find out? So what if I passed out in Mickey's ute? That doesn't mean anything . . . does it?' Simone's eyes grew large as she started to get the hint.

Izzy nodded, waited and watched as it dawned on Simone. She couldn't keep the smile off her face.

'It's Mickey! Mickey's the father? I slept with Mickey? Oh my God.' Her hand clapped over her open mouth.

Izzy began to laugh but when she saw Simone glare at her, she explained. 'I'm sorry. It's just that here you are saying how nice it is that you and Mickey are taking things slow. That you've only just kissed when in fact you've already slept with the bloke. I just find that quite funny and ironic. Don't you think?'

Simone's eyes smiled and laughter escaped her mouth. 'You're so right. God, what an idiot I've been.' Her laughter died down as she thought about it further. 'You know what's worse? He knew, the bastard. This whole time he knew he'd slept with me and that I didn't remember it.'

'Not entirely. He wasn't sure. He thought you might have wanted to forget it happened, and he was embarrassed. Give the guy a break. He's really likes you.'

'Really? You think so?' She smiled at Izzy. 'Do you think he'll mind about the baby?'

'I don't know about that, but you'll have time to tell him tomorrow night. I've invited him around for tea. He should be here by six. Oh, and he thinks it's because you're going to tell Blake about the two of you.'

'Oh, thanks. Nice one, Izzy,' said Simone sarcastically.

'Well, you may as well kill two birds with one stone, hey. Don't worry. It'll be fine.'

'Says you sitting on the other side of the fence.'

'So, do you think you'll keep the baby?'

'Hell, yeah. I do now. Just knowing it's Mickey's makes me want it even more.' Simone rubbed her belly tenderly.

Izzy felt excited about the prospect of a little baby on the way. 'I'm thrilled for you, Simo. I'm a bit disappointed it wasn't Reggie's, but them's the breaks, I guess.'

Simone screwed up her nose.

'You know, I've been at heaps of births so if you need any help.'

'Have you?'

'Yep. Hundreds of baby lambs have been born under my watchful eye.'

Simone picked up her pillow and threw it at her. 'Hey, you can feel free to change a nappy or two. Bloody hell, do I really know what I'm getting myself into?'

'Settle down. You still have eight months left. There's plenty of time. Take it easy, eh. I'll get on the Net later and order you a few books to read. Hey, your mum's going to scream for joy when she finds out.'

'Oh, Mum'll be stoked, but first I've gotta get past telling Mickey. I'm terrified even thinking about it.'

'Just get a good night's sleep and worry about it tomorrow.' Izzy yawned and rubbed her eyes. 'I don't know about you, but I'm absolutely buggered. Were there any leftovers?'

'Oh, yeah. It's in the casserole pot in the oven.'

'Cool, thanks,' said Izzy, closing the door behind her and walking to the kitchen.

Fifteen minutes later, she flopped into bed. Tired as she was, her mind didn't let her nod off for another hour or so. When she finally fell asleep, dreams of Simone holding a baby changed into images of Claire with a tiny newborn and Will standing behind her. Then Claire turned into Izzy and she saw herself smiling up at Will with their baby in her arms.

41

'HEY, Mickey. Come in, mate,' said Blake as he greeted him at the front door.

'Did Izzy tell you she'd invited me for dinner?' Mickey asked cautiously.

'She sure did. Great idea, too. We haven't had you over for bloody ages. It's been right rude of us.'

'That's all right. Here, I hope you like it,' said Mickey, handing Blake a bottle of red wine.

'Cheers. Come on in. The girls are in the games room.'

'Righto.' Mickey headed down to the other end of the house. The room had been added on years ago, just before Blake's parents decided to build a new house. Mickey and Blake had spent a lot of time in it playing pool when they were younger. As he walked in Izzy and Simone stopped talking.

'G'day, Mickey. How's things?' Izzy asked.

'Not too bad. Looking forward to the sale next week. I have my eye on a few good rams already. Oh, wanna hear something funny? Jacko has a girl.'

Simone spluttered, 'No way!'

'For real? Who?' asked Izzy.

'You remember those two girls from the pub? Well, the one with the long red hair and cute freckles – her name was Kate, I think. She's setting up a hairdressing salon in town.'

'Wow.'

'Oh my God,' the girls exclaimed together.

'Yeah, she's Larry Dwyer's niece from Morawa. Jacko's smitten, and get this – she's making him wait.'

'Well, that'd be a first for Jacko. No wonder she's caught his eye,' said Izzy. 'So, Mickey, do you want a beer?'

'I actually brought some wine. Do you both want a glass?'

Izzy glanced at Simone, who went to say yes, then changed her mind. 'I'm right for the moment, thanks anyway.'

'Well I'll have some. How about I get us some glasses,' Izzy said. As she left the room she caught a glimpse of them having a hug and a kiss hello, and she couldn't help but feel very lonely.

Heading to the kitchen, Izzy had two motives. One was to keep Blake sidetracked for a fair while, and two was to get him to open up.

'Hey, look. Mickey brought us some wine for dinner. Should go great with the roast you made,' said Blake as Izzy approached.

Izzy examined the bottle. 'Yeah. I'm just gonna pour us a glass. You want one?'

'Please, that's nice stuff. From down south too.'

'Oh, you're a wine connoisseur now?'

Blake flicked her with a tea towel. 'So, do you need any help with this complicated meal?'

Izzy looked over the kitchen. The beans and corn were cooking on the stovetop and the rest was in the oven, waiting to be served. She just had the gravy to make.

'Christ, Izzy. There's hardly any mess. Maybe you should cook more,' Blake teased.

Izzy and Blake both jumped when they heard Mickey yell, 'What?'

'What's going on?' said Blake intrigued. 'I might just run some nibblies down while you're finishing up.'

'Actually, before you do that, I wanted to have a word,' she said.

Blake leant back against the kitchen cupboard. 'I'm all ears.'

Izzy took a deep breath. She had to make sure she tackled this next bit right. 'You know, tonight would be a great time to tell Simone and Mickey about yourself.' She watched his handsome jaw drop as she went about opening the wine.

'Shit, Izzy. Don't lump that on me. I'm not ready. I haven't had time.'

'Time for what? For you to think about it too much and chicken out? This way is much better. Just spit it out and let them process it.' She could see him back-pedalling. The fear of rejection flashed across his face. She didn't envy him. But if he wanted to start living his life out in the open, he had to try. 'It'll be okay. This is your sister and your best mate. I know they both think the world of you. You have to give them the chance to be supportive.' Izzy got out some glasses and began to fill them.

'You make it sound so easy. Maybe you should tell them for me. Man, I feel like I'm going to have a panic attack. My heart's racing, I'm sweating, I feel sick and I can't breathe. If I keel over, promise you'll look after the farm?' He tried to make light of the situation.

Izzy could see he was struggling – he'd gone all pasty-looking – so she handed him his drink. 'If it makes you feel any better, I think what Simone has to tell you might come as even more of a surprise.' She knew that would make his ears prick up.

'Come on, you can't say that much and leave it.' Blake took a gulp of wine and managed to spill a drop on his clean shirt. 'Crap.'

Izzy was laughing as Mickey and Simone walked into the kitchen. Izzy handed Mickey his wine and they all sat down at the table. 'Well, dinner won't be long. Maybe ten minutes or so.'

'It smells great,' said Simone, helping herself to a biscuit and some chilli dip. 'While we wait, there's something I'd really like to tell you, Blake.' She blushed with the excitement.

'What's so important?' asked Blake, edgy with anticipation himself.

'I hope you're not mad or anything, but it's only just happened,' Simone said, playing with the hem of her jumper.

Blake frowned.

'We are going out,' she said rather quickly, then slipped her hand over Mickey's on the table to make her point.

Blake watched Mickey entwine his fingers with Simone's tenderly. Blake pointed at them. 'You two are together?'

Cautiously, they both nodded.

At first, there was a surprised look, then a smile followed and Blake's eyes lit up. 'Sweet. What a turn-up for the books. I've been so self-absorbed lately I hadn't even noticed. Since when?'

'Just the last couple of weeks,' Mickey joined in.

Izzy wished she had a few ping pong balls to throw into Mickey and Simone's open mouths. They hadn't expected this reaction at all. 'I told you he'd be cool,' Izzy said from the stove as she boiled the kettle for the gravy.

Blake gave Izzy a curious look. 'Did you already know about this?'

Izzy winked at him. 'Hell, yeah. Someone had to nudge Simone in the right direction. But she was worried about how you'd react.'

Blake shrugged. 'Why? I think it's great – my best friend and my sister. It's okay, you can relax now,' Blake said, seeing them still looking a bit uptight.

Taking a moment, Mickey and Blake downed half the wine in their glasses while Simone sipped a Diet Coke.

Izzy moved over behind Blake, put her hand on his shoulder, and gave it a squeeze.

Blake looked up into Izzy's compassionate eyes. The blue depths of them gave him a strength he didn't know he possessed. Her previous words sprang to mind. She'd said that if she hadn't told her father what she really wanted in life, she never would have been truly happy. No, it might not have worked out for her, but at least her father knew where she stood. Izzy felt more at peace with herself for not hiding her feelings and not having to lie. In some respects, Blake knew she was right – he couldn't keep this secret and expect to live a fulfilled life.

'I . . . ah . . .' began Blake slowly.

'What's up?' Simone asked.

'I have something to say too.'

'Well, spit it out. It can't be that bad,' she said, sensing his anxiety.

Blake looked her in the eye before he quietly whispered the words that had tortured his thoughts. 'I'm gay.' He watched as a smile grew on her face, while Mickey's was dark and motionless. 'What's so funny?' He was worried. Did she think he was joking?

'Tell me something I didn't know,' she said mockingly.

Blake's face was pale. 'You knew?'

'Hell, I'm not stupid, Blake. I'd sort of guessed a while ago but didn't know a hundred per cent until I heard it from your lips.' She shrugged. 'I figured you'd tell me when you were ready. I certainly wasn't going to bring it up, just in case I was wrong, which I didn't think I was, but . . .' Simone got out of her chair and wrapped her arms around her brother, kissing him on his cheek. 'I love you, and I'm glad you've decided to trust me with this. I guess it's a big step for you?'

Blake held her at arm's length, tears welling in the corners of his eyes. 'You'll never know how much, sis. Thanks.' He couldn't believe how much time he'd spent worrying about how Simone would react. For the past few years he had pretended to be attracted to girls to keep everyone off the scent. But it was such hard work. All that time stressing and hiding, and to think Simone had known all along. He'd never felt as much love for his sister as he did now.

Blood sure was thicker than water. He hoped his parents would be as understanding.

Meanwhile, Izzy had been watching Mickey. She prayed she had been right about his character – that he was very loyal and never judged people. She could see he was mulling things over.

Simone sat down next to Mickey and took hold of his hand again tightly. All eyes were on him now. The hissing of the boiled kettle echoed throughout the silent house. Breathlessly they all waited.

'I . . . Wow – didn't see that one coming.' He was clearly surprised but what else was to come?

Mickey slowly looked across to Blake and said, in an almost squeaky voice, 'I've never left your side in a fight yet, mate, and I'm not about to.' Then he shrugged. 'Deep down, maybe I knew, but it doesn't really matter because it doesn't change who you are. You'll always be my best mate.' Mickey held out his hand and Blake shook it vigorously before pulling him into a quick, manly hug.

'Cheers, Mickey. It means a bloody lot,' Blake said, as he sat back down. He glanced up at Izzy and squeezed her hand, which had come back to rest on his shoulder.

He rewarded Izzy with the happiest smile she had seen in a long time. It brought a lump the size of a brick to her throat. Quickly she diverted her eyes to a photo on the wall of a bogged tractor, and waited for it to subside.

'Besides, it's nothing compared to finding out you're going to be a father,' said Mickey, getting Blake's attention. 'Did I mention that you're going to be an uncle?'

'An uncle? What do you mean?' Blake screwed up his eyes in puzzlement.

Simone held her belly and laughed. 'Mickey and I are having a baby.'

'Holy shit!' Blake slapped his forehead.

'Tell me about it. I only just found out a few minutes ago myself. We hooked up at the bonfire, which she doesn't even remember, or it was that bad she's tried to forget it,' he stirred, and Simone squeezed his hand in a death grip. 'How romantic is that!'

Blake wiped his hand over his face as he tried to swallow this news.'The bonfire night? But that was ages ago.'

'Yep, so I guess I'm about eight weeks or so.' Simone smiled, reliving the way Mickey had hugged her, felt her belly and asked, 'Is this for real?' She'd nodded and he'd kissed her. 'Is this what you want? With me?' he'd said. She'd nodded nervously again, wondering whether he felt the same, but he'd taken her in his arms and whispered, 'It's all going to be fine, Simone. I love you. I always have.' Simone realised that all she'd ever wanted was right there in front of her and that living in Mullawoon on a farm with Mickey would make her deliriously happy.

With all the commotion going on in the kitchen, Izzy headed outside to drink in the cool night air, away from the overwhelmed but ecstatic group. The moon lit up the garden and cast black shadows over the silvery ground. One of these shadows came from a huge gum tree that was filled with galahs. They were screeching away to each other as they perched there for the night.

She could still hear the muffled voices of the others inside, speaking quickly and excitedly. They had lots to talk about, that was for sure. Izzy couldn't help but feel sad in a way. It was times like these that she missed her family most. At least these guys had a happy ending. Well, more like a new beginning. But what was her future? Was she destined to stay on Erindale forever? She couldn't really picture her future here. No matter how hard she tried, Izzy just couldn't see anything but Gumlea – or maybe she didn't want to.

'A penny for your thoughts,' said Blake, approaching from behind and wrapping an arm around her shoulders.

'Ha. You'll need more than that for my thoughts.'

They stood together quietly for a moment.

'So are you okay, still happy?' Izzy asked.

'Thanks to you, everything's cool. Man, can you believe my little sister's gonna have a squawker, and I'll be an uncle? It's just unbelievable. Simone wants to keep it quiet until she's about three months, but they're going to tell Mum and Dad soon. Mum's gonna flip.'

Izzy nodded. 'I'm glad you're happy.'

'Well, it's a good start anyway. And there's no reason you can't be happy too. Why don't you give Will a call or your mum? Come on, you've made us face our fears tonight. When's it gonna be your turn? It could work out better than you expect, you know.'

Izzy had been trying to tell herself this, but fear stopped her from taking any action. 'I don't know. Maybe. I might after the ram sale,' she said, fobbing him off.

Blake sighed. 'Now you're just making excuses.'

'I don't like being disappointed. And I hate that Dad has this thing over me. He's still controlling my life because he has the thing I want the most, and he's never let me near it.' Izzy gave Blake a weak smile. 'Feel like a game of pool? We could go doubles against the other two.'

Taking a deep breath, he sighed. 'You really are good at avoiding the issue. All right. I'll let it pass, this time. Next time you won't get away with it so easily.' Izzy headed back inside, pretending not to understand, but he knew she was still listening. 'Better enjoy yourself while you can. Tomorrow we start gearing up for the sale next week and I know Wally can't wait for you to look after him.'

Izzy rolled her eyes but was pleased by the change of subject. Wally was one of the best rams they had and Blake's favourite. He had very good balls on him that were gonna make him rich, Blake would always joke. She had to admit she was looking forward to the excitement of the auction and seeing the interested farmers. She'd picked up quite a bit from Blake recently but she still wanted to learn as much as she could in case anyone asked for information on the SAMM stud.

Walking in on Mickey and Simone having a kiss in the kitchen, she soon forgot about Wally and the stud, and instead felt the excitement of new love.

Izzy waved her hand at them. 'Don't stop on my account. It's nice to see a bit of love floating around.'

Mickey and Simone grinned back like silly teenagers before following her into the lounge room with their drinks.

'Come on, you two lovebirds,' she said, picking up a pool cue. 'Let's see what kind of team you really make. Dinner can wait a bit longer.'

42

WILL was so keen to finish making the trailer that he skipped breakfast and began welding straightaway. His father walked over to the shed in the warm sun around lunchtime, carrying a cuppa and a toastie and placed them on the wheel arch of the trailer. Will put down the welder and took off his protective helmet. 'Morning, Dad.'

'Hey, mate. Thought you might be hungry.'

'I am a bit. Thanks.'

'It looks finished,' said Brian, running a hand over the trailer. 'I'm impressed. You've been working hard on it.'

'Yeah, I wanted to get it done so I could get over to Bill's place and check out his gear before the next rain. He's due back in Lake Grace tomorrow.'

'So, how is he?'

'He's up to coming home – well, nearly home – but he still can't talk properly. The right side of his body and the left side of his face are still not back to normal. It's affected his speech and language, and Jean said he has a bit of memory loss as well. She can't move him around by herself so he'll be in Lake Grace where they can keep an eye on him, until he's up to coming home. He's improving all the time. But it means I'll be over at Gumlea a bit.'

'Yeah, sure. They're lucky to have you, you know. You've done a lot for that family.' Will could hear the pride in his dad's voice. He shrugged his shoulders.

'Let me know if you need any help at the Simpson place, but

I won't be around tomorrow. There's a stud sale in Brookton I'm interested in. Think I'll go take a look.'

Will stopped chewing. Hot spaghetti fell to the concrete floor. Something ticked over in his mind.

'That's it!'

'What's it, son?'

'Dad, where's the latest *Elders*?'

'I don't know. Try the loo. What's up?'

Brian didn't get an answer. Will ran out of the shed into the cool midday air, leaving behind his cuppa and half a toastie, and headed straight for the toilet. Opening the door, he spotted the *Elders* lying on the floor. He scooped it up and went into the office. Sitting down at the desk, he began flicking frantically through the pages. Halfway in he found what he was searching for. He picked up a marker, circled all the phone numbers, then lifted up the phone and started dialling.

'Hello. I saw your stud auction ad and I was wondering whether you had a new farmhand working for you called Izzy Simpson?'

The day of the sale had come around fast. They'd been flat out setting up. Even Simone was getting in on the act. The change in her was amazing. The interest she now took in the farm had shocked her whole family. She had just needed a reason to be interested, and Mickey was a good one.

It had been an early-morning start, covering the floor of the display shed with fresh straw and then bringing in the sheep and penning them up. Izzy had been firing questions at Blake and Alan all morning, seeing what needed doing and trying to learn as much as she could.

After they finished, she sat on an old tyre outside and watched the prospective buyers arriving. Half of them were probably only here to look. But hopefully there were some eager buyers out there.

Alan had sixty rams on offer. He would be rapt if they all went for a good price.

Izzy smiled as she looked over the land. She had been here a while now and knew it pretty well. Mullawoon had its low rolling hills, creek valleys and rocky ridges and its red sandy loam soils. But at Gumlea she could drive to all the paddocks blindfolded, and then tell you the exact soil type under her feet without having to dig. The areas where the salmon gums grew were good indicators of nice heavy soil. Likewise the mallee trees, with their many underground stems and branched trunks that liked the sandy loam. Just thinking about it made her smile again.

Shaking her head, she tried to throw the thoughts from her mind. It didn't do her any good to dwell on the farm. It only made her more homesick. Annoyed for tormenting herself yet again, she decided to head inside and see whether she could be of any help.

The huge shed had been purpose-built for farm auctions. This would be Erindale Prime SAMM stud's third year. The smell of straw and sheep hung in the warm air and the hum of voices bounced off the metal walls and ceiling. Izzy noticed a couple of men standing by the yard of one of their best rams.

'G'day, fellas. You interested in our mate, Wally, here? He is one of the stud's best.' Both men nodded. They looked like serious bidders.

'What's the ram's EMD?' asked the taller of the two. He was older, maybe in his sixties, and Izzy got the distinct feeling he was testing her.

'His eye muscle depth is forty-two millimetres and he was a hundred and twenty kilograms at last weigh,' she said while holding Wally's head for them to study.

They raised their eyebrows and nodded, impressed with the figures. She could see they wanted to talk further so she gave them some privacy and turned to leave.

'Thanks, love,' the older man called out.

She waved her hand in reply and headed towards another pen. Mickey and Simone were at this one with another couple. She could hear Mickey doing his sales pitch.

'I've come to buy,' said Mickey. 'I've slowly introduced them to my merino flock, but I've now decided to convert the entire lot, as we're aiming to boost the meat aspect. With their growth rates, we can get the lambs off the farm heaps quicker.'

The young couple looked fascinated by what Mickey had to say. 'It sure does sound great. My wife and I have been interested in the SAMMs for a while.'

Izzy was feeling redundant. She gave Simone a nod and decided to grab a drink. Too many people in the shed made the temperature rise and the air stuffy. The straw scuffed under her boots as she headed down the side of the pens.

Suddenly she stopped.

Will Timmins was heading towards her. At least, she thought it looked like him. Was the heat making her see things? As the bloke walked closer, she expected his face to merge into someone else's, but it didn't. Will stopped in front of her and reached out to hold her arms, as if forcing her to realise she wasn't hallucinating. His blue eyes, bright and electrifying, delved into her soul. Oh, she'd missed them and his strong handsome face.

'Hi, Izzy,' he said in a voice that sent shivers up her spine.

'Will? Fancy seeing you here. I . . . ah . . . didn't know you were interested in SAMMs. Do you want me to show you around?' What were the chances of him coming to this auction? she thought.

'Izzy, I'm not here to buy a bloody ram,' said Will, shaking her slightly.

She raised an eyebrow curiously. 'You're not? Then . . . why are you here?'

'For you, of course.'

'Oh . . .' Izzy thought for a moment, but seemed stunned. 'But how did you know I was here?' She was trying hard not to get lost in his eyes.

'You mentioned the ram sale when we bumped into each other in Perth, so I just rang all the coming stud sales and asked if you worked there. After a handful, I eventually rang Erindale and found out where you've been hiding. Didn't realise you were this far north.'

'Oh.' Izzy didn't know what to say.

'Alan told me that you worked for him but I asked him not to say anything until I could come and talk to you myself,' Will explained.

'I see.' I really need that drink of water, she thought. 'So, what do you want to talk about?' He'd caught her completely off guard and now she was starting to feel angry at him for confronting her like this.

'You need to come home at once,' he said sternly.

Izzy began shaking her head. 'No, I can't, Will. Not yet.'

'You have to. Your dad's very sick. He needs you.'

Izzy squinted at him. 'What do you mean sick?' Thud. Her heart began to beat so hard that she felt like she was standing on a railway crossing as a train chugged past.

Will took a deep breath and glanced around the busy shed. He had hoped to do this in private, but he knew she wasn't going to budge.

'I found him slumped in his wheelchair nearly two weeks ago. He'd had a stroke.' Will let his words sink in.

Izzy felt the blood drain from her body. 'What?' she managed to squeak.

'He's back at Lake Grace now and he's over the worst of it, but, Izzy, he really needs to see you.'

Izzy began to fall forwards. Will could see she was about to pass out. Quickly, he guided her to a hay bale and sat her down. She was pale and staring into space. Will looked up and saw Blake striding towards them. He silently groaned.

'Hey, Will. How are you going?' Blake greeted him, much more cheerfully than Will had expected. 'What's up with you, Izzy? You look crook. Is there anything I can do?' Blake held Izzy's face as he looked into her eyes. He reached over and rubbed her back.

'Some water, mate?' Will asked, hoping he would rack off. This was none of his business. He didn't know if it was the look of concern on Blake's face that had him ticked off or the way he caressed Izzy's back tenderly. Either one gave him more reason to hate the guy.

Blake nodded. 'I'm on to it.' He headed for his water bottle.

'Izzy, are you all right?' Will asked.

'Yeah, it's just a bit of a shock.' She started to stand up but her legs were still wobbly.

'Whoa. What are you doing?' Will gently forced her to sit back down.

'I need to go and pack and head home.'

Will paused. 'You want to go see him, now?'

Izzy turned and looked him in the eyes. 'He's my father, Will. I still love him. I don't want to see him hurt again, or . . .' She was about to say dead, but couldn't bring herself to finish. 'He's the only father I've got.'

'Blake's bringing you some water. Just sit here and get yourself together, then you can think about coming home. Your dad's fine. He's settled into the hospital at Lake Grace and he's not going anywhere. They think he'll make a full recovery, so you don't have to rush home this minute.'

Izzy nodded obediently.

'Here, have a drink,' said Blake on his return.

'Thanks.' She drained the cup in a few gulps. 'Dad just can't sit still, can he?' she said, anger surging through her once again. 'He's always pushing the limits. He's gonna do himself in properly one of these days if he can't learn to take it easy.' Izzy rolled her eyes to prove her point. 'None of this would have happened . . .'

'I know. You're right,' said Will. He could see the colour returning to Izzy's gorgeous face. He had missed her so much more than he thought he would. It seemed so lonely on the farm now. He felt like he was lost most of the time, with no direction or purpose. He found himself sitting by Bill's chair a lot, just talking farming to him. He felt comfortable in their house, as if he was closer to Izzy. A part of him always hoped that the next time he visited Bill, Izzy would be sitting there beside him.

'Do you want me to drive you down?' Blake asked Izzy.

'No,' said Will and Izzy at the same time.

Izzy looked sideways at Will, baffled by his quick reply. Shrugging, she explained, 'There's no use me rushing home, like Will said. I'll go after the sale. It'll only be an extra hour. I can't abandon your dad. This is a huge event for the farm and I want to see it through.'

Blake sighed. 'You win, but I'm still coming with you after it's over. I don't think you should be driving by yourself.' He gave her a forceful look. 'Besides, I've always said I'd love to see your place.'

'Okay.' She knew it was no use trying to argue with Blake.

Blake turned to Will. 'She's not as tough as she makes out.'

'Tell me something I don't know, mate.' Blake knows her well, Will thought angrily. Izzy had her moments where she'd let you see her fragile side, but they were few and far between. He wondered how much Blake had seen.

'I'm still sitting here, you know, and I am tough,' Izzy piped up.

Blake laughed at her and gave her shoulder a squeeze. Will felt an annoying twitch in his neck – or maybe that was Blake.

'Well, I'm gonna find Simo and Dad and tell them that we'll be heading off after the sale.' Blake gave Izzy a wink, then walked away without looking back.

'Are you okay?' Will asked, crouching down to her eye level and giving her the once-over.

'I'm feeling all right. But I'll be better once I've seen Dad. Come on. Let's go watch the auction and you can tell me everything that's been happening on the farm. And don't leave anything out,' she said eagerly. Izzy plucked a piece of straw from the bale as she got up and began to pull it apart.

Will shook his head. 'I can't. I have to keep going. Dad needs help with some stud rams he's bought so I gotta head home as soon as possible, and it'll be dark by the time I get there.' Truth was he didn't want to be hanging around watching Izzy and Blake together. It was bad enough standing this close to her and not being able to hold her.

'Are you sure?' Izzy said, with a hint of sadness.

Will nodded.

'I'll walk you out, then,' Izzy said. She was finding it hard to tear her eyes away from him. She wanted to reach out and touch him, make sure he was real.

Together they headed to the shed opening.

'It's a shame,' she said. 'I would have liked to introduce you to Alan and Simone, Blake's sister. I've been living with her and Blake in their old house.'

Wow, she's living with him now. Will felt his heart drop down into the pit of his stomach like a forty-four-gallon drum. 'So, it's been good, then?' Will said. He felt the green hand of jealousy squeeze at his body.

'It's been great. Simone's like a sister. It's been nice having someone close again, not that she's replaced Claire.' Izzy's voice trailed off when she saw that the look on Will's face was less than happy. Changing the subject, she said, 'You know, I still can't believe you came all this way to find me. Why didn't you just leave a message?'

Will shrugged as they passed the auctioneer, who was waving his arms around like a bird in flight. 'I was worried you wouldn't come, but Bill really needs you, Izzy, and I couldn't take the risk.

Part of me feared you wouldn't come back.' Will saw her expression change and knew she was about to have a go at him. He held up his hands to ward off her words. 'I know, I know. I see now that I was wrong. I shouldn't have doubted how much you love your dad, but he has been pretty hard on you recently and I just wasn't sure how you'd react.'

She was drawn to Will's eyes, and in their depths she saw his sincere concern and worry. 'You really do care about him too, don't you?'

Will nodded and his gaze sent shivers up her spine. Thank God I'm not heading home with him today, she thought. A long drive sitting next to Will would drive me insane.

'We've been through a lot together. I didn't realise at first how difficult he was making your life, but you'll see he's changed when you get home.'

'You know I don't believe you. I can't imagine Dad ever changing. You said yourself, he's very stubborn.'

So was Izzy, and that's why Will didn't bother trying to set her straight. Let her hear it from Jean and hopefully Bill, when he's better. Will climbed into his ute and gave her a quick wave. 'I'll see you back home, I guess.'

She waved as he drove off, with a fierce ache inside her. Seeing him again and then having him leave was like being on a big rollercoaster that she couldn't get off. She didn't move until his ute disappeared from sight.

'So, that was Will?' Simone walked up behind her and put her arm around her waist.

'Yeah, I'd have liked to introduce you but apparently he was in a hurry.'

'Pity. He's a stunner. Don't worry, you'll see him back home.' They began walking back to the shed. 'I'm sorry to hear about your dad.'

Izzy nodded, acknowledging her friend's concern. Having Simone and Blake in her life made her happy and she felt blessed to have found them.

'When will you be coming back?'

'I'm not sure. But don't worry, I'll keep in touch and visit. I'll need to know how you're going with the bub.'

Flicking her hair back, Simone grinned. 'We told Mum and Dad last night. I'm delighted to say they're over the moon. A little shocked but completely thrilled.' Simone watched Izzy's face, looking for a smile. 'And Mickey's asked me to move in with him. He's going to do up the old house on the farm for us. It's so exciting, Izzy. There's so much to look forward to. I could tell Dad was thinking about the farms working together more. Typical bloody farmers.'

At last she got Izzy smiling. 'Simone, that's wonderful.'

'Come on. Let's go inside and watch the sale. I want to see who gets Wally.'

43

IZZY watched the land and trees flash past the window. She had let Blake drive her ute home. Well, he'd insisted. It had made the trip go slower for her, not having something to do. She didn't make a very good passenger. They'd left after the sale and had driven until nine at night, where they stopped and slept under the stars at Merredin. Izzy was eager to get home but didn't want to disturb her mum at midnight. It would be easier to catch up in the morning, when they were all rested. They'd rolled up their swags at seven the next day and started on the last couple of hours to Pingaring.

'I'm so glad that Wally went for two grand. He was definitely worth it,' she said, making conversation.

'I agree. It was our best year yet. And to average just over a thousand dollars a head is bloody impressive. It's been the greatest decision we've made together, getting this SAMM stud off the ground.'

Izzy felt a twinge of envy at this last comment.

'You know, if I knew you lived so bloody far away, I wouldn't have offered to come. We must be past the black stump by now,' Blake said jokingly.

'Keep your shirt on. We're nearly there.'

'You said that ten minutes ago.'

Izzy smiled. They were only five minutes away from pulling into their driveway and she was struggling to contain her excitement. But she was also apprehensive about seeing her father in hospital, not really knowing what shape he would be in. Closing her eyes, she leaned towards the open window and took a deep breath. The wind swirled a few loose strands of hair about, tickling her face. She opened her eyes again, not wanting to miss anything, and took in the familiar road. She looked out over the paddocks – the odd one had been turned over with fresh brown soil. They stood out among the other paddocks that were still bare or left with stained and crumbling stubble from last year's harvest. It looked as though it had rained recently – the trees had vibrant green foliage and their trunks glistened. Deep green weeds poked their heads up out of the ground along the roadside. Someone was spraying out in a paddock on the left and she knew by the ute that it'd be Dave, a contract sprayer. The smell of Roundup floated through the air as they passed him. Izzy couldn't help but smile, knowing she was back in familiar territory.

'Just over there is where Claire rolled her car coming home after a party. She fell asleep and veered off the road. She was okay, though, but the car was a write-off. And over there is where Jim and Betty Cable live. They're our next-door neighbours. Betty's cooking is the best.'

'You and your food,' said Blake. 'So this is the famous Gumlea farm. I feel like I've been here before, you described it so well,' he continued as he turned into the driveway and headed towards the farmhouse. 'Does it feel good to be back?' Blake noticed a sparkle in her eyes that he'd never seen before.

'It feels bloody fantastic.' No paddocks were ripped, and she was delighted to see that nothing had changed. Not much ever did out here. But Izzy sighed after climbing out of the ute. 'Oh.'

'What's up?' He saw her sad expression and began to worry instantly.

'It's nothing. Just for the briefest moment I had this feeling of excitement because I expected Tom to come running out to greet me as he always used to. For a minute I forgot he wasn't here any more. How sad's that?' Izzy looked up at Blake as he wrapped his arm around her shoulder and drew her in. She was wearing one of his large blue and black Warrie jumpers, to keep out the chill, and her work jeans, and Blake was still decked out in his Erindale SAMM Stud work clothes. The uniform made him look tall, sexy and important.

At that moment Will walked out from behind the gate. He skidded to a halt when he saw Izzy and Blake together, arm in arm. He wasn't ready to see them like that. 'Hey, you're here. Good,' he said, turning away to cover his slight embarrassment. He'd been waiting nervously for the last hour, since Jean had rung and told him Izzy would be home this morning around nine. He had hoped she'd come home alone. No such luck.

A smile spread across Izzy's face. 'Sorry we're a bit later than planned. Blake drives like an old lady.'

Blake laughed. 'Don't listen to her.' He shot Izzy a glare, which wasn't intimidating at all.

'Well, did you want to head into Lake Grace and see Bill? We haven't told him you're coming. We thought you could surprise him,' said Will.

'Sounds good. I'll just catch up with Mum first.'

Blake hung back as they made their way to the gate. Before Izzy got to the back door, it swung open and her mum ran through with her arms outstretched. She didn't speak a word, just hugged Izzy tightly.

'Hiya, Mum. How are you holding up?'

Jean pulled out of the embrace but kept her hand on her daughter's arm. 'I'm fine. So happy that you're home.' She beamed from ear to ear but Izzy couldn't help thinking she looked older.

'Will's going to take us in to see your father. But would you like to come inside and have a cuppa first?'

'No thanks. I'm keen to head into town. Is that all right?'

'Sure, love. We can catch up in the car.' They walked back towards the shed where her parents' car was garaged.

When they got close to Blake, Izzy stopped and introduced him. 'Oh, Mum. Sorry, this is Blake MacDougall from Erindale, a stud farm up north where I've been living and working. He kept me company on the drive. Blake, this is my mum, Jean.'

'Nice to meet you, Jean,' said Blake, shaking her hand.

Izzy noticed that Will was standing nearby. He was quiet and almost distant. Normally he'd be trying to annoy the crap out of her. It occurred to Izzy that maybe he'd resented her moving away, taking off the way she had, and leaving him to look after Bill and all the farm work. Or maybe their afternoon together really had changed things between them. How was she to know?

'Blake, are you happy to tag along with us into town?' Will asked him, hoping he'd rather stay put.

'Yep, for sure.'

'Course you're coming. You have to meet my dad. Jump in the front with Will. I'll hang in the back with Mum. We've got lots of catching up to do.'

They piled into the Holden. Izzy and Jean talked all the way into town, while the front of the car remained relatively silent. Blake had tried to start up a conversation with Will but he only got single-word answers back and eventually gave up and listened to Izzy rattle on about her life on Erindale. When they arrived at the small hospital, with its large lawn and gardens out the front, Jean began preparing Izzy again. 'Now, he's lost a lot of weight, so don't be too shocked, love. His right arm is still weak and the left side of his face is a bit droopy. And he hasn't been able to talk yet. He says a lot of garbled stuff, but we can't make any sense of it.'

'Yes, you've told me all this.' Izzy patted her mum's shoulder. 'Don't stress, Mum. It'll be okay – I will be okay. It can't be any worse than seeing his burns.'

Taking a deep breath, Jean nodded.

They walked through the sliding doors and Jean guided them

down the wide passage. They walked past empty wards to the end room where her father was staying. The room was quiet; white walls surrounded a figure in the bed covered by an old white and blue hospital blanket. Izzy headed straight towards her dad. Jean and Will followed but Blake waited by the door. She approached Bill's right side and leaned over.

'G'day, Dad. I hear you're in the wars again.' She studied his face. It was so much leaner, almost gaunt-looking now. She watched as he recognised her. A smile spread across the right-hand side of his face, while the left side remained limp. Izzy reached over, cupped the left side of his face in her hand and rubbed it tenderly with her thumb. 'It's good to see you,' she said with a croaky voice.

Bill reached over with his right hand, and took hers firmly. 'Izzy,' he managed to say quite clearly.

Jean's hand flew to her mouth at the sound of her husband's voice. Will smiled at Jean in amazement. He had a feeling that Izzy would work some magic.

Bill touched Izzy's face lovingly with his hand and began to talk again, but this time it was just a jumble of sounds.

'Oh, Dad,' said Izzy as tears rolled down his cheeks. She was shocked at his show of emotion. Was he really that happy to see her? Ignoring his attempt to speak again, she butted in. 'Dad, I'm going to hang around for a while. Will tells me he's started ripping up on the new land. Seeing as he has his own to do, and after the rain you got yesterday, I'm going to stay and do ours.' She watched his face for any signs of protest. 'I don't care if you don't want me to do it. The fact is you can't stop me. Just face it – you need me.'

Strangely, Bill nodded his head. Izzy looked to the others curiously for confirmation.

Jean smiled while Will spoke. 'I told you he's changed. He really wants you to stay.'

Izzy thought for a moment before shaking her head. 'Until I hear it from his mouth, I still won't believe it.' Bill started up again with the jumbled words, but he soon ran out of steam. Izzy realised that she hadn't yet introduced Blake. She went on to tell Bill all about Blake's farm and the SAMM Stud and how she'd like to introduce them on Gumlea. She chatted on for quite a while. It was actually nice not having her father talk back; she got to say what she wanted for once.

When they eventually drove home, all were silent from the exhaustion of the day. It had been a shock seeing her dad like that but no one could mistake the change in his mood – he was pleased to have his daughter home.

'Thanks, Will, for taking us in. You've been wonderful. I don't know what I would have done without you these last weeks,' said Jean, giving him a hug as they hopped out of the car.

Izzy couldn't help feeling bad – it should have been her supporting her mum. But that was Will – always there when you needed him. 'Hey, Will. I'm gonna take Blake on a tour of Gumlea this afternoon. Can we swing by your place as well?' she asked, trying to include him.

Will shook his head. 'I won't be home. Got a few things to do on Tarramin. I'll catch you later.' With that he turned and headed back to his ute, which was parked up by the work shed. Izzy felt a pang as he walked away. His square shoulder enticed her eyes down towards his narrow waist and cute tight butt. She'd tried to open a door for him and he'd closed it shut in her face, just about. He seemed so distant. Maybe he really was busy – after all, he'd been away from Tarramin a lot with all the work on Gumlea to do.

After a light lunch of salad and cold meat she took Blake for a tour of the farm. He was dying to see where they had rescued Clyde the ram. He was wide-eyed and attentive, like a small boy who'd just heard his first exciting story.

Izzy had convinced Blake to stay for a while and her mum had made up the guest room. If Alan didn't need him, he was going to help out Izzy with seeding. But Izzy knew he had an ulterior motive – Dean only lived a hundred and fifty kilometres away.

That evening they sat out on the verandah in padded wooden chairs after a hearty roast meal. Izzy closed her eyes and could still see the image of the pink sunset they'd watched earlier in her head. It had been a great way to end the day, sitting back with Blake, cold beer in hand and watching the best sunset she'd seen in a while. Pink turned to orange at the horizon. From the verandah, Izzy could see the row of tall gum trees that lined the bottom of the sky with their black silhouettes. A couple of clouds floated in the distance, the last of the rain clouds from yesterday. She took a sip from her beer as she listened to the screeching of the galahs.

'So who was that you were talking to on the phone earlier? Talk about gossip, you were on there for an hour,' Blake asked curiously.

'An old friend of mine, Jess. I haven't seen much of her over the last few years but we used to be good friends. She's been trying to get in touch to invite me to her engagement party. I told her I wouldn't miss it for the world.' Izzy turned to Blake and nudged him with her hand. 'I told her I had you here to help take my place on the tractor so I could go to the party.'

'Yep, use me while you can. How long till you get the last lot ripped up?' Blake asked.

'Well, maybe a few days. No longer than a week, I expect. Why? There's no rush to head to Dean's, is there? I just want to get cracking ASAP.'

'You can't help yourself, can you? You're so excited to be back home and into the work. That's the real reason.' Blake wasn't fooled. He had witnessed her transformation the moment they'd driven onto Gumlea. Not saying she hadn't worked hard for Erindale – if anything, she'd put him to shame. She had restored in him some pride in his work. Izzy made him appreciate what he had and taught him to be thankful that he had a family farm of his own to work. Blake knew Izzy wouldn't be coming back to Erindale. With her dad out of action, there was no way Gumlea would survive without her.

Izzy leaned her head on Blake's shoulders. 'You know me so well, probably better than my own mum. Thanks for bringing me home. I hope you're going to come and visit me lots.'

'Just try and keep me away. Mind you, it took me two hours to get over the numb bum. Anyway, if you're going to buy some of our prize rams next year, I'll be seeing you over our way too.' Blake took another mouthful from his stubbie. He didn't care about the distance really. In Izzy he had made a friend for life and he would stay in touch at all costs.

44

IZZY woke to the familiar sound of the galahs screeching in the glow of the morning sunrise. They were bloody loud, but this morning she took pure delight in their racket. It felt incredibly good to be back. Throwing off the covers, she dressed quickly and headed for the kitchen. She put on some toast and five minutes later Jean and Blake joined her for breakfast. Izzy gave Blake a rundown on the things that needed doing, and he said he'd make a start while she went into town with Jean to see her dad. She was thankful Blake had insisted on coming.

As they drove into town Izzy silently wondered how her mum had been managing all on her own. A horrible sense of selfishness churned in Izzy's stomach for abandoning her mum and leaving her to cope with things alone. Izzy was determined to make it up to her. She planned to learn how to look after Bill's burns and help with his physio. She realised that her mum hadn't had any time off and it was because of her. Things were going to change around here.

When they arrived at the hospital, they were pleased to see that the nurses had moved Bill to a large chair by the hospital window. Izzy sat down next to him. They looked out the window together while Jean ducked into town to get some groceries. The garden was full of birds playing around the birdbath and the bottlebrush trees. A few magpies sat in a small Merrit tree near the verandah and their beautiful gargling sounds were sweet to the ears.

Her dad hadn't spoken at all this morning. Jean said he usually tried to when he saw her, but this morning he'd remained silent. Izzy leaned over to him and said quietly, 'The bush wouldn't be the same without the magpies and their songs, hey, Dad?' She watched him nod his agreement and his brow furrowed in thought as he turned to her.

'Izzy . . . must . . . stay,' he said. Then he took her hand in his and held onto it tightly.

Izzy let out a quick breath in astonishment. 'Dad, you're really talking. It's coming back. Don't rush it. It'll take time.' She suddenly wondered whether this was a one-off sentence, a bit like yesterday.

She gazed across at him. The same face that was once strong and defined was now pale and skeletal-looking. The months of being in a hospital room and confined to a wheelchair were taking their toll. He had lost most of his bulk and was now a mere shadow of his old self.

Bill patted her hand to get her attention. 'I love . . . you. Need you . . . on farm.' It took him a while to get the words out.

Izzy's mouth dropped and her heart stopped. Did he just say what she'd thought? He'd barely said much but they were the most important words ever.

'Take it easy, Dad. It's wearing you out.'

Bill took a deep breath and relaxed.

'So are you saying it's okay for me to be here, working Gumlea?'

Bill nodded and smiled his wonky grin. 'Please.'

Tears blurred her vision. Leaning over, she rested her head on his chest. 'You don't know how long I've waited to hear that, Dad.' She looked up at her father and something passed between them, something that they'd both remember forever.

Izzy stayed like that for a while, snuggled against her dad. He smelt fresh and clean, not a hint of grease or sweat, which was how she remembered him. One day he would be his old self again – she'd see to it. She wouldn't let him rot inside. As soon as the seeding was over, she was going to ferry him around the farm and involve him in as much as she could. She knew he needed to be outside and not cooped up in the house. The fresh air would make him stronger and the land would help rejuvenate him.

Eventually Jean returned to the hospital room with some chocolate for them to share.

'But only one piece for you, my dear,' she said, addressing Bill. Jean turned to Izzy as she adjusted her knitted red jumper over her jeans. 'The doctors have him on a strict diet. No saturated fat, alcohol or salt.'

'It's crap,' Bill mumbled.

'What did you just say?' Jean asked, the excitement at the sound of his voice clear on her face.

'Crap,' Bill repeated for her benefit. She rushed into his arms. After a brief celebration, Jean turned to Izzy excitedly.

'So, what else has he said?'

Izzy smiled. 'For me to stay on the farm. That it's okay. You know, all that but not in so many words.'

Frowning, Jean lectured her. 'Well, it could have been sorted long ago, especially if you'd come home sooner. Will even told you to come back.' Her words were strong but her voice remained soft – she couldn't hide her delight that things were finally working out.

'I know, but it's just one of those things that I had to hear from the horse's mouth to believe it. I'm so happy, Mum. I've got to go tell Blake the good news and then get cracking on the seeding. I might work through the night, as much as I can, while the ground is still moist. I'll meet you at the car.'

'Hey, Izzy. What's going on between you and Blake?' Jean finally asked the question that had been gnawing at her.

'Nothing. We're just great friends. Blake's my best mate, nothing more.'

Jean watched her carefully, then said, 'Does Will know that?'

'I don't know. He's never bothered to ask so I don't think he cares,' she replied, careful to keep the emotion out of her voice. She gave her parents each a kiss on the cheek and headed out the door with a bounce in her step. She pulled up her low-slung jeans as she stepped from the hospital into the car park. Straightaway she saw Will coming in her direction. The sight of him brought her to a standstill. She didn't know if it was the tight jeans or the blue checked shirt open at the front, but he looked so damn irresistible. Other girls would probably laugh at her, but to Izzy, nothing was more appealing than a man in his work gear and boots. Without really knowing why, she began to cry. Will had been her rock through so much. He'd saved her dad and he'd held her so tight when Tom died. All of a sudden, she craved, once again, the comfort of his strong arms.

Will saw Izzy's tears and it ripped his heart apart. He didn't need to speak. He just ran towards her and scooped her up into his arms. She almost flung herself into him, her arms circling his waist and latching on. His whole being reacted to the perfect fit of her body. The effect blew him away. He held her tightly, grabbing fistfuls of her top and pulling her closer. He didn't want to ask her what was wrong, not just yet. She might pull away and he wasn't ready for that. He could feel her tears, which had soaked through his shirt and touched his skin. Brushing back some of her hair, he kissed her softly on her forehead. She smelt just as he remembered – a mixture of soap and sweet lavender. He began to lose control and knew he would have to step away soon. He was scared there might be bad news, that maybe Bill had taken a turn.

Izzy let go first and turned her watery blue eyes towards him. 'Dad's back,' she laughed. 'He's talking. Well, sort of.' She sniffed away a few tears and then reluctantly withdrew completely from Will's embrace. Her cheeks began to redden. 'I'm sorry, Will. I'm just so happy. He's told me to stay, finally. You must go and see him.

He would love to see you.' She stepped back a few paces and added, 'Well, I better go. I'm going to take over from Blake. He's started ripping up.'

She began to head past him but paused. 'And, Will, thanks,' she said, clutching his arm. 'I owe you a great deal. I'm glad you were here for him.' She turned and headed past him to the gate.

Will watched her walk to the car and loved the way her tight top contoured her body. But that hug had him confused. He was sure he felt something in Izzy, saw something in her eyes when she looked at him. He'd seen that look after the gully incident. Did he still stand a chance? Maybe it wasn't quite over yet. With his head full of thoughts he tore his eyes away from Izzy and headed into the hospital.

45

IZZY bounced her way around the paddock as the sun set behind her. She thought about Blake. She could tell he was disappointed that she wouldn't be returning to work for them, but he also knew that it had always been a possibility. He was over the moon that Bill was getting his speech back, and he'd also encouraged her to go and tell Will how she felt. She'd seriously been thinking it was time to get out of her comfort zone and take the plunge.

Izzy was really going to miss Blake. She would have to get a computer so she could keep in contact with him; maybe even a webcam, he'd suggested. Izzy smiled as she turned the corner and watched the last of the dying sun as the horizon sucked it down.

Driving around and around in a square paddock gave your mind plenty of time to think. Izzy's had been going wild ever since she started this paddock six hours ago. She couldn't wait to tell her dad about her plans to introduce Prime SAMMs into their stock. She was sure he'd be interested, and with Blake's keen eye she knew they could get some really good rams. For once in her life, she could plan the future of the farm. It was a bloody good feeling.

It was almost midnight when she turned the tractor and headed up to the highest point on their property. This corner of the paddock was one of her favourite spots – the view was amazing. She could see almost the whole farm and their house from here, and Will's place too. She used to ride the motorbike up here as a kid and hang out under the large gum tree, or sometimes in it. It was her own piece of paradise.

Not that she could see anything much tonight, as it was pitch black. The lights on the tractor only lit up a small patch of earth in front of her and to the side.

A few drivers got lost in their paddocks at night, especially casual workers who didn't know the land so well. Some would drive around for ages trying to find the gate. But Izzy always knew where she was. She had it all mapped out in her head like her own GPS. And she never felt alone. If anything, she enjoyed the tranquillity of it all. Besides, you could never feel totally alone out here, not when you were at one with the land.

Once Izzy reached the top of the hill, she looked around as far as she could see. Out of the darkness of the night shone more tractor lights in the distance, like large twinkling stars. Every farmer was out making the most of the wet soil. She could count ten tractors out at it, and when the train was in at the bin for loading, she could easily spot their floodlights as well, even from this far away.

Izzy wondered whether Will was on his tractor tonight. Lifting her head, she checked the two-way. She had it on scan. Some nights you could catch the farmers telling jokes back and forth to relieve the boredom. Some were highly entertaining. Plenty of housewives turned their radios down at night so they could get some peace without hearing every dirty joke.

Finishing off the paddock, Izzy headed towards the gate and diesel trailer. She wasn't going to do any more as she was low on fuel. She parked the tractor and climbed into the back of the ute where her swag was waiting. She didn't like to go home and disturb everyone. It was much easier to catch some shut-eye, then get back on the job at daybreak.

Izzy stretched out and stared up at the black sky. Only a handful of stars gazed down at her. With the cool of the night on her skin and the smell of the freshness of the soil, it wasn't long before she was sound asleep.

*

At first light, Izzy filled up the tractor with diesel and managed to get two laps in before she noticed a newish point stuck in the dirt. She stopped, ran out into the soft brown soil and picked it up. It was a fairly new one, so she lifted up the plough and checked all the points and found a few missing. Grabbing the hammer out of the tractor, she went and banged on the one she'd found. She stood up to stretch her back. The sun wasn't even up yet. Give it another five minutes or so, she reckoned.

As she worked on the points, Izzy saw a ute heading towards her through the paddock. It was Blake. What was he doing here? It wasn't even six o'clock. Alarm bells rang. Oh, God. I hope nothing's happened to Dad. She'd heard of people turning a corner one minute and then dropping off their perch the next, like a last-minute miracle before giving up.

A soft white fog had settled, lingering in and around the trees. As beautiful as it was, it gave her a haunting feeling. Izzy began walking towards Blake. She tried to shut off her brain and stop the troubled thoughts creeping in. She climbed over the plough and found Blake standing a few metres from her.

'Yo,' she said, still nervous. 'What's up?' He didn't look like someone bringing bad news, and the tension instantly drained out of her.

'I was up doing some work in the shed and thought I'd bring out brekky. Don't stress – I didn't make it. Your mum did.' Blake handed over a square parcel wrapped in foil.

Tearing it open, she said, 'Bacon and egg toastie. You beauty.' She took a mouthful and hungrily chewed away. 'Want some?'

'I've already had one, thanks. Just as well, 'cos watching you eat like a starved cow would make anyone lose their appetite. So you still want me to take over on the tractor some time after lunch?'

Izzy swallowed. 'Yes, please. That would be great. I have to get ready for the engagement party. I feel bad that I didn't even know Jess and Travis had got engaged.'

'Well, you've hardly been around now, have you?'

'Guess not. I'll text you and tell you how much fun I'm having.'

'Yeah, cheers for that.' Blake checked his watch. 'Don't you think it's about time you got on your big green horse and hightailed it back to work?'

'Gonna let me finish my bloody brekkie? Christ, you're just itching for us to finish so you can go see Dean.'

Blake turned her towards the tractor and slapped her on the butt. 'Off ya go now. I'll see ya later.'

She looked back. 'Bring me some more food at lunchtime. Oh, and maybe some cake.'

'Don't push your bloody luck. No wonder I don't like women. You're a bunch of bossy buggers.'

Izzy walked to the tractor and sat down in the large rim of the tyre to finish her breakfast and watched Blake wave before he climbed back into the ute and drove out of the paddock.

Blake had just finished throwing his snacks bag into the front of Izzy's ute when Will pulled up. 'How you doing?' he asked Will.

'All right. Yourself? You heading home now?' Will's eyes were drilling into Blake as he tried to read his face for the answer he wanted.

'Not quite. I'm taking over from Izzy so she can go to the engagement party tonight. Are you going?'

'Yeah. I'll show my face, I think.'

Will was fidgeting and glancing at his watch. Blake could tell he didn't really want to stay and chat. 'It's good that Izzy's staying on the farm now. She's ecstatic about it and I s'pose you are too?'

Will ran his hand through his soft brown hair. 'Oh, yeah. She's a great girl. I'm glad she's staying, for Bill's sake,' he added.

Blake chuckled. 'You don't have to explain anything to me, mate. I can tell you care for her.' Will looked very nervous, like he was worried about stepping on Blake's toes. Blake put him out of his misery. 'Don't stress. Izzy and I are only friends and it will always stay like that. Trust me. I would have said something sooner but I haven't had a chance to catch you alone.'

'Huh?'

The look on Will's face was priceless. He really was a good-looking man. Blake knew what he had to do. He leaned back on the ute and sighed. 'Believe me, she's not my type.' Will looked slightly offended at Blake's words, as if they implied something was wrong with Izzy. 'Don't get me wrong, she's a top chick, and if I liked women, she'd be my first pick, but I don't.' He saw the light bulb go on in Will's head.

Will rested his back on his ute and crossed his arms on his chest. 'Why didn't Izzy say something? I thought you two were together.'

'Izzy's not a gossip. She'd rather wait for me to say something when I'm ready. Being "out" is still a bit new for me, you see.'

Will wasn't smiling, but Blake could tell he wanted to – his eyes had lit up like a Christmas tree.

'I take it this is good news?' Blake didn't wait for his answer. 'I really wanted to tell you sooner, but you've been avoiding me like the plague.'

'Sorry, I was a bit pissed, you know.' Will clapped Blake on the shoulder by way of an apology.

'You know you should tell her how you feel. Give her a chance to respond. A good friend once told me the same thing. I know she cares for you.'

'She does? But why hasn't she —'

'Izzy may be as tough as old boot leather on the outside, but on the inside she's as fragile as glass. She's afraid of rocking the boat just in case she loses you as a friend, and I don't think she could handle you rejecting her either.' Blake studied Will and smiled. 'Mate, it's up to you to make the first move. She's too darn scared.'

Blake had said his piece. For now, anyway. He'd be around to try again if they needed a bigger nudge. He held out his hand to Will. 'I'm off in a few days, so if I don't see you, good luck.'

'Yeah, see ya,' Will replied slowly. 'And thanks.' He watched Blake get in the ute and drive away. Then, in a daze, he wandered off towards Bill's house.

46

WEARING a singlet, shirt, jumper and jacket, Izzy was snuggled up ready for the party. It was already dark as she drove into Travis's farm, heading for his shearing shed. She parked behind the nearest utes and stepped out into the cold. Digging her hands deep into her pockets, Izzy was thankful for the large fire roaring just outside the sliding door of the shed. She didn't stop but kept going on inside to see Jess.

The shed was decked out with a large table covered with dips and biscuits and a small pile of presents, and heaps of chairs, which were mostly occupied by oldies. Trav and Jess had strung up some large coloured lights to brighten the dark space but they did nothing to hide the strong smell of sheep. She noticed a bathtub full of ice and beer against the wall and went and helped herself. Jess came running up to her and gave her a hug.

'It's so good to see you again, Izzy. I'm glad you could make it.'

'Congratulations, Jess. I can't believe it.'

'Me either. Come and sit. We can talk for a few minutes before I go do the rounds. I must catch up with the grandparents before they head off early. I'm sorry about your dad. How's he going?'

'Coming along, making small improvements but they say he should recover fully. I can't wait to get him back out on the farm in the fresh air – do him the world of good. But anyway, tell me about the wedding. Have you set a date?'

'We're thinking a September wedding and that's about as far as we've got. Plenty of time to work out the other details. Just make sure you don't go nickin' off again. I can't have you missing my wedding.'

'Don't worry, Jess. I'll be around and I'll throw you the best hen's night ever.'

The cold beer went down nicely as she sat chatting with Jess, all the while her eyes scanning for Will. Blake had said he was coming but she still couldn't see him. Somehow, the party didn't seem very exciting without him, and after Jess went to circulate, the stuffiness of the shed got the better of her. Izzy headed out into the crisp night air, relishing its freshness. The flickering fire soon beckoned her and she joined the other blokes in beanies and jackets under the black starry sky. She got chatting to Travis for a while but it wasn't until he went to find them some more beers that she finally spotted Will. He was leaning up against the shed wall in the dark, and if the glow of the fire hadn't reached his face, she would have missed him completely. But he hadn't missed her. His eyes were watching her intently. She raised her beer in a wave. He didn't acknowledge it. Instead he just kept staring. He was wearing a large jacket over a jumper with a hoodie. One hand was shoved down deep into the pockets of his jeans. He had her pulse racing just seeing him all dark in the shadows with his vibrant blues still watching her.

Travis came back and handed her the beer. 'Cheers,' he said, clinking his bottle with hers.

She was glad she'd rugged up. She'd brought her beanie too, just in case it got colder.

'Thanks, Trav. Hey, I'll catch up with you later.' Izzy nodded and made her way behind the dark bodies that lined the fire's edge. The entire time she could feel Will's eyes set on her. It took a moment for her own eyes to adjust away from the flames, but she didn't need to see clearly to know where his body stood.

'Hey, Will. I was wondering if you'd turned up.' He didn't reply.

Was he still giving her the cold shoulder? 'You know Dad's been talking more and more, and from what I can gather, you had something to do with his change of heart. I don't know what you said, but thanks. God, I seem to be thanking you a lot lately. You've done so much for our family, and I really appreciate it. I am indebted to you forever. Well, at least for a week.' She tried some humour to see if he'd react.

'No biggie,' he said quietly.

'Holy shit, he speaks.' Will laughed at her attempt to faint on the ground, while keeping her beer upright and not spilling a drop. As she stood back up she said, 'You know, it's good to hear you laugh. You've been a bit distant and I was worried you had the shits with me. I've felt the coldness of your shoulder a few times.' Will wasn't looking so deadpan now.

'Sorry. I've had a few things on my mind, but it's all sorted now.'

'Good, because I was missing the old Will. Now that I'm back for good, we're going to be in each other's pockets, and I can't have you shitty at me —'

'Izzy, I'm in love with you.'

'— or walking around in a strop all the time. It just wouldn't be . . . What did you say?' Izzy finally caught on. 'How much have you had to drink, Will Timmins?' He must be off his trolley, she thought. Either that or he just wanted to shut her up. 'What did you just say, Will?' she asked again.

She must have looked pretty confused because in the next breath he'd caressed her cheek with his cold hands and said, 'I'm in love with you, kiddo. Can't believe I didn't tell you sooner.'

Then his hot mouth was over hers and she felt the tingle rocket through her body. His hand wrapped itself around her waist and drew her closer. Hungrily she deepened the kiss. All the dreams became distant memories as they paled in comparison to this. Her hands instinctively rose up to his chest, trembling at the sensation it brought. Touching Will was way better than she'd remembered.

Will pulled back, but only by an inch. His eyes were alive and the passion in them matched her own desires. Her mouth moved but no words came out.

'What are you trying to say, Isabelle Simpson?'

Izzy brushed back his fringe with her finger and then traced it down to his jaw and lightly across the top of his lips. 'Just that it's about bloody time.' Eagerly she leaned into Will, kissed his neck up to his ear, and whispered, 'I love you, too.'

He quivered as he grabbed her bum and pulled her closer while she devoured his neck. Someone wolf whistled, bringing them back to reality, so they broke apart. Will clasped her hand and led her out the back into the dark. He struggled to walk properly as he practically dragged her to his ute. He needed a quiet private spot. He had tasted her and badly needed more. When he got to his ute he pushed her against the door and kissed her hard. Quickly he attacked her jacket and unzipped it before pulling up her assortment of clothes. He found her warm flesh and searched upwards until his fingers found more fabric. Lifting it up and out of the way, he released her silky skin into the palm of his hand and heard a groan. He wasn't sure whether it was him or Izzy.

Izzy opened her legs and let Will nestle in closer. The heat they were making was melting her insides. She felt for the door handle and yelped when something licked her hand.

The light in the ute came on when she opened the door and Izzy had her answer. 'Oh, Will. You've got a new puppy.' With Will momentarily forgotten, Izzy picked up the most adorable kelpie puppy she'd ever seen. She had a beautiful brown coat with tan spots above her eyes and the cutest floppy ears. Her tiny little paws tried to climb her jumper as she reached up to lick Izzy's face. 'She's gorgeous, Will. What's her name?'

'Well, she's not really mine,' Will said, and saw Izzy's disappointment.

'I actually got her for you. She's yours.' He shrugged, trying not to make a big deal out of his gesture. 'Seeing as you weren't home to name her, I decided to call her Gully. It just seemed to fit, don't you think?' Leaning over he kissed her tender lips again. 'I picked her because she had a lot of spunk and she reminded me of you. I hope you like her. I figured you're going to need a good sheepdog, seeing as you have the family farm to run now.'

Words could not describe how deliriously happy Izzy felt. To think she had spent so many years hating him, and now she was completely gaga over the bloke. She had never known such a compassionate and generous man.

'There is just one thing, though,' said Will, his tone suddenly serious. 'Gully is used to living at my place and I can't bear the thought of her leaving, so you're just gonna have to move in with us.' Will flashed a devilish look filled with lust. 'Don't worry. I'll make an honest woman of you,' he said with a wink before grabbing the top of her jeans and pulling her hips close to his.

Izzy shut the puppy back in the car and snuggled into Will's hard body. 'I'm counting on it,' she sighed against his chest. Breathing deeply the scent of fresh clothes, soap and Will, Izzy was filled with a sense of being home.

Will nuzzled into her neck eager to continue, but she pulled back. 'And don't you think I'm going to be chained to the sink. Oh, and you can wash your own socks too. I've smelt those feet.'

Will laughed, picked her up and sat her on the bonnet of his ute. Wriggling between her thighs, he pulled her close. 'Now, where were we?'

47

TEN MONTHS LATER

GULLY rushed past Izzy's legs and around the side of the verandah. It was early evening and the large yellow sun was making its descent, casting the earth in an orange glow. The floorboards groaned as Izzy followed her dog around the corner. Gully had already jumped up onto the old couch and was greeting Will. Will was rubbing her ears and patting her head, and in response Gully's tail belted the edge of the couch. He smiled into her shiny brown eyes. 'How ya going, girl?'

'Oh, you know, so-so,' said Izzy, appearing around the corner. Her blue singlet and shorts were covered in grease and dust and there was a lengthy gap where her long legs trailed down to her boots.

Will looked up and smiled. The glow from the sun had turned her skin a shimmering gold. 'Hey, gorgeous. How was your day?'

Izzy sat down next to Will. Automatically he put his arm around her shoulders, his fingers absentmindedly stroking the tiny scar on her shoulder. She snuggled into his naked chest and felt his heartbeat against her cheek. 'Okay. Dad's dragged out all the bookwork and we're slowly going through it. I'm loading it all onto the computer and Dad's just completely lost. But I'm happy doing it. We went and did a few jobs after lunch and we're gonna do the fence in the white dam paddock tomorrow and I'm sure we'll butt heads occasionally. But of course, it's nothing I can't handle.'

Will kissed her on her forehead. 'That's my girl. Want a beer?'

'I thought you'd never ask.'

Will handed over a cold stubbie, and Gully curled herself up between their feet. There was hardly a sound except for the crickets and a hiss as Izzy cracked open her beer.

Will tapped his foot nervously against the floorboards. He'd been waiting for her to return all day, for there was an engagement ring burning a hole in his shorts and people hiding in his house. 'Blake rang before. He said he'll be down soon. He's catching up with Dean and wants to drop in and see us.'

'About time he came for a visit. Seeing as we were up there in January, when Chloe was born. With Simone and Mickey's wedding, we'll be back up there again in September. I hope they visit us before then too. What day is he coming?'

Will smiled. 'In a month, so in March some time.' A blatant lie, for he knew damn well they were all hiding in the back room of the house, probably trying hard to keep Chloe from crying out and giving them away. They had their car parked in the bush on the other side of the house so as not to give the game away. He'd told them he was going to propose to Izzy and they were over the moon and insisted on coming down straightaway to celebrate. He couldn't wait to see the look on her face when they came out after his signal.

'Oh, that long,' Izzy said sadly. Leaning forward, she gave Gully a splash of beer in her empty bowl. 'Just enough to wet your chops and no more, okay?'

Will smiled and said, 'We can head up any time you want, kiddo, if you're missing them that much.'

'Go and get some more SAMM rams while we're there, hey?'

Will tilted her chin up and kissed her lips softly. 'Ah, a woman after my own heart, always thinking of the farm. I just hope you think about me that much.'

Izzy kissed him back and then nestled into his shoulder. 'Heaps more.' She took a sip from her beer and closed her eyes against the bright glare. She breathed him in and sighed. 'This is just perfect.'

The sun dipped further down towards the horizon and Will needed no better sign to reach into his pocket. He moved off the couch and knelt on the verandah, while Gully took the chance to lick him. He said the words quickly as his chest was in his throat and his blood pumped in his ears. 'Izzy, you know I love you. Will you marry me?' He held up the engagement ring – a thick gold band with three large diamonds set into it and clusters of smaller ones on the side. Will knew she wouldn't want anything high and impractical – she was a working woman and, God, did he love that about her. He watched her face, which was dead serious, and his heart skipped a beat.

'Took you bloody long enough, William.'

Then she smiled and he felt like a floating cloud.

'Is that a yes, kiddo?' he asked as he knelt there holding out the ring with the sun setting behind them.

'You bet your cute arse it is.' Izzy held out her hand and let him slip it on her finger. 'Now, get off the floor and come and kiss me!'

Will stood up and whistled as loudly as he could as the excitement brewed up from his chest into his throat.

Izzy heard the sound of feet clattering and doors opening and closing and looked up at Will. 'You cheeky devil. Is that our parents in there waiting?' Will just smiled and let her believe what she wanted. He held out his hand and pulled Izzy up before kissing her and spinning her around to face the onslaught of people.

First was Blake with a 'Howdy, stranger'. He was d
and had shaved his head, making him ruggedly ha
followed by Simone, who had already lost w
she'd gained and had her hair back in a nec
'Surprise! I hope you've said yes!' And fina
who was in the prettiest pink dress with matc

cooing at her fingers. Will watched Izzy's mouth drop and her face drain of colour. It took her twenty seconds before she could react.

'Holy hell! What the devil are you lot doing here?' she said finally, then began to hug them all furiously. She saved Chloe for last and prised her out of Mickey's arms for a cuddle and lots of kisses.

Will couldn't wipe the smile off his face and as Izzy turned to him with Chloe snuggled in her arms and a glow like that of an angel, he knew they were going to have a very happy future together. Izzy reached out and hugged him close, savouring the moment.

ACKNOWLEDGEMENTS

Firstly, I'd like to thank my Uncle Mocka and Aunty Di for the use of their farm name Gumlea for this book (even though the farm in the book is fictional). Gumlea is where I spent a lot of my childhood and I have many, many happy memories of time spent there with my cousins and brother Chad.

To Rachael Jensen, who provided the inspiration behind Izzy, from there the story grew.

My dear friends Jim Jim and Lynnie Stewart, and also Aunty Ida – I owe you all a huge thanks. Without your support, enthusiasm and encouragement this book never would have seen daylight.

To Margaret Cole and our writers group, who helped me to believe that what I was doing was important, as well as adding some much-needed self-belief!

To my Aunty Flossy, thank you for your support and endless help in getting these words printed, and Uncle Lionel, for giving me some great pointers and proofreading everything for me.

To Myra Harradine, thanks for all the times my kids came to play at your place; it was the best time to do some writing.

I'd like to thank the ASA and its mentorship program, and Janet Woods for her mentoring. It was a huge learning experience.

Thanks to Arwen Summers for pulling my letter out of the slush pile. It's amazing to have my first book published. To Ali Watts and Anne Rogan from Penguin, thanks for being such an ease to work with and so encouraging.

A special thank you to everyone in my hometown of Pingaring. You make it unique and a great place to call home!

To Jacinta Holmes, everyone needs a close friend when you live where we do. Thanks for always being there. And to Wendy Saunders, you make me laugh – thanks for finding our town and becoming my neighbour and friend!

Thank you to my mum, Sue Hicks, who read everything I wrote hot off the printer, and to the rest of the family and friends who gave their eyes to these words. Also my dad, who I'm like in so many ways – I love you to bits. To my brother Chad, Mel, and in-laws Leanne, Michael, Bob a Coralie – you're an awesome family to be a part of. To my cousins are like my sisters – you guys are the best. I am blessed to hav great family.

But most importantly, to my husband Darryl – where woul your love and support. I got lucky the day they put me to w bin as you. Thanks for putting up with me. I know you partly neglected while this story was born. And to Mac and Blake, you are my little angels. I love yo

Read on for a sneak peek of

Brought to you by Penguin B

1

'Bloody rain. It's harvest, for crying out loud.' Kim cursed again as she tried to peer out of her windscreen into the darkness. Window wipers whipped past on the fastest setting but struggled to keep up with the onslaught of rain. The radio crackled in the background, thanks to the crazy storm happening in the sky above her. The sound of it grated on her tightly wound nerves. Letting go of the steering wheel, Kim snapped off the radio and looked up just as a body of water appeared on the gravel road ahead. 'Crap!'

Kim wasn't driving very fast but a floodway was not something she wanted to rush into at any speed. She stopped just at the edge of the lapping water, the idle motor hardly audible over the rain on the roof of her ute. She could see bushes on the side of the road, and judging by the water levels, she deemed it just low enough to pass through. Slowly she entered the floodway.

It had started raining in the morning, which made it the perfect time to drive the 80 kilometres to pick up a belt for her header. Normally it would have come by post but somehow it had ended up with another farmer's order. Living in the bush, it was usually quicker just to drive to the farmer's place and pick it up yourself rather than wait for them to get it back to town for reposting.

Kim sighed with frustration as she crept through the washe out road, the ute lurching on unseen potholes. She hadn't take back way home in years. She'd only done so to save time. remembered now that it was prone to flooding. The salt all around this area. Neighbouring towns weren't called Lake Grace and Lake Biddy for no reason. When heavy rain came, especially when the ground was as rock hard as it was this summer, the water would flow along the gullies and over roads in no time – but no one would have expected this much rain to drop so suddenly during harvest! Three more days and they would have been finished.

Kim desperately wanted to see how far the water had risen up the side of her ute but the darkness encased her. Before too long she'd made it to the other side, without any water running inside the cab, but from what she could tell, the floodwaters were still rising. Any later and she wouldn't have made it through.

Eager to get home, she finally drove on, the headlights making the gumtrees glisten, the dark trunks shimmering in all shades of brown. It really was a pretty sight, especially after such a long, hot harvest. But Kim would have appreciated it ten times more if it had allowed them just a few more days to finish getting the crop off. Now they'd be set back at least a week, not to mention the possibility of sprouting and staining on their grain. To top it off, her brother Matt had sent her a text earlier telling her they'd had hail. His text had been more full of swear words than anything else.

A murky white mass appeared before her – another floodway. Kim stopped by the edge. This one looked deeper and was running faster than the last one. Getting out, Kim ignored the light drops of rain and made her way to the water's edge. The ute lights drilled holes into the night, allowing her to see the full force of the flow.

'Damn it.' She either had to try to get across, go back through the other floodway, or stay here for the night. None of the options sounded like much fun. She'd been lucky to get through the first floodway as it was. By morning the crossings would ease off and it should be passable – it was just a matter of waiting it out. As her shirt started to soak through, she bent down to pick up a stick that had washed up against the road.

When she bent over she heard a dreaded sound – *plop!* – as her mobile phone slipped from her top pocket into the water.

'Oh, shit. Dave!' Kim fished her phone out of the water, tried to dry it on the underside of her blue check flannel shirt as she went back to the ute.

Her phone, which was a model actually called 'Telstra Dave', had been cursed since the day she'd got it. Sure, Telstra Dave came with one-metre waterproof gorilla glass but that all meant zilch when, only three weeks ago, it had fallen from the truck door, shattering the screen. Some sticky tape had held most of the glass in place but waterproof it probably wasn't. Kim sat in the ute, after slamming the door shut, and turned on the dull interior light. Some chunks of the screen were now missing and drops of moisture oozed out from behind the cracks. The screen remained blank and lifeless. 'God damn it.' Kim threw the phone to the passenger side and hit the steering wheel with her hand. Today was not her bloody day.

Now she couldn't call her brother and let him know what was happening. Kim tilted her head back and groaned. What to do? She knew she was next to Brian Summerfield and Tom Murphy's land and thought about walking to someone's house, but the scary stories about Tom's worker soon put her off this idea. Plus it was dark and she didn't know which direction to try. She'd rather stay in her ute, wet, all night than run into crazy Harry in the dark.

After ten minutes, cursing the rain and Dave, she noticed headlights bouncing their way towards her. It wasn't another car on the road. The lights were coming from her right in a nearby paddock. Was it Tom or Brian out checking that their stock hadn't been washed away? The lights drew closer until a ute pulled up on the other side of the fence line. Kim got out and shielded her eyes from the glare

'G'day,' yelled out a man's friendly voice. His tall stocky sh
walked towards the fence, his wide-brimmed hat protecting h
from the light rain.

Kim stepped towards him. 'Hi.' She tried to see if this was Tom Murphy as she was sure Brian was quite short. She'd met Tom on a few occasions in Lake Grace when collecting chemical and other farming supplies but struggled to make a match in the dark.

'You'll be stuck now,' the man said, stating the obvious, his hands resting on his hips. 'For a good while too. Did you want to come back to the house and get out of the wet? Floodwaters won't be passable until early morning so you're welcome to camp the night and I can bring you back.'

'Is there really no other way out?'

'Sorry, lass. There isn't. I know this place like the back of my hand and when she floods, there ain't nothin' you can do about it. There's a hot stew on the fireplace, if you're hungry?'

It had to be Tom. His wife's cooking was legendary. After all, she was the president of the local CWA. Kim's belly rumbled at the mere thought of food. It was probably loud enough to blend in with the thunderstorm which still rattled on overhead.

'Sure, that sounds great, thanks.' Kim couldn't find any excuses not to. Besides, she could ask to use his phone to call Matt and reassure him that she was okay. Kim headed towards the man and climbed over the fence. 'Thanks so much for your kindness,' she said. 'I'm Kim.'

She held out her hand as a flash of lightning erupted across the sky, illuminating the face of the man in front of her. Her heart raced upon seeing a scar twist across his face, and a feeling of dread shuddered through her as she realised that she didn't know this man at all. This man was not Tom Murphy. And if it wasn't Tom, then the only other person it could be was his worker, and that meant . . .

Kim swallowed hard as his hand slid into hers and shook it. No, it couldn't be Hermit Harry – or Crazy Harry, as some had liked to call him when they were kids. He was almost like a folklaw story, whispered about, told at bonfires or under the torchlight at sleepovers to scare everyone. No one had ever seen Hermit Harry – not in town, not at church, not anywhere – but some said they'd seen his ute driving around Tom Murphy's farm. He'd be burying dead bodies, the older kids had tried to convince her when she was growing up. But the scar on his face, that was real. There were kids who liked to sneak up on his house at night as a dare, to try and catch a glimpse of him, but the shotgun fired over their heads always put an end to that. Until years down the track and many beers later someone was dared again. But someone must have got a good look, as Kim had heard the nickname 'Scarface' used once or twice. She could only imagine how scary that would be to a kid at night. Hell, she was terrified enough now and she was twenty-seven!

'Call me Harry,' he said, as he pulled his hand away after the handshake.

Bloody hell. Kim's knees almost knocked against each other as she tried to keep her breathing steady.

'Come on, jump in and get out of the wet.'

Kim watched him move back to the ute but her feet remained planted to the spot. Her mind raced with ways to back out of the invitation. Maybe she should say her brother was on his way, and that she'd better stay put. Then she realised she was letting the stories of her youth determine her opinion when he actually seemed friendly enough. If he really was all that bad, why would Tom Murphy have had him work for him all these years? Maybe Hermit Harry was just that, a hermit who didn't like to go off-farm? He may have scared away kids with his shotgun, but no one had ever been shot.

Giving Harry the benefit of the doubt, Kim walked towards his ute and tried not to think about her possible impending death and muddy gravesite.

'You're lucky I found you,' said Harry, as Kim climbed into his ute. 'I was just doing a quick check on the sheep and happened to see your lights. A different time and I would have missed ya.'

Right now Kim was wondering just how lucky she was. Unlucky seemed to be more appropriate. She could blame Telstra Dave for being weak and breaking, or the farmer who had her parts and wouldn't stop talking, or even the postal mob for sending it to him in the first place – or she could blame Mother Nature for the bloody rain which had set this whole chain of events in motion. She should have just stayed home. Now look where she was, sitting in Hermit Harry's ute.

'Thank you,' she said, after clearing her throat. 'Were the sheep okay?' she asked when the silence started to scare her. She figured he'd be less likely to kill her if they had a real conversation, right?

'Yeah, they were all up on the high ground. They'll be fine there. I just like to double check. So where you from, Kim?'

Oh, no. Was he trying to find out if she had family waiting for her? she wondered. 'Um, I'm from Lake Biddy way. I work the family farm with my brother Matt Richards.'

'Ah yep. I recall Tom mentioning a David Richards a few times. Tom brought his seeder bar a few years back.'

Kim nodded at the mention of her father's name, then wondered if her dad had ever met Harry.

They drove through the darkness, Harry driving with precision and knowledge of the land that only those familiar with it had. He'd slow down for bumps they couldn't see but she felt the ute lurch a moment later.

'Had you finished harvest before the rain?' he asked.

'No, but we only have a few days to go.'

'Bloody typical. Mother Nature loves to remind us who's in charge.'

Kim almost smiled. He certainly had that right. For a hermit,

Harry sure did seem friendly enough. Mind you, Kim had no prior experience with hermits. This was all new territory.

Soon Kim could see a light, and a small building loomed into sight. It had a tin roof and a large shrubby garden around the outside blocking any real view of the house.

Harry parked in a lean-to off the side of the house. The back verandah light was on, and a sensor light flashed on when they pulled up. She saw two kelpie dogs by the back door, wagging their tails.

'Don't mind the girls. They're friendly. The black and tan is Molly and the red one is Bindi.'

As Kim got out both dogs barked at the new visitor, but upon noticing Harry they soon forgot Kim and rushed up to him.

'See, I wasn't gone long,' he said, patting them. 'This is Kim.'

Kim had never been introduced to dogs before but both girls wandered over to her and had a sniff up and down her jeaned legs. 'Bet you can smell a lot of animals on there.' Kim smiled to Harry. 'I have two pet sheep, a kangaroo and a kelpie dog called Jo.'

'And I thought I had a few pets,' said Harry with a chuckle. 'Come on. Let's get inside.' Harry walked to the door and kicked off his boots.

The verandah was covered with pot plants and had been swept clean. It felt like a woman lived here, it was so tidy. Kim thought hermits lived in ransacked, derelict homes, not real houses with a well-tended gardens and pot plants that needed constant love and attention. Kim could feel her guard starting to drop as she realised Harry seemed like a normal person.

She took her own boots off and followed Harry inside. His hat came off the moment he walked in the door, exposing his thin greying hair. The lights were on and the house was warm. A delicious aroma of the stew filled the air. Inside his house it was tidy, no dirty floor or thick dust on anything. It was probably cleaner than her own house, Kim thought. Old rugs covered the jarrah floorboards.

They were worn through in places but still clean, which seemed to be the status of most of the furniture in the house. The TV was new. She'd half expected some square heavy old-fashioned TV or none at all. Maybe Harry sat in the blue chair with the worn arms watching *House Husbands* like the rest of Australia? Or maybe *Game of Thrones* was more to his taste? Death and gore. Actually, going by Harry's house so far, Kim would guess *Better Homes and Gardens* would be more his style.

On the side wall sat a large black IKEA shelf with rows and rows of books. She would have loved to see what he liked reading. Romance? Thrillers? But it was the sight of two more dogs on the blue couch that caught her attention as they observed their new visitor with interest.

'Ah, the old girl is Pepper. I've had her for a long time so she gets the special treatment, and the other one is Jess. She's terrified of storms and only then does she get to come inside. Both are friendly. Make yourself at home,' he said, before heading off into the kitchen.

Kim could see Jess, the younger dog, shaking on the couch, the tan patches above her eyes almost quivering too. Kim stepped over and rubbed her ears. 'It's okay, Jess.' The older dog with the same tan patches crawled across the couch towards them, hoping for some love. Kim obliged and gave her a scratch on the neck.

'Jess is one of Pepper's babies,' said Harry as he popped back out. 'I kept Jess cos she was the spittin' image of Pepper.' He held out a bundle of linen nervously. 'There's a towel in case you want a shower or just to dry off.' he said. 'And some clean sheets for your room.'

Kim took them from him and followed him down a passage. He stopped by a door.

'You can camp in here for the night. Its only been used on the odd occasion, if we have a good year and Tom gets in a Pommy worker to help out. Other than that it stays empty so I'm sorry about the dust and spiders. I don't usually venture in here.'

Harry's hands fidgeted at his sides and his eyes twitched nervously as he kept glancing at the door. In the light of the passage she had time to really study him. Besides the scar, his face was tanned and lined with wrinkles, like most men of the land who worked long hours in the sunlight. Yet his brown eyes seemed kind, not something to fear. If anything they seemed fearful. Probably because he was not used to having new people around. She thought he was doing all right, considering. Harry must get enough interaction with Tom and the workers who came and went to keep up his social skills.

'Thank you,' she managed to say. 'It's greatly appreciated.'

'Yes, no worries. Right. Um, bathroom is at the end of the hallway, toilet is outside at the end of the verandah in the wash house. I'll go and check on dinner. It will be ready in ten.'

He turned and headed back to the kitchen before she could utter another 'thank you'.

Kim opened the door and walked into the spare room. It was a simple square shape, with floorboards, old flaking paint in cream, patterned curtains that looked like they'd dissolve if they were ever washed, and a single bed. She could tell by the metal bed head and the sag of the mattress that it was an old spring style. The mattress had a few stains but her sheets were clean. Quickly she dried herself off with the towel and then made the bed. There was no way Kim was going to have a shower here. Besides, what was the point when she had to crawl back into her damp clothes? She'd rather wait till she got home tomorrow and use her own bathroom.

Knuckles rapped against her door. She turned to find Harry there holding a pile of blankets.

'You might need these. Just to take the chill off.'

He didn't step into the room so Kim went and took the rugs, placing them on the end of the bed. 'Thanks. Hey, Harry, do you have a phone I can use to call my brother, to let him know I'm okay?'

'Yes, for sure. This way.'

He led her to another room, much the same size as the one she'd left, which had been fitted out as an office with a simple desk, an old filing cabinet, some photos on the wall and an ancient-looking computer. Harry dragged the wooden chair across the brown patterned carpet. It looked like the original stuff that had probably been here since the house was built.

'Phone's just there,' he said, pointing to the antique handset sitting on the desk. She had the same one at home hidden in a cupboard somewhere for when the power went out and her portable ones didn't work.

'Cheers, Harry.'

He left her be and as she sat down Kim wondered, just who did Harry call? Did he have family? Did they ever visit him? Or was this just to talk to Tom?

Picking up the old phone handle, she pressed it against her ear and dialled her brother's number.

'Yello,' came his deep voice and his usual way of answering the phone.

Kim was half expecting it to be Lauren, his wife, but then again she was probably busy making tea or getting the kids into the shower or even bed.

'Hey, bro. It's me.'

'Hey, sis. All sorted with the part? Wanna bring it up and come for tea?' he said, not even realising Kim wasn't back yet.

But she couldn't blame him. He would have knocked off work and gone home and wouldn't have seen her ute still missing.

'Actually I'm not home yet,' she said.

'What? What are you doing?'

'I got stuck between the floodways out near Tom Murphy's place.'

'Ah, shit. Want me to come and get you?'

'No, I'm okay. Someone came and picked me up.' Kim was not sure if she should mention who. She didn't want him to worry.

'Who? Tom? Is he bringing you home or you camping the night? I can come get you if you need.'

Matt was a good brother. He wasn't just her brother, he was her partner in the family farm, and his respect for her was what made her treasure him. Actually, she put her brother on a pedestal. They'd been close growing up and not once did he ever baulk at sharing the farm with her. It had been half each in his eyes right from the get go. She was lucky her parents were the same and so supportive of her desire to be a farmer, which wasn't always the case for people of their generation.

'No, we're water-locked at the moment. Can't get in or out. So I'm staying with Harry for the night. He'll take me back to the ute in the morning once the water's dropped. I just wanted to let you know before you sent out a search party. I couldn't text'cos I dropped Dave in the water.'

Matt groaned. 'Bloody Dave. I told you he'd be trouble.' Matt always teased her about Dave, which was the second Dave model she'd had after accidentally running over her previous one. Matt thought it was funny. 'Hope you never treat your men like you do your phones,' he'd once told her.

'Hang on – did you just say you were staying with Harry? Who's Harry?'

Kim couldn't find a way to answer him.

'Kim? Shit, is that Harry Hermit? Tom's worker Harry?'

'Yes, that's the one.'

'Oh my God,' said Matt loudly.

Then Kim heard her sister-in-law in the background. 'What?'

'Kim's staying the night with Crazy Harry. You know, Scarface Harry I told you about?' said Matt as he held a conversation with his wife.

'No way! Hermit Harry? Tell her to run now,' said Lauren.

'Matt, Matt!' Kim almost shouted to get his attention. 'It's all right. I'll be fine. Please don't worry.' Kim wanted to tell him more – about Harry's house, his friendly dogs, about the yummy curry she could smell – but she didn't dare in case Harry could hear the conversation.

'So, what's he like? Does he really have a scar? Are you scared? Can you get a photo of him?'

Typical Matt. 'He seems lovely, actually. Yes, he does. No, I'm fine. And Dave took a dive into the water, remember?' she said, answering all his questions. 'Now, I'd better go. I'll be home in the morning. Floodwater will have moved on by then.' Even Harry said the same. They weren't the type of floodways to stay flooded – water was just passing through on its way to the end of the gully run.

'If you're not back by lunch, I'm coming over there with the shotgun. Okay?'

Kim wasn't sure if he was serious or not. 'Yep. Don't worry. See ya tomorrow.'

'I hope so. I wanna hear all about it. No one I know has been into Harry's den,' he said with awe.

Kim laughed. 'Good night.' Then she hung up and headed to the kitchen to find Harry.

He stood at the bench where a slow cooker sat, stirring what was inside. She almost licked her lips, the aroma was so strong.

'Anything I can do?' she asked.

'Sure. Help yourself to a plate, load'er up and there's bread on the table too,' he said, gesturing to the pine table in the middle of the kitchen. Harry had a mix of old and new in this house. Like the pale-blue bench top with the old sink, the cupboards looked as if they'd been painted at some point. Cream wallpaper with a little blue flower on it decorated the kitchen from waist height to the ceiling, and floorboards had been sanded and sealed. Harry had obviously made improvements while he'd been here. The ceilings in the main rooms had been replaced, yet the plaster in her room still sagged with age.

Kim picked up both plates and joined Harry. 'It smells good. I think you might be a better cook than me, Harry,' she said.

'I don't know about that, lass. I've had many disasters over the years and got to this point through much trial and error.'

Kim laughed. 'Well, I know what that's like. I'm still going through that stage.'

They loaded up their plates and sat at the table, Harry at the end, Kim to the side. She buttered some of the bread. Harry did the same and then they ate.

It was good stew. Kim looked at the chunks of meat on her plate and suddenly wondered if it was rabbit or roo? Maybe Harry was living self-sufficiently here, with his own veggie garden and an endless supply of rabbit? Her stomach churned. No, maybe she wouldn't ask. It was better to be none the wiser sometimes.

They talked about farm work as they ate. Harry was really chatty, and Kim wondered whether he was lonely. When was the last time he'd talked to someone besides Tom or his extra workers?

'This stew is amazing, Harry,' she said, before scooping up another mouthful. It was hard to talk when all she wanted to do was keep eating until she was full.

The more they talked, the more Kim got the feeling that Harry was impressed with her knowledge of farming as he kept shaking his head as if in disbelief. He'd never been off the farm so how would he know that girls were now out working farms too? He'd assumed she was married to a farmer and quickly apologised when she set him straight.

'Sorry, Kim. I don't really get out much.'

Kim didn't know how to respond to that. She found her focus trained on his scar. She couldn't help it and he caught her staring.

'Sorry, I didn't mean to stare. It's a ripper,' she said.

'Yes, that it is. I was in Vietnam when I was younger than you,' he said.

'You fought in the war?' She wondered if that's where he'd got the scar. 'Was it awful?'

'You could say that,' he said, before getting up and reaching for her plate. 'Sorry, Kim. I don't do personal conversation. One of the reasons I moved out here.'

All those burning questions about his private life – whether he'd been married or had kids, where he'd grown up – died away with his request. She could tell that she'd struck a bit of a nerve, so, keen not to leave a bad vibe, she jumped up and offered to do the dishes. In the end they did them together.

Harry walked her to her room later that night, which she found a little unnerving. She was still on her guard. What if he preyed on his victims when they were asleep? What if he'd drugged the curry? Kim almost laughed out loud at her wayward thoughts. Harry seemed anything but dangerous.

'Now, when you are inside, please lock the door. There is a dead bolt up the top. Please use it.'

Kim screwed up her face as she tried to understand his words. Was this just so she felt safer?

'Oh, okay. Night, Harry. Thanks for your hospitality.'

'My pleasure.'

Kim shut the door to her room and looked up at the dead bolt.

'Don't forget the lock,' he said from the other side of her door.

Kim reached up and slid the lock into place with a loud click, and it was only then that she heard Harry's footsteps echo along the passageway back to the lounge room.

Well, that was strange, Kim thought. At least she knew she was safe. Matt would try to tell her that Harry probably turned into a werewolf at night or a giant bunyip that devoured girls.

Shaking her head, she threw the rugs over the mattress and finished making her bed. In the process she ended up kicking a box-like object, which hit the bedside table, causing the lid to fly open. It turned out to be an old suitcase. Kim was curious and couldn't keep herself from investigating further. She bent down and lifted the dusty half-opened lid. There were some fabric items in there, something that looked quilted, a knitted baby's bonnet and some photos resting on top. Kim picked them up and studied the photo of two young men in khakis. Straight away she could recognise the jungle background from many photos she'd seen of Vietnam during the war. Turning it over, written on the back in pencil, were two names. *John and Harry*.

Kim turned it back and looked at the two young fresh-faced men with their arms around each other. Both had big smiles. Kim wondered which one was Harry. Neither man had a scar, plus they were so young-looking and wearing baggy hats. There was another photo of an older couple by a house and a beautiful girl in a pretty blue dress. On the back of both of them was written *Lake Grace 1969*. She wondered what other things this case contained but felt she'd violated Harry's privacy enough.

Putting the photos carefully back in their place, she turned off the light and crawled into bed fully clothed. Just in case something happened, she wanted to be prepared. Always the voice in the back of her mind kept her wary. Good men were known to hold deep dark secrets. Murderers walked the streets with their families. It was a horrible world that they lived in at times and Kim wasn't about to drop her guard completely. Not even for a talkative, friendly hermit named Harry.

But as she lay there in bed she couldn't help wonder who Harry really was. What had brought him here to this area, and to Tom's farm? What had happened in his past that he didn't want to talk about? Was it just the war, or was there more? As she drifted off to sleep, she couldn't help wondering, what was Harry's real story?